The Life Of Trinity O'Salves

Book One

K. N. Chambers

This book is a work of fiction. Names, characters, places and incidents are the product of the authors imagination or used factiously. Any resemblance to actual events, locations, person living or realistic, is coincidental.

The Life Of Trinity O'Salves by K. N. Chambers
Book One
Copyright 2024 K. N. Chambers
Editing by Jeremy Brown

The scanning, uploading, and distribution of this book without permission is a theft of the authors intellectual property. If you will like permission to use materials from the book (other than for review purposes), please contact the author. Thank you.
First publish: July 2024

Content Warning

This novel contains content that may be sensitive to some. There is death, death of loved ones, mature language and situations, drug use, torture, abuse, and other potential triggering content. Read at your own discretion.

Dang, I am Dyslexic and wrote a book. Something that I been told I would never achieve. Thank you to all who's reading my book. Thank you to all the crazy people around me who believed in me from the very start. Listening to my stuttering words as I try to explain the book. This may not be a literary masterpiece, but I hope you enjoy this story.

This is just the beginning.

Chapter One

My front door hangs open as my friends scurry inside of my apartment, drenched in not only rainwater but blood.

"Get the first aid kit." Daniel barks, his voice mixed with pain and urgency, as he goes to the ground leaning on my couch.

Niel goes straight to my kitchen where I keep it because I tend to slip when preparing food. Which is what I was just doing waiting for them to come over to watch the new drama that's about to air, but now there is a whole new drama playing out in front of my eyes.

June paces around the floor her hair plastered to her body cussing up a storm in mutters. Alix holds onto Daniel's stomach blood pulling out of her fingers. Standing still shellshocked at what's playing out.

Niel came back with my kit and my chest relaxed to see Alix's calm demeanor. Taking a breath braking me out of my fear, walking over to the door, shutting it with a soft click, my hands started to tremble.

Turning on my heel Alix already has the needle prepped. Daniel has a long gouge cut into his midsection.

Grunting through his teeth holding back the pain as exposed meat burns into my retinas. June, now in a fetal position, is comforted by Niels' gentle touch.

"What the hell did you guys do?" My voice trembles as I moved closer.

Even though the words are out, I wish I never said them. Niel looks up at me his blond hair still has remnants of blood in it.

I inquire, "Don't tell me you went over again?"

"They were interested." Niel replies, "Daniel and I have been there so many times without issues. This time, something went wrong."

"Fucking hell, you cunt." Daniel barks at Alix. "Can you be more gentle?"

She tugs his skin as she makes do with my first aid kit, "Stop moving so much; I've only practiced on fake skin."

"Trinity get me your strongest alcohol."

"Good idea I need to disinfect."

Daniel smirk, "That too, but I need a drink."

Rubbing my temples, grabbing my vodka out of the freezer. I don't bother giving him a glass.

I'm the only one sitting on my leather couch, my elbows on my knees still rubbing my temples. "Is that zombie blood on you or did you get June and Alix into whatever the hell you two do?"

Shaking his head, Niels expression solum. "No, they just wanted to see the swimming hole, the one from before high school. When it started to rain they came from everywhere."

Niel and Daniel I am used to sneaking beyond the walls of the city. They can be gone for hours or days and when they come back they don't talk about it. The only reason I found out is because they can't go to the hospital when they get hurt. When I feared Niel was about to die one day, I made them tell me or I would report them. All I know is they sell stuff. I don't know what, or who, and to be honest I don't care. The gray lines muddy to black where we shouldn't tread.

Niel somehow knows all of the blind spots in the city while famously always keeping a neutral expression. Daniel just has to follow Niels' lead.

Daniel let out a holler as Alex poured the vodka over his wound, "This is for almost getting us killed."

Daniel took a swig, smiling despite the pain, "Bitch, but wasn't it fun. To feel alive."

"Since you are feeling so alive why don't you clean my apartment with all this blood." Leaning on my couch, I sigh, "You gave me a migraine."

Niel rose letting go of June, "I got it, Infinity." He wink, going to the kitchen.

Cheeky bastard. I have no clue when he started to call me that but it's stuck. He came back with some medicine for my head.

I ask as my brows closed the distance. "Do you want to talk about it?"

Shaking his head, Niels' throat bobbing the hint of worry that looks like he's just swallowing to others. "We got out of there that's all that matters. I'm worried about June."

Sitting by June, rubbing her back as she trembles. I have never stepped outside of these walls, so I have no clue what it was like to experience a horde.

It has been six generations since the first wave. At least three generations behind these walls. We are trained in school in what to do if we are faced with a zombie, a horde normally done in group settings. Fundamentally, I know what to do, but I may be trembling like June now if I were faced with one.

My nose flares as June remains distant, not saying a word. Pushing my hand through my hair wanting to comfort her. To know what she's thinking at this moment. Her hands tucked beneath her pits, avoiding all eye contact.

Reassuring June, Daniel says, "Look I'm good, we are all good. We are at Trinities. It's safe."

Alex sat on the other side, "Yeah Jun - Jun…Do you want to talk?"

We eyed one another, both the same thought. June always goes to therapy for her anxiety and mental illness, and what happened tonight wasn't going to help her mental health.

"Why don't we all spend the night here? We can watch movies all night, a sleepover the five of us." Wrapping my arm around her, my fingers touched something wet. "June?"

"Hell yeah, I'm down my place is a snooze fest. Niel is stingy and don't let me do shit there…" Daniel sits up, "Trinity, you good girl?"

"Trinity?" Alex asks moving away.

Panic surges across the room as my hand pulls back with dark blood staining my fingers.

I choke not wanting to say the words out loud, "June… How did you get hurt."

"Oh, fuck. She's hurt?" Daniel says grunting in pain as he tries to lean over.

Niel slowly standing. June trembles in fear. I look at my hand, the blood is dark as if it's old.

"Fuck June…" Niel says as he stared at my hand, "You got bit."

A thick air falls over the apartment. I shot to my feet. Finally, June looking up at me. Her doe eyes are red holding back her tears.

Shaking her head, not saying a word, she lean over reaching out for me. I dodge out of her way, fear gripping me.

We all stand well out of arm's reach of her unfair fate.

Alex swears, "Why did you not tell us?"

June's high-pitch voice freezes me to my core, "I didn't want to be left."

"I…I got to make a call." I stumble to the kitchen. My hands trembling as blood smears on the counter. "Fuck. Fuck, fuck, fuck."

She doesn't deserve this fate. She's been scared to do anything all her life and when she finally decided to do something this happens to her.

The world beyond the walls are too cruel and unpredictable. I'm shocked Niel would even allow them to go.

My body tremble as the phone rang. "Hello, this is the hazard department what seems to be the problem?"

Words stumble over each other, "Um…I need the hazard team."

"I am sorry did a loved one die? Make sure you are in a safe room just in case they rise be…"

"No... No... She isn't dead yet." I interjected the heaviness of the situation thicken between the pauses, "She's bit."

A bittern person is more unpredictable than one who has naturally passed. A bite can take minutes to days to fester; the longest recorded time is forty hours, quickest is two minutes.

Silence linger on the other end as she flipped through the protocol for a bitten person. Twirling my finger around the cord, I let out a heavy sigh.

"Ma'am, is she at your location?" The operator ask breaking the silence.

A heavy regret, "Yeah."

"Understood. We have our team going there now. Is there anyone else in the location other than the two of you."

"Three others."

"Their names?"

"You'll find out when you are here. No, no one else is bit. Her name is June Elly Smith." I close my eyes as tears streamed down. "How long?"

"ETA seven minutes. Ma'am, is she showing any signs of turning?"

"Red eyes, blood turning black. She's still aware scared as shit... So am I."

"I understand this is scary, and I know you want to spend time with her, but for the best of everyone get her into a room that can lock, or all who haven't been bitten get out of your apartment."

"I under..."

A loud scream bellows out of Daniel, than his voice went silent. Quickly Niel and Alix screams with clattering of objects. My blood turn to ice, and I press myself against the wall.

"Please, Mother Earth, no…" Before dropping the phone.

I can hear the woman's muffled words as the phone sway. I only can hear Niel saying what could be, go, or no before the chaos stop and silence blanket the room. *Please no.*

Shoving down my fear, sliding backward, grabbing the large knife from the drawer, I held it tight in my hand. Please let me be *overreacting.* My nostrils flare with the strong scent of iron that filled the air. Sickening sound of flesh tearing makes me lose my breath.

Peering from behind the wall a gut-wrenching scene. Daniel, whose wound had just been sewn up, lay there lifeless. Organs torn out from the re-opened wound. Niel bears a huge bite mark in his neck, blood seeping out. June hunch over, digging her hands into Alix's abdomen. June's jaw clicks as wetness move around as she ate at Alix's body.

Unmistakable zombie-like, my body shiver at the sight. I have seen videos where they communicate with weird clicks and chatters. Now in person, I am seeing it with my own eyes from my friend.

Tiptoeing closer, this isn't June this is a zombie. A zombie that just happens to look like my June. Niel's hand twitch signaling me to leave. He force his eyes to look at the door and back at me, back at the door. The unspoken message is clear; leave while I still can.

My lips in a thin line and fighting the rising urge to wail. Shaking my head, my vision blur as my tears form, but I got to do this. This is what we are told if we encounter a zombie we go for the brain. It's better her body dies at the hand of me than a stranger.

Her head jerked sniffing the air. She got the waft there's another living body still in the room. Her chatter stop as I thrust my knife from the base of her skull upwards, twisting it. The lifeless body falling to the ground. Gulping, keeping my gaze on the wall unable to look. Can't bear to see her covered in our friend's blood.

"Niel?" I turn to him, sitting by his dying body, "Why… Why couldn't you save yourself?"

"Couldn't…no weapons." Niel manage to say.

The room reveal the horrible truth he beard. I have vases too fragile to pierce a zombie's brain. Niel manage to lift his weak hand to mine, rubbing my hand slowly. Eyeing his wound, I close mine shut, tears streaming down my face. Only if she tore into him with her hands, Niel could be saved, but she had to bite him.

"Kill…me." He pull my hand forward, my white knuckles still clinging to the knife. "Kill...Ple…" It is too much for him to say as blood poured out of his mouth.

Pulling my shaky hand away, I know he is *suffering*, I know he is in pain, but this is *my friend*… That zombie on the ground resembles June, the one that caused this nightmare to unfold. I *can't* kill him. I cry out, "The hazard team will be here any moment." shaking his head, I whine. "Don't make me Niel. I am not strong enough."

"Infi…nity..." Slowly he let out a blood-filled smile.

"Fuck." I whimper, "I told you guys don't go out there. Now you all left me alone."

"Sor…"

"No, I am sorry… Just close your eyes." Biting my bottom lip, as he closed his eyes, "That night last summer, you thought you were going to be killed with whatever shit you been doing, and you told me you loved me. I told you I love you as a friend. I lied." His eyes open slowly, my voice trembles.

Selfishly all I want to do is say the only thing that always been on my mind. "I love you more than that but since you never ask me out I was too scared to tell you. I still love you, but I was so scared of you leaving me, and look… I was right to be scared."

Closing his eyes, a tender smile curl upwards mouthing, '*I love you too.*' Raising the blade above my head, this moment will never leave my mind. His peaceful smile, the overwhelming feeling of helplessness tearing at my mind.

Letting out a scream of heart-wrenching pain as the cracking of bone vibrated through my hands. Leaning forward screaming at Niel, he didn't move underneath me.

Dropping the knife at the door as I ran out of my apartment leaving them all behind. Descending the stairs, a couple leap out of my way screaming in panic. My clothes, I think covered in Niel's blood, soak me.

Stumbling out of the lobby door's opening into a misty night. Sitting on the curb the distant sirens drew closer. Bouncing my leg as the mist soaked me, my thoughts rattling inside of my head. How did this happen so fast? Why did I not have anything to protect ourselves in my room. We are taught at a young age to always be prepared just in case. We are so safe here I thought it was all okay. Crying in my hands the vehicles screeched to a stop. The weight of their deaths press on top of me; it is all my fault. Their deaths are on my hands.

A group leap to the ground shafts ready to fire. Clad in gray uniforms adorned with dark blue sashes marking they are with the hazard department. Long ago we got rid of guns relics of the past that I only seen one photo of in school. Discarded for the silence of darts with barbed tips, capable of stealthy impact to destroy the brain. Reusable unlike the bullets guns took, but the task of retrieval can be daunting if there more than a few zombies walking around.

Holding up my trembling arms - my head down in silence. Lowering their weapons, I point to the building as a few came forward.

My voice crack as I say, "Four dead, June Elly Smith was the one who got bit and turned. Niel he was suffering she bit him in the neck…" My gaze lift to their faces mask with no emotions causing me to brake. They would had been the ones to take his life if not for me. People who can't even show an ounce of dread, "He begged me to, and the knife is somewhere on the ground."

My head feels heavy as I rest it on my knees, "Daniel and Alix… I didn't destroy the brain."

"Understood." The only one who truly looks at me says.

One gesture of his head and the others are off going inside of the building. The man who answer me sat down.

He asks, "What is your name?"

"For records?" I question, not caring to look.

"Well yeah," A genuine concern in his voice, "Are you okay…Not for the record."

Shaking my head as my shoulders slump forward, "Trinity O'Salves, I just had to kill someone who looked like my friend and my friend."

"You a junior?"

They ask this to see if your mind is all there after a traumatic experience. I reply, "We were all sophomores. Would graduate this summer."

"For the record, how did she get bitten? We need to know if there are more inside."

"Outside the wall. I wasn't there; you can check the cameras." My lids only half-open, remembering the hazy details. "All I know they rush into my apartment. When I ask them what happened, they said they went to have a swim, and a hordes surrounded them."

He nod, jotting down notes on his screen. Putting it back into his chest pocket retrieving a flask in its place. It's the wanderers' fault, really, that hordes still exist. They live like it's the first wave, moving from place to place, making small communities, repeating the same mistakes.

He offers me the flask. Taking it, pausing before putting it to my lips, my nostrils flare handing it back to him. "I don't do Lily."

"You won't sleep for a while without it. Trust me, it helps."

Lily, a drug that grows abundantly which is legal to use. I never felt the need to indulge in it. As I hold the flask, my hands tremble. Tilting my head back, taking a swig.

This is mixed with alcohol; Lily can be consumed in various ways – smoke, eat, or even used in balms. Regardless of the method, it has a relaxing effect.

The burn of the alcohol travel down my throat, soothed by the sweetness of Lily. The Hazard team emerges with a singular whistle. More people went in pairs carrying body bags.

As they emerge out of the building carrying the filled body bags. Closing my eyes I can't see it. Knowing they are in them I take a heavy swig.

The man took the flask with a sad laugh, "That's enough, you don't want too much since this is your first. Glad I could pop your cherry." His brows furrow, "That wasn't an appropriate joke sorry… You have anywhere to go kid?" shaking my head, resting my cheek on my knee once more. "Wait here."

He walks over to a woman in a dark blue uniform with a gray sash. She must be the head of the team.

My leg bounce unconsciously as I sat there. No one talk to me as they pass by as if I wasn't even there. If it wasn't for that man moments ago, I would think I wasn't sitting here myself.

The rain cease, the heaviness of everything making it unable to move. As the heavy droplets fall around me bouncing off the tapestry above. Slowly, lifting my head tears well up at the sight of the two-standing holding an umbrella. Niel's Mom and Dad stood there keeping me safe from the heavy rain that falls around us.

My lip quiver, "It happened so…"

Sandra pulled me into an embrace, not uttering a word to me.

Gabe envelope us both, his deep voice cutting through the silence, "You are coming home with us Trinity. Don't argue, don't say you got this."

His voice stern, "No, you aren't a bother."

Niels' family moved here during our middle school years. This city, born from the downfall from the first wave.

When my parents died, I was too young to take care of myself.

Gabe and Sandra has always been there for me.

In a mutter, I say, "I killed your son."

Sandra's tears fell with ease, "No, you saved him… You saved him…"

Death hung heavy in the air so surreal that he is gone just like that. My friends are all gone before my eyes. Gabe held the umbrella while Sandra and I cried on each other's shoulders making our way to their home.

Days later, standing outside the hazard department building, grief hit again knowing this will be their final time in arm's reach. Their families came to see off my fallen friends, their children and sibling. Gabe and Sandra brought a priest to pray over Niel's body before it gets dumped. Inside the walls, no bodies get buried, a precaution in case the dead return if the brain wasn't killed.

Niel's parent's wanted me to say goodbye with them to be a part of their practice, but the other families made it well known I am not welcomed. June's family served me papers blaming me for her tragic ending. Excuse me that I was outside the walls and didn't keep their child safe.

Gabe, the best lawyer in all the cities unleashed a counteraction lawsuit that he brought with him today. His argument reminded all June had been aware she was bitten and still came back without informing anyone, demanding reparations for my mental trauma. Trusting Gabe in this messy legal battle, I know he will do right by me. Making sure I won't have a penny taken from me nor spend a single day behind bars, everything after that he's free to do as he wishes.

I sip on my tea infused Lily. Every time I close my eyes I only see that nightmarish night, the blood, June's clicks echoing in my mind, and the cracking of Niel's skull.

I won't smoke the crap, nothing going into your lungs is ever good, and it is too early to drink. The guy was right about me not getting sleep without it. Half-done, I leaned my head back and the Lily making it heavy.

Sitting on the bench outside the hazard facility, the doors swung open, out storm June's parents. Looks like he gave them the papers. Gabe puffing his chest out, jabbing a finger at June's father.

My chest tighten to see no one from Daniel's family attended.

Alix's family pass by, her parents without acknowledging me. Her younger sister offered me a sorrowful smile, behind her eyes the silent wish that Alix sat here. Their eyes swollen from crying. Lowering my head with the weight of their grief pressed on me. I too wish they all sat here and that I laid lifeless.

My nostrils flare. Rising, a few inches taller than June's mom, who never told me her name, or cared for my existence after finding out what my last name is.

I stood my ground, allowing her to approach. I place my bottle on the ground, and my arms hangs lifeless at my side. Sandra's futile plea to not hurt me echoes through the air. Before the others descended the rest of the stairs, a slap reverberate across my face.

My head cock to the side I did not react. Lowering my heavy gaze meeting her glare.

"You should have been the one to turn." She spat.

Calmly I stated the truth, "I wasn't the one foolish enough to leave the walls."

Her fist came hurtling towards my face. Jerking my head to the side avoiding a broken nose, her punch landed on my upper cheek. Crumbling to the ground as she straddle me her fists impacting my body, it burns as skin tore and blood came out.

Gabe grabbing her flinging her off with a sharp tone, "Now you have no fucking chance of winning the case, you psychopath!"

Lying on the ground, metallic taste of blood fills my mouth. Sandra lean me forward, each movement sending a throb of pain through my head. This is the price I deserve for surviving.

I say glaring upwards, "If you hadn't sheltered June, she would have known how to fight. They probably risked their lives protecting June while she huddled. All you have is to blame yourself."

"Fucking bitch." Her words lace with venom, "You should had died with the rest of the O'Salves."

Allowing my heavy head to fall to the side with a blood-filled smile, "Yeah, I should have."

Walking away with Sandra, Gabe yelled something about getting footage. I can't escape reality, cursed to bear the pain of surviving.

Snitched my own family out because I didn't know better then. Didn't comprehend the gravity of what would happen. It was too late by the time I realized what the truth costed me. Living in the same apartment that my family once all lived in. The only reason I didn't go into foster care is cause my family owned it, and Niel's family promised to look over me. It's so I didn't get abused for my last name, O'Salves.

*

A few weeks later, along came the court hearing. Confine to a small room with two interrogators, Gabe is outside engaging with the judge. This is not the first time I sat in one of these rooms.

A tall, slim looking man, leans forward, "Why did you not go with your friends outside the wall?"

"I only knew what happened when they came running into my apartment." I reply, guarded with my response.

"They were your friends though. Why would they not allow you in on the fun, some freedom, as one of your friends always claimed? Daniel, he got arrested plenty of times for breaking the rules. A disruption to our society.

"I see you have no records of breaking any rules. Even when his family cast him out, you let him stay with you for a few months before Niel, another rule follower, took him in. Why would you be friends with a person like that?" He push the narrative.

"I knew him since childhood." I assure, aware of their traps. "You looked through my texts, reviewed the videos. You know everything, to reiterate, I was making food to watch the new drama."

I remain vigilant navigating the tricks of wordplay and emotional string pulling as before.

The woman who's been lingering in the corner of the room approach, settling into a chair across the table. My eyes heavy recognizing who she is. She's the one who had me spill the beans. Letting me believe my family would been alright if I told the truth. Elizabeth flip through the slender document on my life.

"You haven't stepped in your parents path yet." Elizabeth says a hint of surprise traces her tone, "I'm impressed. Hmm, but you are reserved, much like your brother was. They were your only friends."

A bitter smile tug on my lips, "Well, that happens when your nickname is snitch."

She flip to a page with her handwriting from years past. "You aren't as talkative as before. Have something to hide?"

"This doesn't have anything to do with the case. That case is closed." I assert, "I am not a child anymore. I know when to speak and when to keep silent. Like the lessons ingrained to be good citizens."

Puckering her lips, she flip to my recent hospital visit. A few stitches inside my lip, a cut across my cheek, and a nasty black eye that is still visible just by looking at me.

Elizabeth close the documents, sliding it forward. Resisting the urge to touch it keeping my hands beneath the table.

"Gabe is demanding hefty compensation for mental trauma, property damage, countering their claims that you caused them mental trauma allegedly knowing about your friends leaving the walls and not warning anyone. Gabe added more compensation due to the physical altercation. Restraining order preventing them from being in the same building as you. Do you agree with these?" She ask, her amber eyes fixated on me.

"Yes." I reply, maintaining eye contact.

Niel's advice echo in my mind: do not look away, or you look guilty.

Leaning forward, she place her palms on the table, "Why are they doing this for you? You killed their son."

My heart stung, "Ask them. He was bit; you see that in the report."

"You are supposed to get out, shutting the door to contain the infected. You did not follow protocol."

And let the hazard team with no sympathy behind their gaze be the last thing Niel seen, no.

Licking the stitches inside of my mouth, I say, "That was my plan. He was bleeding out. He begged to end his suffering." A heavy sigh escape holding our eye contact, "I admit to killing Niel, and it will haunt me for the rest of my life. I did it as his last wish, so he did not turn before the hazard team arrived. What I did was humane, so he didn't suffocate on his own blood."

A subtle rise in her lip suggest I may have revealed more than I should. What she doesn't realize is I've been carefully choosing my words. I know what can happen admitting to killing someone before they turn.

The skinny man loom over me, "Trinity O' Salves, you have admitted to killing someone who loved you," pushing messages forward from Niel and Daniel. "Niel couldn't get enough of you. A man who you wouldn't give the time of day." A cruel satisfaction in his tone, "Poor boy, smother over you, would do anything for you, give up everything for you. All for someone who snitched on her parents, someone who can't get into any colleges because of their last name, a girl who would ruin his reputation."

Tears well up, "This has nothing to do with the case of Junes parents." I insisted on keeping on subject.

Elizabeth interjects with calmness, "It has everything to do with it because you knew June loved Niel."

My heart sank. I did know. She had called dibs on him when his family first arrived. I tried to play matchmaker, but June's mental state kept getting worst, her anxiety would give her a full-blown panic attack with the thought of asking him out. I never revealed Niel's confession to me that night; I convinced myself he was just scared.

It would be the only reason June ventured beyond the walls. She wanted to be close to Niel, something we often talked about during our sleepovers. She wanted the relationship he and I had to be close, for him to rely on her like he did me. She remained oblivious to Niels' often ventures beyond the walls, and the dangers he got into. Instead, she believed it was the so-called 'freedom' Daniel always spoke about.

"Do you think if you told June that Niel was in love with you, she wouldn't had gone?" Elizabeth's calm voice strum a nerve.

My lip quiver thinking about the words before reluctantly replying, "I don't know."

It's deja vu- Elizabeth has a way of trapping me with her questions. She did this to me last time. If I say yes, it can be twisted against me, giving June's parents the win.

"How do you not know?" She tap at the paper containing messages between Niel to Daniel.

Niel's message read, *'I told her. I told her I loved her, and she told me she loved me as a friend.'*

Daniel reply immediately, '*shit man, that fucking sucks. Well talk at our spot man.*'

Elizabeth narrowing her eyes at me. "Where was their spot Trinity?"

Shaking my head, "I don't know where…" My voice cracks, "I thought he was joking with me."

She took the paper, reading from it, "Joking…I am only reading Neil's messages here, 'Man how her hips look in that uniform got me going.' 'I am going to ask her out.' 'June wouldn't leave I couldn't get a chance to be alone.' 'Why would she date that trash. He doesn't care about her. I know he is using her.' 'I can't go tonight reschedule. Trinity needs me that bastard broke up with her. I am going to comfort her. I am her only family.' 'I did something. I need your help don't let Trinity know what happened to her ex.'"

He left me that night after I fell asleep crying my eyes out. The next morning, he returned with torn-up hands. My ex couldn't walk properly for weeks, claimed he had overdid himself at the gym. I thought he always looked on edge when Niel was in the same room as him. Did Niel do that for me?

Elizabeth persist, her tone cutting through the air, ""I need one of your side pieces. I need to fuck someone before I burst. I can't handle seeing Trinity in her pj's without a bra for another second' Seems to me you were wanting them to look," My face is red from embarrassment, "Do I need to continue, or do you see that he was just joking."

"I understand I made the wrong assumptions." I admit, "You can look at June and my messages. You'll see that I actively tried to get them together. It's her fault for not letting her feelings known to Niel."

"Is there anything else you want to confess to before we end this?" The man asks.

I pay him no attention, maintaining my eye contact solely with Elizabeth. Let's embrace the title of *Snitch*. Parting my lips, revealing the secret June had entrusted to me. "Every time we were supposed to practice killing zombies, her parents would purposely take her out of class. They didn't believe it was right for citizens to be so barbaric. Her parents are the reason she got bit."

I stood up, here we go, leaning forward I state, "June's mental state was so bad because her parents sold her body."

Elizabeth drop her mask, unable to maintain her calm expression. You try to ruin my life after I endured my best friends dying. Then I will ruin your life. I am a Snitch, after all.

Standing before my peers, the judge examine the information at hand. His gaze darted from his own notes to Elizabeth's. Reading the end, his eyes flew open with the shell I dropped at the end.

Clearing his throat, the judge says, "Seeing all the information in front of me today, I have made my decision. Trinity is innocent of any knowledge of them going outside of the wall, absolving her responsibility for June being bitten. She did report it as well, following protocol when someone is infected."

June's mom yells disagreeing with him, but the judge continue ignoring her outburst. "She is guilty of killing Niel before he turned. Gabe, you are defending her today; did you have knowledge of that?"

Gabe, standing beside me, "I did know this. My wife and I went over as soon as we got the call. Trinity, the first thing she told us was that she killed him. I understand that is not protocol, but I am relieved that his friend took him out of misery, and a stranger wasn't the last thing he saw."

The judge nod in agreement, "With this, Trinity is eighteen years of age, meaning she is an adult. Since he was bitten, she will not be charged with murder. You will get everything you ask for today. On the condition that Trinity will not live under your roof anymore since she did kill your son. This is her punishment for not following protocol."

My heart fell into my stomach, my legs becoming weak, and dread coming in a heavy wave.

"Sir, she only has a few months of school left, and she can't go back to that apartment after what happened." Gabe pleas.

The judge brought down his gavel. "That is my ruling. Trinity cannot live with you, Gabe. She has to be punished for not following protocol, with the end of this hearing, and winnings of the court today, she can move into a new apartment in no time."

June's mom ball, accusing me of ruining her life, oblivious to what is about to come her way with what I unraveled today. This hearing will be nothing compared to what is about to come their way. Only if the Luners investigate into my claims at least.

Unable to go back to Niel's parents' home, I say my goodbye. They arranged a week in a hotel room. As I sat there, Gabe and Sandra assure me everything will settle down soon. My chest hurt for how kind they are after losing their son.

"We will gets someone to clean your apartment, and you can move back in a week." Sandra says.

Shaking my head, I reply, "Clean it and sell it. That apartment is filled with horrible memories. I am eighteen, an adult who needs to move on."

Sandra ask, "What about your belongings?"

I clearly stated looking her in the eyes, "Get rid of everything."

Her expression soften giving me a small nod ending the conversation, and then they left me alone in that hotel room.

The next day, I return to school with all eyes on me. Bruises still visible yellowing in coloration. The report from my trial were available for all eyes including Niel's messages to Daniel. The thing that's missed is my last comment about what Junes parents did to her. Furthering my feeling that since dead people can't talk they won't look into my confession.

At the end of the day, I open my locker, to put away my schools tablet. Out pour hundreds of folded, crumpled papers, each bearing words like 'murderer,' 'snitch,' 'heartless,' 'bitch,' and even 'killer.' Piles at my feet, closing the locker turning towards the chuckles down the hall. Standing in a corner, a group lean in watching me.

They stood where two halls met halfway down the long stretch.

Confronting them, I ask, "Were you the ones who did this?"

"Most of the school helped. We know you, Snitch. Saved your own ass. You probably watched them die and didn't do shit. Just like you watched your family die." One of them sneer.

Daniel would be pushing to fuck them up. Niel, however, would tell me to be the better person and walk away. What they would say doesn't matter anymore. They are gone.

Grabbing the instigator by the back of the head, wrapping my hands in her vibrant died red hair, and smashing her head into the locker twice before they had the chance to react. Cursing as they pull me off her. Holding her hair most came with me as I lied on the other side of the hall. She cries in a panic as her once-beautiful hair scatter on the ground. Kicking at me their words were no longer audible as I curl into myself. Lights turning black and the distant sound of shoes squeaking on the ground.

Opening my eyes in the hospital, Sandra sat there, her head back sleeping in the uncomfortable chair. Pulling out the needle in my arm, taking off the heart monitor, the machine went crazy. Sandra jerk awake as I try to stand.

Sandra demands, "Trinity, lay down. What do you think you are doing?"

I reply, "Don't waste your money on my hospital bill. I am getting out of here. Thank you, but I want to be alone."

"Honey, you picked a fight. Right now, being alone is the last thing you need."

Rubbing my temples, I explain, "They left the notes in my locker. I didn't start anything."

Slipping off the gown in front of her, not caring about modesty. Putting on my bloody school uniform I limp out of the hospital.

My legs throb in pain, as I laid on a park bench, using my school bag as a pillow.

"You are making Sandra worry Trinity." Gabe says, sitting beside me "Why are you doing this?"

I didn't look at him. Keeping my eyes set on the stars above.

"Trinity, you aren't like this. You don't want this type of attention."

"I am okay being called a Snitch, but not okay being called a murderer." I mutter, "I shouldn't had killed June; I should had been bit like the rest of them."

Shaking his head, he let out a sigh. We sat in silence both gazing up at the stars.

Breaking the silence, I say, "I deserve the hate I know that."

He didn't miss a beat as his head lower, "No, you don't."

"Gabe, I know I do. I see Alex stomach pulled out into the open, being devoured by that zombie that looked like June. Niel using his eyes telling me to run but I couldn't. If I just had weapons in my living room like they recommended, they could been alive."

"It has been six generations since the first wave." Gape explain, "None of us think it's going to happen. Three generations behind the walls, safe from danger, a good generation where the hazard team perfected their call times."

"About to be seven generations. Still no cure." I close my eyes, "Will there ever be a way that we no longer have to worry?"

Gabe put his hand on my knee. "I hope so. Your dad, he was the head of that department, finding a cure to kill that part of our brains that make us turn. I know you don't remember much of his job, but to this day, they are still trying to find out why we developed it, and how to kill it so we no longer turn. Where we pass into the heavens with ease."

Glancing at him for half a heartbeat, I look back up to the sky. I am surprised that there are people who still believe in a higher power all these years later. Monsters we can become, and they still look for a being we can't see for salvation.

My arm wrapped around him Gabe helped me walk back to the hotel room. Opening the door, balloons fill the room, and Sandra held a cake in her hands.

They say simultaneously, "Happy half birthday!"

'*happy 18ᵗʰ and ½ birthday Trinity.*' I laugh as I read it.

Gabe nudges me, "Come on, blow out the candle before it gets all over the cake."

Sandra added, "Don't forget to make a wish."

I closed my eyes leaning over, *I wish that I forget this pain, and that there is an afterlife that all my friends are in.*

Blowing out the candles in one go, they cheer.

Opening my eyes, a pair of keys dangle in front of me. Blinking a few times, my brows scrunch.

"These are yours Trinity." Grabbing them from Gabe, I turn them a few times. "The judge said you couldn't stay with us, but he said nothing about us giving you a home."

"No. No, no, no I can't accept this." I held out the keys, but Gabe walk away, "Please no, I can't accept you buying me a place. Like he said, I'll have the money to buy my own soon."

He wave a dismissive hand, "We didn't buy it, so don't worry. It's Neil's apartment."

My heart sank at the words. His parents are just giving me his place. "Why, why would you do this?"

Sandra, putting the cake down, sat on the bed with Gabe. They held hands as she says, "We knew how close the two of you were. Since you don't have anyone else, we are your only family and want to take care of you. This will be our last way we can make sure you are settled and okay before we leave."

I gulp, "Leaving?"

"Yeah honey. Gabe's mom is getting sick, and she needs help to live. We couldn't get her over here, but they gave us permission to move to our old city." Tears fell down my face, "Oh honey."

Sandra stood coming to give me a hug. "We will help you sell your apartment first, and we will see you walk at graduation, and then we will leave."

I held her tighter. I am losing Niel's parents; I will lose everything I hold dear to me. He never told me about his parents moving away. Was he planning to move with them, or was he going to stay behind?

The next day they pick me up from school, a Lily tea in hand, trembling as we approach Niel's apartment. They always came over to my apartment, I've never seen his before. He lived in the heart of the city, amidst the hustle and bustle, unlike mine located on the outskirts- slower, not as shiny.

My hand shook as I inserted the key, turning it, I hear the electronic hum unlocking the door. Pushing the door open his scent filled my lungs. Hitting the ground, tears of pain fell before the door even closed. My drink scattering on the hard wood floor, as the world blurred.

His apartment decorated in black tones, dark wooden floors, a staircase with glass ascending to the second story. Spacious living adorned with a large C shape couch, three times the size of mine. It is fully furnished everything matching. How did he manage to buy *this* apartment?

As we walked around I went to the wall, floor to ceiling glass windows, a breathtaking view of the heart of the city below.

"Wow, Niel worked so hard for this place." Sandra says in awe.

I turn around, and she is standing in the kitchen rubbing her hands on the counter. "Is this the first time you seen this place?" I ask.

"Niel kept to himself. He didn't even let us know he had been working part-time till he moved out. We always meant to see it, but every time he say it wasn't the right time."

"Why don't you guys put this place in your name, and I just stay here until I find…"

Gabe interrupted coming down from upstairs, "We already signed the place over to you, and you are the rightful owner. I may had snuck the deed in with the documents you sign to sue the people who won't be named. You can't disagree cause everything is finalized. This home is yours. The master bedroom is beautiful, Trinity, you are going to enjoy it here."

I can see where Niel learned how to be sneaky from.

They are so easy to call all of this mine. How am I having a harder time accepting this new reality than they are?

His mom open the fridge, and there was no food-just some sodas, waters and a lot of alcohol. Shaking her head, she closed it. "Why don't I order some delivery and have our first meal in here?"

There was no objectifying to it. About twenty minutes later, a whole meal and more-different pastas, breads, desserts, and any side dish you can think of arrive.

I mutter, putting everything on the dinner table, "This is way too much food."

She came forward with black round plates, "I was worried about you eating. Now I know you'll have food for maybe a week or two. I will wrap it afterwards and freeze it, so it won't go bad."

A soft smile peek through my heavy face. The Lily has been working well making all the thoughts of that night blurry. They are too good to me, calling me their daughter even after what I did to their son. Sitting at the table meant for eight it still looks small compared to the large apartment.

She organize everything in the fridge and freezer for me. Looking up at me, she grabbed the back of my head, tilting it down for her to kiss my forehead.

"You have always been a daughter to me." Sandra says, "Please, I am one phone call or text away. Do not hesitate to ask me for anything or if you just need someone to talk to."

Gabe adds, as he put the last dish on the rack, "Don't sleep on the couch. Niel would want you to be sleeping on a bed." They made it over to the door adding before they left, "I'll pick you up for school tomorrow morning. Sleep well Trinity."

Shutting the door behind them, the sound of multiple locks securing the door echoed through the silence. Laying on the oversized couch, I turned the tv on just for some background noise.

Before I knew it, there is knocking on the door, and Gabe was there waiting for me. Quickly getting into clean clothes, we were gone in ten minutes.

Another month, and it will be graduation. Then they will be out of my life. Three times a week Sandra comes over making sure I am eating, and that I am okay. Gabe will come with her at least once a week. They filled the quiet apartment with much-needed sound.

Niel has three bedrooms - two downstairs, and the master upstairs in the loft area. I can't go up there yet; it hurts too much. Most times I sleep on the couch. I'll try to sleep in one of the bedrooms after a few hours of shuteye. I get jerked awake from nightmares. Then I wander around, putting on a random show and falling asleep for a few more hours before needing to wake up for school.

I should be seeing my best friends walk up on stage, I am surrounded only by strangers silently staring at me. Gabe and Sandra sat with the other parents. They are here to support me. The same person who has made it where their kid isn't here. Nothing is going like we had planned.

They put a memorial of Niel, June, Alix, and Daniel. Their photos flash on the screen above, sad music playing. There was a group photo at the very end. My heart drop to my stomach. Where I once stood behind June and Alix, in between Niel and Daniel because of my height, I was in the middle. I no longer stood there. It is a photo we all had copies of. Our odd family. Someone took the time to take me out of it like I never existed.

Biting down on the stitches which are almost completely dissolved, I held back my tears. My lips quiver, but I'm not going to cry. Slowing my breathing, I listen to all the names called. Niel's parents walked up with a photo of him, accepting the diploma on his behalf. Even Daniel's mom shows up to accept his diploma. So, she can show up for this but not to say goodbye to his body, *two-faced.*

My body shook as anxiety is getting to me. Only a few people away from being called up on stage. I haven't been able to drink any Lily today, wanting to be fully in the moment because today is the last day I'll see Gabe and Sandra, but I am regretting it now. The whispers are loud as they call my name to step up onto the podium. On the stage walking like everyone else did, I feel the glares on me - people who wish I had died, wondering why I live and no one else did. Blaming me for letting my best friends die.

Accepting the diploma, the principle whisper, "I am sorry for your loss. I know the five of you were close."

My lips moves saying 'thank you' and nothing came out. Nodding his head he understood what I was trying to say.

Shaking the hand of a Lunar supervisor, she whisper, "You have done good for the community."

Nodding, I couldn't speak. If so I would had told her otherwise. We look forward for photos, and as we did, boos roar through the crowd. Slurs came at me from every direction.

The principle shouts at them, "Settle down, stop this at once!"

Spinning on my heel, I ran off stage. I didn't sit back in my spot like all the other students. I bolted out of there, the sound of clapping and laughter as I left. Tears fill my eyes as Gabe tries to catch up.

Despite hearing the distant shouts of my name, I didn't want others to see me like this. Far away from the crowd I finally stop. Gabe grab my shoulders, pulling me to him. He hugged me, and Sandra joined in, enveloping me in their warmth as snot ran down my face.

"Honey you did it." Sandra cry out, "You graduated, that is all that matters."

"Niel.." The tears fell, "He should been here Alix, June, and Daniel - they were all supposed to be here. Together."

"I know, honey. They are here in spirit."

I shook my head as Gabe's deep voice penetrate my thoughts, "They are all cheering you on Trinity, so don't let them down, you here? They are watching us making sure we stay on the right path."

They allow me to cry, to tremble in their arms, reassuring me that it's all going to be okay, that the pain will eventually fade.

As the sun dip below the horizon, I had to say goodbye to my last connection to Neil. The last people I called family. Standing at the gate that hardly opens creaking and groan allowing the armored truck to drive through. Waving goodbye, knowing this is the last time I will ever see them in person.

Slowly shuffling my feet on the ground walking alone as darkness of night blankets me.

"Ay, you the girl from the news." I can't tell if he was asking me or making a statement.

I shuffle my feet as the man approach me from the alley. He watch my face, staring at me for a few moments.

"Someone beat you up good."

I still have yellowing from the bruises of June's mom, and then the beating from people in my school, "Multiple." I reply in a soft tone. He went to hand me a roll of Lily, and I shook my head, "I don't smoke it, bad for your lungs."

His raspy laugh prove my point. He took a hit sliding in front of me, he lean in, blowing the smoke in my face.

His tongue play with his lip ring, "You want to drink?"

Lowering my eyes to the ground, I nodded. Before, I would had say no. I wouldn't had engaged with a person like this, but now I need the distraction. I need the sound of others who don't care who I am or what I done - just mindless noise. He put his arm around my shoulder guiding me down the alley he came from.

He opens a door on the side of the building marked VIP. A thick smoke of Lily burn my nose, getting the sensation of smoking it by breathing the air. My eyes flutter shut taking a deep breath in.

His laugh is even horse, pulling me in closer. "You gonna have fun here."

Chapter Two

The thumping of the base vibrates through my body as I sit in my usual spot. A drink in hand, both arms sprawled out, hanging on the couch. Looking over the railing from the VIP spot, everyone below shift, trying to dance on the packed floor. My foot tap in rhythm of the base zoning out.

My drink I'd been babying for all night long slipped up and out of my hand. Slowly blinking at the drunk girl behind me who decided she wanted the drink more than I did. My foot stop moving to the rhythm as she cheered over to her little group sitting on one the stools and packed into a small metal table. Covering their mouths in disbelief, she took a stranger's drink.

I stiffen as her arm wrap around my neck, her breath stinks from spirits, "I can't just not play the game." The drink snatching is done when someone thinks you are attractive. "You wanna come over hmm drink with us, Snitch?"

Tracing my fingertips up her arm, my grin slowly grew as her skin goose to my touch. Tilting my head back, her cheeks flush under her makeup. Making my way to the nape of her neck she slowly came closer to my face.

Tilting my head up, my smile cut off. Her eyes widen as she was about to pucker her lips for me. Gripping the back of her neck, bringing her forward, planting her head and shoulders on the couch. Her legs hanging over the other side, her short dress showing everyone her pink thongs.

"Touch my shit again, and you will be kicked out." I stood up, leaving her in her position.

The sound of her friends' heels hitting the floor, going to help her, telling others to stop laughing. A few mutters of 'bitch' came from them.

Going out of the back door, the bouncer from outside turn to me. The empty alley that I came through with that man three years ago was a special entrance. He was a son of a rich family. A year went by, and he stopped coming. Something like he was promoted and couldn't get bad press hanging here. Lucky for me everyone knew me before he left, and I got to keep using this entrance.

"You good?" Stefin ask, he's been working here for longer than I been coming. "You didn't get into a fight, did you?"

I lean over, our shoulders touching, with a big smile I ask, "Why would you think that?" Raising a brow, I could see the thought.

The slight pity I try to avoid. "Ah, yeah their anniversary is coming up."

"You get more testy when their death arrives." Stefin says, "It's been three years right?"

Moving in front of him, my breasts leaning on his pecks, "Am I that predictable, Stefin?"

He wrap his hands around my waist, pushing me a little closer, "If you were, it wouldn't be so fun talking with you, Snitch. We only know a few things about you here."

Lifting to my tippy toes, voice lowering an octave, "Oh, and what is that now stiffy?"

Feeling his pants bulge, I press a little more. He wrap his hands around me feeling my waist.

Sliding my body down until my heels touch the ground, he let out a slight moan.

Stefin grinned, "Don't call you by your real name. You don't fuck anyone. Just flirt so damn well. Don't mention your past."

I patted his pecks leaning away, "You know me just enough." Turning around, I waved, "See you next time stiffy."

Walking out of the alley, the dead streets meet me. My feet shuffle, the Lily doing its job. I only had quarter of my drink before that girl took it. Normally, I would've been there for a few more hours, but she ruined my mood.

Walking to my old apartment, I stood outside the building across the street. There is a dim flicker of life from the inside. Someone can't sleep without a nightlight, maybe scared of the dark or a small child in my old bedroom.

It's been three years since the accident. I wonder if these new owners know. Everyone knows this is that apartment complex, but many don't know which apartment it happened in. A part of me wants to buy it back, to have a piece of that old life back. Then another part knows it's for the best. Turning around, I walk back to Niel's apartment. I am still living in the shadows, the weight of their deaths always on me while the rest of the world has forgotten them.

Pressing my thumb on the sensor, I open the door. I've added a few personal touches like blankets, flowers, and some girly elements. Other than that, it still looks like when

I first seen the apartment. Checking my phone, I sigh to see it is only midnight. Plopping on the couch, I turn on a random drama.

Raking my hands through my hair, I let out another sigh. I don't like being here. Normally, I won't be getting back till three maybe four in the morning. Two is when everyone is told to leave, and they let me stay until it's all cleaned up and the employees are ready to leave. A few bouncers, bartenders, and cooks take a few drinks and relax. Sounds block my mind from thinking, from remembering, from feeling all the pain I been running from.

Heading to the cabinets I retrieve my jar of Lily tea. I lean on the counter browsing my phone, as the kettle start to simmer.

Sandra messaged me again for the second time today. *'Trinity how are you doing at the Hazard department?'* *'Tomorrow did you want to do a video call after work?'* Tomorrow night is the anniversary.

Messaging back, 'Hey Sandra been busy there. I took an extra shift so by the time I get off you'll be long asleep. Spend time with Gabe on that night.'

A lie. All of these years they do not know what I been doing. Every night I go to the club, lucky to get four hours of sleep before waking up at eight in the morning.

I put two spoons of Lily in my cup, and I pour the boiling water. Watching the dry flowers bloom into beautiful white thick petals as they once were on the trees. Seeping from them yellow liquid bringing a beautiful smell into the apartment. My eyes flutter shut as I breathe it in.

"Some honey…Honey…sweet this time." I mutter to myself.

Drizzling honey into the cup watching it sink to the bottom. Plopping the wet Lily's in the trash, I sat back on the couch drinking the hot drug.

After twenty minutes, my head fell back heavy. My eyes flutter shut and opening half way to see its four in the morning. Too heavy to get up, my eyes shut.

My body jolt as the alarm on my phone went off. Still in my club dress from last night I rush to the bathroom. Cranking the water all the way steam poured out. Washing the night before off my body, the makeup ran down, swirling into the drain. Walking my naked body to the downstairs bedroom, I slip my black bodysuit over my damp body clinging slightly to my skin. Shuffling my hips, I put my jeans over my butt buttoning them. Snatching my bag, running out of the apartment.

Hastily making my way through the gray stone hallway of my work, I froze to see an unforgettable sight. Standing there talking with another worker in a different department is a woman any day I don't want to see, but especially today of all days. Keeping my head down I beeline it to the elevator. Going in, I let out a relief sigh. Pressing G0 to go all the way to the bottom of the department where I work.

Leaning back, the doors slide close, and a hand reaches out stopping it. Tensing, I stan tall trying to hide my eye roll as she walks in. Her face hasn't changed. The cold, deadly expression still holds to this day. Her hair long and straight, virtually the same length as the first time I spoken with her.

A wicked smile form, not meeting her eyes, "Is that you?"

A soft flash of my teeth, I reply, "Long time no talk, Elizabeth. What floor are you going to?" I reach over to press it for her.

Her lips pucker, "Looks like we are going to the same floor."

Awesome, just great. "Well, that makes it easy then."

The elevator slowly descend stopping on the next floor letting two people in. They press just the floor just below us. Sensing the tension inside, they quickly evacuate before the doors even open all the way.

As they got out, Elizabeth turn her body to look at me. Her eyes scan me pinching her lips. I ask, "Is there an issue?"

Elizabeth bluntly say, "With your nightly activities, I wouldn't think they would allow you to do this job."

Another flash of my teeth. "My personal life has nothing to do with my work life." I add, "It looks like you been keeping an eye on me."

"You have odd behaviors, wandering at weird times of night."

I shrug my shoulders, "Is it a crime to be a night owl?"

"Just odd… Oh, today is the third-year anniversary of you murdering your friends."

My body tense, my eyelids falling half way, "I killed a zombie and someone who would had turned." I face the door, no longer looking at her.

I don't need this today.

The door chimes hitting our floor. Halfway open I walk through, not caring to wait for it to fully open. Strutting through the hall, I left her behind. Luckily, where she was going isn't where I work. Going down the stone halls, the bright white, fluorescent beam down. Making my way through the first gate, strong wire latticed together, the door always open. Going through the second, same style. The third, where my desk is inside that room, this one is cover with stone wall and a steal door.

All safety protocols. If the outside door fails, we have this steal layer to keep the zombies or wanderers out. If the Hazard team trained too swiftly take out and the threat doesn't get here in time to kill whoever broke through the outside door, there is the other two doors to keep them in just in case of failure. This is why we are G0, five layers below the main city. Any outbreaks underground, the people above will not find out. I signed paperwork that if I tell anyone any of this, I can get the death penalty.

Sitting at my desk I plop my bag on the ground. Leaning back, I pick up the book I was reading my last shift. They aren't the biggest fan of us being on our phones but have no issue with books or watching something on the work computer to pass the time.

Glancing at the clock, I bow my head. Still four hours left. My phone vibrated on the table over and over. The screen says 'Gabe.' They never call me during work hours.

Answering, Gabe says, "Trinity?"

I question leaning back in my chair, "Yeah, you okay Gabe?"

"Sandra said you are taking an extra shift tonight of all nights."

I let out a sigh, "Yeah, I did."

"Trinity…" I hate when he calls my name in such a doubtful tone, "You do know you are too young to do this."

"There it is. Gabe, thank you for worrying about me but I am okay."

His voice lowers in pitch, "I know you aren't working an extra shift. You sit at that desk, and you guys go out once a week to dump the bodies, where you keep watch to make sure no zombies get too close, and to warn if any Wanderers are around."

Shit, I never told them the job I was doing here. I told Sandra I worked on keeping documentation of deaths on the upper levels.

I lean forward, my head hitting the desk with a small thud. "Did you tell her?"

"She would be worried sick about you if I did. We are your family, and you tell us one lie after another."

I didn't deny it. "How did you know?"

He paused. I heard footsteps on the other side and then a door shut. Gabe's voice lower, almost in a whisper, "I got eyes on you. After a year, I felt you weren't telling us the truth and got some of my buddies to keep watch." I closed my eyes letting out a heavy sigh as he continue, "I thought you were going to grow out of this."

"Excuse me?" I sat up shifting in my seat.

Gabe continued, "I understand what happened was traumatizing; we offered to get you the best therapist."

I interrupt him, "You know how I feel about them. They will just report all that I say to the Luners."

"And you think hanging around that sleazy club you frequent is a better look? A party girl who is never home."

I mutter, "You don't understand."

"I lost my son, Trinity. I understand the pain more than you do."

I hiss, "You didn't have to feel his skull break, puncturing his brain like I did. I still see it in my sleep, still feel it, as if I am doing it all over again. So no, you do not understand. It isn't just about losing my best friends. It is what I ended up doing that haunts me." I paused, waiting for him to reply, "I don't care what others think of me. I am a Snitch, remember. No matter how straight-laced I was, I got dirty looks and whispers. At least now, I am in control with the rumors. A party girl who is never home is fine by me."

Still no reply, "Please don't tell Sandra this. I kept it a secret for a reason. I didn't want to worry you guys."

"Trinity…I won't tell her. Can you tell me if you are safe?

You aren't getting in trouble like Daniel did?"

"A Snitch wouldn't be involved in dangerous activities." The joke didn't go through. "No, I baby a drink, then I wander at night until I am so exhausted I don't dream."

"And um, *cough*, you are being safe with uh, contraceptives?"

My face heat with his question, "Okay, with that, this conversation is done. Not a nice chat but nice hearing you."

He stutter, "It's an honest worry. You are at that age…"

Rubbing my face, I can feel my ears burn, "Bye, Gabe. Tell Sandra I'll message her after my extra shift at the job."

"I'll call a favor. Get you some pills to help you sleep, bye Trinity."

Beep, beep, beep. I let out a grown, rubbing my face, my foot tapping the floor.

I went over to the door to the right of me. *I need to do something.* A small room with lockers on both sides holding extra padded gray and blue suits. Knees, elbows, wrists, and neck had the most padding. A layer of thick leather between cotton inside and a mixture of fabrics on the outside. A hope of if you get bit you can get away before they get to your skin. Leather boots laying at the bottom of the lockers; everything is neatly lined up with nothing to do.

Looking around for anything out of place, I ran my hands across the suits. Making my way to the hatch, all lights are green. Quietness fills the air much like the rest of the building. No music filled the speakers. The light humming above our heads is the only sound you can count on.

Tomorrow we will be going back up there. *I should check the masks.* The stench from the rotting bodies is too much to handle. If we have time, we gather dirt, leaves, and anything else to cover the dead. One for a little more respect, and two to help them decompose. There is at least ten piles we dump the bodies. In my almost two years of working here, I've only been to two. They try to rotate every year or so to give time for decomposition. This one we go to now is in the middle of an old city. Nature has pretty much taken it over, but there is still some life wandering around. Remnants of humans trying to live outside the walls.

I've seen some of the Wanderers before, almost six months ago as the snow buried the ground, covering the stench of rot. A lady carrying a baby ran over to us, begging to save the child, that it wouldn't survive the winter. How was she so stupid to bring a baby into a life like that? A life where they never can stay in once place always trying to get in front of any zombies. Everything inside of me wanted to help her. To help the helpless child who didn't ask to be born in this life. Never to let it know where it came from, but team refused, telling me it was a trap. That if we got close she would had attacked us. To this day, I don't know if that is true. I hope maybe it was a lie and there wasn't a baby suffering from the cold.

A heatwave is coming, and these uniforms are going to make us swim in our own sweat. The masks won't completely help with the abundance of rot that will fill the air, with the huge flies buzzing around, mating in the dead.

Clicking open the mask filter, one after another, making sure they all were intake and there aren't old filters that needs to be changed. Taking away the one bad filter I found. My nose flared as it somehow stinks like rotting flesh as I toss it in the trash. A shutter went down my spine. I feel bad for whoever may had gotten that one if I didn't check it today.

Leaving the room, I shut the large door behind me. My music that I turned on earlier still playing giving some life to the dreadful room. I hardly ever get anyone down here to talk with. My team that I go with outside works on other levels. Two of them work directly with all the dead that comes in, finding whoever has the money to cremate their loved ones. That only happens maybe three times a month, on a good month five.

There are about eight bodies we get a week - on a bad week maybe twelve, good week only three. The others range from outside duties, sweeping the streets, all the way to sitting at a desk like myself, doing odd jobs to keep our minds occupied. There is ten of us in total. We've got three new people joining us this week cause the last three quit. They only worked here not more than a year and 'couldn't take it anymore.'

Eyeing the clock, I only have an hour left. I pull up the security cameras on my floor. I can't see any personal offices, but I can see the main halls and the cameras outside the walls. Flipping through each camera I see two people walking down the hall, just chatting, papers in hands. Another camera nothing - more of nothing. Not much really goes on. My lip raised when I see Elizabeth on one of the cameras. She's alone. Keeping the camera on her, I flip to the next hall she goes down. Why is she still here after so many hours? Then she stops at a door, and someone opens it letting her in.

Bored with that, I check the outside cameras. Lush greenery spreads across my screen. The trails we take every week matted down where the large tires carrying the dead roll. One of the cameras' icons flash yellow detecting movement. My eyes close as I let out a quiet sigh. I like seeing deerlings when they graze the ground looking for food. Some with antlers sprouting like tree branches out from their heads.

Walking through the clearing is a zombie. Slowly it moves, not picking it's feet off the ground. The skin is gray in color. Maybe it is someone who recently died, or it hasn't gotten itself stuck in anything to tear it's body up yet. Slowly the Zombie turned facing the camera. Zooming in on it, the jaw shook chattering to itself.

My stomach emptied out. Never have I seen any zombie just stop like this. There have been times where they walk to the cameras, sniffing it, wondering if they can eat it. Some even try to take a bite out of it. Zooming in, I watch it shift its body again going into the woods disappearing from sight.

Getting into the elevator after my shift, I push the lobby button. Just two stops up, it opens, showing one of my teammates with a new girl. The man with her has worked here for eight years and trains almost all the new people.

A scruffy five o'clock shadow he frequently wears turning more gray every month. Dark, puffy under eyes that seem to make his eyes droop. His hair a little more shaggy than normal, rough around the edges. He scared me a bit when I first worked here, but he just wants to make sure none of us gets hurt. He didn't go into many details, but when he was a newcomer his teacher didn't care about them. He watched too many not be trained properly, get hurt, and killed because of it. He would rather us hate him and us stay alive.

The two walk in, the new girl head is tilted down her breath a little shaky. He has her scared out of her mind.

I laugh, "Randal Saint, you are going to make her cry if you keep showing her the zombie videos of everything that can and will go wrong."

He let out a grunt of approval, "Better to cry now than before we go out tomorrow."

My face flatten, "No, we only have three new people. They been training all week."

He shook his head, "Cat got fired today."

You got to be *kidding* me. I glance over to the girl, "So they are having her come along with us on her second day on the job?"

Randal nods his head, "Trying my best to teach her everything so she doesn't get killed."

The poor thing tense, "Does she know how to use the mask?" He shook his head, "Uniform?" Shaking his head, "She's only watched the video hasn't she."

Randle nodded, "Told them it would be best that we work with only nine, but heads refused, even had a Lunar here as I taught her. At the end she say it's good enough and she can go. Safer to have ten than nine."

That is why Elizabeth was here today. "With her, it is only nine and babysitting." I eyed her, "No offense."

She mutter, staring at the floor. "It's okay."

I would be surprised if she even shows up tomorrow. It would be better for all of us if she quits today. Much more can go wrong with an inexperienced person. She could turn out like June.

My eyes soften as I watch her more. She is acting like June when she got back to my apartment, too scared to speak, too scared to look at us.

Randal say, "Help me make sure the others go slow. Looks like we only have four bodies this time, so it will be an easy rout. Trinity and I will make sure you are safe. Out of the rest of our team believe it or not we have the most compassion for others."

I add, "Stick by Randal the hole time, listen to his words, and you'll be safe."

The doors open and the girl that didn't even tell me her name darts out.

Randal and I gave each other the same look - something we don't dare utter beyond the open elevator door due to any ear that can listen in. A silent agreement of 'I hope she quits.' They are putting everyone's life at risk by having her work on her second day on the job.

Getting out of the building, I walk the opposite way to my teammate. The girl is nowhere to be seen, probably running with tears in her eyes. Heartless Luners do not care about the safety of people. Their concern is only about how other cities perceive us: strong, independent, a force to be an ally with, not an enemy.

*

My hair sways back and forth as I strolled down the dark alleyway from the apartment I live in. These are the only places that don't have cameras. Every one of them are connected to another; you just have to know the right ways to go. Never in my life did I think I'd be using the tricks Niel would mutter to me. Knowing that Elizabeth has been keeping her eyes on me, and who knows who else has been watching me for Gabe. I'd rather them not know all my movements.

Walking out where there is a blind spot, I casually go into another alley. My heels hitting the ground as I approached Stefin.

"Early like always." He says turning his attention to me.

I smile while moving my shoulders forward squeezing my breasts, "You know I like my spot."

His gaze shift down with lewd thoughts on his mind.

Letting out a sigh his mood change, "About that Snitch. You can't sit there tonight."

Cocking my head to the side, my smile fades away. I don't need this tonight.

"Why is that?" I ask.

"Someone reserved it for their bachelor party."

Leaning in giving Stefin a kiss. "Well, they will be more than happy to see a beautiful woman waiting for them. Perfect time for a distraction."

He open the door for me, and the thumping of the base blasts into the alley. Twirling around, I gave him a wink as he smeared my nude lipstick, a few shades lighter than he, off his face.

Shooting straight for the couch I always occupy, with a perfect view of the floor below. Plopping down ignoring the reserved sign. The scent Lily hasn't fully bloomed in the air yet as the night is still early. Within the next hour, they will push the smoke through the vents, ensuring as soon as the partygoers walk in, their worries will be left at the door. It's the unique touch that makes this club stand out.

Pointing a finger in the air my signal for one and only. Ax came, the best bartender ever. I'm just being bias he's the only one whose been serving me. He sat a blue drink down with an extra shot of Lily extract, pulling another vial from his pocket pouring yet another shot for me.

"What's this for?" I say, swirling the drink around.

Ax tilt his head to the sky, "An extra shot of Lily on me. You planning to sit here all night?"

"If the party allows it, yes. If not, I'll sit at the bar with you." I took a sip of the triple-shot Lily, the warmth explode in my body. Hunkering myself in the couch I say, "Thanks for that."

"Anything for my favorite Snitch. If you need a spot, I'll be more than happy to shoo off the sluts who can't keep their hands to themselves." Ax turn going back to the bar where someone is waiting for a drink.

Taking another sip, I lean my head back, savoring the sweet Lily on my tongue. Opening my throat, I let the spirit drug slip down.

Babying my drink as I did every night, the Lily hit harder than usual with that extra shot, perhaps a bit too much even for my taste. I watch the dance floor increasing by the minute. Scraping my thumb nail on my tooth, I stare at a group of men coming to the stairs, hoping to get a chance to get access to VIP. Laying my head on the railing as a man flash his phone to the bouncer. Closing my eyes and reopening them, they are now halfway up the stairs.

Propping my feet on the table, my tight dress crept up. Stretching my arm across the couch, holding onto my drink, I angle my head towards the dance floor. From this position, I can see the men slowing down, perplexed by someone sitting in their reserved spot. The brunette with bleached tips who had shown his phone to the bouncer, step forward.

"Excuse me, but I reserved this spot for my buddy's bachelor party."

I slid my legs open just enough to stroke their imaginations. Planting my feet on the ground, my body wabble as I stood. *Shit,* that stuff is way too strong. Putting one foot in front of another, I swayed my hips side to side.

"Sorry about that. This is my favorite spot, so I just was keeping it warm until you guys showed." Extending my hand, I touch his peck, flashing a cheeky smile. "I'll go sit somewhere else and let you boys have some fun tonight."

The guys' faces flush as their eyes linger on me. Keeping the cup firmly in my grip I went to spin and wobble slightly as I did.

Ice tips grip tighten on my hips squeezing just enough where I know his next move. A grin slipping across my face. "Well, it's up to you guys as well if you want her to leave or not." Icey grins.

Hungry wolves are so predictable. I shoot a cheeky smile, taking a sip of my drink and lifting it in the air as they all cheered. With that motion Ax brought over a round of drinks for the entire group.

"So, who's the groom-to-be?" I ask taking my spot on the couch.

The tall one raise his hand, his head shaved short on all sides maybe an inch long, strong jaw line, scrawny but has muscle tone. "To be married in two days." He says confidently.

Tilting my head, "Aren't you supposed to do this the night before the wedding?"

Icey lay his hands on my thigh, "This one has work tomorrow. The next day is his big wedding day. Maybe get him one last night of freedom."

Taking a sip, I hid the rolling of my eyes. If he doesn't want to be held down he shouldn't gotten into a serious relationship.

The drinks keep flowing and more girls joined the party. Every guy has a girl in their laps calling for more shots. Even the groom-to-be.

A girl in a white dress got in front of me knocking my legs off the coffee table. "Aren't you the girl from last night?" Her question sound more like an accusing tone.

The Lily doing me good, a small grin that wouldn't go away adorned my face, "I frequent here often, yes."

"You the Snitch right?" Her voice sharp, "You embarrassed my friend who was trying to hit on you."

"Oh." The guys shout in anticipation.

My smile grows into a wicked grin, Icey tips moved over to the side unsure of the situation.

My head falls back letting out a chuckle, "You mean the drunk who took my drink. Hope she slept well last night with that extra shot of Lily."

She hiss, "You a fucking bitch."

I wave a finger in the air, "You don't want to do this, Nips."

Her body jolted covering her chest in embarrassment like she didn't know everyone can see them. Her shock is because she thought no one would call her out on it.

Icey put his arm around my shoulder, "Nice view, Nips, but this is reserved area, and you aren't invited."

Licking my bottom lip, I lean in snuggling as I got a whiff of his cologne. Not bad, musky with a hint of sweet, "You are right Icey, you got one more chance to leave before you make a fool out of yourself…Nips."

"My name is.."

Holding up a hand I interrupted, "I don't care about your name."

Standing inches away from her face the sound of her leg hitting the coffee table scooting it back, "You are a stranger that I don't give a shit about. For all I care, Nips, is that you get out of my view and don't ruin my buzz."

"Got to drug yourself twenty-four seven to forget about murdering your friends?"

The girls who were chuckling enjoying themselves stood up in a fright, the guys shooting weary glances. Icey even backed away, making an '*oh*' sound as he made it to the other side of the couch.

My gaze narrow as her lips moved. The gaping hole of her mouth, that red lipstick about to speak. My jaw tense, the heaviness in my head going away as my anger took over. Everything blurs, and there's soon a thud. Screams erupt with the rush of people moving around me.

Opening my eyes, my hand wrap around Nips throat, digging her hand into my arm trying to slap me to stop. I press a little harder. Feeling her quick heartbeat against my palms. She tries to swallow stopping midway, eyes bulging, face turning red, choking, unable to breathe.

"Snitch!" Someone calls out.

Leaning in, I bit out, "Never speak to me again." I held back my tears, "They turned. I saved them."

Pushing off her, she fell to the ground holding her neck coughing up a storm. Stefin standing there with two other bouncers from downstairs.

I wave my hand in dismissal, "I'm going."

Stefin put his hand on my upper back, "Are you okay?"

I shook my head, "I. Didn't. Murder. Them."

Holding my breath, I try not let anyone see me cry. Holding my head high I was guided to the kitchen in the back.

As the doors shut behind, my chest shook as shaky breaths escaped. Ax came over leaving the bar to be watch by someone else. Pacing, I put my hands behind my head.

Ax says, "Snitch, what happened out there?"

"I am not." I let out a sharp breath, "A murderer."

"Shit." He turns around, "What bitch said that."

Stefin reply, "White dress showing off all the goods. Snitch choked her out."

"Really…Scared the shit out of her?"

Stefin answer, "I was watching, and I got scared."

I spat, "Are you two really making jokes right now?"

"Go get a hit of Lily for her." Ax motion over to the back of the bar.

I shook my head, "No, I've had too much already."

"I got to go. I just need to leave."

Ax step in front of me, his hands pushing me back, "You are in no position to be alone. When it's time to close, we'll head out, and you come have food with my husband and I."

"Ah, why am I getting kicked out and she's being kept back there?" Nips screams on the top of her lungs.

My nose flared as Stefin rushed out to help the other bouncers. My hands started to shake in rage, or fear, or I have no clue what I am feeling. "This day has been a fuck fest."

Ax replies, "You are used to fuck fests aren't you Snitch. This is nothing less than what you can handle. I am serious. Come over to our place."

I smile in pain, "It was a mistake coming here today. I just…"

"Don't finish that. We all know. It sucks, and we all know you aren't a murderer; you do what's needed. Stronger than any of us.

"Ha, I talked to my husband about it before. If I got bit, would he be able to kill me? Fuck, we were both crying by the end of that conversation, and realized your balls are bigger than both of ours."

I let out an airy laugh. My hands shaking at my side. Pulling my phone out of a little inside pocket near my breasts. Checking the time it's a little past midnight.

"Thank you for the offer." I patted his shoulder, "Maybe lunch someday. But I don't want to meet your love when I'm a mess. It isn't a good look for myself."

Pushing open the door to see the crowd below spreading as Stefin has Nips over his shoulder. Screaming on the top of her lungs making a fool of herself. Before anyone notice me, I got out of there.

The door slams behind me as I let out a silent scream. Squatting in front of the door tilting my head upwards tears roll down my face without making a sound. Phantom hands wrapped around my heart squeezing it.

Taking a few shallow breaths, I calm myself. Undoing my heels, slipping them off my feet. I chuck them both into the trashcan in my range of sight. The clanking of the discarded heels vibrates. Bolting out of there, I don't care it Gabe gets notified or that the Luners find my behavior odd. I need to run. I need to get out of breath. I need my legs to scream in pain making me forget the pain in my mind and chest.

Running all the way to the other side of the city. Hunching over gasping for air, my body trembles, and the tears that have been falling for the past hour finally stopped. Looking up at the sky where the stars meet my gaze, I bit my lip.

"Why the fuck did you guys go?" I scream, "Why the hell would you take June beyond the wall?" Dropping to the ground, my knees digging into the grass, "Why, just why did you guys have to die. None of you had knives. Daniel, you always carried one, and the one time you truly needed it, you didn't have it. What are you going to tell me? You dropped it running away from the horde?..."

My neck bent as far back as it could go. I stare up with my arms hanging at my side, "It's been three fucking years, and everyone already moved on. Why can't I? Why do I still have to see all of you when I close my eyes?

"Why did I have to kill June. If she was facing me I would been bitten too, and I wouldn't be suffering now. I could be in the darkness with all of you, or even heavens as you and your family believe Niel. I miss all of you so much every day.." I stood up with shaky legs, "Fuck all of you for making me miss you so much."

I ran all the way back to the apartment where now it's almost three in the morning. Pressing my thumb on the keypad, I drag myself in. A small box in my hand that I found in front of the door. Gabe called that favor in fast.

I lay on the cold wooden floor, wiggling my body out of the dress. Sprawl out like a starfish, catching my breath. Bending my head to see the curtains are still open. Whoever is awake at this time can get a show I don't care. They probably wouldn't see me anyway; I am in the tallest apartment building on one of the highest levels.

My legs screaming, and my feet burn as if cuts were all in them. Rolling on my stomach; I am a *sweaty* mess.

The hot shower burns my body in all the right ways. My hair sticking to every curve on my body ending at my hips. Nips ruined my buzz. I was having fun with my distractions, and she had to start shit. I don't even know what she was trying to get out of that interaction.

Tilting forward I jolt. "Shit…did I fall asleep?"

I dry off going to my bedroom downstairs. Scratching my head, pushing this night out of my mind. They are just strangers, they aren't shit to me.

I wonder if Ax was telling the truth of me meeting his Husband. He's always been there when I am on the edge of braking. To be around a normal relationship, a normal life - I don't know if I know what to do being around people like that.

Rubbing my feet, which are still red, with a few cuts on my heel and side. I'll wrap them up tomorrow before work. Shaking the bottle Gabe obtained for me, my lips thinned. This is supposed to help me sleep so it wouldn't hurt. Taking the pill down with half a bottle of water, I lay on the pillow with my wet hair sprawled out. The blanket is the only thing covering me as I forgo any article of clothing.

Letting my head fall to the side I stared at the photo on my nightstand. Niel, Daniel, June, Alix, and I all in the same photo, all so happy. They were my family when I had none, and I lost them like I lost my birth family. My eyes drift close, and I force myself to look at them. I can't meet Ax's husband. I am bad luck.

I've been alone for almost three years now. I could keep this up for the rest of my life.

Chapter Three

Sitting at my desk, waiting for the others to get here. My hair up in a high ponytail and both my feet and legs bonded from over pushing myself this morning. I drank Lily tea today to ease myself, then downed a cup of coffee. I have to be fully aware going outside the walls. We already have four, hopefully, only three new people to worry about.

My expression flatten as I see my team walking down the hall. The girl *didn't* quit. She is standing extremely close to Randal, looking terrified. Elizabeth ingenious idea is putting all our lives at risk.

Behind her two people I didn't recognize, and unfortunately, I recognize the third newcomer. He is the groom-to be at the club last night. I grip the edge of my desk as I stood up.

His eyes slowly widen as he sees me emerge from behind the desk to greet them. In front of the desk, one hand still gripping it, the other cheekily waving.

Flashing a smile, I say, "Well it is nice to see four new faces on the team. I am Trinity. This is where I spend my days making sure that door over there is shut and nothing malfunctions." Turning my desktop so they can see the cameras pulled up. "Been checking for the last ten minutes and haven't seen any zombies or Wanderers. Did see plenty of birds flying around, and I know Randal warned you about the animals. Not every sound is a predator. Pay attention to us and you guys will be good."

Randal cough, "We are a team. Outside these walls we are the only ones to protect ourselves. Trinity and I have shafts and extra darts just in case. Every suit is equipped with knifes for shortrange fighting if needed." He glared at the new people, then turned.

As everyone change into their uniforms, Randal guided Abigail on how to put it on. Turns out she is the same age as me, graduated from a different school. Chad, the groom keeps glancing over at me, probably trying to figure out if I am that girl from last night. Checking the other two as their suits were on, face mask around their necks. Pulling at them making sure no skin is exposed.

"Strap your neck tighter." I instruct, "One slip-up their teeth will get your neck."

Alexander complains, "It is so hot. I'm going to die of the heat."

I hate that his name is so close to hers, "Crybaby, it's better to almost die of the heat than to die by a zombie attack, and one of us needing to stab your brain."

He stiffen at my cold glare, instantly fixing his neck. Before I made it to Chad, Randal is already pulling on his suit.

Pulling up my digital pad, which fits into my pocket when folded double - checking everything, I gave a quick nod to Randal.

"Bring the bodies." He orders.

The two who deal with the dead went out, and they will come back in less than three minutes.

"Okay, you four stay close to us. Stay in the middle if that is possible. Eyes and ears open, do not talk back, and do as you are told."

He press some buttons opening the top hatch. Up the steep incline, there are notches to put the wheels in to automatically pull the bodies out of here. Checking the cameras again, the people who've been here a while went outside to wait. Since there are eyes up there, I fold the digital pad and put it back into my pocket.

The two who walked out came back with…I recounted making sure it is correct.

"Five now?" I ask, "I thought there were only four."

"Someone died last night." Randal says in a somber tone, "Overdosed on that drug circulating."

I blurted in shock, "Calm? There's still people taking that crap?"

Randal patted my shoulder, "It just been going unnoticed for the past ten years. Looks like it's gaining popularity again." As the five bodies got lifted up passing our heads, he added, "Okay you four get ready. Abigail stay by my side."

Loosening my body, I prepare myself to go up - the beauty Niel and Daniel craved for. The illegal things they did out here, which I'm still not sure what that was. Now I go out once a week. Just another reminder of them. When seeing a wanderer, the thought always crosses my mind; Were they involved with these people?

Outside, we walk slowly. Randal leading the group with Abigal by his side, the two controlling the motors of the catty the dead are on, are in the middle. The new people found their spots with the others as I stand in the very back, as I always do. My head on a swivel for the thirty-minute walk - possibly longer, as we aren't moving as efficiently as we normally do.

Halfway to our destination. Chad moves to the back of the group creeping closer to me. The others making fun of the new people, jokingly threatening to leave them behind. Poor Abigal yip at the statement, almost grabbing onto Randal in fear. How are we the same age and yet we are so different? I wasn't even that scared my first time out.

"How long have you worked here for?" Chad finally spoke to me, stopping to be by my side.

I flash a smile, "About two years now. You'll get use to the sounds. Especially after you see the cute little animals that make them. You'll yearn for it so you can hopefully see them."

A moment of silence, as if he's trying to find something to say. He whisper, "You're okay to carry that?"

My brow raises, "What do you mean by that? I've done this for over a year. Probably six months in, I got trained. So, no worries, I know how to work it."

"I mean you were pretty drunk last night, and..."

I cut him off, "I wish you didn't mention that." My brows raised a little more, a permanent small smile, and a curious look all turn flat. "What happens outside of work stays that way. What happens in that place stays in there. Learn the rules."

He gulps, "Well you were..."

I put my mask back up angling my head to the side, "I wasn't anything, and if you mention anything again, I will let them know about your drinking fest. You had what? Seven drinks before I left. You are probably hung over;

that's a no-no. I had half a drink before a drunk pissed me off. The end. Get back with the others. Learn from them."

"What if I wanted to learn from you?"

Surveying the woods I reply, "I don't teach people. That distracts me from seeing danger before it comes."

"I am curious about the murdering thing the girl claimed…"

Growling my reply, "She was a drunk."

Chad push the subject, "But you became very agitated."

"Randal!" I holler, "Get this one up front with you."

Randal stomped the ground coming to the back where I stood, "What the fuck is wrong with you Trinity for yelling?"

My lids shut half way, "They are laughing louder than my shout. Can you tell him…the…rule…"

His eyes slid over to Chad as I bit out the last two words, and he says, "We don't talk about our past, what we do after work, or what we do out here. We are a dysfunctional team. If someone wants to talk about something, they can, but if they make it clear it isn't a subject they want to discuss, you shut the fuck up before you get punched. If you get hurt it is an accident. You understand?"

Chad's face turn pale and hurried to the others. Who are still chatting like they weren't in ear shot of that conversation.

"You okay Trinity?" Randal asks.

I reply clenching my jaw, "Seems like my bad day followed me to a new day."

"No worries I'll let them know. Just breathe the air in and find one of them scurrying animals you like so much."

He gently nudges me, "Hey, if we get a zombie, I'll let you shoot the first one, my treat."

I gave a wink, and he went back into his position. Randal always lets them know just enough about my past, so they won't ask me. Randal has his own past when he worked with the Luners, he would rather not most know himself.

Three months ago, I discovered it when he was drunk in the alley beside the club I frequent. When I reached his place, he poured his heart out. My information is all public because the news and media publicized it, but his life is locked down. What the Luners made him do made my eyes tear up. Knowing he was one of the people who tortured my parents, made my blood chill.

He tortured many bad people, even innocents, but he couldn't stop. He had to follow orders no matter what he felt. That's why, when it was time for retirement at a young age, he took it and came straight here. When he saw me, it hurt him because he knew exactly who I was. He is kind to me because of that, understanding I got the short end of the stick, just like himself.

I would never let anyone know his history. For all they know, he lived a simple life doing odd jobs, and for some odd reason he's stuck with this one. He isn't anything like Elizabeth, and I am very grateful for that.

In the front, Abigail gasp as we turn from the thick tree line, giving way to a path leading straight into a once thriving town. Now reclaimed by nature the life of humans not allowing it to completely crumble to nothingness.

Randal order, "Alright, masks on. After this point closer we get the rot will blind you."

Figuratively, it will blind you, like how onion stench does. As we get closer to the inner, nature showed signs of disturbance buildings with broken glass, entrances covered in wood, glass that didn't match frames. All sign of Wanderers. Eyeing my other teammates, we pick up our pace. There are signs of recent life.

"What the burning earth is that?" Crybaby spat out.

I laugh, "You didn't put your mask on correctly. Now you got to suffer crybaby."

"It's Alexander."

I cringe at the name, walking past him pretending not to hear him. A pile of dead creeping on us, bugs swarming for their new feast. I don't understand how the Wanderers can survive in conditions like this. Are they unable to smell anymore for survival?

The buildings that once stood tall crumple on one another, some flatten to the ground, bits disturbed for peoples use, and somehow, some still stand. We've never gone inside them. Curiosity always lingers when we come, wondering what the inside may look like. Are they destroyed or have they frozen in time, allowing us to see how people lived before the first wave.

The newcomers spat out in disgust as they view the pile of rotting bodies. My heart sinks a little every time seeing it, knowing this is the fate my friends' bodies met. When I first started, they just moved from the pile where they were laid. It's probably for the best I didn't see them. I would had to fight the urge to go looking for them. They would been rotten flesh and majority bones by the time I got there. Shifting my mask, I took a deep breath. I never miss spraying perfume in my mask, it helps maintain a pleasant scent especially during the hot seasons.

The guys did their job tossing the bodies onto the pile. One after another all five got heave up. Randal glance around and went to the catty that the bodies were on pulling out shovels that were stored inside.

He toss the first one at Chad and says, "Since this was a small load, let's try to get all the dirt, leaves, and biodegradable on these things. If we get enough, next time it shouldn't stink so much and maybe Alexander won't suffer." Crybaby retorts, "I'll get it right the first-time next week."

Everyone except Randal and I went to the wood line, piling the dirt and anything else on top the catty. Randal watching them. I decide to walk around the pile, making sure nothing sneaks up behind us. On the other side of the dead, peering further into the town, spotting a zombie in the distance moving away from us - too far to even worry about.

I gulp, the thought of how far that thing has walked, and how long its lived in that state. Not all cities are as merciful as us. Some don't stab the heads of the dead to make sure they don't turn. They think it is giving back to Mother Nature, allowing them to turn to eat whatever Wanderers may still be out here.

The Celestial City is known to have a celebration every time they roll out a dead, believing that their festivities keep the zombies from attacking them maintaining the harmony. If they didn't do that, maybe we wouldn't have to worry about zombie hordes.

Continuing around the pile, the zombie moves out of sight.

A whistle blew from Randal on the other side, jogging around, seeing the others coming back with the car filled with debris.

Rounding the pile, Randal smile at me, pointing his thumb behind his back. "I told you I'll let you kill the first one to let off some steam."

Coming out from an alley where two buildings lean on one another, a zombie coming towards us. Pulling the shaft from my side, I walk forward. Randal patting my shoulder getting behind me.

He enjoys playing with these things when we only encounter one. Putting a dart through their leg, maybe the shoulder, watching them still move to us not stopping. After he gets close enough, he will point - blank shoot it. For me, it is a little too cruel. Their bodies are forever moving, never able to rest, decomposing as time goes on. They have suffered enough.

Taking a deep breath in leaving the sight on the head, as I exhaled pulling the trigger. Taking them down and giving them back to Mother Earth is what's best. Allowing them to finally rest to whatever unknown awaits for us.

As the dart flies through the air, barbs extending out, the Zombie stop moving, falling to the ground with a loud clank sounded. My shoulders sag. The zombie hit the ground with a thud, the loose dirt flying up around it.

I mutter, "Crap it hit the building. I hope it isn't damaged."

Randal, his back turned to me, say, "Only way to find out is by getting it."

I mocked him, over - exaggeratingly bobbing my head with a smile as he glanced back at me laughing. He focused his attention back on the rest, who going towards the woods again. Fixing my mask, turning loading the shaft with another dart.

A blood trail from the exit wound splatters far beyond where the body fell. Creeping up on the lifeless body. A person you would have to worry about faking being dead so they can attack you at close range. These things don't have that thought process. I just need to make sure it hit the head - a clean shot slightly above the eyes.

Narrowing my eyes at the lack of a jaw. Someone made sure this thing couldn't bite anyone. They can still do harm if they... That thought stopped as both of the zombie's hands were removed, and blackened blood - stained gauze wrapped around the nubs.

What psychopath went through all of that, mutilating this body? A shiver went down my spine, knowing the same people who did this can be close.

Taking in my surroundings, the only life is my teammates still by the pile of dead bodies. Darting my eyes back down at the zombie woman, at least the body is no longer restless. I am glad to be able to do this. The family could been too weak to see their loved ones like this, unable to kill them themselves. I know they would be happy to know it's over.

I still can't convince myself to think that way about my friends. Wishing I myself was too much of a coward and ran off out of that apartment, allowing the Hazard team to kill them.

The two buildings leaning on one another creaks as I approach. The soft wind causing them to sway, shuffling my feet around, hoping the dart bounced off the building and came back, hiding within the gravel and tufts of grass growing. The last place we were at, none of the buildings were this preserved. Nature took it over forgotten by humans.

It is scarier seeing this part of time still surviving because that means Wanderers frequent here. The clouds uncover the sun catching a part of the dart. A shift of light disappear as the clouds move back in.

Shimming my shoulders, annoyed with where it landed, tilting my head up, windows broken out from the tops where the two collided allowing the sky to shine through. Nature barging it's way in twisting around the two buildings. It has been up this long me going under it won't cause it to break. Why of all places did it have to not bounce back but go more inside the alley?

Putting the shaft at my waist freeing both my hands. Dipping down, grabbing the dart, holding it in front of my face examining it. Letting out a sigh as one of the barbs are lodged inside the canal of the dart. The other three are still fully erect. It must have slid across the building when it hit. Shaking it to the side, the bit of blood left flew off onto the ground. This didn't help dislodge it. Pushing the switch, it all went back into place. Back in its container it goes with the rest of them. The repair guys are going to have fun with this one.

Randal is no longer where he had been standing. He's further from where the tree line is. The others getting behind him as a zombie approach from one of the buildings. Aiming with ease, the thing start limping. Shaking my head at his actions.

Shuffling of the gravel behind me, I pivoted. My hand already going for my knife, strong arms grab me dragging me backwards. The mask is yanked off my face scraping my head as it's pulled off. The horrible smell of rotting bodies makes me gag. My nostrils flare as the hand cup my mouth, dragging me further into the alleyway. Unable to scream, I kick my legs. The arm wraps around me making it impossible to grab anything to protect myself.

My body being pushed against the wall. Thrashing around, hitting the person's leg, but it isn't stopping them. Grabbing the back of my head, my mouth still covered, my head strike the wall.

Moisture dripped from the side of my head, my vision blurring, they made sure not to knock me out.

Chatter sounded in my ear. Zombies don't have the mental capacity to grab and drag me away from the sight of others. My stomach drops a foot. This may be a person who's been bitten, trying to fight the disease off but losing the fight.

Slowly putting my hand in front of me going for a knife, he felt the movement, and in one motion he took both my hands into his. Moving my wrist, the hands gripped tighter to the brink of breaking my bones. Letting out a painful groan, they let up only a hair. The body leaning on me, his body cool to the touch as I radiate heat. Pinning me in place, breathing in the stench of death that fills the air, the veins on his arm bulging from his tan, graying skin.

Shit, this person is turning into a zombie, and I am going to be his first meal. Still in control enough to know to keep my mouth covered, he lift my hands all the way up to my chest. Squeezing my face, he forced my head to look in the sky. Getting closer to my cheek, the chatter from its jaw happen again.

Today is going to be the day that I get the ending all my friends got three years ago. Plus, it is a day after their anniversary, kind of fitting in a way. His blond hair drift into my sight as he try to look at my face. Making sure I can't see his face of whoever is about to turn and kill me. Lifting my neck further back exposing the bit the uniform doesn't cover. If he gets a bite, it will be mainly of my jaw.

I am going to see the same end as my friends. Know how they felt as June tore into them like a crazed starving beast. I will know how Niel felt this day. As soon as he turns, he will no longer hold onto my mouth. Then I can scream letting the others know I am in danger.

He chatters again in my ear. I let out a whimper. I know Randal will put me down before I have the chance to turn. Maybe I'll have to beg him like Niel begged me. A crazy change of fate. I feel bad though that I am someone he wanted to protect. In his drunken state he told me how he wants to see me survive and live a happy life, to prove to Mother Nature that the short stick can still grow into something wonderful. Now he will be ending my life. Looks like my stick was shorter than his after all.

Staring between the broken building into the blue sky, some dark clouds overhead. Exhaling long and hard, I want to see the sky before the pain hits. When it changes and takes a bite out of me, I will be able to get away. To end up laying on the ground to only see the beautiful sky above. Gabe and Sandra will be sad they couldn't see me. That they couldn't get someone to pray over my body like they did for Niel. My eyes flutter as tears finally came up, pouring down my cheeks, soaking the hand of this man.

My heart bottom out with what the man behind me said. A voice I never thought I would hear in my life, raspy and older than I once remembered. It could be due to the head injury that I am hearing this voice. My head throbs in pain as he moved me off the wall slightly still unable to confirm my identity.

"In…fin…ity." The raspy voice utter so slowly like he hasn't spoken in a long time. "Infin…ity…"

My body utterly still. No tears, not a ripple of my body, my hair didn't even sway as a soft wind blew by. This can't be happening.

"Fuck yeah, you caught one." A female with a hoarse voice say. Not enough hormones to keep her voice light and flowy. She sounds like a young boy going into puberty. "We can do it now, and the others won't even notice she's gone."

He says, "No…not this."

"This was the fucking plan, Second Life, you got one of them."

Second Life? I never heard of that term before.

Another female, a higher-pitch voice, "Wait if he's saying no, there must be something we are missing that he caught."

"You Second Life's just stay together…"

"Don't start that now. He is the reason we have gotten so far for so long."

He let out a grunt of approval with the other female. They bicker back and forth, a few other voices chiming in.

How many Wanderers are here? How were they so light on their feet? I didn't hear them approach.

His grip started to loosen. My first instinct is to bite down on his hand, but if he is turning into a zombie, I don't want to get infected. No one ever bit a zombie before, so would it work that way? I don't want to be the person to find that out.

He let go of my hands but pushes me more into the wall. I let out a grunt. His jaw chatter not to me but to the others. His hand still on my mouth, his upper body turning to the voices talking that are more in the alleyway. Slipping my hand in my chest pocket, I pull one of the knives. Stabbing outwards, sinking the blade into the arm holding my mouth, he let out a grunt of pain. Kicking him off, I turn to get my answer of who held me.

Falling against the wall my legs tremble beneath me. Blacken blood coming out like a normal human, he pull the knife out with a small grunt, tossing it to the ground. Holding both his hands up, he slowly lower them again. *No.* My body trembles at the sight.

"No…No…No...No." I keep repeating, "You. I. I.. You.. no. You aren't you." My chest jump, unable to catch my breath.

"Infi…nity."

I jolt taking a step forward then back to the wall again. "I killed…I killed you." I pointed with a shaky hand, "You are dead, Niel. I killed you."

Chapter Four

The soft chatters of the Wanderers went to silence. He's so much tanner than when he was alive, now with a gray undertone. This can't be possible. He can't be *alive*. I stabbed him in the head. Gulping, there is a scar on the left side of his face going through his eyebrow.

I utter, "I still feel your skull cracking in my hands."

A single tear fell down my face. Niel stepped back, and I slap both my hands on the building, forgetting I'm already against it. Sidestepping, getting myself away from the wall, and closer to where I can run. I cup my own mouth, letting out a painful, deep cry. Niel's expression soften, reaching out with one hand as the other covers his cut.

"You are her?" a girl with a similar gray undertone says, "Just come with us. We can explain everything. Niel isn't use to talking, so I can explain it all for him."

Niel eyes widen chattering at her, causing the girl to frown.

The raspy-voiced girl step forward. "Listen, you don't come, we kill you."

"Maple!" the gray-tone girl gasp.

Niel squared his shoulders at Maples comment.

Maple snap, "Fuck, Lavender, you say my name, I say yours. She snitches, we both are in deep shit. Grab her, run off the rest."

No one followed her command. A few eyes dart to Niel and Lavender. I've been scooting back little by little as they turn to each other to bicker.

They let that zombie go to trick one of us into getting closer. They know that we retrieve our darts. They have been watching us. Niel has been watching us.

Niel chatter, and Lavender say, "Niel wants you to come with us. He didn't realize who you were before he attacked if he did…"

My face flatten, my gaze leaving her. Just on the outside of the two buildings, a horde of zombies coming down the small curve of a hill in our direction. Whatever she is telling me isn't registering in my head. Behind the zombies, other Wanderers are wrapping up shiny metals. They wanted to kidnap one of us and send a horde for the rest to run back to the city. When they realize one of us is missing, they will just assume a zombie got them and wouldn't come to look.

Turning my body to the side, kicking off the ground. I heard Niel's voice calling out. Sprinting out of there, both feet off the ground, one slamming springing me back up. My flight or fight kicks in, and I choose the path to survive.

"Run!" I bellow, "Run. Leave it all, get out!" The other see me, pausing in what they were doing, and start to walk forward. "Fucking run, Wanderers, zombies, run now."

Almost all at the same time, their legs kick up, running where we came from. Only Randal ran to me. The whites of his eyes vibrant over the mask he still wears. Both taking a beeline running parallel, meeting side by side. I shouldn't look, I can't look, but everything inside of me is itching to know what's going on. Looking behind my shoulder at what's happening. Wanderers kneel at the ground pointing at us. Zombies despite being slow are following us.

Loud deafening bangs rings through the air. A buzz races past us at an alarming speed, dirt leaving the ground as the small object impacts. Cupping my ears desperately trying to muffle it all, Randal took me by the elbow.

As more small objects buzz around us, and a few hitting the ground only a foot away. Randal pushes me in front of him, shielding me from the lethal objects. More than ten feet ahead of us Abigail is flailing trying her hardest to run in these heavy uniforms. Her body stills and moves in a way like an invisible force is bushing her. Then the scream erupts in agony as her body hit the ground.

"Abigail!" We shouted in unison.

With that, the bangs and buzzing all around stop. Sweat beading down, soaking the inside of my suit more than before. Blood stains Abigail's uniform.

I ask looking back as the Wanderers are already gone, "What were they using just now?"

"That, Trinity, were guns." Randal replies while his focus is on Abigail.

I heard that they were loud, but never have I imagine that is what they sounded like. The sounds would attract zombies from long distances. No wonder we got rid of them.

Randal heaves Abigail into a fetal position, her cries of pain filling the air while in his arms. She clung to him as pain pulsates through her wounded leg. Staying beside him, my shaft in position ready to fire at any threat. Ignoring the ringing in my ears and the rapid racing of my heart, ignoring the fact I just saw Niel alive. Everything that's going on, shoving it deep inside, to stay focus on getting home out of this chaotic mess. Yesterday's shit show truly followed me to today.

Making it up an incline of rolling land, the others been out of eye shot leaving us behind. Panicked screams came from the others below.

"Go see what's going on." Randal demands, "Save whoever, and do not let them lock us out."

A quick nod at Randal, picking up the pace peeking over the land where it dips down I crouch down before anyone seen me. Wanderers dragging two of my teammates into the woods. The remaining of the group abandoned them without a second thought, despite us outnumbering them. They chose their own life rather than following protocol. Clenching my jaw in frustration at their blatant discard of another human. Unable to identify my teammates, their mask still covering their faces.

Save whoever. Aiming the shaft at them they move differently from zombies - from the shuffled movements, slow sway of their bodies. They jerk, with quick movements, shit I don't know if I can get the shot. My teammates struggle desperately to brake free. One manage to free an arm striking anything within reach. They wouldn't be in this situation if the others came to their aid. Yet they fled at the first sign of danger.

Taking aim, I steady the shaft, focusing on the Wanderer dragging my helpless teammate towards the edge of the woods. The back of their head creeped into my sight. Taking a deep breath in, aiming past their head, pressing my finger on the trigger releasing the dart twirling through the air. It's only a hum, mask by the nature around. Holding my breath watching as the person fell with a hard thud, the other Wanderer scream in panic. My heart sinking deep inside my chest the heaviness of my actions bearing down - I just took a life.

The teammate who I saved ran deeper into the woods. Fuck, what is he doing? The other Wanderer chose to follow leaving only two of us.

I call out. "Who just ran?"

"Alexander," Chad responds between heavy breaths, "He was the one with me."

Loading another dart, breathing heavily mixed with exhaustion, "We can't… shit, we can't go after him. Let's hope he finds his way back before we close the door."

"Screw that! Everyone for themselves. I will not die because he decided to go who know fuck where."

I bit back frustrated by their actions, "Follow protocol! We stick together and hold out as long as possible when there is no sign of direct threat."

He flip me off before running away. We are a unit of ten, to overpower anything that threatens us. Yet, at the slightest inconvenience, all unity unravels.

Catching my breath, I wait for Randal, he came over the edge in a steady jog. Some of the zombies still followed as others seemingly forgot their motive.

Randal yelled, "What are you doing here? I told you…"

Cutting him off I explain the situation, "I'll make it no worries. No protocol. They're doing a free-for-all."

Randal brows wrinkled, "You got to be fucking kidding me." he order me as Abagail softly cries, "Keep that door open. Do whatever you must until it is too late." Hesitating a flash of worry must have shown because he push me forward, reassuring me "We will make it. Just go."

Pursing my lips, ramping up my speed back into a sprint. I have to get there before they chose to close that door on us.

Approaching the city, I no longer hear Abigail crying. Nearing the door, the others tumble and shouted as a fight starting to break out. No Wanderers, no zombies, there's absolutely no sign of danger.

Bengerman shouted, "We don't have the code to re-open it."

"They fell behind, they get locked out." Chad counters. Bengerman now in Chad's face, "That isn't how it works."

"I will not die for an old man, some cowards, and a murderer." Chad pushed back, "I have a future I have my wife I need to worry about."

Pointing the shaft in Chads back, their faces pale. I will not leave them behind because of some coward wanting to shut the door prematurely. Standing his ground, I push harder, his heels digging down trying to show dominance.

Sweat pouring from every pore of my body, speaking through my teeth, a heavy breath between every few words. "Get the hell back. Or your soon-to-be wife, she'll be a widow."

Finally, the pressure let off the shaft as he step away. Chad's eyes seethes with rage. Chad lingering in the doorway waiting to shut it. Positioning myself my foot rests on the door itself, where if he tries to shut it, well we will fight.

"Get back." I warn.

Chad scoffs clearly unintimidated, "You're going to get us killed."

He has a good foot on me, and despite being lean he has some muscle mass.

Taking a few breaths before replying, steadying the shakiness wanting to creep out, "There no Wanderers, no zombies, this door stays open until otherwise."

Chad took a reluctant step back, eyeing me as my shaft still pointed at him. Trailing his every movement as he plays casual. I know he is waiting for me to put my guard down, so he can shut this door. Mother Earth I wish he would just go inside like everyone else.

Glancing over my shoulder, wishing that they peeked over the horizon. Once we leave to dump the bodies, the door can only be re-opened from the outside once. With Randal being the only one with codes, we would need to find someone else who has clearance to get these doors back open. At that point it can be too late for Abigail. All I know she may have already passed in Randal's arms. Their only other hope is to find the illegal entrance or bear the journey to the front of the City. Her life bleeding out of her, I don't think she will make it any longer.

No one has called for help yet. They are just sitting around, some already out of their uniforms, others stiff staring at Chad and I. If I go down there myself, Chad most definitely will seize the opportunity to lock out the others. Only minutes pass which felt like an eternity watching a lifeless horizon ahead. My foot tap the ground as murmurs of agreement grew among the group.

I assert my position, "Until I see zombies on that horizon and no sign of our teammates, this door stays open."

Glaring at Chad and his crowing smirk knowing I am slowly becoming outnumbered; my heart sinks as part of the original horde emerge from the clearing. Dropping the shaft to my side, as my arms lays limp.

Chad let out a cruel chuckle, "Close the damn door." I shook my head, refusing to budge. "Close the door before you get us all murdered you psycho!"

I lift the shaft pointing it at his head. "I am trying to save lives."

Chad mocks, "By letting the Zombies in the city."

I hiss, "You don't know a damn thing about any of this. Its only your first round. If you were out there, we'd be doing the same thing for your dumb ass. If you don't shut the fuck up, I will get the video of that woman you were fondling at the bachelor party."

His eyes widen in shock. I have more leverage to play with than he ever would dream of. If he wants to bring up my personal life on the job, I will play the same game. I will play whatever hand to buy myself enough time.

Breaking through the tree line, all three teammates who been left behind finally emerges. A sigh of relief escape as I waived them down, pointing at the zombies who are making their way to us. Randal and Crybaby are each supporting one side of Abigail. Abigail whimpers loudens with each hurried step.

They need to hurry. Chad making unnecessary comments behind me, causing him to be shushed by others. We are now all standing quietly urging our teammates on. In the final stretch, Randal and Crybaby lift Abigail's feet off the ground. Braking into a sprint as the sounds of chatters strengthen as zombies close in. She scream in pain as her body swung around. Roughly twenty zombies remain, still far too many to fend off after seeing the lack of support of the team I can't rely on any of them.

Barreling through the door, Crybaby and Abigail fell to the ground huffing. He held her in his arms as her cries reach a crescendo. Her pail skin contrasting the blood - soaked lower half of her suit. Randal and I hurriedly pulls the door close. As I flipped the handle up to engage the main lock, Randal dash down to the control panel.

Red lights flash above my head - slowly stepping away in case of any failures. Watching the sequence of red, yellow, green lights, another set going through the sequence, the third yellow, green, my heart ease as the last light turn green.

Dropping the shaft to the ground in relief, the tension in my shoulders easing. Crybaby sat visibly shaken, unable to move. They have made it safely, we didn't lose anyone today.

Panic lace Randal's voice, "Where are the medics?"

Chad sarcastically says, "We were too scared to call one cause this maniac pointed the shaft at us."

"Says the guy who was trying to close the door before I even got here." I retort, "It was at you only, by the way."

Randal and I lift Abigail by the shoulders, each step pushing out a cry from her.

Randal whispers, "Told you the two of us will have your back." He gave me a reassuring smile.

Two floors above, we got Abigail in the right hands with a group of medics already tending to her.

"Did she get bit?" Someone ask trying to stop the bleeding head down unable to tell who it may be.

Since Randal is our boss he is supposed to do the reports, but he is struggling to breathe, so I explain for him. "Wanderers, they shot at us. We had to leave everything behind. No one got bitten, and everyone has made it back."

Rolling her out of the room as they cut up her uniform exposing the needed area.

My heart still pumping like I am desperately running for my life. A nurse came up to me handing me some water as she guiding me to sit down.

Nurse asks examining the wound on my head, her eyes widen with curiosity etched on her features, "How did you get this wound on your head?"

Finishing the water in a few gulps, I recounted, "I went to retrieve a dart and they were waiting for us, like they've been watching us. I almost didn't get away. Fortunately, I got a chance to pull my knife and stab the guy who did this to me."

"Well lucky for you, I'll only need to use butterfly closures. Let's hope you hit an artery in the arm where he isn't lucky." She commented while dropping a professional demeanor.

My throat closes up, knowing who it was, but not too sure what he was. I don't think that would matter since he's already dead. 'Second Life's' they called him. Maybe he isn't dead? Tightening around my heart recapping where the knife gone in. A part of me hoping I didn't hurt him too bad.

A hiss escape my lips when she applied the alcohol to clean the cut. I am going to need a drink tonight, maybe two. After we were left alone, Randal yanking out the fluids they were giving him. Rising from the bed, he pull back the curtains that concealed us. Side-eyeing him noticing his uniform discarded on the bed. Glancing down at myself forgetting I still have mine on.

Randal settle beside me. I only stared at the crack between the door and floor, as if it held any hope of answering what I seen today.

His voice cut through the silence, "I am proud of you Trinity."

I didn't meet his gaze, "I killed him."

He reassures me. "You saved someone by taking a life. You did good."

My eyes darting towards him. Oh, he believes I am struggling with taking the life of a Wanderer. No, Niel *I know* I killed him. Could someone survive it without medical attention? Closing my eyes rubbing my face seething as I touch the wound. He was bitten by a zombie he should had turned into that.

"I know your first kill isn't fun. It doesn't get better, but you dwell on it less. You saved us - one life taken to save three, maybe even more." His hand patted me in an attempt of comforting me. "I am proud of you."

"I will vouch for you too. Chad will report you for pointing the shaft at him, but he wasn't following protocols. You reacted to which you felt best to keep as many people safe. If he had his way, Abigail would had died before we got inside."

Turning my upper body to face him, the words slid off with ease. "It isn't my first kill."

Pushing my chin up, Randal sternly respond to something he knows too well of what happened. "Niel was bitten, and you saved him. It was two zombies you killed before even coming to this unit, and that is what helped you get this job. You are quick to make the right decisions without panicking."

My mouth opens and closes soundlessly. Randal nudge me, with the silent look in his eyes *'what's on your mind,'* I can't reveal what I witnessed, who I had seen. Secrets hide behind my blank expression.

The door opens and my head throb as the person who walk in triggers a sudden surge of fight or flight. Randal stand diverting his attention to her, as if I no longer sat here. Elizabeth didn't even acknowledge my presence in the room, and oddly, I welcome that. He followed her out with one subtle jerk of the head, softly shutting the door behind him. Their muffled voices are the only two on the other side.

Standing, my body sways, pain shoots up my legs finally feeling the aftermath of it all. Blinking a few times, Niel stands in front of me. My breath hitch as his arms extended tenderly, devoid of anger towards me. Instead, there is a look of understanding of why I had done what I did. His pain appeared undeniably human. Tears braking through - he isn't human. He'd been bitten and I killed him.

Even if that's not the truth, that the stab wound wasn't good enough, he still would have turned into a zombie. Yet, there he was. Here he is. Shaking my head, the sight of him vanishes. It's all my imagination.

Undoing the straps around my neck. The way he chatter is the number one sign of being one of those things. The other girl, Violet, no Lavender it was, too, bore a resemblance to him. Though she spoke normally, in contrast of Niel's slow, broken speech. If they are both Second Life's. Shaking my head; it challenges everything we have been taught.

When we die, we turn into a zombie if our brain is not killed. No cure has been found to say otherwise. Plus, he was bitten, an automatic zombie sentence. I'm trying desperately to make since of it all and no matter how many times I repeat it the information sounds wrong.

Shimmying out of the suit as it clings onto my sweat soaked tank top. Plopping it to the ground tilting my head to the door as their voices cut off. Pure silence met me inside of the room. Brushing my hair back, thinning my lips. Niel being whatever he is defies every rule of the world we thought we knew.

The door swing open, and Elizabeth stiffly enter with Randal stepping out coming closer to me. Elizabeth purses her lips, eyeing my clothes sticking to every curve of my body. My workout shorts riding up too high from all the running and sweat. Her head tilting in a gesture, I didn't pull my shorts down. We are all adults here, need be no embarrassment of how I look after running and fighting for our lives.

Randal says with a sharp tone, "She saved all of us."

Elizabeth responds with a wicked smile, "You pointed a shaft at your teammate."

I chose my words carefully, "He threatened me after I shot and killed a Wanderer to save him. I may be paraphrasing from all the chaos I can't remember word for word, but his words were under the line of 'everyone for themselves' before running off. Watch the cameras and ask the others. He wanted to shut the doors before any threat of danger, leaving four of his teammates behind, while one was severely injure."

She stared at the butterfly bandages on my head, skepticism in her narrowing eyes. "You don't look that injured to me."

Emphasizing, I moved my hands together. Speaking at a slower pace. "Abigail, the poor girl that you forced out on her second day, she got shot. If you did your research before questioning me, you'd known this."

"You get harsher with your speaking every time we talk." Her voice calm, "Defiant in a way."

I flash a smile, "Read the laws. Nothing says anything about tone of voice, as long as I answer you as best as I can. I'm also not in an interrogation, so technically, I don't even have to answer. Unless you are interrogating me before getting everyone's testimonies."

She push her lips out as if she was sucking on something in her mouth. Glancing at Randal for a heartbeat, spinning on her heels, whipping her hair, slamming the door behind herself.

I wince in pain. Turning to Randal I ask, "What did you guys talk about?"

Randal looks down at me, "She wanted to know if you are following protocol, my opinion on the matter, and if you have any signs of…"

"Being insubordinate." I finish his words, "She's suspicious that I am involved with them?" Randal nods, "You know what. I am so happy you aren't like her."

Randal reply holds a hint of pain, "Don't let me fool you. Elizabeth trembled at the sight of me when I was a Lunar."

My brow raises, not entirely surprising. Randal carries an authoritarian aura around him. I assure him, "There is a difference between you two that is clear."

Observing him as he narrows his eyes, and I flash a smile, "You have compassion for others, where I doubt she has a heart. She fakes power with fear tactics, where you radiant a natural power that people respect."

He smirks in response. I know he technically isn't allowed to talk about his past, but I know how to fill in the blanks. Unfortunately, filling in the blanks is what got my family killed.

After all that happened today, we decide to leave work early. Tossing my bag over my shoulder I eye the empty room. Blood drench where Abagail laid, footprints spreading it further. My teammates' uniforms scatter the floor all the way to the door. Thankfully, it isn't my job to clean this up.

Leaving the building to go home, Randal stood outside waiting. He ask which sounds more like he's telling me, "Let's go have dinner. My treat."

I cock my head to the side. From the two - ish years I worked here, we always left at the same time going our separate ways. Never have either of us offer to do anything together out of work. People pass us as he awaits my answer.

I flash a tight smile, "Why not?" After all that happened today and yesterday, perhaps two unlucky people can get a nice dinner together.

Getting a spot in the middle of a restaurant, we sat in silence. The waiter arrive with menus leaving us to look over the options. Okay this is *weirder* than I was hoping. Shifting in my seat unable to focus on the menu, the silence hung around us as the rest of the people laugh and enjoying themselves. I should have changed and took a shower before coming. My body is sticky with sweat and there's trace of blood in my hair.

Randal order himself some spirit as I got myself a Lily tea to soothe my nerves. Before the waiter could set the drink on the table Randal took it drinking it half empty. Guess I am not the only one needing something to settle down.

Rubbing my finger along the rim of my drink, Niel's voice ring through my mind, *'No. Don't leave.'* When I sprinted away, the words didn't register, but as I sit here replaying all of it in a loop. He had ask me to stay with the Wanderers, the people who have relentlessly been trying to destroy our lives within the city walls.

So many memories flood my mind, running together, then Gabe's voice louder than the rest came in. While we sat at that park bench, I ask if we would ever beat the disease. What would he say if I told him his son is still alive, or half alive? Would he be happy at the news? Would he even believe my words?

My voice low as I ask, "Do you think we will ever beat the disease?" I ran my finger round and round the rim. I still haven't taken a sip of the Lily tea.

Randal lift two fingers, signaling for another spirit, matching my tone he reply, "I hope so. One day, future generations would get to see the world without the walls." He nodded in gratitude as he received his second drink, "Why do you ask?"

My jaw clench forcing Niel's name down, "I thought I was going to die. I couldn't get out of his grip." *Niel's touch*, "I remember how Niel begged me to…you know. I had the thought that maybe you would have to be the one to end me." His eyes drops to his drink, "I would have left them all to make sure you got back in time to be saved."

Not if it was a zombie who bit me, or a Second Life's as they say. I want to tell him that there may be a possibility.

I ask, "What if…they found a way where we didn't go mindless, like animals when we turn? What if we retained our memories, our control somehow." Maybe Niel found a way on his mystery trips to not turn, I finally stop circling the glass with my finger. "Do you think they would tell us?"

Randal ponder my question. His eyes drifting off as if he never thought about this himself. It isn't the first time I pondered death. Hope after death we didn't die, but after today that hope may be a reality.

My face heated up as Randal focused on his meal no longer talking to me. The deafening silence between the two of us rises like a fog. By the time half our meal is finished, Randal drank another three spirits. His eyes hazes as it took its toll. The Lily they serve is a bad grade I can't feel the effects at all.

Swaying in his chair, he try to reach for the check the waiter put down. Without hesitation, I put my card on the light up screen paying instead. A flick of my wrist signing to approve the payment. So much for the meal on him.

The waiter peer at the name on the receipt, O'Salves, she side eyed me. Reaching to finish off my Lily tea, she jump in fear. Rolling my eyes, chugging the rest of my glass as she scurried off. My family history, how I snitch out my flesh and blood, or even murdering my friend. Any of that gives anyone the fright. They may not remember what I look like but this name of mine, every household knows of it, fears it, or down right hates it.

Standing, Randal lift his head, confused where the waiter just ran off to. Still fumbling to get his wallet out of his pocket, he mutter a few unrecognizable words. Leaning down beside him, I manage to get his arm around my shoulder, heaving him up. Stumbling at his weight, I wobble to the door.

"Aw, your dad had too much to drink. So sweet of you to care for him." An older lady comments as she enters, leaving the door open for us.

"Thank you. Yeah, he had a few too many." I reply, choosing not to correct her. There's no need to share my true story - a drunk father is more acceptable.

Getting closer to Randal's home, his body became heavier with every step. Groaning, attempting to stay on my feet. Stumbling grounding my feet as I nearly hit a building.

"Help me out a bit here." I grunt trying to stand him up more, "You need to lose a few pounds."

He moan in response. His words slurs, "I make a bad dad."

So, he can hear, just unable to reply at a reasonable rate, "Yeah no drunk makes good dads."

"When you say run, I thought you got bit." Randal trails off before adding, "I needed to know you came safe…Came home."

His hazy eyes stared at me, "You don't live in that apartment still."

It sounds like he was telling me, but I know it was supposed to be a question. I shook my head as an answer.

Approaching his home, his head lifts recognizing the area. He stood up suddenly wobbling backwards. Reaching out to grab him, he heave all of his dinner on the ground.

Turning to the side, avoiding the splatter zone, glad he was too far away, or I would be covered in his dinner now.

I gag at the putrid smell, pinching my nose shut as Randal stands. With one eye more closed than the other, he pointed at me stumbling around.

"You live safe?" He ask with sudden concern in his drunken state.

I rub the bridge of my nose. Why is he caring about if I live somewhere safe all of a sudden?

I reply, "Yeah, I live somewhere safe. Randal, come on, let's get you home."

He shook his head pointing again, "Your home."

"You aren't coming to my place."

Rolling his head back in an attempt to seem sober, his feet shuffling around unable to keep still, "I need to make sure you are safe."

His voice dropped to a whisper, "Elizabeth will do anything to get you."

My heart quickening at his warning, maintaining a natural expression, acting as if what he say isn't anything new, never knowing who's watching the cameras. Putting his arm around my shoulder, I guide him across the street. Taking him somewhere only Gabe and Sandra knows I live. Not even the Hazard Department knows my exact address. It isn't required, so I left that blank.

"To answer before. No, only the rich and Luners get that privilege." Randal says, his choice of words implying knowledge beyond what the public knows.

Get that *privilege*. Staring up at the camera ahead, my jaw tightened. He isn't talking about the future. They know things and keeping it secret from the rest of us.

Laying Randal on my floor, dropping my bag by the front door more exhausted than before. He reeks of alcohol and puke stains his clothes. Flopping on the couch, I let out a long - needed sigh. Eyeing Randal on the cold wooden floors, I pick myself up. Rummaging through the linen closet for spare blankets. From Niel's time living here. His face, his smile flashes before my eyes.

Shaking it off, I took a pillow and tossed everything on the couch.

Nudging him with my feet, I ask, "Can you get up?" He didn't answer. Getting both my arms under his armpits, dragging him through the apartment, "I swear, if you get poisoned by how much you drank and die, I hope you became whatever the hell I seen today so I can kill you for being stupid."

His leg hit the door frame and I wrench at the thud. I don't think he will feel that tomorrow. Flopping him sideways on the bed, kneeling down removing his shoes, setting them at the door before leaving.

I need some Lily tea.

I plop on the couch turning on a show as I sip the steaming hot Lily tea. Eyeing the time on my phone, I could go to the club tonight. Leaning my head back, swishing the tea in my mouth, a wave of warmth radiating from my core. If he wakes up and I am not here, Randel may freak out and possibly go through my things, figuring out who's place it is. Kicking my feet up on the couch, my eyes closing. Sipping Lily allowing my mind to go numb.

How is Niel alive? Whatever a 'Second Life' is it shouldn't be possible. The others said his name, said my name knowing who I am. Putting my empty glass down, I start to rub my head, seething in pain as I press on the wound again. Mother Earth that hurts. That scar on his face, I caused it. He healed as if he is still alive, yet his body has that gray undertone that happens when you die. Wanting to scream I flung myself down on the couch, rolling into the blanket.

None of this makes since and it is making my head hurt.

"Infinity, let me explain." Niel pleas.

Pushing him away walking through an unknown building, I respond, "You left me. You disappeared without a trace, and you never thought to contact me. I told you I love you, and this is what I got in return."

He grab me by my wrist, his head tilt down allowing me to lean back, holding me with ease. His pupils widen his skin kissed by the sun as if he's trying to hide the grayness of his skin. It is still there, showing he is other than human. His lips part leaning closer moving my hips closer to him. His jaw chatter making my body tense.

A small movement curls on his lips before saying, "That is all I needed. I needed that love to get you here." I try to push him off, but he held tighter. My body leans on his as both arms wraps around me. "I knew when you saw me, you would need to know more."

Niel brushes my hair behind my ears. No hint of happiness on him. Niel look at me with a cold dark expression, "Haven't changed all these years. Now that I got you…"

His mouth went over my neck. Screaming in pain, he tears a chunk out of me. Falling to the ground kicking my feet getting away from him, blood seep through my hand as he chew on my flesh.

I cry out, "Why, why would you do this?"

"Ah, I haven't eaten in such a long time. I just couldn't help myself." He explains, kicking me to my back, pulling a knife from his pocket, "Maybe we can have matching scars since you were so willing to kill me."

I gasp, air quickly escaping my lungs, "You, You begged me."

"You didn't put up much of a fight. Luckily, I got this second chance for revenge." Niel taunts waving the knife around. Getting on top of me and lifting the knife over my face. He sneer, "A murderer doesn't deserve to live."

The knife came down as I let out a scream of terror.

Flinging the blankets off of me, grabbing at my neck and face in a panic. Spinning around seeing the familiar view of Niel's apartment, the room is dark, the tv is still on. My heart beat slower realizing I am not in danger.

Pushing my hair back, getting my phone to see its early in the morning. There is a message from Sandra, shit, it was from yesterday. 'hey, sorry a lot happened yesterday I didn't get on my phone and passed out at home.' It's five in the morning. Yeah, there's no way I'm going back to sleep after that messed - up shit.

My nose flare as I caught a whiff of myself. I didn't even get into a shower last night. Didn't even know I fell asleep.

Niel filled my vision, even in the steam of the shower. Not the Niel I knew before, the one bleeding out before I killed him. No, this vision is the new version of him. Holding my neck, the steadiness of my heartbeat in my veins. Is he seeking revenge for me killing him? That could be the true reason he called out to me to go with the Wanderers. Perhaps that nightmare is a warning to me not to ask any questions. It could also just be my guilt manifesting in a new way.

Chapter Five

On my way to making my second pot of coffee, I lean over the steam pouring out of it. My head heavy for all the Lily I put in my first two cups, desperately wanting to drown out my thoughts. Maybe I overdid it a bit.

Halfway through the second pot, my leg tap the floor uncontrollably. A creek, and I jolt out of my seat to see Randal peeking out from the corner, confusion plastered all over his face as he took in the scene.

"Theres coffee." I say, tilting my head to the kitchen.

He slowly ask, "Where are we?"

"You don't remember?" I say in shock, but I shouldn't have been since he was drunk. I could had dumped him at his place then.

Pinching the bridge of his nose, "No, I mean yes. I asked to go to your apartment." He say in disbelief that this is where I live.

I sat down, drinking more coffee, "Technically it is." I look around, "At least legally in my name. Niel apparently bought it I don't know when. His parents gave it to me."

He sat down and my nose flared with the reek of puke that came off of him. Looking the other way, I cover my nose.

Taking a deep breath of my coffee, Randal survey the area the high ceiling, the loft above the kitchen where I hardly ever go into, where Niel's room lies.

"You live good." Randal states, clearly surprised.

I reply, "Niel lived good. Bathroom is at the end of the hall. Use whatever you want. Take the toothbrush under the sink. It hasn't been used."

He made his way back into the hallway without any hesitations. He probably could smell himself as much as I did.

Sinking into my seat. It is weird to have someone else here with me. I could've refused to let him come, dropped him inside his apartment, and left. Yet, I brought him here without a second thought.

Randal made himself a cup of black coffee with no sugar. Sitting beside me at the dining table.

I say in a flat tone, "Don't tell anyone where I live. It isn't their business."

Randal laugh, "You think they will treat you like you are rich if they knew?"

I lean my head back, buzzing with random thoughts that don't stick, "When they find out who's, the names will start. The assumptions will resurface." Tilting my head to see him, "Only you know this...Other than Gabe and Sandra, of course." I turn my heavy head back to the ceiling, rubbing the rim of the coffee cup mindlessly.

"I won't tell. I should go give my report on their bad behavior and not following protocols..." He say as his phone rang inside of his pocket.

"Hello?" He answer walking into my room, which I allowed him to sleep in.

That was weird. His eyes lower upon seeing whoever called him, even deepening his voice, as if it was someone higher up. Honestly, it would be great if it was his boss seeking the report. I don't know how to tell him I want him to leave as soon as possible and sound nice doing it.

I've only had my friends over at my other apartment, we could stay together for days, and I was fine with it. They were allowed to leave and come at any part of the day or night without a raised brow from me. I don't feel comfortable with others being where I live, only those four were the exception.

Randal came back into the living room, his expression tightening. He sat down, sipping his coffee. He isn't looking at me anymore like he was before, no longer examining the apartment in awe.

I couldn't resist but to ask, "What was that call about?"

He took another drink, closing his eyes, "The team won't go back to work until further notice."

Slowly lifting my gaze to him he didn't look at me. "Why would they do that?"

Randal shrugs, "Since it was traumatic, they want everyone well-rested and mentally stable."

I slowly blink as I peer without moving my head. The buzz of my body internalize as I became still. They have had people who faced worse outside the walls. Almost whole teams wiped out. The few survivors, cover in blood, didn't give them more than two days off. Never have I heard of a unknown time off.

"How much Lily did you drink this morning?" I lean back in my seat, "Enough..."

Enough and too much coffee, making me want to run and stay all at the same time. My mind vibrating with nothing. My toes tap the ground once more.

"You are too young to do this to yourself. You need to lay off."

"I can take care of myself."

"You are smarter than this."

My ear touch my shoulder as I stare at Randal, "This protects my mind."

"Trinity." I hate people using that tone with me as if they are worried, a mixture of pain and disappointment in his voice. "You aren't here when you are like this. I can see it; I can hear it in your voice. You need to keep your mind fully here Trinity." I rolled my eyes at his comment, staring into the empty cup of coffee sitting in front of me.

Of course, he is going to say that to me, that I need to focus on my future more and stop doing Lily to numb my mind. I thought after what he told me about his past, he would be one of the few people who would truly understand me.

"Do what you want but keep your eyes open with who is around you. We have the butt of life on our shoulders. Still, there are people out there who will try to make sure it's worse." Randal down the rest of his coffee.

He push the chair where it once stood, walking to the door. I didn't move my head to look at him. Keeping it tilted down at my cup, only my eyes follow him. The door click shut, and here I am alone in this apartment again.

The quietness fills these walls, and his words turns in my mind. Lifting my head to the door, I stare at it. He doesn't understand. This is to stop the memories. To suppress it. I am here; I hear all. I am aware of who to trust and who not to trust within these walls.

*

The dance floor pulsate with bodies. The AC had broken right before the place opened. The smoke of Lilly and the height of summer, it isn't a pleasurable time. Beads of sweat drips between my breasts as I just sit watching everyone below. Avoiding eye contact with anyone, trying to keep a low profile. I need to stay out as long as possible this week since I have no work to distract me during the day. The pills Gabe called a favor in for helps me sleep during the day. Keeping the black out curtains shut, to wake up right before Vixen's Club opens.

Ending the night, only a few stay at the bar hoping to get one last shot. Ax, plop down beside me as the VIP section is already cleared other than me.

"You been here earlier than normal." Ax states.

I watch as they locked the front door, responding nonchalantly, "They gave us the week off. Have nothing else to do, you know?"

Ax inquire, "Why'd they give you the whole week off?"

"No important reason." I reply, not diving into specifics. I couldn't risk sharing details about my job, what goes on outside the walls, breaching confidential information with civilians could end my life. Despite there was no breech in security, I can mention what had happen. After all, people know the Hazard Department has the most risks.

Randal's warning bounces off the inside of my skull. I refrain from discussing the recent incident just in case that was why he warn me. Stepping out of my apartment yesterday, I noticed a Lunar tailing me. Notably out of uniform, attempting to be discreet in street clothes. The mistake he made is that he photographed me as I passed a window reflecting him peering from the corner of a building. Wandering around the city, going unusual paths, he continued to trail me.

I can't talk with my teammates to see if I am the only one experiencing this, or its due to me escaping the Wanderers.

There are no cameras in this club and nothing recording our conversations. This is a dead zone for all surveillance, underground enough to be legal but edging the line of illegal.

Leaning my head on his shoulder, I mutter, "It's been stressful more than normal, you know?"

Ax drapes his arm around me offering comfort. "Yeah, some days it gets like that..." he pause lifting his arm off me, "Eww, you are sweaty." I chuckle, pushing him away.

Vixen came from the back, "I don't care that you stay after hours, Snitch," She kicks Ax's leg, "but you get your ass up and clean."

Ax groans, "I'm just keeping our best customer company since, she's had a bad week it's the least I can do. Can't get mad at good customer service."

Vixen playfully kicks at him. This time Ax dodging her, "One drink a night isn't a good customer." I smirk at her as she took Ax's spot, "Anyways, I am the boss; I get to sit first before you. Or do I have to tell your husband you're flirting." She glances over her shoulder.

Ax snorts, "Oh yeah, he is gonna be really scared that a girl is going to steal me from him."

Vixen with drink in hand, lounging her feet on the coffee table. She doesn't like to appear during work hours for when she does, there's a frenzy - every regular recognizing her. Nowadays, she may pop out an hour before closing to see how the night is going. Before she open this underground club Vixen was on track for a law career like Gabe, she shifted gears after a few years of legal study.

Vixen went to parties and people got busted for having underage drinkers with drugs involved too. She got into a bit of trouble being 'involved' so she decided to flip off the Luners by opening this club. Purposefully navigating the murky waters, it's the gray area of club life, carving a unique niche that others still hadn't dare to explore.

In the early days, persistent attempts were made to shut her down. Almost every night, Luner's barged in trying to interfere. After it became a regular thing, Vixen turned it into a game, a spirit game no less. A list of phrases posted and if Luners say it, drinks were on her bringing in even more of an audience. Now they come once in a blue moon with 'complaints.'

"You know, you're always here. Why not just work here already." Vixen say staring at her glass, "You carry yourself well, hot, detect people who will start shit before anyone else, and you're the perfect person to round out my group."

"You don't want me, trust me." I reply, swinging my legs over her lap, "What is up with this AC?"

"Mother Earth, your ass is a sweaty mess. Get up and walk around to dry that mess."

"You should feel my breasts. If my dress wasn't black you would see the mess going on under here."

She shamelessly stare at my chest, raising a dismissive brow, "They aren't big enough to worry about."

"Oh, sorry I am not blessed like you to have curves and honkers."

"Do you want some of these? Here, I will give you some." Jumping on me, slipping her fingers around my drink, both of our cups clank together as she put them on the table.

Taking both her breasts, I squirm underneath her, Vixen press squeezing them down on top of me. "Come on, Snitch, take some already. I need some weight off my back I'm getting too old for them."

I laugh still trying to squirm out, "You are only like ten years older than me. I am perfectly happy with my body." She pressed harder, "I don't want your saggy things."

Leaning up, her hand on her chest, she let out a dramatic gasp. Her thigh wrap around my hips. Grabbing at her own breasts, she looked down at me making a pouty face as she drop them.

"They do sag a bit don't they."

Snorting, I buck my hips causing her to squeal. Her hands fell on my midsection as I move a few inches on the couch, resting my head on the armrest.

Reaching out, she took a section of my hair. My lightish brown hair that shimmers red in the light. She pulls it to her in admiration as it glides in her hand. Vixen ask, "How do you get your hair this long and beautiful?"

My hair that is almost at my hips, laying in natural waves, I reply, "Washing it once a week helps."

Twirling her fingers in my hair, "Have you ever cut it before?"

"Actually no. I was supposed to get it cut when I turned eighteen, an O'Salves tradition or something, but never did it; my hair never needed a trimming and still doesn't. Kind of want to see how long it gets."

Ax cough, "Do the two of you need a room?"

I smirk, "Aw, do you not want to join us?"

Vixen leans into me our breasts touching again as she kiss my hair winking at him, "I don't think he can deal with the both of us."

Ax grumbles, dumping an ice cube down her back. Squalling, she jump off of me.

"Get this damn AC fixed, please." Ax took his place on the couch. The others who wanted a late - night drink finally joining.

Vixen says after the ice fell to the ground, sliding away, "They are coming tomorrow morning, so everyone's balls and breasts won't reek up this place. The bouncers warned everyone, and I even took a loss, offering half off entry cause of it. So, stop grumbling about one night of heat."

A bar tender that works below huffs. "And somehow it was more packed than normal due to that half - off."

They started to pour drinks, relaxing, and unwinding.

Leaving the club close to four in the morning, Ax caught up with me as I went from one alley to another.

"This isn't the first time I seen you go down alleys."

I ignored the comment which sounded like he's been watching me. "It is easier this way sometimes." I lower my voice to a whisper, where no audio could pick up, "Someone is keeping their eyes on me, and I'd rather make it harder for them to know my movements."

He match my volume, "Snitch, don't tell me you are getting involved…"

I stop him, "My name alone is the issue. All I do is go to work and this club, and maybe go for random runs to clear my mind. Still, they are watching me."

A hint of concern trace his words, "Do they think you are going to rebel like your family?" I shrug my shoulders.

I was too young to understand then. Still, I don't fully comprehend why my family would try what they did. They came through ransacking my family's apartment taking all of us for questioning that night. If I knew better, I would have stayed silent. I shouldn't have been so nosy listening to snippets of private conversations, filling in the blanks when needed. I shouldn't have gone into that room that was always locked. I should never have trusted the Luners. I think the only thing that saved me from receiving the same fate as the rest of my family were the squiggles of words I couldn't read.

My shoulders sag from the memory. I stopped walking, and when Ax realize I was no longer following he turn around. We were still in the alley, one of the safe places cameras don't reach - a huge flaw. Since I started walking it more and more, it brings up weary thoughts that these so - called 'flaws' in the structure of this society seems intentional. All the blind spots are perfectly positioned for walking from one alley to another with only a few cameras on the outside and a few pointing at the wall. I could walk to any end of the city, and no one would know.

"This is your street." I say with a blank expression.

His eyes widen, darting his head out of the alley, "Dang, it is. Before we leave, I want to ask you something." He continue not waiting for me to reply, "You want to go with my husband and I to another club on my day off?"

My nose flared. Rubbing my hand underneath trying to stop it. I reply, "On one of your days off, you go to another club?"

"You can't say shit. You go to clubs every day. Come on, get into a new environment. It's small, there aren't as many people like Vixen's club. You'll enjoy yourself Snitch." I ran my hands through my hair wanting to tell him no, but then he continued, "I still got your number. I'll text you the address."

Glaring, I let out a sigh realizing he isn't going to take no as the answer, finally nodding in agreement. He flash a true smile waving bye before leaving the alley.

*

Sitting in my office after a whole week off feels strange. Drinking my second cup of coffee waiting for my team to arrive. Trying to wake myself early in the morning after sleeping during the day, it has my schedule all wonky.

The distant mutter of voices grow louder down the hall. The rest of my team is coming to work. Abigail limping into view, a reminder how horrible the last time we went out. I am surprised she didn't quit after that. She must be stronger than she acts.

Chad avoiding eye contact with me. After what happen last week I don't want anything to do with him. Crybaby, along with the other new person isn't here. Even an old member seemingly quit. So, we are going with only seven people, and considering Abigail's limp it's more like six. Before I even open my mouth, Randal shoots me a warning look. Telling me to keep quiet about the demise of our team. Chad takes the lead, entering the room to change.

I can't help muttering to Randal before we walked into the room with the rest. "He thinks he's all a big shot now?"

Randal snaps. "Shut it Trinity." His cold demeanor freezes me to the core, his tone carrying an underlying tension as if he's been waiting for an opportunity to snap at someone. Stepping aside, I let him rush into the room barking at everyone to hurry. The muscles in my arms tense. Looking over my shoulder with a flash of thought, I could just leave I don't need to be treated like this.

My eyes widen as two slip away without my knowledge already bringing the catty in. Normally, they would get dressed then retrieve the bodies. Changing with the rest of them revealing my tank top and running shorts. Pulling my hair into a high ponytail to keep it off my skin, noticing Abigail wearing fewer clothes this time. At least she learn quickly. I hate that they are still making her come with us despite having that horrible limp. Her expression has hardened already, eyes still set on the ground. That fear of before no longer remains.

Randal and I inspect everyone's uniforms. While he focuses on the two new people, I just glimpse over the ones who know the drill. Approaching the panel to see a missing mobile device.

Turning around, I ask, "Why is one missing?"

Randal shot me a glare, as if I should know the answer already. My nostrils flare as I got a glimpse of his glossy eyes.

He reply, "It wasn't in your uniform when they checked." My lashes flutter looking back at the panel. I put it inside my chest pocket. They must have misplaced it or washed it by accident and blamed it on me.

Swiveling to address the rest of the team, Randal's voice cuts through the room. Finally, a glimpse of the Lunder officer he once was. "Since the Wanderers have been watching us. We're changing our course. We won't return to our previous dump spot. We'll head to station C, throwing off the Wanderers because we have no clue what information they have or if they know our entire route."

I can feel all their eyes collectively burning holes in my back. With shaky hands I took the mobile device off.

Checking the feed, ensuring the coast was clear before giving Randal the nod to open the hatch. Reaching the third camera, the hatch beeps signaling its opening. Startle, quickly turning my head toward the door as it swung open. Chatters of a Zombie is on the other side turned to the open door.

"What the hell!" I shouted furiously at Randall's carelessness.

He strut past me as if what he did is natural, swinging the shaft upward, firing a shot that silenced the zombie. Randal barks, "Come on lets go."

My jaws clinched glaring up at the shadow of Randal. Something is off. He never engage to risk anyone's life so recklessly before. The glossy look in his eyes is the reason he isn't acting like his normal self.

I waited to be the last one to get up grilling my thoughts over.

Chad snicker as he's second-to-last, "Looks like you've fallen out of his favor finally."

My nostrils flare, "What did you do?"

His snicker morph into a ruthless grin, "I'd suggest you to be nicer to me, Snitch. Maybe a little bird will tell the Luners how you handed a mobile device to the Wanderers."

I bit out word for word, "What. Did. You. Do?"

"Simply told my father-in-law how a murdering snitch works here and pointed a shaft at me. Your days are limited, and Randal seemed to receive the memo to keep you in check." The fury inside me surges, blood heating up my core wanting to hurt him. His marriage into a powerful family shot his ego to the sky.

Flipping my ponytail over my shoulder, maintaining a dignified stride passing him. Keeping my head held high holding my urge sock him.

Station C is where they are at, Alex, Daniel, and Junes' bodies were dumped. Where I also thought Niel laid. It has been three years, so I know there isn't any part of their body that will be recognizable. A part of my heart pulls tighter the closer we get.

Niel lingers at the front of my mind. He probably woke up atop our friends. Did he grapple with the reality of what he became? Niel could had spent days, weeks, or months mindlessly consuming others before regaining his control.

Fuck. Before I knew it, we were on the spot. The increasing tightening in my chest dissolves into an indescribable emotion. Where there should be a pile of bone, it's all gone. Bone fragments lay scattered, but the mass of it disappeared. Closing my eyes, tears slip through tracing down my cheeks. A painful grin grace my face.

A round clearing surrounded by trees, a poignant juxtaposition against the natural beauty that thrives here. The summer heat taken a toll wilting the surroundings. I envision the vibrant colors that paint this land in the fall, when snow lays in blankets, flowers bloom, when the heat isn't wilting the leaves, and it's all so beautiful in my mind. They rest peacefully, embraced by nature.

Watching as the bodies were easily dumped due to no mound to toss them on. Randal directing the others to gather dirt, wanting the bodies completely covered. As they went into the wood line still in view, the swaying of trees rustle as the warm summer breeze came by.

"Don't test him Trinity. He isn't worth it." Randal says stumbling slightly, "His new Father-in-law… he has a significant pull over the Luners. We can't afford to lose his donations."

I reply in a flat tone, "I can't let him step on me and do as he wishes."

Grinding his teeth, Randal slurs his words, "I put my neck out on the line for you. Don't make it all for nothing." My brows scrunch as I turn to face him, "So, because he married into money, he now has a say of who gets fired? He has me around his fucking hands like the Luners?"

He snaps, rage twisting his expression, "Shut it Trinity."

I hiss, "Make me silent." I challenge him getting an inch away from his face, his stare avoiding mine, fixated on my shoulder as if my face is too much to bear. "I do good here. I've done nothing wrong, and I saved your lives while he was a coward wanting to close the doors early. I can prove my innocence and ruin their family name. Before getting on my ass, remind him not to mess with a Snitch. O'Salves ruins lives, remember?"

Randal open his mouth, attempting to find words. As air escapes from deep within, I caught a whiff of it - he is drunk.

My throat closes. Randal is well aware of the repercussions he would face if they discover he's intoxicated on the job, especially the day we go outside the wall.

Randal's voice lowers, carrying a raspy pain, "Elizabeth was going to interrogate you. Chad say he saw you talking with the Wanderers before making a run." My eyes widen at the claim. I can't deny it outright; I was speaking to them, but I can't tell them that because Niel was there. No one would believe me even if I did tell the truth.

My stomach turning on itself with the new lies being spun because of the cheating groom. He forgets that I saw him with that girl in his lap, his pants becoming tighter as he kissed her neck. That alone makes him a cheater. Since everyone is believing his lies now, what does my words have? Nothing.

Wait, he couldn't have seen me from where he was standing. If he did, that mean he was waiting and didn't warn the others danger is afoot.

I counter folding my arms, "Why didn't he warn you guys before I came screaming like a madman."

"That is what I said," Randal's eyelids drops with weariness. "Trinity, tell me the truth. How did you get free?"

As the team approaches, covering the lifeless bodies with dirt, I kept quiet knowing he will be listening.

Facing them as they did their job. Chad position himself obviously to watch me. If Randal and I talk too much, he will think Randal is on my side and make this harder on him. 'Tell me the truth,' sounds similar to 'you can tell us the truth,' the trusting words that are venomous lies.

The team came a second time, the dirt thickening. Their talking is now distracting Chad who is no longer looking at us.

"You didn't have to stick up for me. I've been interrogated by her before. I know how it goes."

Randal's voice rises briefly before lowering to a whisper, "You don't understand - not like before. It's 'if she doesn't spill her guts, I'll pull out her nails until the pain forces her to squeal.'

"I told her we have no ground, no other proof other than a newcomer in my team. She smiled." He paused, his lips quiver, and continued. "She didn't care if you lie, as long it's what she wanted to hear - that you are going against the city, trying to start a revolution like your parents."

Raising my voice, "That isn't true!" That's the narrative they *fed* the public. "You know of all people that isn't close to the truth."

"Not like the truth was any better." Randal admits, blinking a few times and widening his eyes. "What happened?"

I sigh, "They weren't going to let me go. I stabbed the one who grabbed me, and that's how I got out of their grip. They started arguing - one wanted me dead, the other two wanted to take me in for information. I took that moment of distraction and ran.

"Please tell me you weren't on Chad's side."

Randal reassures me, "We won't do that to you."

Turning my head to the side, I press, "What do you mean 'we' Randal?"

He shook his head, dismissing me, "It wasn't anything. Just leave him alone Trinity."

Flashing my teeth, "You are right. It's best I keep my eyes open." My expression turned blank, causing Randal to slowly pull his head back, "Once a Lunar, always a Lunar. Don't pretend to care about me. I am an O'Salves, my name brings me trouble and I snuff it out. Go make sure your team is good, and I'll stand here."

"Trin…"

"Leave, Randal, and report back to Elizabeth that I say I have nothing to do with my family. That I am trying to forget about the deaths of my best friends and being alone. So, fuck off."

For a heartbeat he kept my stare, not to dare me, but showing remorse in his eyes.

My chest expands and flattens as he walks off. Chad standing there with a smirk as if he's the shits, that he is now untouchable due to the family he married into.

'We,' Randal say we as if he is still part of the Luners. Are the rumors true? Could you truly never get out? When I found him drunken, could that be part of the plan to get close to me. In hopes I would reveal my connection of continuing where my family left off? Eliminating the last O'Salves.

Your kids do not fall far from the tree. Any time a parent commits a horrible crime against the city, Luners, or disturb the peace, the kids inevitably follow in their footsteps. Somehow, I stand as the exception so far. Possibly it's because they've framed all the others and haven't managed to get me on anything. I glare over to Randal; they are getting desperate if they are using him.

I use to believe Luners cared for us. A commitment to keep the peace and render fair judgment. As time passes and I grow older, I find that's furthest from the truth. It's a lie. Despite my feeling for Luners, I could never do what my family were about to do. It's a horrible disaster that would never go right.

The remainder of the day I remained in silence. Despite

Chad constantly provoking me, I remain silent. This isn't the time for me to act. I am a Snitch, not a liar. I'll get the right information to bring an end of his inflated ego.

Finding the hidden button the hatch opens, allowing us to go inside to safety of our city. Once we leave to do our trip, one time to get in. It's for the safety to protect the citizens of the city.

Stripping out of my uniform, snatching my bag off the floor, and not bothering to finish the day. Striding to the elevator, catching a glimpse of Elizabeth heading in my direction and my heart skips a beat. Jumping into the elevator I press the quick close, not taking the chance for her joining me.

In the apartment I live in, preparing myself for the evening, releasing my hair letting it fall down to my waist, brushing through my waves. Staring at myself in the mirror, holding a chunk of hair in front of my face.

Why don't I cut my hair? Make the change and cut it to shoulder - length or even shorter. Imagining how my hair would bounce at that length, I shook my head. It would make me look like any other girl. My length makes me stand out. While I don't need my hair to help me stand out. It helps me stand out in a good way.

I slip into a tight skirt, it's hem stopping halfway to my knees. A slit runs all the way with only string lace holding it together preventing a glimpse of my underwear. Pulling at the bottom, I revealed more of my leg stopping just short of exposing what lay beneath. A lace eggshell crop top with a nude under piece. My three - inch heels echo my steps as I strut down the hall.

Ax texted me the location earlier today. I don't even remember giving him my number. If anything, it probably happened around the first anniversary of my friends' passing. That whole month is a blur. The amount of Lily and alcohol in my system during those days were enough to last the rest of my life.

On the other side of the town, my legs start to burn far before I got to the club. Why did this club have to be so far away? Standing outside, a steady flow of people went into the building. It's nothing close to Vixen's club. By now, there is a line wrapping around the building.

As I waited near the building for Ax and his husband to show, people's gazes linger on me as they past. They should have been here by now. My foot tapping impatiently on the ground. A group of people a little older than me, ran into me nearly pushing me into the street. The girls laugh, offering no apology.

Flipping my hair I mocked, "Ha, if you needed more room to walk, you could just say 'excuse me.' I know livestock tend to sway, so I would had understood."

Before anyone had a comeback, I heard Ax's voice in the distance. They couldn't gotten here any sooner? Placing a smile upon my face, I made my way over to him and his husband.

Ax introduce, "Snitch, this is my husband Henery."

I wink, "It's nice to meet you, husband Henery. You're late. I thought you two stood me up."

Ax explains, "Sorry, we are used to others being late when it comes to club night. We tend to run ten minutes behind to avoid waiting ourselves."

"Well, for future reference, I show up early." Clapping my hands together, "Anyway, you guys got here just in time before I got into a fight."

Henery, with his smooth voice, rang familiar in my head, "As you walked to us, it looked like two girls were trying to say something to you."

I shrug, "They tried to push me into the road. I called them livestock. Fair game."

Henery's smile radiated pure joy as if he never experienced any pain his life. "You're right; I like her, babe." That voice tickled my brain, and it feels like I have heard it before. Not just once but constantly. It bothersome I can't pinpoint it.

Sitting down at a small table, they begin telling me how they met. Henry's soothing voice wrapping itself into my mind, pushing out every other thought. Both had been stood up at the same restaurant.

Henery was not out yet, so he was waiting for a girl. Ax had known his preference since puberty, where girls didn't stir any excitement, but the locker room he experienced his first arousal. His ears turn red at that story, embarrassed to this day it happened. Henery just gives his love a cheeky smile in return. Smiling at Ax's demure behavior around his husband, its nothing like how he acts on the job.

It was Ax's third date with the person, and getting a breakup text, he found himself drinking endlessly at the bar. Henery, already at the bar, was uninterested sitting alone with his date. Their parents had set the whole thing up, so Henery was prepared to express that he wasn't interested. So, he drank to celebrate her standing him up.

Ax, started to drunkenly flirt with Henery after learning that neither of their dates didn't show. They exchanged numbers, stayed in touch, and a few months later, Henery ask Ax out. Ax, oblivious to Henery's sexuality, thought of him as a friend.

Henery adds, "His cheeks flushed, stumbling over his words asking if I was sure. Ha, sounded like he was asking himself that question. I told him he could think about it, and that's when he cut me off with a kiss."

"That is so cute." My hands cup to my face, "I can just imagine the look on your face Ax."

Ax took a sip of his spirit, "I felt dumb I didn't realize it earlier, or I would have already put the moves on him."

Henery kisses Ax's cheek lingering in true love, "Sure, you would have babe… By the way, um, Snitch, if you don't mind, what is your real name? It feels wrong calling you that."

I flash a tight smile, "I don't mind. It's a nickname I got in grade school, and it's stuck."

Curiously Henery asks, "Why would they give you a name like that? Did you tell teachers whenever students cheated or made out in the bathrooms?"

I stare in his eyes, replying, "O'Salves." That is all one needs to know for it to click. Not everyone knows my face, but that name - they all know my family's history, or at least the version told. Henery sucked his lips in, his brain working on everything he has heard.

Straightening his back, Henery clarifies, "You mean the O'Salves who started building this city, help start the Luners. When the Luners became what we know now, kicked them all out of power for controlling too much."

I blink, confusion plaster on my face. It's almost like he is praising my ancestors. His face isn't contorting like others, disgusted that we were such an important part.

He continues, "The same O'Salves that were going to betray, oh, Mother Earth," He cover his mouth, and I lean back, my hand resting on my cup, "You're Trinity

O'Salves, the only surviving member due to your age and aiding them to stop your family."

They told me they wouldn't die, and that I would be saving them. In every generation, we O'Salves got the short end of the stick. My ancestors built this place, allowing people in for a new society, and the thanks they got was being kicked out of their luxuries because it wasn't fair for the others. Now look - there are people with more power because of money.

Henery place his hand on mine, offering comforting words, "In life, we do what we believe is right. Never allow others to deem your worth by the actions they may not agree with."

There's a smooth calmness in his voice. Sincere in every word that came out. He isn't judging me. Even Ax had a shocked expression when he found out my true name. Yet, Henery, he isn't looking at any of that. Looking beyond it all into the deepest parts of me.

It suddenly click why I know this voice to my core. "You are the guy who holds the pod show I listen to, Lovely Crest."

He smile, "Oh, you're a fan? Well, I'll let you know," He leans in closer, "I am a fan of yours too."

I scoff, "I haven't done anything in life but party."

Henery counters, "You do things I can't even fathom. Bravery that, if I was in your shoes, I don't think I would have made it." Ax nod in agreement with his husband's words, "How you make decisions to save yourself and others, I strive to be like that."

I pound my spirit with one shot of Lily, slamming it on the table, and say, "No. No the hell you don't." My face contorts in anger that he would say something so foolish.

Truly someone who hadn't suffered in his life thinking I am someone he should strive to be like.

Snapping I want to grab him by the shirt, but I didn't. "You have someone you love, where I killed my family, killed my second family, and even a Wanderer to protect my teammates. Yet, I am being treated like a criminal by the very team I saved. Cause I pointed that fucking shaft at Chad, he has a vendetta to ruin my fucked - up life even more."

Ax got out of his seat, rubbing my shoulders shushing me trying to calm me down after I got it all out.

Henery ask, "Wanderers? Only the hazard team can go out there."

I point at my head no longer caring who knows what happen out there. At least at this moment. I may regret it later. "That's how I got this wound. I was almost taken by Wanderers, and Chad, whoever the dark moon he married, is powerful. Spreading lies that I am aiding Wanderers, that I am leading in my family's' footsteps. That's why you don't want my life, Henery. Everyone is out for me one way or another."

I held back my tears of frustration. No matter what I do I am the bad guy, why not tell a few people the stress I am facing. It's not like it breaks my contract. Ax went to the bar to get me a straight shot of Lily to calm me down.

"We won't tell a soul, I promise you." Henery assures me, patting my hand, his soothing deep voice suffocating my brain. "If anything happens to you, I will use my platform to set the truth free, to let all the cities know you are innocent. Ax talks about you almost every night, how you don't dance. You just sit there, motionless watching below, frozen as life goes on around you.

"You keep it all in, and through the years, you've become easier to get a rise out of. Your body is getting tired of holding it all in." Henery smiles as he touches my hand, "I am happy you let some of the pain out. I know Ax will be thrilled too that you trusted us enough."

Ax returns with only half a shot of Lily. They refused to give him anymore, stingy bastards. I took it, dropping it in my other glass. Tilting my head back, I let the smoothness slide down my throat. Henery's voice repeating, keeping me calm. I haven't listened to his pod show in a year, I've forgotten how it used to calm me down.

The music reverberates through my body, and suddenly, Ax and Henery stood. Smiles plaster on their faces as they guide me out of my chair. Ax spun me, handing me off to Henery, where he did the same.

"You are going to finally dance." Ax laughs, "With two hot men at that."

"I wouldn't consider you guys hot, but easy on the eyes, yes." I pause, leaning into Ax, whispering "I don't dance."

"No one truly dances on this floor. You let the music in, and you have fun with it. Follow our lead." Henery says as he guides me to the floor.

Spinning on my heel, people bump into each other. They pass me to each other, doing their own special moves. Henery touches the back of my head, spinning me in three tight circles. Where Ax helps me sway my body back and forth.

Before I knew it, another man chimes in, stealing me from my dance partners, and surprisingly I didn't fight it. Allowing him to guide my body, I follow his moves. My back against his chest, allowing him to feel my body. Ax cheer me on as they pass me, dancing with one another.

Bashfully smiling, this feels good.

It's true, I never step on the dance floor because the man who took me to the club for the first time wasn't a big dancer himself. We both sat in what's now my spot, just talking, giving enough information to feel close but not enough to show our cards where either could ruin the other's life. He taught me the 'tell just enough' rule that I've been following. Sometimes, I did wish we had exchanged numbers; it would be nice to message him finding out who Chad's new family may be.

Tilting my head back, the man place his lips onto mine. His tongue intertwines, pushing just a little more, getting a better taste. Not bad. He doesn't have any other smell on him other than his cologne, meaning he hasn't been doing this to all the girls tonight.

Leaning into him as we back out of the crowd, our hot breaths collide. We didn't stop. Getting behind a pillar somewhat hidden from the crowd. He press his body against mine. Shit this is going too far. He presses upwards, ready to do more than just kissing. I only wanted to kiss, not this.

Pushing him back, I kept my head down, my face burning, "I am not that type of girl. I am sorry. I just wanted to dance. Thank you for the kissing, but I'm going to go."

He tilt my face, giving another kiss his tongue wrapping around mind. Pulling away, saliva drip from his tongue.

He groans kissing my neck more, "You taste so damn good. Just calm. I can take us to a hotel."

I push him away. My hands on his pecks keeping distance between the two of us. "Tempting but I don't do flings."

My legs feeling weak, I don't know if it is from Lily, or the intense kissing. Moving away from the pillar, waving my hand at Henery getting his attention. He spots me bringing Ax in my direction. I am glad Henery is tall so it's easy to spot him in the crowd.

The man came up behind me, wrapping both of his arms around my midsection. His hard cock presses against my ass as I try to push away.

He whisper in my ear, "Shh, just calm, it's all okay." His hand slip in my mouth, "It's all okay, let it be, and you will feel good."

He lays something on my tongue. My eyes widen, my heart rate increasing with what he just gave me. Slamming my head back, I hit him in the face. He stumbles back letting me go. Spitting the substance into my hand.

I curse, "What the fuck is this?"

Henery took my hand that has the quickly dissolving pill in my palm and says, "He gave you Calm."

Ax kick the man in his cock, causing him to double over in pain. Henery snapping his fingers in the air singling someone to come. I froze staring at the pill, the bitterness lingers in my mouth.

"This man has Calm on him and try to drug my friend." Henery says averting his attention on me know. "Trinity, are you okay?"

I shook my head dropping my hand, "I… I have to go before the Luners come."

Ax states putting a hand on my shoulder, "Let us take you home."

"No!" Backing away from them. "Don't let them know it was me. Trust me, if they ask, say you don't know me. I am just someone you met at the bar, and you don't know where I went."

If this gets out, they will have any reason to say I took it because I wanted it. They will spin the story like they did with my family, but in my case, make it way worse.

Pushing my way through the kitchen, people scream at me to get out. Ignoring them, I found the exit in the back.

Hearing the sirens in the distance, I dart into another alley heading towards where I live. My feet stumble as the silence of night follow me. Rolling my ankle, I fell to the ground.

Everything around me vibrates. What is going on? Squeezing my head, trying to make the world stop moving using the wall as a guide, continuing to stumble further.

Peering into the street, this one has a very narrow blind spot. If I'm not careful, they will see me. One step in front of another, I wobble my way to the other side. The world tilting again, and I stumble to the other side of the alley. The world tilting, I slid down the wall trying to ground myself.

My head is spinning, or it's the world. Well, the world is always spinning. I grab my head, trying to keep it in place. The Calm did this. I spat it out almost instantly, and I am reacting like this. No wonder people are dying because of it.

Closing my eyes, waiting for the disorientation to ease up. My nostrils flared breathing in a sweet, earthy scent, cider mixed with a hint of vanilla, and a smell I am unaware of. Niel used to smell like nature, a constant reminder of hours, and even days spent beyond the walls. There is a lot of things I don't know about Niel. Things I still don't understand.

Curling my legs to my chest, resting my head on them. He is breathing, moving, and somewhat talking. tears runs down my face. I want to ask if he is okay. If he is angry at me for stabbing him. Angry that I didn't do it right and he has to exist as this… Second Life. My chest bounced as I cry to myself.

Makeup smears into my knees; I wipe my snot on my skirt.

"Infinity" Niel slowly says.

Looking up my vision blurs, Niel approaches his head tilting to the side. A wrinkle forming between his brows in a familiar expression of concern. The scar on his perfect face - a scar I caused - pulling on my heart with what I did to him. My lower lip quiver as I let out a whine.

I cry out, "I know I'm hallucinating but why does it have to be of you?"

Niel knelt a few feet in front of me. "You need. To go home."

Shaking my head, I utter, "I am so sorry. I'm sorry I killed you. I'm sorry about it all. I've fucked up over and over, and I don't know what to do. Niel, I am scared."

He had his life together more than I even knew back then. Here I am, three years later, more of a mess than before he died.

I stare at him, as he mirror my gaze not getting any closer. I long for the warmth of his hug, willing my mind to have the hallucination to hug me.

Rubbing my face, I let out a groan, "I am tripping bad."

Niel forcing each word out slowly, "What did you do?"

"An ass tried to drug me."

Muffle voices from the main road came closer and Niel stood, he says, "Home. Home now. Sleep. Everything locked, okay?"

When I didn't move, he came forward and the chatter of his jaw made my body tense. I don't want to remember that part of him. I got up. The world no longer violently shifting, I am able to walk in a straight line, leaving the fabric of my imagination behind.

"Wakey wake, it's time to shake. Wakey wake, it's time to shake."

My arm shot out, muting the alarm. Daniel has such an irritating alarm. After all these years, I still don't know what 'time to shake' is supposed to mean. Groaning, I roll over in my bed, my head pound with every move. 'Calm' my ass, that shit is a trip. My body hasn't felt like this in a long time. The equivalent of an all-nighter of non-stop drinks. Wearing bright pink pajamas with black polka dots pajamas I haven't worn in years.

"Shit." I mutter getting to my feet.

June, Alix, and I had the same matching pajamas for our girls' night. This thing was tucked all the way back in my bottom drawer.

Shuffling through the hall, I still at the sight of my living room, snacks set up on the coffee table, open containers all over the dining room table. Rushing to the kitchen at the sound of running water, steam bellowing out of the faucet. Cooked noodles laying inside the sink and a jar of sauce set out.

"What the fuck." I say out loud, confused at the sight.

"I need coffee."

Getting the coffee ready, I stare at the party I was apparently preparing for. Shutting my eyes, slumping over in realization, remembering the hallucination of Niel last night. The pajamas the girls would wear, making dinner for everyone - it was what I'd always done when expecting them to come.

I hope that ass who forced that Calm in my mouth got tossed into a cellar for a few weeks.

Cleaning up the kitchen while waiting for the coffee to finish brewing. Shoving everything into the fridge, saving for tonight's dinner. With the coffee done, cup in hand, staring at an open - faced down photo album on the dining room table. Made from lightly color leather scratched up from use. Where did this come from?

Pulling the album closer, I flip it over, and my lips pulled to a straight smile. Clearly, I must have been missing them. The page the album was set down at displayed our first-ever photo together. First time meeting, and at the end of that year, we became best friends. The teacher captured this moment for us.

I don't have many photos where I smile with that amount of joy. My eyes squinting to the point where it looked like they were closed. Niel in the back, wrapping his arms around Daniel and I. Alix looks like she's being choaked out by Daniel. I remember that she was standing a little forward when the teacher told us to get closer. That's when Daniel wrapped his arm around her, pulling her in, and we all laugh, especially at her squeal. June stood close to my side, our heads bonked as the photo was taken, and we just laugh keeping our heads connected for the photo.

Flipping through the pages, there's a lot of photos of Niel and his family. I must have gone into Niels room and found this when I blacked out. Slightly smiling at his baby photos, including a few tinny baby butts, I couldn't help but to laugh at. In my mind, I can almost hear him scolding me not to look, and that he would be trying to take this away from me.

I got to see a bit of his life in City Beta. He stood at the gate; his eyes puffy as if he was crying but forced a smile for the photo. This must've been the day they left to come to City Alpha. My ancestors built three cities - Alpha, Beta, and Omega - each slightly different to determine which would work best. One mistake tarnished my families name.

City Omega, turned out to be a colossal failure. Not even a full generation in, people were murdering one another. I only know about it because some old - timers used to give my dad a hard time, blaming our bloodline. According to them if we hadn't been kicked out of position, the same fate would befall City Alpha.

It's no longer taught in history class. By now, the old timers who remember are all dead. With that their knowledge has also died off. We're only told in school that the walls failed and the soil in the region couldn't sustain crops.

Other cities sporadically popped up over the years seeking help from City Alpha. Sometimes, we would send them resources if they agreed to certain contracts. Other times, pretended not to hear their pleas. I'm not sure of any new cities that have been built in the past generation, or if they have, the information isn't being shared with the public. The news use to talk about what happen in other cities. Now that I think about it it's been years since the last time I heard anything about them.

Pages of photos, memories I long forgot flood my mind. Flipping back to our first year together, my smile grew wider. It feels like they are still with me. Pulling the photo out, a second slip from the album, sliding across the table. Tilting my head, reaching for it, bringing it closer.

Jerking my hand back as if it hurt me, my eyes widen in disbelief. Gulping, I can't believe it. Niel casually taking a photo of himself, my parents and older brother directly behind him. My heart skips a beat. It's surreal. They all face the camera, fully aware of the moment Niel was capturing. Inside that dark room, I wasn't ever allowed it.

Tears stream down my face seeing my brother with his recently cut hair, short on the sides, and shaggy in the front, tied back out of his eyes. My mom, with her beautiful curls that bounced effortlessly, not even shoulder length. Her headband sending them in every direction behind her. My dad, who kept his hair pretty much buzzed, winking at the camera. It has been so long since I saw their photos. Luners wouldn't leave me a single one, fearing I might mourn and follow their path.

Slowly, I close my eyes, my head spinning with maelstrom of thoughts. Why was Niel in that room - the room where I found out what they were doing, the room that led to my actions getting them killed. Rubbing my hand through my hair, ink on the back of the photo catches my eye. Flipping it over, my stomach bottoms out. This was taken a week before I snuck into the room myself about a month before Luners questioned them. A month and a half before they took me and needed to know what I knew. If only I kept quiet about what I'd seen, my family might still be alive. Then again, they could have caused irreparable harm if I didn't speak. Every day it nags at my mind - what if I made the wrong choice?

Tears of happiness turn to sadness, pushing my face into my hands, crying. Memories flooding back, overwhelming me. Darkness filled that room, only a few lamps giving light. Papers adorned in a language never seen before, test tubes filled with black, red, clear, and white liquids, actively being mixed together. Photos of zombies plastered on the walls alongside random numbers scribbled haphazardly. The history of the first wave highlighted in red and rewritten as if they were trying to pinpoint where it all went wrong.

Dad was supposed to be working to cure the disease. The language scrawled inside notebooks and only my family knew what it meant, evident from the Luners reaction. In that room, small lifeless animals confined in cages marked with signs that read 'failed.' It was clear they were experimenting with a new strain of disease. Blood samples, black fluid that oozes from zombies, were labeled with X - except for one, which bore the mark of an O, black like the rest. Whatever they were attempting, they had succeeded.

The last time I saw my parents, I told them that the Luners know about everything I had seen, their faces drained of color. As the pieces of the puzzle fell into place in my mind, I realized in that room they were crafting a new strain of disease to put out in the world. My mom ask how did I figure it out. To be honest, I still do not know how. Everything clicked into place in my mind. Naively, I reassured them, saying, '*It's okay. They promised you will be safe now. They will show mercy as long as you stop.*' How stupid I was to believe the Luners would show mercy.

I lean in the chair, air laying heavy in my lungs. It's a memory that had been buried deep within the recesses of my mind for a long time. Niel must have known what would happen if they found these photos. Taking out all the photos from the photo album more were hidden behind other photos. Getting every last photo out of the album, my chest tightened.

"Who the hell were you?" I mutter to Mother Earth.

Scenes unfamiliar to me. Spaces beyond the walls, an environment I'd never laid eyes on. Rooms stripped of windows, illuminated only by dim overhead lights. There, in the photos spread across the table, Niel stood alongside Wanderers as if they were friends.

Niel and Daniel standing together. It couldn't been more than a year before they passed. They were carefree, unfazed by the constant threat of zombies outside the walls.

Sandra, Gabe - there they were alongside my family. Squinting at the photo, Niel and my brother seated in the background both perched on a worn couch, the walls adorned with books.

All these photos of a life I hadn't known. A reality where they were free, not tied by the fear of zombies. Everything I knew shattering beneath me. I was the only one in my life in the dark.

Were they all involved, and I was the only one left in the dark? Niel had been involved with Wanderers long after my families death. We are the same age; did he truly understand what he was involved in? We weren't even ten when my family passed.

Landscapes I never seen before, it explains why he would be gone for days, falling off the face of the world. Theres a world beyond our walls, a world where Wanderers aren't always in distress as the city portrays them as.

Gazing around the lavish style Niel apparently had. People outside of these walls were willing to pay for all of this. Showing Wanderers aren't these impoverished and helpless people. What did Niel give in return for this life?

Putting everything in the book in a hurry, I slammed the album shut. I thought Niel was honest with me. I thought I knew who he was. Instead, he was closer to my family than I was, Gabe and Sandra as well. If only they included me in their secrets, perhaps I could have talked them out of it. A lifetime spent in the shadows becoming abundantly clear.

Chapter Six

Weeks have pass and I haven't moved the photo album off the table in the apartment. I can't touch it. Racking my brain over everything I have seen; I can't rationalize any of it.

Leaning in my chair, mindlessly buying time down here isolated from the rest. The baron gray walls bored me giving me nothing to silence these thoughts. Attempting to read my book, my mind keeps wandering, still on the same page since I got in. Even at the club my thoughts choke my mind out. Diving into my memories for any telltale signs, some sort of obvious behaviors I was oblivious to, but there's nothing. It's frustrating.

I chose to not pay attention to Daniel and Niel going beyond the wall. Assuming it involved drugs or giving supplies to Wanderers in need - both honestly. The photos suggest it went way further than just supply runs. Niel's lavish apartment, he did way more than drug deals. They both spent time with people that have been trying to tear the walls down. Just what could they have been doing for these Wanderers?

There were no signs, nothing before I snuck into *that* room. Never did I think they spent time together. The few times Gabe and Sandra would talk to my parents, they were very short interactions like any other adult talking to their kid's friend's parents.

Starting to send Sandra a message, 'Were you and my parents close?' Before pressing send, I hesitate. If they were close, she will be tip off I know something. Staring at the ceiling, I delete the message, unable to shake this unsettling feeling.

I haven't even done Lily since that man attempted to force Calm in my mouth. My friend's deaths are no longer on the forefront of my mind. Somehow seeing the beautiful area and that Mother Earth accepted them had helped heal that part of me. Knowing Niel is whatever he turned into, that I didn't truly kill him is echoing in the back of my mind. Perhaps it is because I never truly knew him.

Normally, Randal would come here a few times a week just to say hi and talk for a little bit. Chad ruined it all. However, it may have been a necessary buffer. Randal still sees himself as a Lunar. He could be genuine when wanting to be kind to me, but I can't fully trust him not to report to Elizabeth.

A sequence of unfamiliar sounds disrupt my thoughts: Click... Click... Clank... Bang. I jolt pushing my chair away from the desk. What was that? Creeping towards the adjoining room, heart pounding, reaching the door and cautiously pushed it open. Peeking my head in revealing an empty room. Letting the door swing the rest of the way cautiously making my way inside.

As I stand in the silence of the room, my nostrils flared, questioning the source of the sounds. Could it have been the docks above? The creaking could be due to air blowing through another part of the building. Butterflies flutter in my stomach, urging me to flee, yet I stand my ground.

Clenching my chest wanting my heart to go back into place.

Tiptoeing across the floor, closing my eyes, I inhale deeply, willing my heart to slow. As I reopen my eyes, I set on the mobile device that's missing. Panic surges. I know it was in my chest pocket. How did it just disappear? Could a nurse have taken it? Could Elizabeth be involved in the missing device to frame me?

A cold shiver ran down my spine as I stood there. My eyes fixates on the door above, with normally all green lights, and one is now red. The hatch is failing. Reaching up to retrieve a mobile device, shakily logging in, the surveillance reveals a nightmarish scene. Zombies pressing against the hatch. Overwhelming mass of relentless hunger and decay. My breath hitch as each camera has the same horrific display. How are there so many of them outside, and no alarms blaring their warnings? Panic clutches me as my feet stumble backwards.

Calling Randal, I dial his number from the mobile device. The first call drops, staring at the red lights, I called again. Slowly I back away terrified. If they knew I'm down here somehow, it would trigger them to ram into the door even harder.

On the second call he picked up, "I am in a meeting Tri…"

Cuffing my hand around the phone, I whisper urgently, "The light is red. The alarms are not going off, even though there is a huge herd right outside the walls."

"Theres a herd? That's impossible. We gotten…"

"Check the cameras then, Randal." I bit back, "I am seeing it myself. Get your ass here…Fuck."

Another light has turn red. The door groans and creaks as another light went straight to red. Retreating with soft steps, not wanting to provoke a heave from the zombies on the other side.

Muffle yells erupts from the phone, as Randal deliberately cover the voices.

"Randal." I call out, "Randal, send the Hazard Prevention now."

Silence lingers on the line, my pleas unheard, drown out by the chaos unraveling on his side. A dread intensifies as natural light spills into the room.

Casting eerie shadows of impending threat, silhouettes dance on the walls like monsters from childhood stories, to teach kids to not go out at night, and especially never beyond the walls. Slamming the door shut, twisting the emergency latches as I stand on the side of safety.

Hanging up on Randal, he clearly had no intentions of listening. Frantically dialing the emergency numbers contacting everyone in the lower levels.

My voice echoes over the intercom, "This is not a drill. This is not a drill. Code Black. Zombies have breached the exterior hatch. Code black, I need Hazard Prevention in G0, ASAP. They are stuck in the lockers for now. Exiting the office to seal the iron door as we speak. Repeat, Code black, Hazard Prevention in G0."

Throwing my bag over my shoulder, leaving the comfort of my office. Kicking out the stand that kept the door open all the years I have worked here. The door groan as it fought against me. As I pull at it, my heart pounds.

A loud bang from the other side echoes. Eyeing the door behind me, pushing with all my strength unsure if that door will stand the weight of all the zombies.

"Why the fuck is it not moving!" I scream, frustration and fear mounting on top my shoulders.

The door resists everything. It's hinges are not use to being closed for so long. Another bang echoes from the door behind. Panicking, I ram my shoulder into the iron door as the alarms finally blare through the halls. My shoulder throbbing, I persist with the groaning of the door intensifying behind me. Dropping my bag, I kick it into the hall. Wrapping my hands around the door, I pull with all my might, and it eventually gives slamming shut right as I got my fingers out of the way.

Sweat beading down my face, I took a deep breath as the sound of metal slams shut behind me. My chest tightens, and I rush to the metal lattice door, shaking it in disbelief. Then the second set of doors shut beyond my reach. Pulling on the open handle, the gate wouldn't budge. Panic welling up inside.

The mobile device in my hand vibrates. Pushing myself off, scratching the back of my head seeing it's one of the offices on G0 calling.

Chad's voice came from the other side, "The Hazard Prevention is on its way." His voice callous.

Grinding my teeth realizing where he is calling from. Looking up at the camera with a cold expression, "Open the gates now, Chad."

I'm not sure if that room has cameras or not, but in the off chance there is, I want him to see me.

Unusually relax, as if he is leaning back in a chair, he reply, "I don't think I should risk other's lives by opening them up."

"They are not even through the iron door. Let me out so I can get off this floor." I remind him, "These doors should be shut only if the Iron door has signs of failure."

He ignores my words, "How did they get in?"

"What the fuck are you talking about?"

He didn't answer, "Let's hope the Hazard Prevention gets to you before the zombies do." He pause letting his words sink in, then continue, "Snitch, I told you not to mess with me."

"What the fu…" The phone hung up, but I didn't stop, "ck… are you that insane that you are going to keep me here despite them not getting in yet? I swear when I get out of this, I am going to destroy you Chad!"

I hope whatever cameras were watching could read my lips understanding the curses I'm sending his way.

Kicking the gate, it recoils, shaking in a loud metallic sound. Behind me inside of my office, there's a muffle bang. I let out a whine as there's an even louder thud as the door broke. The zombies are in my office, flooding every part of the room. Me making that loud noise must had triggered them to push harder.

Checking the cameras inside my office they are pushing one another. Two of them moved differently from the others, going right to the door, understanding a task at hand. Never have I seen zombies move like this. They must be Second Life's. Niel wouldn't do this would he, put everyone's lives at risk inside the city by unleashing zombies?

Kicking the gate again, desperately trying to get out. Even if I manage to escape this one, I still have a whole other one I got to deal with. The door behind me groan as the dead press against it. Following by a loud bang, and another, shortly after, the Second Life's attempting to force their way in. Wedging my fingers in the hole for a handle trying to push upwards, hoping to feel the lock.

Yelling in frustration, backing away trapped like an animal because of that bastard. Dumping everything on the ground, desperately looking for anything to help. All I found are my perfumes, makeup, hair ties, an extra charging cable, loose papers, and pens. Grabbing a pen, I play with it in my hand, thinking.

Before jamming the pen into random places, I tried calling Randal again, but it went straight to voicemail.

I scream, hoping my voice echoes through the walls. "Get me the fuck out of here!"

Violently scratching my head, I pace around. The iron door could hold for a while until the Hazard Prevention Team arrives. The door behind me groans, as if telling me another story. A surge went through my body, my mind going blank. Logging into the system to see how many zombies there are, an error appears. 'access denied.' My throat closes up. I just log into it; how did I lose access?

Trying to call Randal again, he still didn't pick up. Cussing with each step I took, jamming the pen up where the lock's at, hoping something would happen. Even if I manage to escape this first door, I have a second one to deal with. If the zombies brakes through the iron door before I get out, I'll be like a small animal ready for the taking.

Since he won't pick up, I decide to send a voice message, "If I fucking die here, it's your fault. Chad has locked all the gates, leaving me right beside my office where zombies have gotten in. I lost my access to call the overhead to let anyone know, and whatever the hell you're doing where you can't pick up, I hope it's trying to save..." I bit out every syllable. "My. Fucking. Ass."

Chucking my mobile device, it shatters against the wall, and I flip off every camera I can see.

They are wanting this to happen. The alarms still blaring, and the Hazard Prevention Team should've been here by now. Lifting my head, my body trembling at the sound of the iron door groaning under pressure. This barrier, which has stood for at least two generations - possibly even longer, might have never been tested and weakened over time. Straining against the pressure, which in theory it's supposed to hold up against zombies and direct blasts.

An air duct above me twists through the whole building. Grates possibly large enough for my body to fit through if I can reach it. Scaling the wires, my hands burning half way up, digging into my flesh, and my feet struggled to find a stable grip. My feet hardly fitting through the hole, slipping out from underneath me, and a painful whine escaped my throat as my body fell.

Going again getting a little further this time. Reaching out, my hands finally able to touch the grate. A bit of hope surged through my body. The slits were small, and my fingers barely fit inside. Tugging at it while trying not to fall, refusing to budge.

A loud thud reverberates the hall as the iron door crashes to the ground, its hinges finally giving away. Zombies flood in, their hands reaching up for me. Scrambling to get my body higher, getting my feet out of their reach, I bang on the grate, my fist red and sore.

The ones that moves differently than the others, shift their heads, staring up at me. They aren't Second Life's.

Their skin doesn't have the same grayish hue. Their bodies are torn to shreds like other Zombies. One had both eyes missing, yet still senses me looking from its empty sockets. Their constant chatter seems almost like communication between them as they move forward. Two of them, as if following orders continue, grabbing at the door, prompting a few others to follow. My jaw hangs open to see them working together.

Some didn't follow. Instead, deciding to reach up for me, their hunger taking control. Kicking my foot, fending off those just tall enough to get their fingertips on me. Desperately positioning my legs higher, I can't reach for the grate without falling.

Someone cut my access to the intercoms. They want me to die here, holding up the Hazard Prevention, hoping I wouldn't make it by the time they get here. The halls echoes with the groans and clicks of the zombies.

With another forceful hit, the grate shifts out of place. Pulling it down, I press my body against the wall. As it fell, it landed on the top of a few zombies, shuffling them in every direction. Stretching for the opening, as a zombie grab my foot, trying to drag me down. Kicking my foot with all my might, my body is pull down. Holding on, I shove my foot deeper into the wires. Despite the burning in my hands, I refuse to let go. I will not die here.

Pulling my foot up, shaking it free from the grasp of the zombie. My shoe drops, hitting the floor below. Getting my second foot on the gate, curling my toes around. Catching my breath, as my body is stretch out holding onto the ledge of the duck.

Breathing deeply, I grip tighter as I wiggle my foot loose. Pushing my feet off, my body swung, lifting one elbow up getting it inside the ducts. Heaving my body upwards my arms shook holding up my upper half safely inside. My legs kicked, catching the other side with my toes, pushing myself further in. Safely inside laying on my stomach as their groans echoes as if they were up here with me.

Crawling away, moving cautiously, not risking the ducts giving out beneath me. Getting to the end of the ducts, passing the second closed gates before the hall turns. Thunderous steps came down the hall. Hollers came from a single man, having the steps slow to a stop. Peeking from a grate overhead, looking down on the men dressed in tan.

Loud deafening bangs erupts. Covering my ears as the distant noise of bodies hit the ground. A few calls I didn't understand then everything around booms in a loud ear rupturing echo. I lay there unable to move seeing that even Hazard Prevention has guns. We were taught they have been out of use for generations. What else have we been taught that are lies?

The constant blasts of gunfire pierce through the air, unlike the sporadic shots from Wanderers. Silence fell, no guns, no groans from the zombies. My hands tremble underneath me. Glancing down as sounds things were being drop to the ground, they were taking long black cases from the bottom of the guns, replacing them. The man mutters some words, where everyone aimed again. The short - lived silence ends as ear - shattering blasting resume.

Crawling away from them, everything around me rang. The gunfire are so loud I can barely hear my own thoughts. If I didn't get out, if I were still on that gate hanging on for dear life, they wouldn't have hesitated to shoot me dead.

Treating me as if I was an infected myself. Someone higher up wouldn't risk the city just to kill me off, they had to use this at their advantage.

Remembering the turning halls, twisting into doors, each air duck leads into every room. I can only hope he is still in that room. There's only one room where anyone can shut the doors if there is a breach.

Peering through the grate, a smile creeps on my face as I spot Chad alone. Oblivious that I am perch above him, leaning back in the chair as if he owns the room, proud, as if he knew the outcome of my dire situation. The grate scrapes as I lift it. His neck tilts looking up. I descend as he jumps out of the chair. Legs dangle out of the grate before dropping to the ground with a thud. My knees buckling, not showing sign of misstep catching myself before I fell.

Glaring up at Chad, my eyes burn with rage. His mouth agape, as if caught off guard by my unexpected survival, locking his phone taking a side step to the door. I stood slowly and steadily keeping my eyes locked on him.

My breath heavy, but managed to keep my voice steady, "Who took away my access to the intercoms. Chad? They riddled that room, not bothering to check if I was safe or infected." I demand. "What higher - up did you manipulate?"

Chad stutters, "I…I told you not to mess with me."

"I didn't do anything to you."

"I saw you talk with Randal. You were planning something."

A smile plays on my lips as my eyes widens. "Did you let them in? Were you involved in turning the alarm systems off?" Chad chuckles nervously, stepping behind the desk, "No, that was just convenient timing."

My nostril flares, "You are scared of me. That's why you are trying to take me down."

"Why would I be scared of you? You better get out. You, you probably got bit and," I took a step closer, and he flinch, his voice raising. "If you do anything."

My heart beat is in my eardrums, "What? What would you do?"

"My family, they are going to destroy you."

I flash a smile, "Looks like you are already trying, so why not give you all a reason."

Dodging to the side, he ran in the other direction. Planting my hands on the table, I slide across it, my feet gliding out in front, both landing on his abdomen.

Tumbling to the ground, he didn't have a chance to react before my fist connect with the side of his face. My nails dig into my palm, sending pain through my arm as I struck again. His new wife won't be able to look at him after I am done. Trying to buck me off, I didn't stop, connecting and disconnecting, each blow revealing more blood on his face.

Letting out a scream, Chad digs his nails into my side. In that moment I pause going to get his hand off my side. He manages to fling me off. Stumbling to his feet, leaning on the wall helping him to stay upright.

"So, you like to play dirty? Put your hands up and fight like an Alpha Citizen." I challenge.

He spat blood in my direction. Coming at me, a laugh bubbles up. The shakiness stop as the pent - up tension eases with each hit I land, and each hit he manage on me. Falling to the ground, blood quickly filled my mouth after the third punch to my face. Looming over me, his stance wobbles.

Grabbing his leg, I flip out positions, stepping on his chest as I get the upper hand. He wheeze rolling on the ground. Reaching out for me I kick him in the face. The sound of the door open. *Shit.*

Everything told me to look who it is, hesitating I stop. Chad, at that moment of hesitation, digs a sharp object into my leg.

Randal's voice sound behind as he yells, "What the hell is going on?"

Rage boils inside me as he took the knife out. Everything overwhelms me telling me to finish him. I didn't reply to Randal. Kicking him repeatedly, my hair fell in front of my face, as Chad tries to crawl away.

I stop myself as Randal stood between Chad and I. Chad crawl to the wall, leaning against it, breathing in rough gasps. My face burning with a mix of rage and pain.

I bit out, "Why the hell did you not pick up the phone?" Directing my anger now at Randal. Who's seemingly coming to Chads rescue. Perhaps that's who was on the phone when I came down.

Chad let out a low chuckle, Randal eyeing him as he explains, "I was on the phone with Chad. He was saying how the zombies passed the iron door and kept talking. I told him to just stay here. I tried to call you, but it didn't go through."

Grinding my teeth, I reply, "I threw it against the wall after over five fucking calls. I even texted you. He locked the gates before zombies even got close, he cut off my intercom access somehow. Chad wants me dead." I lock eyes with Randal. Dropping the anger to show him the fear I feel. "They shot without checking if I was there. If I didn't climb into the vents, I would have been killed."

Chad glares at me, spitting blood, "You will be dead after my wife and her brother come here." He shook his phone at us, "They are on their way."

"You did what?" Randal voice quickens, "Why would you tell them to come?"

Elizabeth is in the doorway, my shoulders slump as my boss stood by her. Rubbing his balding head, he's filled with panic. My body cover in blood which is mostly from him. I let out a long breath as Elizabeth stares at me.

"That was impressive." She eyes the air duct where the vent is missing. "Crawling through to get away." Her words didn't sound like an observation, but she watch it all with her own eyes, "Too bad you beat the son of one of the largest donators for nothing. Do we have to test you for being infected?"

My expression mimics her own calm demeanor, "It was self - defense, Elizabeth. As you probably watched, he locked the gate before danger, which is against protocol, and I, Trinity O'Salves, came to protect myself."

A string tugs at her lips, "You allow your team to beat one another, Randal?"

He pause unsure on how to reply, finally Randal says, "No, I do not. This is an investigation matter. There is too much that went wrong today we need to…"

Chad butts in, "When my wife comes, this whole place will be under fire if she isn't taken care of."

Our boss made a call getting nurses over. Sweating up a storm clearly scared of what's going to happen, nurses rush in, tending to Chad. One came to me, but a click of Elizabeth's tongue made her back away, confusion twisted her face as she look down at my bleeding leg.

"Since you are the team leader, you decide." Elizabeth making it clear what she's getting at in her words.

Randal shot me a pitiful glance, "She got stabbed, can we take care..." She shook her head before he finish. Giving me another look Randal is underneath her unable to argue. "For now, you are not allowed back to work for two weeks. If the investigation shows you are innocent, you can come back to work. If you are not, you are terminated."

"She's going to wish she was dead soon." Chad threatens as the nurses helps him up, "Just you wait. You are going to regret what you did today."

I took a step forward. Everyone in the room tighten in worry, I smirk tilting my head to the side. "The only thing I regrated in my life was killing my best friend," *And* snitching on my family, but I can't say that. "If I had the chance, I would do this all over again."

His eyes flare with rage, realizing he couldn't intimidate me. I already wish I was dead, so whatever family he married into isn't going to do much worse.

Heading to the elevator, I don't wait for anyone. Inside I watch them chatting, my blood trail on the floor that they ignored. Except for Randal who's giving me a look of remorse. Keeping my head high, seeing Elizabeth eyes suddenly widen for half a second at me, the doors cutting my view off.

My boss didn't say anything to me. Even walking, he wiped his sweat, clearly apologizing to her. She was showing who's truly in charge in this situation and who's 'boss' in name only.

There was no reason for her to be here today. She's hanging around our department on my floor, and all of a sudden, we are having these issues; the alarm not going off with a horde, the hatch failing, my login not working right after I made a call. Chad clearly wants me gone, and maybe his loud behavior is giving her a chance to pin something on me. Even hoped that I wouldn't make it out. Either the horde or the Hazard Prevention would take care of me.

That is why she must've watched the cameras to confirm my death. Then went to find where I landed after. Because she only muttered about making sure I didn't get bit once, which is against protocol. I should've been fully evaluated. Yet, they allow me to walk out.

Stepping out of the elevator, a small pool of blood is left behind for the next passenger to witness. Straightening my back, lessening my limp, I hear people just out of view. I won't get this job back. Not like I really want it. It isn't like I need the money. I was doing this just to keep myself busy. No matter what, Elizabeth is going to find a reason to make me the bad guy.

Keeping my head straight, not paying attention to the two in the lobby talking with the front desk employee.

"Snitch?" A voice asks. Tensing my shoulders, the voice became cheerful, "Snitch, is that you?"

Peering over, there's a man wearing a suit, his hair cleanly cut, and piercings that didn't match his clean demeanor.

A man I have never seen before is smiling and coming to me. He flick his lip ring subconsciously. My eyes widen at the mole on the outer corner of his eye. Only one person I'd seen with that mole.

"Mr. VIP?" A soft chuckle escape from me.

"Ay, I never thought I would see you in a place like this." Mr. VIP pause checking me out. His eyes lingering on my foot with a missing shoe. "Once again meeting up and it looks like someone beat you up good."

I smile, remembering how I wanted to be beaten up then. "You should see the other guy."

I haven't seen him in years after he went to represent his family business. Before that, we spent every day on that couch just talking.

His voice was raspy for smoking too much Lily back then, accompanied by shaggy hair covering his eyes, and always wearing nice dress clothes. As we got to know each other better, he became comfortable enough to lift his hair, revealing his birthmark beneath his beautiful hazel eyes.

Now, his hair is neatly brush back, still longer but stylish leaving parts tuck behind his ear. His voice is no longer raspy and is dress in a light blue suit with a white undershirt.

I remark, "Your voice cleared up."

His smile never dropping, "You were right. It was bad for my lungs."

It is as if we left off at the same spot, like years haven't passed. Every week, I made a comment about his smoking habits.

"I am glad I convinced you." Bluntly I ask, "Why are you here?"

He stretches as if boredom brought him, "My little sister forced me. More importantly, I know they have a nurse's office inside this building. Why are you walking around dripping blood?"

Eyeing where I was stabbed, the bleeding has slowed down but still making a pool underneath my feet.

I can't dive into the breach details that would land me in more trouble. However, I can share anything about my personal issues.

"I had a few issues with this new coworker. Let's say he did something reckless a few times, almost getting me hurt and maybe killed if I didn't react quick enough. So, I defended myself, hurting him."

"Where is this coworker of yours, did they kick him out?"

A laugh, not of joy but annoyance came out, "He married into a family that is apparently powerful. He's already got my bosses breathing down my neck to," I quote with my hands, "'not to mess with him.' They are scared to lose funding."

Mr. VIP crosses his arms, tilting his head to the side. His smile falls, a rare sight to see.

Even if drunks messed with him, he would continue to smile at others, mistaking him for a fool. In fact, he didn't want them to know the truth. A valuable lesson I learned from him with our times together. Never show others the extent of your power, the depth of your knowledge. Let them think you are a fool, a party girl, and when the time to assert yourself come, they'll be fumbling under your weight. For they have already revealed everything while you remain a new entity, never seen before.

This is why I kept the name Snitch at the club, not talking to others. It's why, until Randal, no one had seen my apartment, knew about the money I have from the lawsuit of June's parents, or witnessed my strength. It's why I could quickly subdue Chad. No one knows that he cheated on his fiancé that night at the club, or that I possess the ability to feel others' emotions at times. I keep it all to myself, just as Mr. VIP taught me.

Mr. VIP put his hand on his jaw, staring at the few cuts on my face and the blood continuing to pool at my feet. I didn't look away from his gaze, my expression remaining unwavering despite the throbbing pain in my leg.

"You've learned well, Snitch." Mr. VIP softly smiles, uncrossing his arms laying his hand on my shoulder. "Whoever he married isn't as powerful as my family. I donate at least forty percent to this place alone. The highest donations in the city." He leans in, "Not to mention our contributions to other cities."

My breath hitch, as my eyes widens. It clicks in my mind why he is here. His hair fell from behind his ear, and without saying a word, I reach out, tucking it back into place with a toothless grin.

He straightens standing tall, giving a wink, "Little Sister." Mr. VIP calls, "Come meet a dear friend of mine."

Her steps clicks on the floor in her high heels, a tight dress grips her curves as she moves. Her lashes large and full, with makeup design to enhance her beauty, not cover it.

Her nose crinkles seeing the state I am in, yet she reaches out anyways to shake my hand, "It is nice to meet you. I am Chrisy. I don't think brother mentioned anyone he knew who worked here. Do you know where my husband is? He told us to get here fast."

She furrow her brows, genuinely worried for her new husband. It is a shame someone seemingly pure falling in love with a power - hungry man like Chad.

Sucking on my teeth unsure what to say. Mr. VIP put a hand on his sister's back, "Go give him a call Chrisy. Just because she works here doesn't mean she knows who your husband is."

"You are right. It was nice to meet you." She walks off, putting the phone to her ear.

Mr. VIP whispers, his lips grazing the top of my ear. "How long did it take?"

Staring into his hazel eyes as he backs away. They are a little greener than normal, "When you say you donated here."

"Not bad." He gave me a wink with the eye that has the mole, "They will learn not to mess with you, Snitch. They mustn't known you yourself have a powerful friend by your side."

"No need for that." I say, turning to the door, "It was nice to see you again…"

Mr. VIP interrupts, "Ieronim."

"Trinity, but you've known that from the moment you saw me."

"It is better to have heard it straight from your lips, dear Trinity."

He reach for a handshake. Shifting my weight, blood smearing on the floor, I face Ieronim for the first time.

Extending my hand, I wince as pulling it back. My hand is torn exposing the pink flesh and blood. Ieronim took my hand. His warmth radiating as he gently cups his hand around mine, aware of the damage I was trying to hide.

"She's the murderer." Chad yells out holding onto his wife. "She is the one who beat me babe."

Chad eyes bulges out of his head. Nurses have bandage him up and wash the blood off getting him a new pair of clothes. He probably enjoyed them stripping him more than he should as a married man. Elizabeth and Randal standing behind him. The boss has dispersed, allowing the true person in charge to deal with the matter.

Ieronim kept our hands intertwined a few seconds longer than normal, making sure they see this interaction. Raising a brow at his smug expression. He kept me talking long enough hoping they would see. Smart. Chrisy, giving her brother a weary look. Holding back my smile as Elizabeth's calm expression melts away. The person she holds something against shaking hands with the main donor. Her fingers curls then relaxes, masking her worry with that calm expression I despise so much.

I stood there with my arms at my side as Ieronim stride over. Elizabeth closes the distance, giving a fake smile. Words I couldn't hear, than she says, "We took care of the issue and will investigate the matter."

Her eye glaring beyond his shoulder at me, conveying that I need to leave. Ieronim turn his body ninety degrees, extending his arm at me. I stood hesitating, not wanting to go closer.

"Brother-in-law, she's the bitch who did this to me."

Chad shouts, "She disrespected the family."

Ieronim calmly states, "Trinity O'Salves, please?"

My chest tighten as he called my name. 'Please' making it impossible to deny. Obliging him, limping as I went to him.

He says, "Why is this worker of yours clearly hurt? She's leaving a trail of blood on your lobby floor. Why was Chad taken care of, but Trinity O'Salves is left beaten?"

Ieronim lays my last name on thick, not stuttering it as many others do.

Elizabeth clears her throat, "Well, there was an altercation between these two, and we deemed it better for Trinity, with her record, to be sent away from Chad."

"Record?" He ask, playing dumb, "What type of altercation and record?"

"Well, what has happened is confidential."

"Zombies came in…" Chad blurts like a fool, "I locked her inside because the zombies were going to come in, and we needed to wait for the Hazard Prevention to come."

My body fell limp while standing behind Ieronim. Chad indulge in information not even a quarter of the Hazard Department has access to, to civilians at that.

"Before I knew it, she came through the vent and tried to beat me to death. Brother-in-law, I warned her not to mess with me, and she didn't listen. She's a murderer. She pointed a shaft at me, threatening my life before this. Help me."

Ieronim tilts his head, flashing that familiar smile with the unfamiliar non - raspy voice, "Trinity O'Salves, what do you have to say?"

We sign a contract saying we are not allowed to speak about any breaches in safety to the city. Something that should be fresh in his mind for how new he is.

I remember my leg wouldn't stop shaking as Randal told me the rules on my first day. Laying it on thick of if that rule was broken, you could kiss your life gone.

I say, "I am unable to talk about anything that may or may not have happened due to the contract we signed when accepting the job," I pause. Ieronim about to ask, so I continued, "Anything that happens in our department that may cause a worry of public safety cannot be shared - one example: outbreak," Which *did* happen, "another example weakening of the walls." Which been bad before I was born. Maybe even on purpose.

I finish only looking at Ieronim, "If told to others, imprisonment, and even death penalty."

"Well," Ieronim smile at Elizabeth, "Chad has just told two civilians about a possible breach and outbreak. What will happen to him, Elizabeth?"

He is testing her. Elizabeth stutters, not knowing what to say. She eye Randal as he pretend not to see her struggling.

Chrisy whines, tugging at her husband's arm. "Let's get you home. Let's forget today. Brother, let's go."

There is a plea in her voice towards Ieronim as if she seen this side of him before. Her eyes wide, darting her eyes to me in a pathetic expression hoping that I can stop this.

Ieronim stood his ground, "Are you saying Chad is above the rules? Elizabeth, the head of Lunar's intelligence and safety is allowing someone not to follow the rules? Is this because he's been using our name to get away with harassment, bullying, and putting an employee in danger."

His chest expends as he stare at my face. His eyes tracing my body down to my leg which has practically stopped bleeding.

"Where Trinity," Reaching his hand out to me, "Still bleeding is told to leave and probably not to come back to her work? What if I told you, that Trinity…is my lover. Are you now going to give her the same leniency?"

I held back my own shocked expression at Ieronim's outrageous claim. Have I had ex's pretend that they weren't dating me, yes. Have ever had someone pretend they were dating me, never.

Elizabeth's mouth hangs open as she tries to gather words. Her mask gone as fear swarms. Her vocal cords are unable to let out a syllable. I soak in her expression, loving that someone caught her off guard. That arrogant calmness wiped out of the building. I want to pull out my phone to take a photo to savor that expression for the rest of my life.

Ieronim reaches over, grabbing me by my waist. My spine straighten as his fingers wraps around the bit of bone that protrudes. My face heats as he lean in closers placing a kiss on my cheek, he lingers there. His soft lips press firmly, and a flick of a smile came from him before he pulls away.

Elizabeth stutter, "He, he is new. We are also in the safety of the Hazard Building, Sir."

Ieronim spun me around, both of us now facing the door walking away. Pressing on my back making sure I kept walking.

He turned his head saying, "If I find out Trinity O'Salves has been fired, and that Chad has been manipulating you and this company, I will pull all of my donations. Elizabeth I hope you react accordingly."

Elizabeth voice is still clutched in the grips of fear. He didn't wait for her to regain her composure as he slams the door open leaving the lobby.

Walking too fast, I couldn't keep up, limping horribly. It worsen as he push me on. The tapping of Chrisy's heels on the pavement catching up to us.

Chad demands as if he has any authority, "You cannot be her lover. She has poisoned you."

Ieronim spun, his hand planted around Chad's throat in a quickness I've never seen. He leans in, "You just got into this family, and I will disown you and my sister from it all.

How dare you use our name to your liking to hurt others." Chad's face redden, "How dare you slander Trinity via our name."

Ieronim releases his grip. Chad falling to the ground panting for air. His wife throwing herself beside him, making sure her love is okay.

"Little sister, teach your husband how to be a man. If not, if I hear him use our name for his own business, and if he dares act like I am his family, you will have to choose. The money and title or your husband."

He turn to me, brushing my hair back as a lover would do. "You would be better suited for our family than that boy ever would be."

My face blushing from it all. A reaction I am not use to. Feelings surfacing that I haven't felt in a long time as I been numbed by Lily. Being the one to always tease I am not sure what to do in this situation.

I slow down, unable to follow his speed anymore. My leg throbs with pain.

Breathing heavier than normal as the pain seizes my body, I say, "Thanks Mr. VIP for the help. I got it from here. I'll just go home now."

He turns, his lips tighten before saying, "I thought we were over the nicknames."

I flash my teeth, "It's best you don't associate yourself with me. You've done more than enough, but I can take care of myself. I am an O'Salves, my family kicked out of their rank due to a power issue. If people know the most influential family is interacting with me, there will be an uproar."

Ieronim didn't argue, he only ask me, "At least let me walk you home."

"No, it's okay." I don't need more to know where I live, "It isn't too far from here."

He follow a few paces behind. Working my jaw unsure what to do. He sped up, standing beside me once again as we approach the apartment building.

"I am not following you." Ieronim reassure, "I live in this direction as well."

Oh, grate. I didn't say anything. My head twist, wondering if I should walk in another direction to see if he is telling the truth.

Coming up onto the building, Ieronim points, "Well, that's my building, top floor. How much further do you need to go?"

My shoulders sag, eyeing the building he's pointing at. Why am I surprised *this* is where he lives?

My nostrils flares, unsure of my next move. I could keep walking circling the block before going in. The throbbing in my leg reminds me I can't go much longer. I let out a heavy sigh, passing Ieronim going into the building.

He perks up, following behind with a grin as we walk in. Placing his hand on the elevator pad, which allows only residence or authorized guests to use it. He presses the top floor. He wasn't joking when he say he lived at the top.

Leaning over, I push my button only a few floors beneath.

I say, staring at the elevator door, "I am not going to your apartment. I happen to live here too." He took a step back unable to restrain his disbelief. Side eyeing him, I say softly, "Don't tell anyone. I try to keep it a secret."

He flicks his lip ring grinning mischievously, "I won't tell if you show me."

Glaring at his smirk my expression relaxes instantly. Shit, he reminds me too much of Daniel. "You're a dick, you know that?"

His smirk widen, "I've been called that a few times by you alone. So, the O'Salves still lives a good life."

Getting out of the elevator, he follows me down to the end of the hall. Slowing down, my eyes trace the floor, the doormat I have has been moved. Placing my thumb on the pad, the door opens.

Extending my arm, allowing Ieronim to enter. Clicking the door shut, making sure everything properly locked. Glancing around the main room, nothing seems out of place. No one should have been this far down the hall. They could have been at the wrong door by accident, but for the three years living here this has never happened before. I hope Randal didn't betray me informing Elizabeth where I live.

Ieronim nod as he spun around to look at me, "Impressive. This is one of the most expensive living areas, other than my own. How do you manage to pay the monthly rent?"

Pushing the thought that the Luners could had been outside my apartment. My eyes flew open as the photo album still laid on the table.

Going over to the table, I say, "I don't. Niel is the one who bought it." Scooping it my hands, I kept talking as I put it away on the bookshelf, "After his death and the judge saying I can't live with his parents, I was gifted his home."

"Niel?" He is staring at me as I turn my back to the bookshelf. His eyes seem darker for a few seconds before adding, "Wow for someone who was still in high school, its impressive he managed to buy this place."

Shrugging my shoulders, "Would you like something to drink?"

"Got any beer?"

"How about a tea?"

"Not living up to that party Snitch I knew."

"Lily is what I did, remember?"

Ieronim sat on the couch, "You are correct. You aren't under the influence right now. Why is that?"

Setting the kettle on the stove, waiting for the water to heat, I pick my words carefully, "Nothing to block out at this moment."

He nods his head as if I was still talking. Ieronim turning the TV on making himself at home before the kettle even simmers.

Setting his tea down, I took a sip of my own. It is strange not having the taste of Lily on my lips. I've done it for so long pushing my memories down and out. Now knowing Niel is somewhat alive, something's changed. Everything I had done, tearing at my mind and heart, is healing after all these years. I no longer see Niel with the knife going through his skull, no longer the feel of bone breaking in my arms. Now I see him standing there, his soft eyes staring at me before I ran away.

"I can't believe all these years, you have lived in the same apartment as me," Ieronim says, taking a drink of his tea, "This is good."

I reply, "I try to keep to myself for the most part. I had no clue you were such a big shot yourself Mr. 'I'll pull all my donations'."

"Hmm, all in the family title. Oldest son runs family business. It's an old tale before the first wave."

There wasn't much talking after that. When he finished his tea, he got up and wash the cup himself. He let me know if I ever need him, he is one knock away.

Staring at myself in the mirror, the swelling on my face is worse than I thought. Ieronim only mention it once and never again. He sat there with me as if I looked normal, and my clothes weren't stained with blood.

The water stung my body as it ran down, and the soap intensifying the pain. Limping out with nothing but a towel, I grab the first aid kit I still keep in the kitchen. We have been so close, and neither knew it. I never thought he saw me as a friend, but today it shows I have someone powerful on my side, someone who even made Elizabeth nervous. Not like I am ever going to use him like that.

"Mother Earth, my head hurts." I mutter taking a painkiller.

Doctoring my leg, I took a deep breath as the alcohol stung. Limping to the couch, propping my leg up, watching the show Ieronim had on. Day became night, and my whole - body throbs in pain. It's too much to get up and make Lily to numb me.

*

A week passes and I hear nothing from Randal about my job. I haven't seen Ieronim as usual. Living here for three years, and we just found out we live just a few floors apart. Sitting in my spot, a beaten face turning yellow from healing, makeup covering it up from wandering eyes. Sipping my half - shot of Lily, the time ticks by. There's more people in VIP than normal - special groups, reunions, a few show - offs with their 'big paying jobs,' and a divorcee who won his case. Their voices are loud, never realizing who may be listening in. Even for a weekend, this is unusually busy.

As the night ends, the crowd thinned. Stretching my leg on the coffee table, waiting for everyone to clean up before we had one last drink of the night.

Stefin sat on the opposite couch with two other bouncers, "How do you feel?"

I chuckle, "The pain is gone, but sometimes it gets a weird tight feeling."

"I can't believe he stabbed your beautiful leg."

I turn showing the healing wound, "Next summer, you won't even remember this was here."

Ax chimes in, holding a tray of drinks, "Someone tried to drug you at the club, now a man stab you. I feel there's some sort of connection, Snitch."

I raise a brow at him. The one at the club had to just be some druggie. I don't think that it would be connected. Only a convenient situation to get rid of me if Elizabeth found out.

Ax continue, "We are still very sorry about that, by the way. Henery feels especially horrible."

"Yet still, she stands strong as ever." Vixen snatches a drink as she pass him, plopping down beside me. "I saw him on the street the other day. You got him good; he looks like shit."

I told them about our fight but never about the zombies. Simply said, we were needing to work a task together, and he almost got me killed due to not listening. Leaving out Mr. VIP involvement as well.

As it became closer to three - thirty, I depart, following my now usual path. No longer limping due to my stab wound, though it still looks nasty with the scab not fully healed yet. I have to put a bandage over it at night or I scratch it off in my sleep.

Halfway down the hall, my nostrils flare, stomach emptying out seeing a light gleam from the end of the hall. Unstrapping my heels, holding them stilettos side out, one in each hand. My footsteps press softly on the floor, making them almost inaudible. My knuckles turning white holding my shoes tighter as the door is ajar. The deadbolt out keeping it from closing all the way.

Gulping, I listen and heard nothing. Pushing the door with my foot, it swung half way. Setting my heels on the floor, reaching behind the table near the door, pulling out a large knife Niel stashed. I found many weapons around the apartment through the years. He did it right - anywhere I go, there is something in reach to protect yourself.

Leaving the door how they had it, moving across the cold floor beneath my feet. I don't hear anything. Going down the hall, every room is open, but no items are out of place. Thud. My head tilts upwards. That's where Niel's room is. I only go upstairs, not even once a month to clean. Forcing my body up every step, I stop, seeing that Niel's room is crack open. Whispers became clearer, revealing a man's and woman's voice inside.

My heart flutter with joy at the thought of Gabe and Sandra coming to surprise me. They asked me when my off days were just a week ago. Lowering my hands to my side picking up speed to show them that I am home.

However, my legs stop almost at the door. My hand wrap around the knife tighter, the scabs on my hand cracking under pressure. My face sag, willing that it's their voices who I heard just now.

"Just find the shit." A deep voice clearly from a man says.

Why couldn't it had been Gabe and Sandra? Putting one trembling leg in front of another, two strangers dressed in torn clothes shuffle around Niels' room around.

How did Wanderers get into the city? More importantly, how did they get into my apartment?

"We need to hurry. She will come home any moment. She should be leaving the Club around now." The female says.

What should I do, should I leave, should I call the Emergency line? Why do they even know my moves. I just want a quiet life and yet so many people are interested in my daily activities.

I always lock the door before leaving the house. We have fingerprint sensors to get up the elevator unless they took the maintenance stairs.

"She is ruthless." Her voice at a whisper, "From on top of the hill, she killed my partner who was supposed to be doing this. If it wasn't for my quick thinking, killing that dude, and taking his uniform, we wouldn't have this opportunity."

Crybaby is *dead*. A dread fills me. No wonder he didn't take his mask off after going inside. Why he 'quit' all of a sudden. She helped Abigail and Randal out as a trick. *I* allowed a Wanderer to get inside the city. If I call the Emergency line and they catch these Wanderers, and they let it known they got in because I didn't close that damn door, I will be labeled as conspiring with them.

Everything stilled. The humming of silence behind me stops. The movement of objects seem to stop as well. Taking a step forward, nostrils flare in anger. I have to deal with them myself. About to reveal myself, ready to fight, a hand came around my body. Squealing in a panic as a moist rag is held over my mouth. The burning smell of chemicals and Lily fills my lungs. Twirling the knife in my hand, slamming it into his thigh, he screamed out in pain, alerting the others. Lunging forward, I cut his hand getting him out of my way.

The air shifts behind me. Twisting around, the girl yips backing away, blood seeping from her arm. Grabbing her face as if this is the worst thing she's seen in her life. My legs wobble missing steps as I race down the stairs. I slipped tumbling over the last five steps.

My body feels numb, no longer able to move a muscle. What did he put over my mouth? Fighting, trying to force my body to move, my mind is stuck, wanting to run, and nothing is listening. My head hit the ground, eyes flutters shut, seeing nothing but darkness.

Chapter Seven

I didn't even see the third person. How did they manage to get inside? There is a key, but it wasn't used. I get notifications, violent alerts informing me if it's used. I should had knocked on Ieronim door and took him up on his offer that he is only one knock away. He probably has guards at his disposal like many of the elites do.

Calling Lunars were out of the question. What would I have said, 'Wanderers are in my apartment that once was Niels.' Elizabeth would had the apartment searched, found the photos. Gabe and Sandra would been taken for questioning. I couldn't make that mistake.

Soft mutters ran through my mind. Like buzzing nonsense too distant to decipher. The urge to swallow halted by a dry throat. Uncontrollable small coughs clearing my throat. My head throb as my eyes squint. One hand tied, and both legs are secured to the chair. Barely able to open my eyes due to the overhead light. The mutters and whispers I once heard are no longer here. There's a silence in the room like they left before I woke.

Stripped out of my dress, I find myself in baggy pants and a loose - fitting shirt. Shifting my breasts still supported by my bra. I try not to imagine who was in the room when they undressed me, hopefully it was only women.

Time passed and I hear nothing as if I am alone. Perhaps that's what they want me to think. My eyes adjusted to the light, able to fully keep them open. A tray of bread and water rests on the side of my free arm, untouched. No clue how much time has passed. No ticking of a clock. No signs of restlessness as if others were with me, just silence.

My nostrils flare as I roll my head. Alone, *truly*? Picking up the water sniffing it cautiously. Something is off. Setting it down, I reach for the bread, sniffing it.

They couldn't have left me alone. Sitting there, staring at the void beyond, remaining motionless. This doesn't make since. The sliding of a shoe sound in the room for just a heartbeat. Bingo. Someone is with me. I didn't move, my stare pretending I heard nothing. It was on the opposite side of my free arm. Are they seeing if I will try to set myself free?

More time went by, and I let out a heavy sigh. My mouth becoming more parched, grabbing the glass. Is it safe to drink? Pressing my lip to the glass, there's a subtle shift of air. I pause, taking my lip off staring into it.

Chucking the glass to where I heard the movement, shattering on the wall, followed by a few swears and screams. Then, the lights turn on, revealing four people in the room, all but one seated by the wall where I tossed the glass.

"We were kind enough to give you water, and that's how you repay us?" A younger guy wearing a hat remarked.

My voice groggy trying to respond through the dryness, "No, interrogations are never nice."

A lady with short blond hair closes in, sneering, "And some wall dweller, a sheltered bitch would know?"

I let out a pitiful chuckle. They think just because I live inside the city, I am sheltered. "I guess you do not know who I am."

She smiles as if I am a mouse a cat caught, "Some bitch who we need info from."

"Language." I say jokingly, "Who broke into my place?"

The one who stood alone, dons a long jacket with a glossy coating. He took my hair into his grip, pulling my head back. "You managed to hurt two of our people you know."

Good, one of them killed Crybaby for his uniform.

"Are we going to play nice and tell us all you know, or will we have to hurt you?"

Rasing a brow, masking any fear I harbor. Hoping they can't hear the thumping of my heart that's desperately trying to burst out of my ribcage. Masking I say, "Well, ask me, and we can see from there."

A gasp escape my lips as his hand print burns on my face. Glaring with rage, biting my tongue suppressing the words I want to say. *Barbaric Wanderers.*

"You can't be cocky here. This isn't your home, sweetheart. This is our territory." His eyes holds nothing but hatred towards me.

I try to hold it back, but the invisible strings tug harder than my muscles could resist. Smirking, I push my head into his hand. "I like it harder than that baby."

"For fuck sake." Someone mutters. I can feel their eyes roll from across the room.

The man's brows rose caught off guard with my words. Reaching into his coat pulling out a large knife, my muscles involuntarily tighten.

Flicking the knife on my cheek, cutting a layer of skin, I hiss from the pain as he asks, "Who is involved in your operation?"

My brows furrow at the strange question. They have no clue who they are talking to. I shook my head in disbelief, I am being interrogated not for who *I* am, but who they *think* I work with. The man points the knife at my throat, halting any further movement of mine.

I slowly state, desperately wanting to defuse this. "I don't know what you are talking about. You have mistaken who I am."

"Fuck sakes," the same man cursed again, this time noting who say it. His hair is dark, almost black, and a scar on his cheek, "They all say that before they break. Let's make it easy on you. We were told to chat with you. If you didn't get violent in the first place, this would had gone easier."

He really has the balls to say that when they killed Crybaby and kidnapped me. Mother Earth, what the hell do they think I am involved in? I held back rolling my eyes since they are a temperamental group.

He gesture with his head and a fist collided with my temple. Their faces blurred. Finding myself facing the ground, groaning in pain, unable to scream how sudden it was. I didn't even do anything and got hit.

Getting my hair yanked back, hissing in pain I quoted his words, "'They all say that before they break.' Meaning you got information you need from others. If you allowed me to speak before abusing me, I would have told you. I work in the Hazard Department, task with removing dead bodies from the city. I know nothing about anything that you think I do." Screaming out in pain hurling myself forward as he plunges the knife in my arm, quickly yanking it out.

Holding back tears, he wipes the blood onto his coat. Leaning closer, he grips the chair with both hands; pulling my face away the back of my neck digs into the chair. My heart pounds like machines at peak hour. Slipping my hand under the table, he look down about to get something else out, pulling the small metallic table up and over. As fast as I could swing it at him, he fell to the ground and the knife in hand slid across the floor.

Holding onto the ledge, rearing my arm back as much as I could, tossing the table at them. They move out of the way with the weak toss. In the chaos, managing to get the other arm free. They rush towards me as I went to unbuckle my leg. I have to get out of here. They are going to kill me thinking that I am lying to them.

Grabbing one arm, another person tries to get the strap around me. Burying my nails into him chaos brakes out more. Fists came in contact with the back of my head, my shoulder, and my neck, trying to get me to let go. They came from all positions. Someone hitting me in the ribs, but I didn't let go. I can't let go.

Digging my nails deeper, the man screamed as I pull down with each tug they do to get me off him.

A second person grabbed my arm. I can't hold it like this. Doing what any zombie would do - sinking my teeth into his arm. The taste of iron pours into my mouth. My eyes flare open as a knife sank into my thigh in hopes I will scream and let go.

I did scream - a deep gut curdling cry from within my throat as I bear down harder breaking through layers of skin.

"Get her off me!" He screams, sheer terror in his voice, "Its coming off. My skin is coming off."

He manage to yank away, as someone else pulls my head back. My teeth slide across his skin; I shudder as I feel human flesh inside my mouth, quickly spitting it on the floor trying to stop my own bowels from following. The door across the room hangs open as blood trails behind him, screams of terror lessening as he got further away. My mouth moist with blood, I didn't dare swallow. My stomach turning on itself one more sip of blood going down my throat is going to make me vomit.

Another hit the head. I spat out what was in my mouth. Blood trailing down my chin, and my world tilted. The chair with my legs still strapped in fell to the ground. Covering my head, hands wrap around the back of my neck, curling up as they kept kicking.

Stepping on my long hair sprawled out over the floor, not daring to let them know how much pain I am in. Tears tracing down the side of my face I took every kick. They yell how ruthless, insane, and what a vicious monster I am. Says the people who broke into the apartment I live in and kidnapped me.

"Hey, stop it's enough." The woman says lowering to the floor. Maybe she is more willing to listen to me. Finally figuring out I know nothing. She pulls my head to look up at her sideways, "They took you for a reason. You know something, and that's our jobs to get it out of you. The first person who managed to get us all worked up - impressive. Didn't think anyone would be crazy enough to act like a Zombie. Now, how many is in your operation, and when is your next attack?"

My eyes flutter shut. Why can't they listen to my words? Stopping the whine from creeping out I lay there for a few seconds.

Breathing heavily, only one eye can open all the way.

Gasping I reply through the pain "I work for the Hazard Department. Just listen I don't know…"

My hearing goes out in one ear, as she slapped me with an open palm on the side of my head. My words stops replace with screaming out as my hand is being crushed under another's foot. Enough for pain but not to break anything. She stood up walking out of my sight.

Desperation takes over as I cry for the first time. The only name that crosses my mind I scream. "Niel, Niel!"

My body trembles as he releases the pressure. Pulling my hands underneath my body, the room went eerily quiet. Whimpering I can't even look up at them. Every inch of my body is thumping to my fast heartbeat.

A knife dangles in front of my eyes. My head resting on the cold floor, unable to move.

"See, they always squeal the truth when the pain gets too much," The man in the hat laugh. The others slowly joining in. There he says smug, "You know of him. So, who else do you know, and when is the attack?"

Bearing my teeth, I say with an unsteady voice, "I am the one who killed him."

The man with black hair who hasn't said anything loud enough for me to understand until now mutters, "I think we beaten her crazy."

The girl racks her hand through her short hair. Eyeing her as her skin drains of all color. "Oh no, no, no we fucked up." I smile in her direction; she knows the truth now.

She ask, "Eric, please tell me they told us to torture her."

The man with black hair and the scar reply, "They told us to watch and chat. Why else would they put her in this room if we aren't to chat and extract the information she knows? Why would they drag her all the way here from that Alpha City if not to find out their plan?" Eric continues reaching for the girl shoulders, "Why are you freaking out?"

She violently pointed at me then waved her arms as she spoke, "This bitch is Niels childhood fucking friend from the inside. The one who stabbed him a few weeks ago and he didn't kill her. Do you not listen to Lavender at all? She told us to never attack if she's seen."

As if Mother Earth herself summoned him to us, the door swung open, crashing on the cement wall bits crumbling down.

His eyes flare as he stare at me. There are three people by him - two I don't recognize, and one with the same gray tone as him, Lavender. His jaw clicked at a rate never heard before. Lavender steps in front quickly, grabbing the door slamming it in Niel's and the other two face's, locking it. She moved quicker than any human, any zombie I ever seen.

She cries in a panic, "What did you guys do?"

There's loud banging on the other side of the door, startling even me. There's no windows to be broken out. Niel screams in rage on the other side.

The other girl pointed at Eric, "He told us. We thought he had the orders to extract information. We just found out. Please Lavender, tell him we didn't know."

She cover her mouth seeing the bloody mess that I probably am, "If we didn't stop Jesus running through the halls like a mad man to hear who the hell bit him, we wouldn't know she was up."

Niel's voice punctures my brain as he screams my name and to let him in on the top of his lungs. My heart stops as it is the same scream of pure torment after I killed him. Pain and sorrow rushing through my veins.

The door handle violently moves before breaking off as he tries to get in. Lavender moved, hurrying to unite my legs. Lifting me up, I see them at the far wall in the room. Eric's face pale as the door bent to Niel's banging.

Lavender reassures me with a wobbly smile, "We aren't bad people, I promise. It's just we live differently. Desperate times here."

She speaks normally. If it wasn't for the skin coloration, I wouldn't ever guess she isn't human.

The door creeks and bends before slowly opening on its own. No longer is anyone standing by Niel. He chatter unhuman like, his head twists like a predator hunting eyeing every person. His eyes soften as he sees me sitting up, taking a step to me. Lavender chatters, stopping Niel. He turn his attention on Eric.

Eric desperately explains, "We were told to chat, I took chat as extract. I didn't know who she was. I assumed…"

Lavender translated Niel's chatters, "You always try to play your own game. You forgot your place one too many times now."

Eric went to run, but Niel took him by the head. Eric scream out in pain as the familiar sound of skull breaking rings in my ears.

My breaths halt as June came to mind, right beside my vision of Niel. How she dug through Alix's organs for a first meal, and now Niel - his jaw extend beyond normal capabilities devouring Eric's neck. My mouth water unable to look away. Twitching on the ground, blood coming from his skull and neck. Eric isn't dead yet.

This isn't Niel. I gasped for air sporadically, unable to get a full breath in. He is not my childhood friend. This is a monster we have never faced before, a mutation of zombies. He had a life I wasn't aware of, keeping secrets from me as if he didn't declare his love to me. Niel did die that night. I killed who I thought I knew three years ago. Standing up, Lavender reach out to help and I push her away. The other two people stood there in silence as the body on the floor stop moving.

"Kill the brain." Lavender translated for Niel, "He doesn't deserve to see if he has a chance to be a Second Life's."

Run.

Run.

Run!

Everything inside of me surges forward. The stab wound in my leg didn't stop me. My limp didn't slow me down. Exiting the room, I heard that man call me by Niels nickname. That isn't Niel.

His looks fooled me. That familiar voice I once wish I could hear just one more time is a mimic. It isn't truly him.

Rushing down the hall, people split ways, confused at this apparent odd behavior. The bland halls resemble those on G0. The winding halls open up to a mass cafeteria. Dim lights shine down in the large room, with random paintings scattered on the walls. Wanderers lifting their heads, gasping at the sight of me.

"Dead woman running." A bodiless voice yelled within the area.

My only exit I see is being blocked by people with guns in their hands, dressed in dark and tattered clothes from age. Spinning around, stopping to see Lavender and Niel. Now he's wearing a tank top, shedding the shirt where another man's blood spilled. His face is now clean, bearing a familiar worry. But he is not Niel.

Looking at my options, finding myself stuck, leaning forward, my hands on my knees, breathing heavily. What's the point to run even if I somehow manage to escape them. I don't know how to get out.

The people with guns came closer. I waited for that new sound I heard not even a month ago. A older man steps forward. Short peppery hair, age thick on his skin, naturally bronze not just by the sun. He looks me up and down before turning his attention to Niel and Lavender, who snuck up behind me. My body jerk, almost tripping over my two feet how smoothly they moved. Niel, only an inch away from me.

"What is going on?" He ask, closing the distance, guns still pointed at me. His dark eyes narrow on me, despite his words being directed at Niel and Lavender.

My stomach growls at the smell of food unable to focus on their words. I don't know if this is breakfast, lunch, or dinner. There's no windows to indicate time of day, or how long I've been out for.

Lavender replies, "Can we go to your office to discuss, Maxwell? We've ran into a small issue."

Maxwell reply with a head twitch, "Fine, get that one, put her in a cell."

"No." I wail, "Take me home. I am not whoever the fuck you think I am."

Niel slowly says, "Its, okay. I'll be with… you soon." I shook my head, limping back, "She needs doctor." He says looking at Maxwell.

Lavender agrees with Niel adding, "Maybe its best she comes, and we get her looked at. It's the least we can do, with the mistake that has happened."

He grumbles, indulging he wave two of his people forward. They went behind me pushing the gun against the upper part of my back.

Niel, an octave too deep, growls, "Don't."

He went behind me and flinching as his shadow grew. He didn't touch me the whole way as we mosey down the halls. His shadow just lingers. The feel of his body close enough that he can just lean on me.

The four of us are sitting inside Maxwell's office. The men who were with guns are probably waiting outside the door in case they are needed.

My body weakening with pain, my heart throbbing with every movement, I want to fall. Struggling to keeping myself upright.

The room is slightly brighter than the lunch area, with old brass lamps in the corners. A bookshelf filled the brim beside his old wooden desk, and a clock hangs on one of the walls. It's nine. I don't know if that's in the morning or at night.

Lavender made herself comfortable lowering herself in the worn leather chair. Niel and I stood on opposite sides. My muscles tighten in disbelief at how well I know that face and yet it looks so foreign. It hurts to see him, that scar I made, but I can't look away.

Lavender gave a report to Maxwell of all that happened. Eric is probably cleaned off the floor and being sent to the incinerator at this moment. Maxwell let out a heavy sigh looking at me from over his hands. Unable to say anything to an outsider, someone raised within the wall who should never been here from the start.

The door slowly opens revealing a woman holding a first aid kit. Maxwell pointing at me, taking a step back stumbling with the pain. Niel came forward reaching out to grab me. As I got my footing, instinctively recoiling from his touch. I faced the ground. He is a monster mimicking my best friend. I dart my eyes to see him slowly stepping back. The muscles in his jaw clench.

I say, desperation lacing my words, "I want to go home."

Maxwell calmly wave the woman over to me saying, "Please sit. You can get infections out here easier than in your perfect city." His words carrying an undertone of concern.

I did as he said, facing him as I sat. I beg cupping my hands together, "Please Maxwell let me go then. I don't belong here."

My words hung in the air. My expression soften as he held no resentment towards me. Like I hadn't just bitten one of his people. He has to know I don't belong and that I need to be sent back. Being kept out here is a death sentence for me.

"I can't do that mis…" He pause as if he just realize he doesn't know my name.

Keeping a natural expression. He only need to know a name that I am called, and it's not what he is looking for, "Snitch." I say.

The muscles on his head wrinkled before saying, "Not a good case for freedom with a name like that don't you think, Snitch?"

I held back the hiss as the woman doctor up my wounds, I added, "You say I can't do that before you knew my name."

Niel butts in, "Yes, Inf….nity can go."

Maxwell shift his body in his chair. His face harden, "You have done a lot for us Niel, but asking to let her go after seeing this. It's too risky."

"Trust me." Niel forces out, "Let her go."

They stare in a silent standoff. Both refusing to waver a subtle way showing off dominance, until, Maxwell broke. His tone sharpens, "She stays here for a week. If by the end of it. I deem you pose no threat to us here. Then I will permit you to leave."

"I have people who will worry about me." I push, "They will look for me."

Niel's expression shifted, painfully look at me again. Maxwell dismissed my concerns.

"Niel will have your phone. Any messages that come in, he'll supervise your contact." I try to protest my words being cut off before the second syllable when Maxwell adds, "Niel, Lavender, make sure she behaves, and we have no more issues. One of you, figure out temporary living arrangements."

As the lady, a nurse, maybe doctor if they even have that out here. I don't think they would have schools as we do. Cleaning my leg, she tells me I need stitches, but I waved her away. The cleanliness of their tools are too risky. I will rather take my chances allowing it to naturally heal. She could use a dirty or poisoned needle just to kill me.

As we walk out of his office with my leg wrapped in bandages. All of my words were for nothing. No one listen to my pleas. I am a dead woman walking out here.

Maxwell suddenly says from his desk right before the door shuts. "Its nice hearing you speak, Niel."

Niel gave a half - ass look over his shoulder giving a half nod. I can't shake the feeling that this week is going to be more than a test of my loyalty.

Lavender suddenly left Niel and I alone. They were chattering in that zombie language before she walked off. A part of me feels Niel is the reason she suddenly had a task that needed to be done.

The room we are in is furnished with newer items, contrasting the worn belongings I saw the rest of the Wanderers bear. How is this possible without them stealing from our cities?. Unless, their society is more advances than we are told.

"Where can I lay down?" I state, attempting to steady myself as my body threatened to sway.

Blood cakes every inch of me. Each time I talk the blood around my mouth cracks. It is cold in the room, which is a relief against the heat radiating from every cut on my body.

I don't want to be alone with him. I eyed him as he freely moved around me. There are no windows, it's just a square box housing three doors. Hopefully, one is a bathroom I can wash this blood off.

The Wanderers wore torn clothes, and only some were presentable. Niel on the other hand, everything I've seen him in is new, almost tailored to him. What on Mother Earth what does he do to have this type of treatment? Even Maxwell, I believe is the head of this place, bent to Niels request.

There's a small two - burner stove, and a smaller microwave. There's minimal overhead cabinet, a glossy wooden table stood in the center of the room adorned with rich red wood grain, while the couch is covered in a soft tan fabric. This place looks as if we could be in the city if it weren't for no windows.

He return with a stack of papers in his arms, setting them down a small first aid box was between his chest and papers.

"Leg now." Niel demands, patting the coffee table, "Sit."

Sitting not because he asked, but because my body is begging me to.

"Infi…"

I stopped his words, laying down my own thoughts. "You are not Niel. Despite how much you look like him, you have no right to call me by that. You will call me by Snitch." He shook his head, "No…" Then he stop. Dragging the paper to him, writing down words then handing it to me. My heart ached seeing his hand writing again. The curvature made his writing hauntingly beautiful.

"Out loud." He demands, poking the paper.

I read aloud, "'Stop this behavior. I am him despite my looks, despite my voice, I am still your best friend. Now let me take care of that leg before you get an infection'…" I sigh, "Just no, Second Life. You look like him, but Niel wouldn't lost his temper like that. He always used logic and the legal system to outsmart people, rarely using violence."

He handed me another paper, Niels' handwriting pleading with me to understand. "Infinity, there with you, violence wasn't needed, but there is a lot you didn't know about me." I stopped reading interjecting my own words, "Yeah, like all the photos I found you with my parents in *that* room." His face somehow pale in color.

Continuing to read, "I don't talk with these people, so it's hard for me to speak now. I let Lavender do the talking for me. She's friendlier, even in her first life, talkative. Since I saw you, I've been talking more. Once I can talk with you not like this, but how we once did, I will tell you anything you want to know. Stop arguing, give me your leg. Why the Snitch name? You hated it when people called you that."

Niel took my leg his hand. Gripping my leg with strength I've never felt before. It's effortless, yet he keeps me in place. I answer his question, "It's what I'm known for, so I play into it."

Tensing as his chatter emanated from his throat. He let out a grunt ceasing the sound, slowly lifting his eyes. He rolled up the baggy pants gifted to me; his eyes fixate on a sight he wasn't expecting. The same leg I just was stab in, is the one Chad stabbed. His grip increase slightly, grimacing at my almost perfect leg.

He twists my leg in a uncomfortable position getting a better look. His rough callused thumb rubs around the scab. A tingling sensation erupts where I almost don't want him to stop.

Niel ask, "How?"

I can feel my anger bubble up, and that warm tingle subside. Knowing Niel had to be involved with the zombies who broke in, "With that stunt of yours, getting the zombies through the hatch," His gaze met mine. Niel's eyes darkening with dread as I continue. "My office is right beside that place. A dick, Chad, who hates me for being an O'Salves, for 'murdering' you. He thought it be best I got trapped. I got out, just like I will get out of here, and I attacked him. Trust me, he got most of the damage."

"I almost died because of that stunt. Second Life, do you hear me?"

Niel's muscles tense, his gaze challenging me to act how we once did. To push him to talk, getting on his last nerve, but still laugh after it all. I am treating him like Niel, but he isn't my Niel.

"Pain." He rolled the pants the rest of the way up, undoing the blood - soaked gauze. "I'm sorry. To leave you." I didn't let the 'don't be sorry' out of my mind. He isn't Niel. I have to keep reminding myself of this. Despite him caring for me like before, it's just an old habit of unconscious behavior of who he once was. That's all it is.

My phone rang inside of his pocket. Pulling it out, his eyes glisten with joy. He answer it before I even saw the name, putting it on speaker for him to hear who's on the other line. Then I saw Sandra's name.

Sandra's voice came through, "Trinity, honey, are you busy?"

Calming my voice, as I eyed Niel, "No, I'm not. Why, what's up?"

"You haven't answered my texts in a few days, so I was worried."

Niel stared at the phone, more enthused in hearing his mom's voice than the conversation. Just as I would be if I could hear my parent's voice once more.

Quickly, I thought of a truth I can manipulate, letting out a sigh I told her, "I am sorry Sandra, just somethings happened and I…"

Niel took my arm, silently mouthing the words 'no.' I shook my head at him, 'stop' I mouthed.

"Trinity are you okay…Hello?" Sandra's voice of concerned now became panicked.

Before Niel could intervene, I blurt out, "I've been working in the Hazard Department to dispose of dead bodies, and I got suspended due to beating up a teammate cause I almost got killed by the dude." Niel let go, leaning back on the couch, visibly relieved I didn't tell them the situation I am in. "I'm sorry. I knew you would worried, and that's why I didn't tell you. I've got hurt pretty bad, and I just been wanting to be alone."

Gabe's voice came through the phone, "What the hell, Randal did not…" he stopped, and I can hear the curse under his breath.

I chuckle, displeased, "Randal. So, Randal is the one keeping tabs for you." out of the corner of my eye I see Niel writing things, but I ignored him, "I can't believe you had my lead report back to you. Can't believe you had a former Luner report back to you, Gabe."

"Trinity." Gabe replies in a low and calm voice, "He's a good man. I trust him."

"Ha, I thought so too, but he is not the man you think he is. He reports to Elizabeth, the lady who made sure I couldn't live with the two of you." Niel scribbled more things, ignoring him I continued, "Randal let it slip he still reports to them. I am in danger, and I am not sure if I am going to make it. There's so many things I don't fully understand, and I don't truly know what to trust anymore. I am drowning in my own blood like Niel did, but I have no one to end my suffering.

"I got lucky, knowing someone in power near me, but that's going to end soon enough." The longer I am outside the walls, worse will come to me. I let out a shaky breath, "I love you two. You are my parents, but I feel like my whole life has been shrouded in secrets." A truth I don't fully know that I can't say.

Gabe states, "If you haven't done anything."

"I see the patterns. She's waiting for one slip up, one questionable action. I see Luner's everywhere I go, waiting and watching. She wants the O'Salves eradicated for some reason. It's just a matter of time."

They bicker, their voices blending into an incomprehensible mix. Sandra's voice prevailed, reassuring me, "Honey, it will be okay."

"If they try anything, I am right there as your family and the best lawyer anyone can have. You will be safe."

I didn't let the words out. The ones where I ask about the photos, about their past with my family. I end the conversation. Ending their worries with, "Yeah I know, I just worry. Thankyou."

"Honey, go to sleep. It sounds like you need it."

He took the phone as the phone call ended. Starting to rub my face halting due to the pain, momentarily forgetting my face is messed up.

Niel hands me the paper. Crumbling it, tossing it at him. Slowly standing, I say, "Take me to my room, and do whatever is necessary to get me out tomorrow morning. By the way that wasn't a lie, I know she wants me dead. I just don't know why. Being here is risking my life, Second Life."

Niel remain silent. He obliged opening one of the three doors. Peeking my head in, this doesn't look like a vacant room. There's not much in here other than for a few books on an end table and a small dresser.

As he stared down at me, I can't help but to wonder, "Do you Second Life's sleep?"

He smirked, his throat working to try and speak, "Yeah, you here. I'll be on couch."

Shutting the door behind me, alone in the room still coated in blood. Some of it is from Jesus. I feel bad for him.

He was just following the orders of a misinformed man. At that moment, my life was at risk, and I reacted accordingly.

I didn't lay in his bed. Just like in his apartment, I never lay in his bed. Resting my body on the cold floor, my heartbeat rushes through my body. Constantly reminding me of every part that's bruised or cut.

There's a soft knock on the door before Niel peeked his head in.

Grunting as I try to get up, Niel slowly came in keeping our distance, "Use any clothes. Change, okay?" He forced the rest of the words, "Night…Clothes on top."

I reply, "Thanks, Second Life."

He turn leaving without saying another word. Finally standing on my two feet, slowly rolling my sore neck. If this was Niel, I would had told him I would take a shower first. It isn't him. Mother Earth but it looks like him, sounds like him, but it just can't be him. Staring down at myself debating if I should take him up on changing.

Then a door on the outside shuts. Did he leave? Reaching for the door stopping myself only an inch away. No, I don't care. The clothes cracking with dry blood, making my mind up. That I will take him up on a new set of clothes.

Opening the top, I gasp. The clothes laying on the inside are brand new. It isn't exactly like the ones I've seen in stores but damn near it. Could they be making their own? Are there others from inside the cities giving Wanderers old stock of clothes that weren't on sale? I gripped the drawer knowing all my questions won't be answered. Not now at least. Taking out a cotton pair, tan and gray strands woven together. Elastic where I can tie it at my waist. Still feeling dirty, I am a little more relieved to get out of the blood - soaked clothes.

As I lay on the floor, exhaustion overcomes me. My body aches, every fiber screaming at me, and somehow the cold floor easing some of the ach. My mind drifting finally feeling relief.

My nose crinkles waking me from my sleep. It feels like someone is in the room with me. As my eyes flick open; it was too late. Niel hovering over me, quickly placing a rag on my face as he sees I am awake. I let out a cry of panic already unable to move. His face soften, picking the back of my head up. It's the same chemical smell mix with Lily as before.

Niel repeated, "It okay, okay, home now... going home."

My head heavy in hand, my body surrendering as my eyes gave up. The last thing I feel in the darkness is his hand wiping my tear.

*

Waking up, I let out a shriek of fear jumping off the bed. My legs collapsing beneath my weight. Looking around to familiar surroundings. I am back in the apartment. My chest rising and falling quickly, I ran to the bathroom turning the sink on. Shoving my dry cracking lips underneath the facet, moisture gradually returning.

Pulling my head away, water splashing everywhere. I glared at the mirror. Both hands curl on the ledge. My face is busted up; my eye isn't as swollen how I thought it would be. Stripping the clothes, reminding myself none of it was a fever dream. My body looks like a leopard we see in history books. Burses cover every inch of me. The gauze is dry but stained a deep red.

I held the clothes I had just stripped. Stumbling into Niel's room where his bed, it's now a mess from me being in it. Walking downstairs practically naked it's not an unusual practice. The curtains wide open, as if I forgot to shut them. The apartment is silent, devoid of any sign of Wanderers, not once but twice. Sullenly going to my normal routine, I turn on the coffee pot, glancing out the large windows to see its about midday.

The phone sat on top of the dining table, perfectly placed on the ledge to catch my attention. The clothes slip out of my hands as I sway to the phone. Tapping the screen, the display lit up. Two in the evening. Sinking into the chair beside me, a coldness settle in. Five days have passed since it all happened - almost a whole week gone by, and I could only remember part of a day. No wonder my body forced me to the bathroom, it was in instinct mode in fear of dying.

Sitting, the curtains are now closed, my coffee in a cup caramel in color, and a sandwich in front of me.

My voice, small for no one to hear, "What the fuck?" It rose to a raspy call, "What the actual fuck?" They were in Niels' room looking for something. The memory triggering a sudden outburst, "What the actual fluckite fuck, fuck, fuck happened! Coming into this apartment, fucking me over,"

My mind spun as I shoved food in my mouth, not giving enough time to fully chew up before swallowing.

Maxwell insisted I had to be there for a week. That night, Niel got it where I can go home. In a method I would rather them not done, but still, it shows somehow Niel has a very powerful influence. Is it possible that he finished making the new outbreak?

My tongue graze over the busted part of my lip. Groaning as I got out of the chair, my body begging me to stay seated. Going to the kitchen for some medicine to stop this constant ache. Stepping on the pajamas on the floor they crinkle under my foot.

Swallowing the pills, almost done with the cup of water. I stop. Cotton doesn't crinkle like paper. Bending down one of the pockets crinkle in my grip. Throat closing at the sight of the handwriting.

Infinity,

I've spoken to Maxwell. He is convinced to let you leave. I just have to do something first, and I hope it doesn't scare you too much. Don't worry, I'll be beside you the whole time. You'll be safe. I will never call you that other name, and it annoys me that you let others use it. They don't know the truth about you, not like I do. Despite you not seeing me for who I am. I'm still your best friend. I'll change your mind soon enough. When I can talk how we once did, I will be there for you. Theres a lot you don't know, but in time when its right, you will. It saddens me to know the suffering you've been through, and I wasn't there to help you. Still, I am happy to know at least you have my parents there when you need them. Life isn't what you think it is, but maybe you already figured that out.

Take care, live free, and always be you my infinity.

-Niel

I stared at the letter. My chest tightening with a mix of emotions. Three years have gone by without a trace of him in the world. Now all of a sudden he is just here back again.

Three years had passed, and now, Wanderers are coming back, as if they knew all of his belongings would still be here. Skipping steps, going up to his bedroom, I stood at the door. They knew his parents wouldn't had sold his stuff off, but did he know I lived here? A room which I only came in to clean, I never dared look through his things as if he may had come home one day.

The note he wrote me, 'I will know when the time is right,' my ass. Pulling out his clothes keeping it neat, as I try to find whatever they were looking for. Anything unusual that looks out of place. The photos he hid were out of place yet exactly where they belong. This is going to be hard since I don't even know why they were here.

Is it something that may been moved through the years as I cleaned? That would explain why they were frantic about not finding it. Not like I'll remember myself what's been shifted. Niel's parents also came here before me. They mentioned 'cleaning up a bit of a mess.' as we came up to the apartment.

Sorting through every drawer, everything on top of his dressers and nightstand appears normal. Gritting my teeth, my nostrils flare in frustration.

"What in the Mother Earth were they looking for?" I say to nothing, "Everything looks normal, just like his life. Just like with the photos, it all looks normal, but it isn't."

Taking apart the dressers drawers, scattering across the room. Sitting on the bed, breathing heavily, sweat beads down from my hairline. Half the room torn apart, I look over things again and again. Everything is normal. Running my hands through my hair, pulling it back. Everything is normal, just like everything before the accident, his life looked normal.

Walking backwards, I stare at the half - destroyed room, his clothes lay neatly around.

Living normally is *key*. In my room, I squeeze into some leather pants, a tight black tank top to cover the bruising on my torso, while a long-sleeve fine lace garment covered every part of skin yet keeping the essence of showing. The black attire camouflages the bruising. Complementing with the final touch of black heels that gracefully wrap around my ankles. Checking myself in the mirror to see majority of the bruising is concealed. Only looking up closely you can tell something is not right.

Draping a tan raincoat over my arm, I went off like nothing ever changed in my life.

Be normal, just as it once was. Sitting in my spot, I gaze at the crowd gathering below. Sipping my drink, laced with half a shot of Lily. Bodies rubbing against one another, dancing their hearts out. It is all *normal.*

Vixen sitting by me, closer than anyone gotten to me all night. She blatantly stared at my outfit. I'm no longer with the coat, its where the employees kept theirs.

"Isn't it too hot to wear your fall and winter outfit?" Vixen ask.

Sipping on my drink, swishing the bitterness of alcohol with the ever - slight sweetness of Lily. Swallowing, I leaned in, my ear touching my shoulder, "Have you noticed, throughout the history of our city, any family that tries to speak against the Luners somehow end up dead within a few years? All following in their family's footsteps?"

Vixen shuffle uncomfortably, taken aback by the question, "If you haven't noticed that at this age, you're blind to the truth."

"I think my days are in its final moments." I confessed, my face relaxed as I look into Vixen's dark brown eyes, an odyssey where all the worlds words stay. "Remember, it is all lies. My family - that was a lie to maintain the calm. Whatever they say, I am not following in my family's footsteps."

Ax appears before Vixen had time to process my words. He looked at me and Vixen as he sat on the coffee table.

I took his and Vixen's hands, holding them tight as we were the only ones here. "Thank you for seeing me for who I truly am."

Vixen's mouth hung open for moment before she reciprocated, holding my hand back, "Whatever is going on.

I am telling you I have your back."

My heart swells with worry, and I flash a small smile, bringing a frown on both their faces.

Ax says, "What's going on Snitch? Is this something to do with a Luner asking me about you the other day?" My eyes widen as he continues, "They stopped Henery and I at the park. Asking if I have seen you recently."

Vixen, now accusatory, crossing her ankles, "And what did you tell them?"

"Oh, like I would tell them peace of shits anything. You weren't there at the club when she got drugged. She ran off, frightened, saying they couldn't find out it's her."

"Well, that wouldn't had happen if you were here at my club." She says side - eying him.

Ax rolled his eyes, continuing, "Snitch, I told them you come to the club practically every night. When we ask why they are asking, the dude smiled and walked off."

Shaking my head, I let out a heavy sigh of relief. They don't know what's going on, yet. He willingly lied for me despite not knowing where I've been the past week.

My mind wrestles with itself to tell them. Really tell them the truth. Just do it and they will understand. Yet keeping it away like I have been all these years may be best for them.

Abrupt, loud knocks echo through the front of the club; I froze as they hit the door another time. They were hard, impatient, one after another. I shot up as the knocks wouldn't stop. One of the bouncers on the bottom floor look up at his boss. Vixen already standing, gently placing her hand on my shoulder before spinning on her heels leaving Ax and I. The other workers who were still cleaning up gather. Their curiosity piqued. While dread fills me.

"We are coming! Stop that knocking, we hear you." Vixen shouted, getting halfway down the stairs. The bouncers line up at the door awaiting her orders. "Open it, see who's trying to come in after hours." She said that yet we all knew whose outside the doors.

They know I left outside the walls. They are going to take me. My legs shook. The knocking resonates in my mind, triggering memories of that night. My fingers wrap around my neck, my body weaken as fear overwhelms me.

It was late at night, much like this. I was sleeping in my bed when heavy knocks abruptly woke me. My mom screamed in panic bursting into my bedroom. Dad was in the living room yelling and a crashing made him stop. She kept whispering in my ear *'Nothing will tear us apart. We will always be together.'* If only I did not open my mouth that may have been true.

My back heating as the memories floods my mind. There she stood – Elizabeth - calmly, almost serenely, with her unnaturally dead eyes scanning the room. I wish Ieronim was here to panic her once more. Her gaze lift landing on me, her brows raising slightly, if I am not mistaken I have taken her by surprise.

Vixen cut straight to the point, "What fake claims do you have this time Luner's? I follow the law here."

A man handed her a few pages, retorting with a smug expression, "If you followed the laws, we wouldn't be here."

"No, if I followed it to the extent you want, you wouldn't be here. I'll have my lawyers look at these and get this out of court like all the other times. Anything else you'd like?"

The whites of Elizabeth's teeth could be seen, her smile not touching her eyes, "I see everything I needed." Her voice echoes in the empty club. "I guess they didn't lie to Luner's after all. Because as you know, lying to us is punishable by death." That was a direct threat aimed at Ax.

Vixen snap to the bouncers, who promptly closed the doors on the Luners, "Always overstepping your authority with them loopholes."

This wasn't just about serving her papers. They'd done that plenty of times during normal hours. This was to keep eyes on me.

My chest heating, peering to Ax. If they had kept me outside these walls for the week, I wouldn't be back yet. The lie Ax did for me would had gotten him killed.

Clenching my jaw, Ax put his hand on my shoulder, "Nothing is going to happen. See? I knew you would be here." He winked with that confident smile of his.

Vixen approached, grumbling about the nonsense they try to tag onto her.

Quietly, I spoke for both of them to hear, "They were here, looking for me. I am sorry to involve you guys."

Vixen laugh, "Don't be sorry. I've been dealing with their shit for years."

Ax whispers, "They need to be taken down a few notches. If they mess with you, I'll go to battle."

A statement that hung in the air all too possible. With the Wanderers asking about an operation and attack. I believe Luner's are doing something bad outside these walls we don't know of.

We stopped talking about it once others start to circle to get their late - night drinks. Wandering ears lead to blabbering mouths.

Vixen pass the papers around to her employees. They joked about how if it gets shut down they better get paid extra for the trouble. Her empty threats of firing them erupt an outburst of laughter. I stared at Vixen and Ax truly watching their movements. Their lives are perfect the way they are. I can't allow them to get them involved with this.

*

Sitting on Niel's bedroom floor in my workout clothes, out of breath once more. My back leans against the closed door. Marveling at the absolute mess I made. Every corner of the room has been turned over, the bed pushed against the wall, the boards underneath scattered. One dresser remain on its side, and I feel too exhausted to pick it up.

If only I knew what they were looking for, this task would have been much easier. If it was something small maybe a flash drive, some notes, or an object that was out of place for Niels' parents, they could had put it where they deemed it belonged.

Slumping over, the dread crept in. What if it was the photos they were looking for? Nothing in the photos warranted breaking into the city. They are just snapshots of his life. Unless…he wanted them to protect his parents.

No, he wouldn't have waited three years just for photos. After catching my breath, I got up, prioritizing the task at hand. First, get the dresser upright. Pushing it against the wall, feeling for anything out of place - any wobble, loose bit, anything that might reveal a hidden compartment. Yet, once again, I found nothing unusual. Putting Niels neatly folded clothes like he had them to the best of my memory into the drawers.

My phone rang disturbing the song that was just playing. Wiping the sweat from my forehead, planting my feet in the path I made.

Confused I answer slightly out of breath, "What's up Randal, why are you calling?"

Randal replies, "Why are you out of breath?"

"First off, none of your business. Second off, working out." Not like I am telling him a lie.

"Well, good news." Randal went on, "You can keep your pay, and only work twice a week. They found that you were not guilty during the investigation, but since Chad was badly hurt, you are on probation."

"What about Chad?" I ask already knowing the answer.

He stumbled over his words, "Well, he is still working with us. They-"

"Elizabeth." I interrupted.

"Deemed he was doing what was the best to protect others in an incorrect manner."

I bit out a laugh, knowing that would be the case, "What if they didn't know Ieronim was with me? If he wasn't there that day, what would the outcome be then?"

Randal stay quiet, and I waited, wanting to hear the obvious answer. To hear the hypocrisy, the reason my family was demoted so long ago for this exact reason.

They said my family had too much control back then, and that is why they stripped everything from the O'Salves. Because with power you can skew results, and influence citizens to think a certain way. Now, a few generations later, the same thing is happening, but it's not being stopped.

There had to be alternative motives that died with that generation. A hatred for my family that's gone down to me.

A secret I do not know, not just 'too much power in one family is bad,' there's something else going on in history I don't know about.

He broke the silence with a sigh. I could hear him rubbing his head. Clearing his throat, he finally says it. "You would had been fired for the fear of losing funding. Trinity, let's not do this. You should be glad you'll be keeping your full pay."

"But now they are scared to lose funding due to if I wasn't there and Ieronim finds out." I pace around the room mindlessly within the path. "I think this job has become too much stress for me, and it isn't like I need the money. Elizabeth being there is bringing back too many bad memories for me."

"Trinity," Randal begs, "Next Friday, come to work. Not for Elizabeth, but for me. I need you on my team. You are someone I trust here, so please don't run away on me."

A reluctant rumble escaped un - enthusiastically, "You better not show up at work drunk ever again." Randal grumbled in disappointment, not with my words but with himself, "Make sure Chad doesn't fuck with me. Mother Earth, if he does, I will walk out. Plus, if I find out you report anything to Elizabeth…"

Randal cuts me off, "I only report job information to her. I know your history with her," a mutter almost to himself, "I know her history way too well than do that shit to you." He cleared his throat, "Thank you, Trinity, for coming back to work. Thank you for not doing your nickname and spreading about my mistake."

Flopping onto the sideways bed, slowly sliding down as I lay on it, "I figured you were under a lot of stress. Just not again, or I will own up to my nickname and snitch."

With that the call ended. I can't believe I agreed to work there again. My music play on its own - an upbeat song that doesn't match how I feel at the moment.

Rolling to get off the bed it slip more, getting caught on the end table that's in the way. Pulling myself up, attempting to step off, my hand hit something unusually hard on the lip of the mattress. Grabbing the rim, squeezing, I felt it. Pulling the mattress back slightly there's a seam of Velcro large enough for two large hands to easily fit in. Dragging the mattress back onto the bed.

My heart started to quicken its pace. The music creeping up in volume. Pulling apart the bed, peaking at what could be inside. My face prune as I pull out tan enveloped stuffed full. Sitting on the bed, I slowly open one. Pulling out random cuts of cloth, no its too skinny, it's almost like paper. Gasping as it hit me, I fumble through the other four envelopes with similar looking things inside. They are notes. It's something they used to commonly use before the first wave. Some cities tried to bring it back, attempting to keep the old ways alive, but ended up giving into the plastic currency.

Still, these can be used in dark markets; we learned Wanderers are known to carry them around. Notes from before the first wave are collectible and known to be bought for large amount of currency. My hands tremble to see many are from before the first wave, and slightly off looking ones.

Perhaps these were the attempts after the wave. This is what they must've been looking for.

Lifting the flap open seeing if there's anything else inside. That's all in the hidden pocket. At the back, its sewn messily as if they hurried to get it done. My tongue slid over the cut in my lip. Getting both my hands inside, I pulled, breaking the threads.

Flashing my phone light, I see multiple things inside another hidden compartment. Breaking the threats free, my hand stings from the way it dug in. Taking out multiple books, all are in a plain black binding, indistinguishable from all the other notebooks inside Niels' room.

Flipping through the pages, my legs hit the ground. These are what they were looking for. My heart caught in my throat, and I couldn't make a sound. My hands weaken and the book slips out falling with an open page.

Unable to move, I stare. He was continuing my family's work. The difference this time is I can understand the words on the papers. He didn't write it in the weird language as my family did. The page it fell open to has a sketch of a body, pointing to the small part of the brain that seems to activate when one dies, the one we are all now born with. My chest doesn't move despite breathing, the music despairs. Is he this Second Life thing because of the work my parents started?

Loud and hard knocks on my door broke me out of my spell. Clasping my hands to my mouth stopping my panic squeal threatening to escape. My breaths quicken as I shove everything back into the bed where it once was. Rushing down the stairs, they knocked again.

"Coming!" I try to keep my voice calm, but it cracked letting the panic be heard, "I'm coming."

Both my hands resting on the door as I look through the peeping glass. To see a distorted figure of someone unexpected.

My shoulders sag in relief that it's only Ieronim. As I show myself, his smile grew, holding out a bag of grilled meats.

As he got a better look, Ieronim's smile flattens. "You were not this bad last time."

Spinning on my heel he follows me in as I say, "I don't want to talk about it, Mr. VIP."

"We are past that point Trinity, and you are just being stubborn. I've seen your apartment. How many men can say that?"

I chuckles, "Not many."

He set the food on the table, moving to the kitchen as if he lives here himself. I would protest his unannounced presence, but the food smells so good.

Picking at the bag, aroma filled the air with pork and chicken. Ieronim handed me a plate as he took everything out laying it on the table.

"You hungry?" Ieronim ask.

Before I could answer my stomach growled as if his words woke it up. He side - smile as my face heats from embarrassment. If my face is as bright red as I think, he's pretending not to notice.

Putting his hand underneath mine, bearing the weight as he puts food on it for me.

I sat at the end of the table as I often do, and he sat beside me. He pointed at his own face in a circular motion than pointed at me. My eyes flutter shut not wanting to talk about it. Ieronim then leaned over and pulled my plate away.

"Hey." I called out, "I was eating that." He just stared at me, "I got into a fight, okay? I don't want to get into it."

He slid the food back, and I wrap my arm around it. Taking my fork, I stab a chicken wing on his plate. "Payback for taking my food."

Ieronim ask, "It wasn't my brother-in-law was it?" I shook my head, "They gave you your job back. Chad was bitching at it last night during family dinner."

"I'm not the biggest fan of keeping my job cause I know someone."

"Think of it this way." He took the wing off my plate, taking a bite before saying. "Your job wouldn't been threatened if Chad didn't marry into my family. It was simply leveling out the playing field and allowing you to keep what's yours."

Picking at the food on my plate he did have a point. Only thing is, he doesn't know Elizabeth is the main issue in my life.

"Why are you here anyways?" I ask, "You've been gone high and dry for years."

A soft, genuine smile appeared, "I had to. Not much of a choice to go MIA. When I saw you broken that day, it reminded me of myself. Lost and wishing someone would be there for me.

"Everyone around me now sees my money, the power. Where you knew me as a stranger with too many secrets. Genuinely showing care for me as a person, not what can be gained.

"You leave a mark on the people you meet. Whether good or bad, it's undeniable you have a gift. For me, the mark you left made me want to be friends afterwards. For Chad, he wants you dead." He chuckle taking another bite. "Either way, it's rare, but you, Trinity O'Salves, impact people one way or another.

"Now that I met you again and we live in the same apartment building, get used to me dropping by. We are friends despite you still having your guard up."

"O'Salves are known to be bad luck. Aren't you afraid to lose everything?" For reasons you don't even know yet.

His grin widens, touching his ears, "I am ready for a new challenge. My life has been smooth sailing lately, why not spice it up?" We paused for a moment then he added, "Bad luck is in the eye of *others*. Sometimes the bad is there to make sure you go on the right path." He mutter, almost inaudibly, "History they try to hide teaches us that."

My eyes narrow as he stared at his plate. A moment of honesty, a blip in a thought that wasn't meant to be spoken out loud. Not letting him know his thoughts were spoken, I continued to eat.

*

Standing before the mirror, preparing myself for the club. My phone vibrating, to see Ieronim's message, 'I had fun let's do this again.' Somehow, he convinced me to give him my number. Leaving it on read, putting my phone down.

Taking my coat, long pants, and a flowing top covering my bruises. Heading towards the club. Normality is key.

A few sprinkles hit me as I stood in the alley. Strangely Stefin isn't here. Checking the time, it's always when I come. Knocking a few times without an answer, scanning my surroundings, I step out from the alley, seeing the main door where no one stood. There aren't even anyone waiting to get in. Nostrils flaring my hair trailing behind me, retracing my steps back to the VIP entrance.

Moving the plaque telling people 'no smoking, no underage, VIP entrance only' revealing a handprint scanner. Pressing my palm against it, the door unlatch. This is one thing I never thought I would use. Vixen always talks about me working here, and one day on a whim, maybe not a whim for her but felt like one to me, she had me in the system to get inside if ever needed.

Entering the club, met with yelling from Vixen and few other voices mixing. Anger surged within. The scent of Lily hasn't begun to permeate the air. Peeking over the edge, Luners officials stood below. Bouncers surround the agitated employees preventing fights from breaking out.

"My lawyer already contacted your fucking people." Vixen's voice cuts through the air, "You have no right disturbing my business telling my customers to leave!"

Elizabeth respond calmly, "Until that is proven, you are not allowed to keep your doors open."

Vixen try to push forward, but her people kept her back. Elizabeth step forward taunting her.

With one swipe of my thumb, ringing someone on the other end, hoping they will pick up.

"That's not how the law works, you overstepping Luner's." Vixen retorted, taking a few steps back, "I went to law school. You are not allowed to stop a business until they are proven guilty. I told you search the place. Go see for yourself nothing illegal is here, then leave!"

Elizabeth declares, "We have cause, and as long as my men and women are here, your business cannot go on."

Gabe who heard that part of the conversation on the phone intervened, "Elizabeth is that you? For someone so high up, I would advise you to revisit the handbook. An owner who has not been proven guilty can keep their business open as long as it does not disturb your investigation. From the sound of it, you are not investigating, so the Vixen's Club is allowed to have her customers inside. Disturbing a business to cause significant loss of sales, and if they are then proven innocent, they are allowed to sue for up to five times the amount of revenue lost. Additional compensation for every employee, losses on products that went bad due to the disruption, not to mention utilities, rent, and well Vixen knows the rest."

I didn't hide the smile that's plaster to my face. Every head tilts up at me as I lean carelessly on the balcony. I thanked Gabe and hang up the call. This time I would not miss the pure rage in Elizabeth eyes. Forever getting it captured.

Resting my elbow on the ledge, my fingers tracing along the side of my face. The eerie quietness with only the sound of feet moving around.

Elizabeth looking up with pure shock. "How did you get in?"

"From the door like you guys." I flash a smile.

Elizabeth taking a step forward is blocked by the bouncers. The Luners backing her and my stomach hollows. Tension rises from below as I stood safely up here.

Her lips pucker, "Maybe you are following in your family's footsteps after all."

My heart presses against my throat. From an outside perspective, the meaning is nothing, but from where I stand, I knew that's a threat. She warned me three years ago and now she's trying to make it a reality.

I say, "My parents weren't much of the party type. They preferred to stay home. It looks like you are losing your touch in your later years." Her cheeks redden, and I pressed. "Maybe it is best to allow someone younger to take your place, so you don't get anyone hurt for false accusations."

Her expression calms once more, the mask being forced on top of her red cheeks, "Looks like we became talkative once again O'Salves. See you next Friday."

My lips thinned as I wave her goodbye. Plopping my butt in my spot. My expression flattens as they left.

The thumping of my chest came to the forefront. Everyone came upstairs where I sat, my fingers curl into my jacket, trying to stop them from shaking. Vixen came over, her brows lower at me. I looked away as she pulled my arm, and I follow without a fuss.

Every bad thought coming to mind getting whisked away with one action.

Her arms wrap around me, her large breasts pressing into mine, almost at the same height with her tall heels. Staying still shocked, she lean her lips against mine earlobe.

Less than a whisper, Vixen says, "The papers served were bull shit. They are after you, trying to get anyone caught into their webs to grab you." She pulled away speaking for all to hear, "Thank you so much for the help. Alright everyone, get a round of drinks and let's open this bitch up!"

As everyone scattered, she went into the back. I followed Vixen into her office. Ax calling me from behind the bar.

Already seated at her desk, Vixen looks weary. Shutting the door behind myself, taking a seat.

I ask, "How do you know she's going after you to get to me."

Vixen replies as she turned her computer around, "She ask Ax and his husband about you on their day off. Now they are doubling down to get me out of business. Its putting one and one together Snitch. More importantly, I need to know what you are involved with."

Leaning back, I kept calm, "I am not involved with what my parents did."

"That may be true, but something is going on. Snitch, I need to know to keep myself safe."

The door crept open. I turn to see Ax coming in. "Henery was followed to work and home yesterday, and I recognize one of the goons standing with Elizabeth today."

Now they are being involved when they have done nothing but be nice to me. I knew I should have kept them far away from me. Nothing good comes from being near an O'Salves for too long.

The chair scraped on the ground as I got up. Ax pressed on my shoulders, urging me to sit back down. Pulling up my loose-fitting sleeve, I showed off my cheetah prints.

Vixen flinched at the sight of me.

"You are in trouble, aren't you." Ax asks, "Why did you not want them to know you got drugged, why did you disappear for a week?"

My eyes burning as I held back the tears, my voice unable to come out. Words I never dreamed of saying. Never thought they would have been said.

Vixen plays a video on her computer, and both of us turn our heads. I wish I could have melted away. On camera, the Wanderers who broke in are carrying my unconscious body over the guy's shoulder. She presses a few buttons, and there I was in the pajamas Niel gave me.

I'm curled in his arms, Lavender and two others, a female and male are with them.

When the video stopped, I stared at the empty street. The Luner's already know I wasn't in the city. There is no more denying it, it's over. My head becoming light, as if the Lily I never took finally hit.

Vixen explains as she sees the fear on my face. "This is my personal camera Snitch. This covers a blind spot the Lunar system doesn't cover."

Somehow that doesn't release the building pressure. Ax rewound the footage to a better view of me in Niels arms. Niel looking down at me pulling me closer to his body. There his gaze seen the camera, and that's where Ax stopped the video.

Leaning in, Ax asks, "Why does he look so familiar?"

Vixen nodded, "I couldn't pinpoint him either, I was thinking maybe an old regular."

Tears drip down my face as I say, "That is what's left of Niel."

The room became cold like winter has come early. Their expressions blank, remembering the name I've said so many times.

I continue, "They are called Second Life's," I pointed at Lavender, "And she is one too. You can't tell but they have a gray undertone."

I told them everything. My life is already at risk with Elizabeth wanting me dead, so why not get it all off my chest. What I've seen outside the walls. How there's walking paths of blind spots all over the city. The zombies who broke in and no alarms went off.

By the time I finished telling them almost everything, leaving out the truth of what happen my family were doing, the photos, and what I discovered today. Their eyes gloss over trying to compute all the information given. Fidgeting with the edge of my jacket, awaiting their reaction. Vixen leans into the computer, scrutinizing Niels' face as she move the video back where he stared down at me.

"He's handsome…You guys dating?" Vixen ask in all seriousness.

Blurting out a laugh in disbelief she would just ask that. The laughter caught on where Ax and Vixen couldn't contain their amusement.

Wiping my tears, I say, "Out of all that you are wondering, that is the main one?"

"Hey, I may be a little older, but if you aren't I will. Look at that face." She got out of her chair, coming to us, "Now that we know your dirty business, I am most definitely in."

Ax's voice lowers trying to make it make since for himself. "We were taught the Wanderers were the violent ones. Yet it sounds we are attacking them… My sister…" His voice cracked, "She could have turned to one of these. Her cancer - it may not had ended her."

My lips curl inwards seeing the pain on Ax's face. He's now questioning everything he has been taught in life.

I shrug my shoulders, unable to answer, "I know nothing about that. I only was awake for one day. They mistook me for, I guess, a Luner or whatever else they may have."

Ax seemingly ignoring my words blurted, "I am in. I need to know the truth."

I shook my head, running my hands through my hair. "No, no, you guys are not involved. You two need to pretend you don't know anything." Laying my hand on my chest, "This is my issue."

Ax brows lowering into a dangerous glare. "My sister had a chance to live, Snitch. I don't care if it was one in a million. It was still a chance. I need to know what other secrets they are keeping. They got us involved; you can't push us away."

"He's right. Luners are pushing their luck, and more people are getting sick of them." Vixen brush her shoulder on his, "So, what's the deed, how do you get in contact with them?"

I just want to pull all of my hair out. Standing up I went to the door saying, "Just stay out of it for now. When I know," I sigh in disbelief what I am about to say, "I guess I'll tell you. Give Vixen my number."

"Wait, Ax had your number before me!" Vixen shouted as I left the room.

Rubbing my face, full of worry with no clue what life will hold. O'Salves bring bad luck for others, and its exactly   what   I've   done.

Chapter Eight

Things have returned to normalcy, before the Wanderers grabbed me, and finding out Niel is still alive. I sat in the quietness of the office, it's clean as if zombies weren't here. A new iron door stands propped open, this time painted dark blue. Down the hall came new people and some regular faces I am used to. Already standing in front of my desk, clad in my tight workout shorts and tank top.

Randal's eyes widen as his gaze falls on my yellowing blackened skin. Though my lip is almost healed, I can feel the crease of the cut when I rub my tongue against it. It's been a few weeks now since I came back to work. This isn't the first time Randal has seen me like this, but he still looks at me as if I'm as beaten the first day. Gabe hasn't ask about it, so I'm not too sure if he's told him or not.

Chad still pretty beaten himself. Ignoring all the looks burning into my skin, I tilted my head with a smile, flipping the screen around.

"I know Randal has scared you guys with his methods of teaching, but it is to help keep you alive." I say in a cheerful voice, pointing at the screen, "I checked the cameras, and as you see in the furthest wing, there is a zombie. We don't have to worry. It is walking the other way. So, follow me, and let's get changed.

Randal and I will check the uniforms before exiting to make sure every crucial part is covered. It's hot, but better to be alive than bitten."

Chad snakingly says, "Or attacked by a teammate."

Randal bit back, "Chad, that's enough out of you."

As he rolled his shoulders, back stiffening, his expression causes me to smirk instead.

Checking Chad's uniform, his eyes burn into my forehead. I pulled at his neck, it all looked good. Giving Randal a nod, he stepped over to the keypad putting in his numbers.

"Okay, stick close, follow our leads, and don't step out of line." Randal directed to all the new people whose names I don't care to remember, "Remember where your knives are located in case you get blindsided by a zombie. Trinity and I both have shafts with extra darts, so we are the main ones in charge of making sure you all are safe. Now let's go."

Randal and Chad made their way up first with the new people following. The nine bodies were next, with the two who deals with them, and I am last.

The cool breeze hit my face, providing some relief from the heat. Sweat still rolled underneath my uniform as I pull at the neck brace, hoping the cool air will help my suffering.

Arriving at our designated spot, they start to drop the bodies. Randal backed up to me. He looks at my face that's covered in makeup but still can notice my busted lip.

Randal asks in a quiet voice, "Are you going to tell me the truth now?"

I reply, "Like I said, got into a fight."

"You look like you got the shit beat out of you." Randal voice hitched, "It wasn't Luner's, was it?"

Side - eyeing him, I match his low voice, "If you have to ask that, it means I need to worry about them."

He sucked in a sharp breath, forcing his body not to turn to me, "I heard…You may want to have a grab bag Trinity."

"Grab bag?" I tilted my head, ensuring no one could read my lips, "What are you getting at?"

"Clothes, water, unperishable food. I know you know where the blind spots are, meaning you know where the holes are in the foundation, right? That knowledge is setting off Elizabeth's alarms, and she is planning to turn the heat on you."

Randal question as if what he just said truly hit him. "How the hell do you know every blind spot in the city?"

I counter back, "Someone unimportant taught me where the blind spots are. Are you telling me to get out of the city? I don't know where the holes are in the foundation."

"Well, you may ask them where it's at. I am only saying, as the last resort, if they come for you, you have to leave. I can't stand by and watch…" He stopped catching his words, "I know what they will do, and I can't allow it. Promise if they come, you get out, run as far from here as possible."

"Is that why they are talking to people I know?"

His back straighten stunned at my words. "Cut ties now or they will be drag down with you."

My heart shatters with the words that falls out of his mouth. I put them in danger already. They know information they shouldn't. I know they won't just let me cut ties, I've tried that, and they doubled, tripled down, and they want in.

I ask, a strain in my voice, "Randal, will you be safe?"

"I will be fine, and them too if they hadn't done anything, maybe."

"Maybe, maybe isn't a good…"

A loud squeal of pure panic came from one of the new girls, cutting me off. She trips over her own feet as a zombie moves in the tree line.

Randal whispers, "Worry only about yourself." He loudly say for the rest to hear, "Get back. This is Trinity's shot!"

Crawling away from the zombie she squeals as if it's on top of her, which its nowhere close to her.

Passing them and the catty, the girl finally getting to her feet running. It hover in the woods not breaking out into the open. Getting a little closer cautious at its behavior, could it be a Second Life's? Closer I got, it's hand's torn off just like the one before. Scanning the area in the thick woods, I couldn't see anyone waiting.

As it turn going little deeper, I let out a breath, releasing the trigger straight into the head, hitting my target.

The body shift before falling sideways. Chad laugh, "Now you have to go get it."

I flash my teeth, "You're welcome. Maybe next time you can try to shoot one and keep everyone safe."

Before he opens his mouth, Randal clear his throat getting them to go back to work.

Walking into the woods, plants scatters the ground snagging and twist around me. Grabbing the dart not too far from the body, my eyes graze over the zombie. The hands aren't wrapped like the last one, it's been chopped off haphazardly.

Cleaning the dart off in the greenery some leaves are becoming brittle. Putting the dart in the used slot, cool wind blew releasing the constant torment inside the uniform. Fall is going to hit before we know it. Mother Earth warning us with her plants which aren't as vibrant and resilient as normal.

A clean piece of paper sticks out from the zombie's chest pocket. Surveying the land around me seeing no other life beyond my teammates. Squatting beside the fallen zombie taking the paper.

Unfolding it, I lost my balance and fell flat on my ass. *Infinity,*

I trust you are the one who will see this, if not, I failed you. Our group was attacked the other night. The situation demands my return to my district. I need to be there to discuss further matters and to counter these attacks. Luners are threatened by us, they know of our existence, and fear what would happen if the cities find out. Soon I will find you, and then I can tell you everything.

Take care, live free, and always be you my infinity.

-Niel

A pin remained in the zombie's pocket, quickly scribbling a reply, I tuck everything back in, hopefully Niel will see my question before departing.

My heart races as I dust the dirt clinging to my body. Exiting the woods, my heart thunders inside my chest. Passing the others, I can't shake the feeling they can hear my heart racing. May be paranoia, but I feel Chad's gaze, questioning why I lingered in the woods. With Randal's warning I have to take this chance and find the answer on how to get out of the city. I just hope I get the answer before it's too late.

Stripping out of the sweat - soaked uniform, I chug down my bottle of water I left on the desk this morning. As I sat there, Chad exit first. Flashing him a smile as he pass he stopped in the doorway.

Over his shoulder, he says, "I don't care that you are one of my Brother-in-laws many lovers. He will see you for the murderer you are sooner or later."

My brow rose at his threat, "Are you planning to frame me?"

"You do enough damage that it isn't necessary. I wonder why you stayed in the woods so long?" My throat started to close on itself as he continued, "Maybe the Luners would be interested to hear that?"

Flashing my teeth in a grimace, I retort, "I bet Ieronim would love to hear how his litter sisters husband threaten his lover. Maybe I will tell him as my legs are wrapped around his strong waist, and he's deep inside of my wet..." I pause as a wicked grin took over my grimace, "Ha, you probably never experienced a wet pussy before, have you?"

His eyes bulge before turning and leaving without a word. Smirking, I wave where he could see me as he turn the corner.

*

"I think its best I don't come back here." I say, sitting in Vixen's office. Ax leans on the wall behind her. "He couldn't tell me if you guys would be safe or not."

"Not this again." Vixen sighed, leaning back, "How do we know he is on your side? Cutting ties with us would show them you are like your family. You say it yourself, they weren't club goers."

Fuck she makes a good point. Brushing my hair back my mind going crazy on what is best.

Ax mutters like a note to self. "I need to tell Henery to pack."

I clapped my hands together standing up, "This is why I said not to get involved. O'Salves bring bag luck. I can't bring you guys down with me. I am serious now. They ask you anything, you don't know shit. I am just a regular that is all."

Leaving the office, my shoulders sag as Ax says, "You have stood up for Vixen. They see us together at a club. It's too late not to involve us. We are older than you, Snitch. It isn't like we are some kids. We know what we are getting ourselves into."

They don't understand what is at stake. They have never been treated like I have by society. It would break them.

Pushing through some people who stood too close to the employee doors, they're almost knocked over. Getting in my spot, Ax brought me a shot of Lily, with a spirit of his choice as always. Pinching the bridge of my nose, I didn't look at the crowd below.

Zoning out in the middle of the open space above the Lily making my head heavy. Mother Earth, they can't be involved with me. Strength like the trees, roots strong to keep them where they belong. As I flutter past, just a blip in their memories. Keep them protected at all costs, and for me, bear me no mind.

Opening the door to where I live, a piece of paper peeks out from underneath my foot mat. My body sways as I bend, fingertips untucking the note. Inside, the door locked, my back lean against it as I read it.

Infinity, what have you gotten yourself into? There is only two unknown to the Lunars. Strip of the Clubs where the black and white merges to gray. There is your best hope if needed to escape. Please, stay long as possible so I can explain everything. I leave tonight having someone else deliver this for me. Take care, live free, always be you my infinity.

-Niel

The paper was written quickly, the lines aren't even as if he was already on the move.

Absorbing the words, where black and white merges with gray. The only club that deals on the edge of legal and illegal is Vixens club. Collapsing on the couch, my head throbbed with the weight of impending decisions, lives at stakes because of me.

On the dining table, photos of an unknown world lay scattered. Three books are sprawled open; pages filled with cryptic information. Panic creeps up. Positioning myself to see the front door always on edge that this moment, the Luners can rush in. The fear telling me they are coming any moment.

Scooting the chair back, I went to the kitchen to make myself a cup of Lily tea. I can't constantly live on edge like this.

My eyelids grew heavy, dropping halfway shut as words on the papers blur. This can't be true. The photos showing them all together, capturing moments when I was home, yearning to have someone to talk to. Texting Niel during the quiet hours alone. Unaware he was with them.

A shiver course through my body as there's a knock on my door. Quickly gathering the scattered pages, shoving the photos back inside the books, placing them atop the bookshelf as if they were any ordinary book.

Without bothering to check, I swung the door open, revealing Ieronim holding a large box of pizza.

"Nothing on?" Ieronim ask, attempting to engage in small talk.

Not in the mood for idle conversation, I hand him the remote, taking a seat on the far edge of the couch. Opening the box on the table, he took a second slice. "How's work?"

More small talk. In a small voice, I say, "Fine."

"Your mind is not all here, is it, Trinity O'Salves." It sounded more like a statement that a question.

My body wrench as he called that name. Slipping through my lips involuntarily, "O'Salves... bad omens," unlocking memories from ages I no longer remember. Stories of generations of misfortune settling on my shoulders, "Old - timers would often tell my dad. Once thought of luck and fortune. In one generation, we fell. Ever since, we have gone downhill. Now, there's just me left, and soon all will forget when I am in a pile."

I paused, my mind a jumble of thoughts, reluctant yet compelled to speak, "You aren't the first you know. That I stick to people, unable to get out of their minds. They would stare at me, a shy child too young to understand and say..." I closed my eyes, memories too painful to say out loud.

Ieronim turning to me, my words sinking, "What would they have to tell a child?"

My eyes blurry from putting too much Lily in my tea and getting a second glass. Heavy memories trickle out. Memories that were supposed to be kept at bay.

My tongue slip the painful memory, "'It's as if she never leaves the room.' 'I can feel her unblinking eyes still looking at me.' 'I felt like she invaded my body, reading my mind.' 'You won't get anywhere in this world.' 'They want a revolution leaving that thing alive.' 'She snitched out her own family'… Blood is on my hands in more ways than one."

My thumb rubs every fingertip, acknowledging the hateful words hold some truth. Ieronim picks up a slice of pizza and puts it in my hand.

"I don't give a shit what ignorant people said about you before they got the time to know the true you."

Chewing a few bites of pizza, I pondered, "Do you think you are more powerful than Luner's?"

A prideful smile show as Ieronim nods, shoving the crust into his mouth. That cocky smile moves his mole upwards. Daniel would had tossed that back into the box unless we had dip. Than he would slather it and eaten the bread.

"Can you promise to help keep three of my friends safe? They don't deserve the bad luck I bring."

"Your bad luck is in the eyes of the beholder. I see no bad luck in you - just people who don't like you, trying their hardest…" He stopped as I stare deeply into his eyes, his throat caught before saying, "Tell me who they are, and I will try my best…"

"Vixen, Ax, and his husband Henery. They are good people."

"The two from the club?"

I nod, a little relieved he remember who they are. "Thank you."

He didn't push the question on why. That's something he had taught me - answer only what you need and keep quiet when necessary.

*

Summer has turned to the sweet release of Fall. There hasn't been a trace of Niel or any Wanderers hanging around. Ieronim comes to my apartment at least three times a week, to the point I'm excited for his knock. Always coming unannounced.

Chad seems to have lost interest in me. Still only working two days a week, I find pleasure in having more free time. Somehow knowing Niel isn't exactly dead healed a part of me. Now, Lily provides a comforting fog which I don't need as often, not just a daze of nothingness I once felt.

The smile I had fell when I held my door open to see three unwelcome guests in front of me. My glare didn't leave Ieronim as he only smile.

Vixen push through, thrusting flowers in my hands, "This is where you live, and you chose to spend time at clubs. Like, I am flattered but girl I wouldn't leave here!"

Ax hands me a spirit he snatched from the club, offering a simple "Wow" as he pass.

Henery took the flowers and spirit, holding a box of baked goods saying, "Thank you for allowing us in your home. I'm guessing uninvited judging by your eerie stillness."

Ieronim pointed, "Kitchen is over there, Henery." And that is exactly where he headed with my gifts.

Grinding my teeth at Ieronim, "Why the hell are they here?"

"Keeping them safe for you. You were right. They are good people. I'm glad to have them back in my life that isn't the club life." He nudged my shoulder, "See? You aren't all bad luck."

Pinching the bridge of my nose watching them wander around the apartment, making themselves at home. I can't believe this is happening to me. The corner of my mouth turn upwards as Ieronim pass holding bags of food and setting it on the table. Laughter finally fills the air, as it once did many years ago.

Slowly, my lungs filled with air. Six invisible hands touching me, beckoning me forward. Telling me not to stand on the outside any longer. Giving me their blessing to live again, that I have people in my life who are here for who I am, just like how they once were for me. Thank you Alix, June, and Daniel for being with me as kids.

Tears ran down my face as the nudge got a little harder, guiding me towards them. They set up the table as if they've been here a hundred times before.

Ieronim wrapped his arm around my shoulder, brushing away the tears, "They better be because you are happy."

A grin so wide and pure spread across my face, catching him off guard for a second. His expression falters before returning an equally big smile. None of us went to the club, staying hours laughing, enjoying our time. Vixen hogging the remote to watch her favorite drama.

This has become my new life. They came almost every other night, all together, like my original group once did. In the absence of their liveliness, the quiet creeps back in, a reminder of what is to await me. By my bedroom door, I kept the bag with all I need to leave. Now understanding what my parents were trying to do. The bag I take everywhere has an extra set of clothes, a little food, and water which looks like a lunch, just in case I can't go home.

Fall turns to winter before I know it. No need to wear air masks, the bodies on the ground are now frozen. Unable to bury them because of the frozen ground, we leave them there. I shiver as we walk back cold to the bone. Forgetting a mask to go cover my face, my lips numb from the relentless wind.

Not even half way back, a woman cries in the distance. My back stiffen as I see her silhouette come out from the woods.

"Do not engage, keep walking." Randal orders.

Her cries grew louder, stumbling over her two feet as we got closer. She kept walking in our direct path begging us for help. She carries a baby in her arms, wrapped in a dirty blanket. Randal and I exchange weary looks. The last time, the woman didn't get this close. The two guys who work in the morgue slow down, unsure of what to do.

Chad cursing under his breath as she tripped again. My body jerk, between wanting to help and knowing what Wanderers can do, secrets they've hidden from our eyes. Not making a move. The two girls we have lean in closer to the morgue workers.

Chad braking formation, Randal yelled out, "What do you think you are doing."

Chad bitch, "Teaching these Wanderers not to fuck with us."

"I told you not to engage!" Randal follow behind, "Chad, get back here. Have you learned nothing about protocol?"

Never engage with Wanderers. They are violent individuals who will do anything necessary to survive.

As Chad nears the woman, she cowers, looking suddenly at me. He took the blanket, revealing nothing in her arms. Then, he pulled a knife out of his pocket. The ground turned red, and I fell back, my weapon slips from my hand as I just witnessed the brutality unfold. She screams on the ground, covering her face kicking her feet, getting herself away from the maniac. Any animal that might have been sleeping are stirred awake, the echoes of her blood – curdling cries sound through the once - quiet woods.

Randal acting fast, grabbing Chad disarming him as the woman ran into the woods. Turning to hear distant voices coming in our direction.

"We have to go." I urged as no one listen.

Chad and Randal is locked in a brawl. Edging closer to the woods, stopping at the blood on the ground. Multiple people scream as if that would get them to stop. Their voices too elevated to hear the braking of twigs from within the woods. Only three of us stood outside the group - Randal, Chad and I.

On the ground lay a stained note, bearing familiar handwriting. Squatting down, I covered the handwritten note with my foot, pointing the shaft at Randal and Chad. Touching behind my foot, sweeping the note, crumpling it in my hand. Steadying my shot, taking a breath in, hitting a mere foot away from Randal, he pushes Chad off, both looking in my direction. Placing a finger on my lips, signaling for silence.

Running away as quickly as possible, I had them stop in time where the Wanderers didn't get anywhere near us. My body heats as my finger tips and face frozen from running.

Collapsing on the ground inside the warm room, the new hatch shuts behind all of us. Dropping the shaft onto the floor, getting out of my uniform quickly, shoving the note into my pants pocket before anyone notice.

They are too engrossed in the ongoing fight between Chad and Randal. Chad is press against the wall as Randal's arm is pressed against his throat.

"You are suspended. What you did was moronic and put us all in danger." Randal's face twisted in anger, "No one needed to get hurt."

Chad red in the face, spat back, "What, are you a Wanderer sympathizer? None of them deserve to live."

Breathless, I interject, "And if not, if she lives, you disfigured her face. They knew where we were coming from. They could hunt us for what you've done."

Chad dismiss me with a click of his tongue.

Randal let's go of Chad, stating, "Trinity has a point. I will report this to the head council to see what needs to be done. You get out of here now."

Chad insisted, "You can't do that. I'll get my father-in-law."

I rolled my eyes, stepping forward interrupting him, "I will let your brother-in-law know all that happened today when he comes over for dinner." Tonight is when they all come to my apartment. "I think he will be furious knowing you are using their name for threats again for your poor behavior."

Chad came forward, his finger pointing into my chest, but I didn't back down. Randal between us, I push him away from me. I am so sick of Chads actions, and him always getting away with shit.

Chad spit in my face, "You psychopath, you shot a dart at us for what I did to that poor Wanderer," He looked me up and down noting the bit of blood that got on my hands.

I didn't hide them. "I did it to save all of us, and neither of you two got hurt. I killed a Wanderer to protect you guys before. You just were playing big bad strong man, when you are just weak for attacking someone who didn't pose a threat."

I stumble back as his fist connect with my face. The two girls shout slurs at him as they held me up. The pain heating my frozen face. All the guys exiting the room, Chad caught in the middle of them all.

"Sit, sit." The girl with bright blond hair always perfectly curled guided me. "He is such a dog, attacking that poor woman. I am sorry, I'm not a sympathizer, just… They have a hard enough time. Then punching you like that."

The girl who's scared of the smallest sound, even after months of working here, sides with her, "I hope he gets fired. If not I will complain to HR that I don't feel safe."

Randal came back, there was no more yelling. We were good to go, and he assured me it will be a while before Chad is allowed to come to work.

In a steamy hot shower heating up my frozen core. My eyes shoot open remembering the note in my pants pocket. Getting out, towel wrapped around running to my bedroom where my clothes were stripped. Taking out the paper, blood is dried on it from the poor woman.

Infinity,

I'm unsure how long it will take to reach you. I'm still in the North, unable to leave. My thoughts are consumed by you, and you will see I am the same person you loved before. As soon as I return, I'll find you. There I can tell you everything you dream of. You worried me wanting to know where the hole in the wall is. Since I haven't gotten any news, I assume you are still safe. I hope it stays that way. We are having issues here, not where I am at, but other known districts are. We are located far away where Luners will never go. It's beautiful here. Someday I hope you can see, but not how life is now.

Take care, live free, always be you my infinity.

-Niel

Sulking in my bed, the poor girl was just there to deliver me a message.

Lily stewing, golden streams fall down heavily and slowly. Hearing a knock on my door, downing half in one go. I answered the door and quipped, "Your brother is more insane than I am."

He scowl as everyone entered, muttering and laughing.

Ieronim corrected, "Barely brother-in-law let alone my brother. He say something similar about you. My sister called me with his twisted story on what happened. I'll believe your story before his."

After relaying everything that happened, I pointed at my cheek, swollen from Chad's punch.

Ax laughs, "He should be happy you need to behave yourself. I've seen you fight for less before."

Ieronim sighed, "I'll just cut half their allowance. My sister should put him in his place with that."

As we ate dinner, there's another knock on the door. Henery, the gentleman he is, got up to see who was there. My spine rigid trying to think who could be coming here. Suddenly, there's a thunk, and our heads turn as his foot blocked the door from opening further. His long arms cascade grabbing the top of the door.

Henery's voice, smooth and heavy when he speaks on his pod show, now carried irritation, "What I am doing here has nothing to do with you." Unintelligible mutters could be heard behind the door. Henery retorts, "Do you have a warrant? If not, come back when you get one."

Attempting to shut the door, a hand stopped him. Pushing the door wider, I stood, knocking my chair back. My body froze as I saw Elizabeth standing there, three men behind her. Smugly she smiles at my fear.

Ax and Vixen stood, both coming up from behind. Ieronim turn gently in his chair, acknowledging that his presence alone is a threat to them.

With an air of calmness, Elizabeth says, "So, Trinity O'Salves isn't sleeping with a married man then."

Henery remains unfazed, not allowing her to enter.

Elizabeth's eyes darted to Ieronim, her jaw flexing. "We received a report of treason and possible rebellion. Trinity O'Salves, you are under arrest."

Ieronim simply asks, "Vixen, are they allowed to without proof?"

She shook her head. I can feel her smirk behind me, "Innocent until proven guilty. Without papers of proof, Trinity doesn't have to go."

Elizabeth face twisted, unsure where to go with this.

Ieronim slowly rises, speaking deliberate, "If I find out my brother-in-law made any false statements against her."

He walk to the door, standing a few inches taller than Henery, both looming over Elizabeth, "You can kiss all that money goodbye. He punched her today, threatened her, and is unstable. I know her coworkers would attest to that. Now we are having dinner, and you are disturbing us."

Elizabeth extended her hand, likely about to say something, when the door slammed shut. Henery quickly locking it, keeping her at bay. The room's filled with joyous smiles, but I stood there, fear consuming me.

They won't stop at this, not by a long shot. Closing my eyes, darkness surrounds me, their joyful laughter will soon be a distant memory.

Ax putting his arms around my shoulders, "Snitch, we always got your back."

Breaking free from his embrace, wrapping my hands around my throat, feeling like I can't breathe. Their expression's darken as I slowly backed away. Without saying a word, I sprinted to my bedroom, grabbing the go bag. *This* is the day Randal *warned* me about. Henery stepped out trying to stop me. Dodging him making my way to the bookcase, I took Niels secret books and the photo album.

Ieronim grabs my shoulder stopping me. I stare at the bookshelf in front of me, while the rest circle around, unsure what I was about to do.

"I need to leave before it is too late." I stated, "You tell them I ran away. Do not protect me anymore from them."

Ieronim asks, "Where are you planning to go?"

Turning abruptly, his hand knocks into the books, my eyes widen as the photo album slips from my grip. Loose photos scatter across the floor.

Fluttering away, Vixen picks one up, passing it to Ax, who gave it to Ieronim, Henry picked one up on his own. My face burned with fear, a world they should never know about within their hands.

Vixen ask, "Were these your parents and brother? He looks so young."

I reply my voice cracking as my shoulders sink forward, "He was only nineteen when they died. It was my fault." Getting to the ground scooping the photos.

Ieronim squats getting to my level. Laying a hand on top of mine. "You were doing what's best. They were going to revolt against the city."

Shaking my head, a whimper escaped, lifting my gaze one by one as I say, "Luner's lied to not have panic rise." Tears drip down my hot face, "I was wrong, and I got them killed because of it."

Ax asks, "What were they doing then?"

I can't allow them to know, if I do I will put them in danger, "Zombies are evolving. Second Life's is what they are called, and him." I pointed at Niel's face in one of the photos. Information Ax and Vixen already knows, "He's a Second Life. He found me, and I think the Luner's know that." A *lie*, "I have to leave the city to never return." A *truth*. Ieronim ask, "When did you find this out?"

I shook my head, reluctant to share. I looked at him in the eyes.

His face didn't pale like Henery's, who had no clue. It isn't filled with confusion as Ax and Vixen when they found out. His brows raised, touching his hair that's fallen in front.

"You already knew this?" A statement that came out like a question.

Ieronim nodded, "Everyone sit…"

As the others sat around the table, I neatly put the photos inside the album while Ieronim says, "This must stay between us. It's a rare phenomenon, so rare they are still unsure what percentage of its occurrence. Celestial City reported it two generations ago. Their first case, they were waiting for the zombie to rise and walk off. The person rose and turned, asking them what had happened. No cities believed them. Maybe twelve years ago, they had two people not from their city again. Everyone gray in color but acted human, coming to their gates.

"Something changed, the cities didn't laugh but listened. The words spread to the wealthy and powerful. We don't kill people right when they die. We have specialty Luner's, and Special Force Hazard Team who wait for them to turn. If they turn into that… Second Life's as you call them, Trinity.

We got none here by the way. We are told if it ever happens they would be sent to Celestial City. We aren't told much about them. Celestial City keeps quiet now about how many they may have."

Ax clenched his hands, rage filling him. He must be thinking about his sister who could had turned into one, because of our class, we had no clue. Killing her brain like so many of us had believed is the only way.

Clutching the books near my chest. The truth, concealed in these pages, has the power to reshape what we know. What Niel has been trying to finish, and on paper looks complete. Now I understand why a rebellion is the notion Luners used more than ever.

Shoving the stuff in my bag, I headed to the door. Their voices synchronized telling me to stop. My back stiffening, releasing a long sigh.

Ieronim says, "Let's make it official. They already think we are lovers, Trinity. Let's tell everyone we are getting married. Then they can't make these fake claims on you like with your family."

Vixen always quick - witted chimes in, "That sounds like a sweet bargain to me. I want to be your maid of honor."

A bitter chuckle escaped my lips, "O'Salves are bad luck for anyone to be around for too long. It is time I leave. And for the four of you to be happy."

A heaviness in the air, an inevitable departure that is well overdue. A proposal of a mock marriage sounds good for a temporary fix, but in the end I will just drag Ieronim down.

Henery's smooth voice wrapping around my brain caressing my thoughts, "How about you stay with one of us. Let things calm down. It will take at least a week for them to get the right paperwork."

Ieronim slipped his fingers between mine, effortlessly taking the bag out of my grip. I didn't bother arguing. I just need to leave at night when everyone is sleeping.

Ieronim says with a smile, "Well then, lets pack up the rest of the food and bring it up to my apartment."

Vixen shouts, "You live here too?"

He gave her a wink, "The very top."

Walking down the short hall, only one door belonging to him.

Vixen practically left a drool trail as we walk inside. Five bedrooms, two of them are master bedrooms with their own bathrooms. Vaulted ceilings similar to Niel's, a spiral staircase leading upstairs. His television is three times bigger than the one Niel owned. Ieronim's apartment is a stark contrast, decorated in whites and light tones, while Niel's blacks and dark colors.

As the night wanes, Ax got drunk on the fancy spirits Ieronim owns. Owned, since there are five empty bottles laying around now. Vixen giddy, just buzzed, as Henery and I stay sober sharing a smirk.

Ieronim offered everyone a place to sleep, "Trinity, you can have the spare master bedroom."

I reply, "I think it's best the couple gets it."

Ax leaned his body onto me almost knocking me forward, slurring his words, "Aww, my Snitch does care if we have a room to fuck in." Henery shook his head, ears turning red with embarrassment as Ax continues, "You are someone great. I wish my sister could've met you. The whole city, all the cities will see your greatness."

My jaw tensed at his words. He truly thinks the city won't see me as a Snitch, as bad luck. Somehow, he could convince them otherwise. Patting his head and he sunk into it; he sees me as a false reality that I admire.

Henery swept Ax up holding him in his arms as if he were a child. Henery turned his head, "I promise you we won't have sex in your room."

Ax playfully kisses his husbands neck, "Not if I have anything to say about it."

Sucking in my cheeks trying to hold back my laughter. As the door latches shut, Vixen and I no longer could hold it in.

Vixen, gasps for air between laughs managing to say, "He's never going to live this down. That bad boy outer shell is such a fake act."

Wiping away tears, my jaw aches from the size of my smile. Something that wasn't even that funny but due to the stress we have all been under in our lives, it was a pleasant release to see Ax as his true cuddly self.

Ieronim downed the rest of his drink, interjecting, "They better not make that room a mess."

Vixen rolled on the ground laughing harder than any of us.

Before we knew it, she passed out on the couch nearing two in the morning. I sat on the other side of the large living room in a reading chair hardly ever used.

Ieronim seated at the end, "Are you not tired yet?"

I reply, "Every night for years, I would be coming home around four. I don't need much sleep, plus, I don't know how much more time I got."

"I wasn't joking earlier tonight about marrying me." Ieronim's eyes glistened, slightly buzzed, "Take it as a marriage of convenience. It's very common among our class."

Gazing away, fixated far outside his window, I see the trees over the city wall, I reply, "No one would accept it. You will be cast out just like the O'Salves."

Ieronim says as he leans closer to me. "Do you believe the stories? How they felt your ancestors had too much power, and that's the end of it? Never have I seen any documents about your people."

I filled in his words, "As if they've been erased… I have always found it weird. My parents said they were involved in helping to create the cities, and since the

Omega failed, they blamed it on the O'Salves solely. That was the start of our downfall, but nothing to confirm only mouth of word."

I absentmindedly played with my long hair, "You know we had a lot of superstitions: don't cut the hair till eighteen or your body will be weak, believe in your gut feelings - they'll bring you to the truth, and never be too still - or they will know your fear. All weird old - timer stuff they kept at heart."

Without asking, he touches a strand of my hair, bringing it out to his lips. My back stiffened as he says, "You told me before you've never cut it. Do you not want to follow in their traditions?"

Shrugging my shoulders, I took my hair back, "I just never felt like it. A few times, but something told me not to. As if it wasn't time yet."

"Your gut feeling." He smirked at me.

This feels nice, one last good night before I escape, leaving the city, not to return.

Jerking awake, I lay on a bed not my own. The smell of meats cooking filled the air around. Creeping out of the room, encountering a disheveled Ax, holding his head tight and messy hair not yet tamed for the day.

"Slept good?" I ask with a wicked grin.

A glare telling me to shut it caused my smile to widen more. The both of us wonder into the kitchen side by side with a unusual view. Ieronim wearing an apron, in a long sleeve knit shirt, cooking us breakfast. Vixen sat holding a coffee too close to her lips while not drinking it, her hair a complete mess going in every direction. She looks almost as rough as Ax. He sat by Henery who gave him a cup of coffee more milk than anything else.

One by one, they all left, leaving only Ieronim and I inside his apartment.

I confess, "I don't even remember falling to sleep."

Ieronim grinned on the other side of the counter, "We were only silent for a minute, and your head fell to the side, passed out. I carried you to the room if you don't mind."

Raising my brows, my silent response of 'I don't care.' Brushing my hair back, as Ieronim took another sip of coffee. I was supposed to leave last night. This ruined it all.

Getting up grabbing my bag that sat beside his front door, Ieronim stood behind me, quietly watching. Turning to bid my farewells, he only an inch away, causing me stumble back. His arm reached up leaning on the door. His eyes half shut, staring not at me, but through me reading my mind.

Ieronim asks in a lower octave than normal, making my body tingle, "What are you hiding? Luner's wouldn't be going after you only for knowing about Second Life's as you called them. You never answer when we ask what were your family was doing if not planning to revolt, is that what this is about?"

I shook my head, lowering my sight to my feet, "I can't tell any of you. It is better only I know and leave, so all of you stay in the dark. That way, no one will be in danger."

"Is it that bad?" Ieronim stepped back, allowing the light of the room to shine back onto me.

I nodded, "It would cause a panic, a disbelief in a way, more so than I ever imagined."

He took my hand, I grip tighter on my bag as he tried to take it, "Stay one more night. I will find a way to keep you safe… Trinity, please stay."

His plea came out as a beg. One finger at a time, the bag slips, allowing him to take it. Just for tonight. I can't leave during the hustle and bustle of morning anyways. His smile met his eyes, as if my agreement to stay was an accomplishment for him.

Chapter Nine

What is it? No, I have… Okay. Okay calm down… I will be down there in a moment." Ieronim says, rushing down the spiral staircase. Hanging up the phone at the last step, he turned to me, "I will be right back. I just need to let someone up."

Before I could even reply, he was out of the door. My heart sank as I heard the latch from the outside, locking me in. Nostrils flare, foot tapping the floor, something isn't settling right. Trying to wait it out, the tapping became more sporadic, out of control. Looking at the time, it's not long before sunset.

Jolting upwards, the door flung open with Henery pushing his way through, Ieronim following behind.

Henery demands in a panic. "Whoever you know you need to tell them to get you out now."

Ieronim raised his hands, attempting to calm the situation. "We aren't sure yet. Just calm down and wait. Explain what just happened."

Henery thrust my bag into my arms, almost knocking me back, "There is no waiting. They are at Vixen's Club now. They got papers to arrest her on criminal acts." He eyed me, "I know you didn't do any of it. Chad testified she tried to kill him multiple times and is using your family name as leverage. Your sister is standing by his side."

Ieronim's brows knitted. The veins in his neck pop as he paces muttering to himself how they are going to regret it.

He continued grabbing both of my shoulders, ignoring Ieronim's mutters, "As soon as they leave, Vixen will text me. She's trying to buy you time, but they will come here after the club."

Throwing my bag over my shoulder, everything happening too fast. My heart pressing against my ribcage with thunderous beats. I should had left last night.

Shit, I have to go to the club to get out. They are going to see me if I go there.

Ieronim, looking down from his window says, "There are people already station outside."

Henery tries to tell me. "Who are you meeting, tell them…" I interrupt, locking eyes with him. "Theres no one. Anyways, the only way out is towards Vixen's Club."

His shoulders sag, color draining from his face, "You can't go alone; you'll be…" His throat closes unable to say more.

Killed, rape, or worse, lawlessness with no governed everything is possible. Ieronim cursed under his breath as he closed the distance.

"You have warm clothes in there right? Water, food."

I squint my eyes shut, "Motherfucking Earth." I prepared this back during the summer, "I only have clothes for the heat."

Ieronim yank the bag off my shoulder, tossing everything on the couch. He pulled out all my clothes putting them to the side.

Notes fell to the floor sliding out of the sleeve, catching both Henery's and Ieronim's eye.

Putting them back inside, I warned, "Do not ask information that can get you in trouble."

Ieronim took my now - empty bag with him upstairs. Sounds of things falling to the floor made my body shake.

"Trinity, they just left." Henery warned, "They will probably wait till Elizabeth comes before raiding here." On cue, all our phones go off in a rarely used alert system.

I want to pass out. Henery came up behind me, as if sensing the overwhelming sickness. He held me tight, gently petting my hair back, soothing me with hums.

The television echoes the same sound as our phones. The emergency news broadcast came on, "Trinity O'Salves is under arrest for treason and revolting against Alpha City. Everyone, keep your eyes out. She is a dangerous sharp shooter who has already tried to kill multiple people whose tried to stop her. Do not engage and follow proper protocol calling the Hazard Emergency Lines. If you are found harboring her in any way, you will be arrested and charged accordingly, which can be a sentence to death."

My legs gave out. Falling to the ground Henery wasn't quick enough to catch me. It feels like a boulder is on top of me. It's been three years since Niel been here, the wall could have been fixed by now, or the Luners know it's a way to get out and will be waiting for me to leave there.

"Mother Earth, I am going to ruin him and my sister. I will make them regret today." Ieronim is fuming as he came down, a jacket over his hand and my bag filled. "They should fit you. They are my winter clothes when I was a kid. Luckily for you, I am a little bit of a keepsake person."

Turning me around helping me into the thick black wool jacket that hangs past my knees. A matching black beanie already warming my head. Ieronim helps the bag on which is heavier than before.

Yells comes from outside we can hear all the way up here. All three of us rush to the window to find more Luner's than before.

"Shit, I can't get out." Both my hands lay on the window feeling as if I may fall again.

Ieronim says, "There's a fire escape in my room, and it leads to the back of the building."

We ran upstairs, Henery staying behind calling Ax.

Inside Ieronim's' room, there's a pile of clothes in the corner. Multiple windows inside, one sits in the corner with a thicker ledge. Peering over, it goes straight down.

Ieronim darts into another room, returning quickly with a leather bundle.

"This has been passed down since the first wave, even before the history was lost." Ieronim quickly explained, "This has been in my family longer than I even know. Take it and be safe."

Holding out two crescent moon - shape Damascus blades, long with deep bows. Long handles darkened with beautiful wooden grains. The blunt end is brushed with gold, and the base heavier with gold on the end. Putting one in my grip, my fingers moving it with ease. My throat bobs. The large bows are clearly meant for decapitation to easily get around anyone's necks.

I reply, "I have a few knives. I can't take something so precious from your family."

Ieronim taking it back, placing both inside the leather they sat in for many years. The outside is stained with many colors. He pushes them into my arms.

Buttoning up his wool coat, which is now mine, Ieronim says, "Just take them and promise to survive. Be the Snitch who can survive anything. We will help to clear your name."

He rushes me out of the window, and I turn my head, peeking back in as the sun sets, "I will take them, but do not speak up for me. Trinity O'Salves will be dead; you know nothing about me. So, only Snitch will survive in your mouths."

Both of his warm hands caresses my cheeks.

My eyes widen as his lips press onto mine. His fingers move to the back of my head, going underneath the beanie, intertwining them in my hair. His tongue tracing my lips guiding them open. I let out a gasp as my body heated, the sensation overwhelming me. Pulling away, his eyes darken with dread, Ieronim's jaw tenses as he released my hair.

"I need you to live." Ieronim says, his voice shallow.

My voice catches half way up unable to say anything.

Henery rushed into the room, yelling out Ieronim's name. My face hot, I back away as Henry tells us, "I went to check things out. They are ransacking your apartment as we speak. This is your time. Be safe out there, I hope to see you someday."

Finally getting my voice out, I managed, "I hope so too."

Giving Ieronim a quick glance, I turn not to say another word. Running down the stairs, the cold air against my hot cheeks. Never have I had a reaction like that before to a simple kiss. Why in the Father Sun would he do something like that at a time like this? My chest rises and falls rapidly as I reach the ground.

At the edge of the alley peeking out. There stood a group of Luner's in front of the apartment building. They surround a couple who try to walk out and now being question. Tucking my hair within the beanie, going the opposite direction. I can't go from one alley to another without them wanting to stop me.

Vixen calling me, I quickly picked up. She says, "Every way out is blocked. Tell me you aren't here."

My feet stumble at her words. Getting back into a normal stride trying to stay calm. Eyeing those around me, no one's gaze lingered on me as if they recognize me.

Choosing my words carefully, never knowing who is around, "No, not yet. No worries, I will get there on time, but when I do, I can't talk for a while, okay?"

"I understand. Be safe, Trinity." Then she hung up.

My heart sunk as I saw a group of four Luner's on the other side of the road checking down alley ways. My back stiffening, I kept going. I can pass as a shorter guy, they didn't put my height out, not where I live, they only showed my face.

Where can I go, how the hell can I get out without being seen? Am I stuck here?

"Hey, have you seen Trinity O'Salves?" A man repeated himself.

Turning around, he stopped a group down the street from me. I kept walking a little faster than before.

Colliding with someone, I fell to the ground. The leather I was holding unfold showing the knives sheathed. Quickly folding the leather back, the sun now gone. Hoping that they didn't notice. "What is that you have there?" The man asks, dressed in the Hazard Department blue and gray uniform.

Getting up before answering, he got a glimpse of my face. Eyes wide, his hand slowly reaches for his shaft. Hazard Team is meant for smaller cases and potential zombies. Luner's reserved for more severe cases. Elizabeth must have spread some major lies to get this mobilized.

Before he disconnect his shaft, I push him back into the alley, ensuring no one sees. Grabbing his hand, the shaft fell out to the ground. As he pushes me away, he went for the weapon, and the moment his eyes left me, my leg shot up, connecting with his face. He fell hard on the ground, no longer moving.

"Shit, I am so sorry." I apologize. About to leave him it clicked. This is exactly what I need to be free. I turned around, "The Hazard Department will be empty. They probably disconnected my card, but yours….Sorry again."

His chest still moving showing he is alive. I took his ID card for temporary use.

Inside the building after hours, no one is guarding the front entrance. I didn't dare use the elevator. Running down the stairs all the way to G0. Sprinting down a hall not to my own area but to Randal's office, his door locked. I took a deep breath in. Twitching my head to the side, backing up, I had no time to think. Hitting my foot slightly above the doorknob a few times, I need in that room it is the only way I can get out. If anyone else were here they would have been alerted by the loud bangs. Finally, it broke open. Luckily, they didn't make these rooms out of iron doors, but normal wood.

My leg twinge in pain as I stepped on it. Ransacking his desk, I found an emergency number to get the hatch open.

Writing the number down leaving his office, I am going to make it.

I stop, a name that hadn't seen before. Elizabeth has an office right beside Randal's. Everything's telling me to leave, but a small voice beckoning me inside. Kicking her door in my leg screamed at me. She tricked me as a child. She try to blame me not following protocol right when my friends died. Elizabeth is pinning everything on me with lies. She has to have a reason, an agenda against me or even my family, but what?

Looking around for any answers, I gave myself only two minutes. If I didn't see anything, I would leave. Nothing sparked until I got to a drawer locked in the middle of her desk. Kicking at it until the thing bent, I shove my hand inside, pulling out a bunch of weird items. Among them are books and maps with points of posts outside the walls. The Wanderers weren't being suspicious for no reason; they are attacking people outside the walls. Ledgers with names on them, I can't get through all the papers. Taking my bag off, I shoved a few of her items inside.

On top of her desk lies a candle, recalling the top drawer had matches inside. Lighting the candle, the nice smell of outdoors whiff my nose. The pillar half way burned before I got in.

"They are so dangerous to keep burning without being watched." I say, knocking the candle over. "They can fall over at any moment."

Tossing papers of the people's names on top making sure the place burns. The flames rises in an instant, backing away slowly as they travel outside of the desk. Ensuring myself no evidence of what I took. No one will be working at this time anyways. Perhaps the building burning will give me extra time to escape without being followed.

Going down my hall, suddenly the lights turn off all at once. Darkness only lasts momentarily. Emergency lights turn on blinking red and white. Picking up my speed, my foot ached in pain running up my leg with each time I put weight onto it.

Elizabeth's voice came through the intercoms, "We know you are here, Trinity O'Salves. We deactivated all your numbers. You have nowhere to go. Turn yourself in, or we will kill you on sight. I see where you are, and you'll see me soon enough in your office."

She won't kill me on sight. Randal warned me she will torture me first. Flipping off the camera as I ran through them, I hope she saw that.

Running down my hall, the metal gate slams shut behind me. Jolting, peering behind me momentarily. I have been locked in again. Not like I am trying to get out. Getting into my office footsteps rumble. The second gate shuts. Bodies hit the gate shaking it in anger. Curses filled the air.

Smirking at their I'll timing I watch her.

Standing at the iron door, narrowing my eyes. Elizabeth stood at the very end, her face scrunched up. Pressing her hand on the keypad, the first gate opens, and she ran in front of the rest of her group. Before getting to the other gate, before any words were say between us, my smile turns into wicked grin. Water pours from the sprinklers as the fire must be ablaze now. Her face twists with pure rage as her eyes bulge.

Shutting the iron door silencing everything.

Taking a few steps back, trying not to pay attention to the shaking in my body. Unlocking the hatch, the green lights going red as it opens. My stomach curdles, fear bubbling up. This will be the last time I ever step foot here. Gripping the leather tight in my grasp, waiting for the hatch to completely open. Taking a shaft and extra darts, tucking them on my side. Not looking back. I left for good.

Chapter Ten

On the ground shivering from the long night. It's the first time I saw the sun rise from outside the walls. My legs burned in pain as I lean on a tree. My face feeling like it might freeze. They yelled for me. They screamed my name. It all went by so quickly.

By the river, I wash blood off the knife Ieronim gifted me. Layng the knife beside me, yanking the beanie off, the cold winter air freezing my head as it touches the sweat. Closing my eyes, I don't know who it was or where I was. I don't even remember getting it out of the leather it had been in.

An arm reached for me, pulling away they wouldn't let go. Closing my eyes tight as the memory fuzzily went through my mind. There were too many voices to tell if it was a man or woman. Spinning around, the grip firm and tight, and hearing a thud on the ground. Screams of agonizing pain filled the air. I think I cut their hand off, but I am not too sure. I let out a whine as the memories flash. Nothing but darkness in sight; all I can remember are the voices.

Sipping the water, it's too cold. My throat closes not wanting to accept it. A small bite of food to keep me going.

Looking at the papers and books I stole from Elizabeth, in my tired state managing to stretch a weary smile. I know where every Wanderer has districts, outposts for temporary stay, and every path Luner's take to get around secretly. It's all plain - pathed out for me. They are much more advanced than what we ever were taught. Putting my beanie back on rubbing my heavy eyes it's time to get further away.

*

"We have to check your bag before coming in." The man at the front gate tells me.

I ask, my voice airy, "Why, I have personal stuff inside."

He let out a uncaring laugh, eyeing the shaft, "We all carry personal stuff here. Not lucky to stay in one place to keep it in our home." Eyeing my shaft a second time and the wool jacket that's been keeping my body warm these past few days, he added, "We take payment to let you stay here. Judging by your look, you may got good things."

Shaking my head, my feet unsteady as I backed off leaving without a word, struggling to go further.

My hands burned pulling myself up on a rocky ledge. Wedging myself to get away from the cold air. *Zombies cannot climb. If you find yourself outside of the walls and without shelter, get high, preferably where you can only get to if you climb. Then you only need to worry about Wanderers.* Eyes getting heavy, warmth from Ieronim's wool jacket, my eyes shut without a second thought.

Keeping my distance I didn't make a sound as zombies pass me. They seem to not notice me if I stay more than ten feet away. As long as I don't run into any hordes everything should be good.

Rummaging in my bag pulling out a few notes, hoping I won't be laugh at. Shaking, I showed my notes at the front gate of another district. The people there took half the money that was in my hands and didn't even ask about checking my bag. Feeling like I am about to collapse, I couldn't enjoy the sight. This is a town of its own, not nearly as big as any city but impressive in its own right.

People cheer as zombies were in a ring. Someone in the middle has a knife fighting them off. Passing the cheering crowd, the smell of warm bread fills my nose. Inside the bakery, buying a piece of bread, getting notes and coins back I took a seat shoving them in my pocket. I don't truly understand the currency and it isn't like I can just ask.

The lady brought me my bread and a hot cup of something I didn't order. She looked at me for a moment as I pointed at the drink confused.

She says, "It looks like you need it."

Her hair is up in a messy bun, gray coming in from the top and the back still a dark rich brown. Her eyes sag, tired from this lifestyle. My smile wobble from the week of walking, having only a few hours of sleep altogether. Needing to get furthest away as possible from Alpha City.

Niel mentioned where he was is too far for Luner's to attack. Meaning further I get less likely they would come to find me.

I mutter, "Thank you…um, is there a place where someone can sleep…safely?"

She sat at the table, tossing her rag on top asking, "Well, it depends what type of person you are. How did you get that thing? I've only seen a few, and normally they aren't carried by good people."

I patted the shaft, only using it a handful of times when zombies got too close. I say, unable to keep my eyes completely open, "I took it from them. They attacked and chased me."

She leaned in, grabbing the rag, "Have you killed someone that isn't a zombie?"

My eyes became heavier, only seeing a sliver, "I have notes to pay with. I am not asking for handouts."

I can see her judgment through the haze of my stare, "So that means you have killed someone."

I drank the hot tea that she was so kind to give me, warming my insides, "yeah," my voice just above a whisper, "My best friends, one that turned, the other bit by her. I had to kill both. And I don't know who but..." The memory of the Wanderer attacking my teammates flash, "They attacked someone I knew. I was trying to protect him and killed one." I tapped the shaft, "One of them... maybe not killed but it was so dark I think I cut their arm off..."

Her eyes soften, "All in self - defense it sounds like."

The bread melts in my mouth as I took a bite, swallowing before speaking, "Some could argue I am a murderer."

"You are the kindest murderer I've met. You can stay upstairs with us. Women only so you will be safe."

Pulling out notes from my pocket she only took a few, handing the rest back, "You are not from around here. Others would take advantage of you and take all the money you have. Come, I will teach you what things are supposed to cost; what each note and coins represent. Where you from anyway?"

Too tired to lie, or something deep inside telling me lying would get me nowhere. I told the truth, "I am from within a city. They were going to kill me, so I ran away. I am Snitch by the way."

"Nice to meet you, Snitch."

*

Winter became spring, and with each passing day, I learned much about the world beyond the walls. What the currency is worth. They try to remember the fragments of life before the first wave. Although a lot of the information has been missing, the city lied about much of it, making up their own truths.

Throughout the winter, a constant flow of people came in and out. My heart quickened with each dirty face and desolate soul. Working with the mistress who had took me in and taught me, I got to talk to many who came into her bakery. I got to learn Luner's are getting closer to this place. Showing Wanderers no mercy driving them further from the cities, killing them, and kidnapping who aren't fast enough.

In the quiet hours of night, I pored over the stolen materials from Elizabeth. Trying to find the path they are taking, if they are going to come here, or when they will make it. I read by candlelight, the gentle flow flickering, as electricity is cut off after sunset.

Alarms shatter the serenity. Hastily dressing in Ieronim's clothes, I ran out of my bedroom I been lucky enough to have it all to myself since I work for the Mistress.

Alarms echoes through the air. The other girls stumble out of their rooms, confusion mirroring my own, while the Mistress raced up the stairs.

"Get your belongings and run as fast as you can." Mistress yells passing me, fear popping out of her veins, "Luners are here."

Leaning against the wall for support, my legs felt like led. They shouldn't have made it here by now. Spring has just graced us with winter still on our necks. The sounds of gunfire erupt from all directions.

Over fifteen of us got downstairs with our things including the Mistress. Shots came from outside the door. Slowly I sunk into the group until I was last. Both crescent moon knives gripped tightly in my hands, I crept to the stairs, my nostrils flaring.

The door splintered; squeals came from the girls. Already halfway up the stairs adrenaline coursing through me. Seeing the familiar Hazard Prevention uniforms as they came through the broken door. The Mistress and a few girls charge the three men, a brave and desperate attempt to save themselves.

Helplessness seizes me. Cursing under my breath knowing I can't help. Getting to the last step, gunshots fired, screams of agony went silent in an instant. Reaching my room, hastily locking it and shoving the unused dresser in front of it. My breaths shook knowing none of them are left. *I am sorry* Mistress but even if I was there the same fate would been bestowed on me.

As I step out of the window, gunshots went through the wall. My grip slip from the windowsill before getting my footing. Losing myself on the slippery roof, the knives came out of my hand falling to the ground. Right behind them tumbling with a hard thud. Wheezing on the ground, thankful in the fact my bag softened the fall. Struggling to my feet, reaching for my knives, commands from Luners surrounds me.

Going to peek beyond the building a hand reaches out grabbing my bag, pulling me down. Reacting swiftly, I swung my knife mid - fall, stopping just short of harm. Two men, armed with guns, loom over me. Behind them, a cluster of frightened children seeking refuge from the nightmare unfolding.

"You know how to use one?" One of the men ask, handing me a gun.

My voice tremble as I reply, "A shaft, yes. This can't be much different."

Coming from behind a woman with a slight limp, her face stained with blood, cradling a child in her arms. They are desperately trying to save as many kids as possible.

She stare not caring by my presence, "I made an exit, we can get out from here."

"We can't get this many kids north." The man skinnier than the other says with a underlying woe.

My ears perk hearing them mention north, "What's north?" I ask.

The man still holding my bag replies, his voice filled with hope, "It's the strongest district in a remote area. The issue is there's too many zombies out there, and you need to know someone to get in."

"Unless you have kids." The woman added, passing the young child to an older kid. "They take anyone with kids."

The less joyful man corrects her. "They take kids. They can choose to leave us dry."

"Let's do this." I say, my voice still shaky, "I know someone who's there. We can get in as long as someone from within listens to us."

The trio exchanged weary glances, and the decision was made.

Keeping all our heads down and staying within the shadows. One skinnier man, seem to be about my age, blacken hair. He went out first with over half the kids behind him. The woman her hair cut to her shoulders, went in the middle, and the remaining children following. With the quickness of it all, I don't even know the names of these people.

Gunshots rang above us. My body tumbles to the ground as the man who's been behind us all. The one who grab my bag from the start cover me as bullets buzzed by. His body larger than mine kept me safe. When the gunshots stop I turned to fire back, but he stop me.

His voice somber, "Go now. If I get out, I know where to follow."

My eyes widen, I protest, "No, they need you to protect the kids. Let me hold them off."

He push me back, his face wrenching, "You know someone within. They need you more than me to get in." He shouts, "Grab her and leave!"

Two hands tug my bag, dragging me on the ground. My eyes filling with tears as more shots fire. My chest sinks deep inside as his body moved out of sight.

Stowing my knives to my hips, leathers I have that are perfectly shaped for these unique blades. My knuckles whitening from my grip on the gun. Screams filled the air, my heart ached for those left behind.

"Trinity! Call Elizabeth, we had eyes on Trinity!"

"Where did she go?"

"I don't know. Someone shot at me, and I lost sight."

Choking on my breath, not due to the chill in the air, but the realization they are here hunting me. Why would they still be looking for me? They could had told the people inside the city I was dead.

Keeping in the back of the group, we move along a small goat trail. The children whimper for their lost parents. Dragging my feet, a twig broke. Looking out in the woods, darkness is all that welcomes us. Anyone or anything that made the sound is covered.

Multiple kids scream, animals flew to the sky with the disturbance of peace. Spinning on my heel, a Hazard Prevention member held a child by gun point. The other two draw their guns, tension rising as the child hung in a chokehold.

"Just give us Trinity, and all of you will be free." Panic fills his voice the realization I am no longer standing there, "Where did she go?"

"She was just there." The woman stammered.

As everyone has their guns drawn, I became a ghost, lurking in the darkness. The moonless night shrouds me, rendering me invisible. Mother Earth cloaks me in her bear forest helping me move without a twig braking. My eyes narrows as the shaft pointing at his head. Inhaling deeply, my fingers posed on the trigger, hesitating, unable to shoot.

He's moving around too much. The child gasping for air in his grip, I can't get a clear shot. Securing the shaft back to my side, my fingers tighten around my knife.

Sneaking behind him, knife poised around his neck, I say, "If they find you alive, tell Elizabeth I am nothing like my parents. I am a murderer, where as they were trying to fix the world. I was too young to understand then, but I do now."

My hand glides smoothly, the knife cutting across butter. Crimson blood spilled out as the girl fell out of his arms. The rest fell into silence. Scooping her up, I carried her not meeting their gazes. I had no other choice. I am truly a murderer now.

The sun nears the horizon, and we found a spot for the kids to rest a few hours before continuing. The three of us are unable to sleep, our eyes fixed on where we once were, hoping that guy makes it.

The woman says, "So, Trinity is your name. Why do they want you?"

I blinked slowly. I was hoping they weren't going to ask. Letting out a sigh, I reply, "It's Snitch now. I knew of this world and knew of Second Life's. Knowledge I wasn't supposed to have threatened them, so they are hunting me down like the rest of you."

"Wait, you guys didn't know about Second Life's?" She ask, and I shook my head in response, "Shit…Well, thanks for saving the kids with us."

Flashing my teeth, saying, "Can't let kids die…They haven't done anything wrong to deserve a fate like that."

After a few hours of silence, she woke the kids up to keep moving. The spring warmth help keep us moving during the day.

As we took another brake, the sun no longer giving light, they made a fire as I kept watch. Rummaging came from the darkness. I point my shaft in the direction. Not wanting to attract anything with the boom of the gun.

Lowering my weapon almost smiling to see the guy we left behind limping out, "You made it, Tobias." I say with glee.

Winking, not questioning how I know his name, he replies, "I sure as hell did, and saw that body you guys left behind."

Sophie ran out giving him a hug, while Brent patted his head. My heart heavies at his words. A part of me wish the Luner made it, or was he Hazard prevention? Either way he was only following orders. Rubbing my head, a dreadful feeling consumes me within not knowing how long we would be walking as a zombie, restless.

My legs burn, needles piercing every part, wanting me to collapse. In overdrive mode just wanting to get to the end. These past few days have been extra hard. Out of the sixteen little kids we got out, five of them died. The girl I saved died in her sleep; he must have broken something in her neck because her face and lips were blue when we tried to wake her. Exhaustion killed three, we assume, and by the looks of it, one had internal bleeding we didn't know about. Only eleven are left with us four adults. I tilt my head to Tobias, noticing his foot is swollen the size of a cantaloupe.

I ask, blatantly gawking at his swollen ankle, "How many more days?"

Tobias replies, "At this rate, maybe tomorrow evening or the next day."

Sophie chimed in, "I think it's best we show up when the sun is out."

I mutter, "Does he even have that long?"

Tobias, whom I learned is in his mid-thirties, had lost his wife and kid a few months back due to birthing complications. He gave me that half - filled smile, trying to make it look like he is okay, but I can read right through it.

As we got closer to our destination, attempting to climb high on the mountain edge. Below us zombies wander, unaware of our presence. The edge is barely large enough for adults to pass. Our fronts press to the side of the ledge, the kids, surprisingly accustomed to this life, keep quiet. I know at any of their ages, I would been bawling my eyes out, scared out of my wits.

Tobias leg, bigger than the day before, couldn't stay on the ledge well. His leg slipped about to fall I didn't have time to think. I shoot my arm out grabbing onto Tobias. My body hating me for the overexertion, my arm tugging as I help him regain his footing.

"You okay?" I ask breathlessly.

His face pale, and I held back my expression. Sweat beaded down his head nodding in response.

Getting to a safer spot, we sat to rest for the night. Raking my hands through my hair, there's a bit of the sun left in the sky. I sat near the ledge, looking down on a valley below stood a building and zombies surrounding it. My nostrils flared, my mind trying to wrap around how we will get through that.

"We just have to get to that building." Tobias say, breathing harder than normal.

I didn't look at him. "I never seen that many before."

He patted my shoulder, "We got this far. You guys can make it."

Arching my brow, I ask, "What do you mean, you guys?"

His lips thinned as he pulled up his pants leg. My breath taken away as his ankle is now purple, and he says, "I will get them all away as you get the kids to safety."

Tilting my head up looking him in his eyes, he patted my hand trying to calm me. He looked down onto the valley his mind set.

I barked frustrated that he's going to do something so stupid. "You are not going to risk yourself."

A sad smile reach his eyes, "My wife is waiting for me with our baby girl."

My throat bobs, "She would want to see you live."

Propping his leg further out, he says, "They won't take me anyways. As soon as they see this, I will be turned away." He patted my head, grunting as he stood, "But you guys…They will take you all. Saving fourteen and losing my life is well worth it. Because you all will live long lives and hopefully have kids too, meaning I've saved even more lives than what I see now. It's worth it."

He walked off ending the conversation. He smile as some of the kids tug at him for attention. People like that should live long lives, not someone like me.

He slept with the kids all around him; he's a natural - born dad. Brent and Sophie is still awake talking around the fire. I haven't moved out of my spot since we got here. A light in the middle of the building glowed. A beacon you can't see until you go round the mountain. Standing, I held both knives in my hands with the moon in the sky matches my blades.

Tobias, you *deserve* life more than me. Descending the mountain edge, trying to be quiet as my front leg slides out, my elbow behind, slowing my speed. Getting to the bottom, trees cover the moonlight, blanketing the darkness of night. The clicking of the jaws sound to the right of me. Gasping, I swung, barely getting the skull. Falling to the ground with the zombie, my hands shook. Get ahold of yourself; they need you.

Following the beckoning light, the clicking of zombies follow me. Swinging my arm out as one got too close striking it down. Picking up my speed, with each kill, until I got to a full - on sprint.

Over halfway to the building, all the air knocked out of me as a zombie pounce. My eyes bulge as it pushed against me. No, I've gotten too far. Pushing back, getting my arm over my head, swinging down. Keeping my mouth shut, black blood spills on me. The light on the building went black as I lay there. Zombies all around as the moon gave little light.

Scurrying to my feet, panic wells as I hardly can see anything in front of me. I'm going to save them. Swinging at every moment, my hand hitting I don't know what. Tripping over manmade objects, a smile pulls on my lips as my hand hit the doorhandle. This close, I can see many lights glowing from inside.

As I pulled, every light went black. Heat fell over my body, my legs dropping to the ground, my hand still gripping the handle. No. No. This isn't right. It is all dark.

I beg, "Please…There is eleven kids and an adult who is hurt they need your help." The zombies lost me for a moment as I stood on the steps. My voice beckoning them to me. "Please, I know you are in there. Someone!" Putting my bag on the ground, I stood with an uneasy stance, "Don't let me die like this!" I shout.

A light turns on above my head showing the zombie that's about to pounce. They know I am here. Why are they not letting me in? In a quick motion killing the zombie. Right behind it, another came. Then after another. Four down, I gulp my body still wanting to give out, but my mind not allowing it to.

"We need you, please!" I shout even louder than before. "I know you can hear me."

Two came at me at once. Swinging at both with the blades, a third came at me as I dislodged my knives from the skulls. Kicking the third making it fall off the stairs.

My back pinned to the door, I let out a wheezing squeal, "Niel, I know Niel, tell him Snitch is here!"

I was met with nothing as tears stream down my face blurring my vision. Another three lay in front of me. Kicking them off, they rolled down the steps. My knees buckled, begging me to stop.

"I am Snitch. Also known as Trinity. Tell Niel, he's a

Second Life. I am here, ah!"

Slicing the throat of one, it didn't stop. Stumbling back into another, I let out a whine as the black blood oozed out.

Picking the bag up, swinging it knocking them back, tripping over their own kind that were slayed. My body stumbled forward losing strength with every move.

The lights from inside turned on. The sound of the door unlocking, I didn't hesitate pushing my way through.

Falling inside as there was no resistance, I lay on the ground. Met with a gun pointed at me. I remain motionless.

"How do you know his name?" My face pointed to the ground, unable to see who spoke. They pressed the gun to my head, "Speak now."

Panicked, I reply, "We are childhood friends. He told me he's going north. Please tell me this is where he is."

"Do not move."

I followed his orders, not daring to fight back. Not like I could even if I wanted. We have been walking for over a week now, only getting maybe half an hour of sleep - an hour if I was lucky - every night.

My body didn't care if I was on the cold, hard ground; it was happy knowing it's indoors once again. Unable to hear the groans and clicks of zombies outside my breathing eased. The guy nudge his gun in the back of my head from time to time, reminding me of the position I am in. I've already let go of both of the knives, inches away from my grip.

Lavender says on the edge of surprise and confusion, "Oh wow, it is you."

Niel says, his voice almost the guy I once knew, "Infinity."

As they acknowledge me, the guy took the gun away from my head. Reaching out to help, I took his hand, understanding he is just trying to keep safe in this world.

I say, skipping formality, "Theres eleven kids and three adults with me. One has a hurt leg and needs help. Please, we need to go now."

Lavender eyed Niel as she communicated in their language. His eye lids lower, replying in the language no human can understand. A strain in my heart being reminded he isn't human.

"Where are they?" Lavender ask, "If they aren't far, we can help."

I reply, "Just on the edge of the clearing up the mountain ledge."

With these Second Life's presence, no zombies came close. Niel didn't say anything to me. I try to hold back my shivers from his clicks as he spoke to Lavender.

Getting up the mountain, I have them stay back. Sophie on watch, ready to fight as she hears me coming up. Both my hands up, only holding one knife just in case a zombie did attack on our way.

Sophie face pales seeing the black blood covering me, questioning, "Where the hell did you go?"

I closed the distance, "Making sure you guys got to the district safely. Get them all up its time to go."

That's when Niel, Lavender, and the guy who stuck the gun to my head came out from the shadows of the night, daylight threatening to break through.

With a smile that didn't reach my eyes, "I told you I knew someone."

Her smile, on the other hand, reached her eyes. Tearing up overjoyed, knowing they are going to be safe.

Everyone is on edge as we walk beside the zombies in the valley. Some of the older kids pretend to push one another out of the group, as zombies pass us.

Sophie snapped at them, "Stop that shit."

Her and Brent carried Tobias since there were no more worries about safety. His face paler than before I left. I know he wouldn't had made it through the night.

Lavender move forward to the front of the group. Some younger kids yip, not understanding what she is yet. I roll my eyes underneath my lids, knowing Niel sent her off so we could be alone.

I say with a generic tone, "Thanks for the help."

His body rubs against mine, his skin cool to the touch that sent shivers down my spine.

His gaze descend upon me. His tan skin couldn't hide the undertones of gray.

His lips parted, words flowing out slower than he used to. "What happened?"

Sucking on my teeth, I released a heavy sigh, "Second Life, I knew more than I should, and that was a threat to the City. Every willing body was out to turn me into the Luners."

His eyes sag, a subtle plea as he says the familiar name. "Infinity…"

I flash a smile, dragging my foot a step behind, where he could no longer look at me. "If I had been caught, they would have found the beautiful photos of your parents and you. Then Gabe and Sandra would be arrested for treason as well." His body moves about to turn. I demand, "Don't look at me. You were close to them…" Trying desperately to mask the pain in my voice, "All of you kept secrets from me in a life I knew nothing about. If I was involved maybe I wouldn't had said anything. Maybe then my family would still be alive."

Everything could had been different if I just knew. Stepping forward wrapping my fist around his shirt pulling him down a rage bubbles inside of my chest. He doesn't resist, allowing me to do what I wish. Both knowing how much stronger he is as this creature.

"You all smiled at me, pretending as if nothing had happened. Like open books, I thought I knew every page. Sandra, Gabe, and you Second Life." Pushing him away he didn't stumble back, "I found your books by the way. Looks like your parents hid it before giving me your apartment." His eyes widen, "Do you have them?"

My nostrils flare, after all I said, that's what he asks. Really I shouldn't be surprised. My jaw tensed, I swung my bag to the side, thrusting the books and photo album in his chest.

He clutch them as if I might take them back.

Leaning in, grinding my teeth, keeping my voice low. "The work is impressive, but the tests are too small." I poked the books, trying to keep my control, "You are all deluded, thinking everyone would willingly become

Second Life's like you. Activating that part of the brain before death…Well you wrote down everything that can go wrong already. The worst is that they all can become zombies, not Second Life's, not make them stronger. Only weaker, rapid degenerative, anger, self-mutilation, too many things can go wrong."

The only thing that could go right, what my parents were trying to do, wasn't to cause a second wave. "And if it does go right…You guys are what like immortals?"

His throat bobbed, struggling to respond, "It isn't for everyone, only blood that can accept the compound." He inhaled deeply with a long pause before continuing, "Before I tell you more, I need to talk to someone else. Let him know you brought this to me. I need approval before revealing anything. When I get the okay you will know it all. No more secrets."

His speech is slower than how Niel spoke over three years ago. Always reminding me that he isn't my childhood best friend.

I waved my hand leaving him behind, "Don't worry about it. I'll never expect you to be completely open with me, Second Life."

Niel reached out, tugging my bag back, calling out a name he doesn't have the right to say. Half - turning, slipping the knife out of my leather holder, pressing the dull side against him.

As Niel pull his hand back and leaned into the blade. I pause baffled he didn't step back. Not fearing that with a flick of my wrist I can cut him.

I hiss, holding back any sadness I may feel, "Snitch is my name, and stop fucking calling me that other name, Second Life. I know everything I need from those books.

As your parents would say, 'Pray for the best.' Good luck for everyone's sake I hope it works. If not, you are sending them to a painful death sentence."

Putting the blade back into its leather, I left Niel in the rear joining Tobias, Sophie, and Brent. Passing Lavender as she went back to Niel's side.

Inside the building, we follow shoulder to shoulder, on the first floor a door opened to steep stairs. Tobias is going to have trouble getting up these.

The man in front of us pressed his hand on the wall where a door opens hidden in the stairs. Steps mirroring in steepness but these are going down. The man went down, followed by Brent, Tobias, and Sophie, the kids follow, and I waited to be last in my group. Lavender, and Niel behind me.

Lavender remarked, "This isn't the normal entrance. Others will teach you all easier ways to go in and out."

The length felt three times deeper than where I worked on level G0 in the Hazard Department. The air grew heavier, my heart rate rises as we are stuck in a narrow path. Light beams in as the man opens another door. Greeting us is a large hall covered in gray walls.

People are walking around living normal lives down here. Dim lights giving barely enough light in the halls. Curiously looking into rooms that were open, welcoming light shines out. Nods and smiles meet us on our journey down here.

Lavender says, "Okay kids, over here. You are going to wait for nurses to check all of you out. While you wait enjoy the toys and snacks."

To our right, a brightly colored playroom, filled with younger kids playing. The older ones, casting hesitant glances towards Sophie, who only needed to give them a soft grin, and they ran in drawn to the table with food and drinks. The next stop is a white room with nurses already positioned waiting for the three of us.

Lavender says pointing with her hand, "They are just going to check you three. To treat any medical needs, and make sure no one is bringing in diseases."

Each nurse approach us, one assigned to me stating, "You can strip behind the curtain so I can check your body…What is your name?"

"Snitch," I reply.

She began writing then paused. Looking up from her bangs then eyeing Niel who hovers in the corner.

Annoyed he is who she looks at for confirmation on my name. Grinding my teeth I demand, "Write 'Snitch'." Dropping my bag starting to undue my clothes, "I'm not shy."

Each layer of nasty clothes drops in a thud heavier than they ever should. Seeing myself in a full - size mirror for the first time since I left Alpha City my throat closed.

In the mirror, I catch a glimpse of Niel. His hand covering his mouth, his longer hair falling in his eyes hiding his gaze. Lavender's brows furrow seeing how my ribs protrude out, my knees, elbows, and feet covered in cuts and bruising.

Sophie didn't miss a beat, shedding her clothes out in the open saying, "We are all adults here. We shouldn't be ashamed of what Mother Nature did to us." She eyed me, "Some people had a harder time surviving than others."

She wasn't discrediting me, but a way of lifting me up. She gave me a wink. Her body is bruised, but the weight she lost isn't nearly as close as mine. As she's probably used to this style of living, it's all new to me. Muscles on her body, where my body ate at any muscles I once had.

I can't believe I kept going, seeing I am only flesh and bones now. Possibly I didn't look this bad when we first started our journey here. I wouldn't know because the mirrors in the Mistress's home were enough just to look at our faces dingy in color. Lifting my arms, the nurse checked my body. I stare through the mirror at Niel's sharp gaze. His hand never lowering from his mouth.

Lavender moved about the room, collecting our clothes. "Let me get these washed for you. They will be returned later tonight to your rooms." She adds, "We have spares we will give to you four."

I reply, as I now sat on an examination bed, "I have extras in my bag that are clean."

"Oh. Um…" She looked back at Niel clicking, then she says, "I am sorry, but all clothes need to be washed in case anything is on them."

I inhaled sharply, as she took the clothes out of my bag, keeping them neat.

Niel came forward pulling at the folded clothes messing them up, "Men's?" he questions.

Lifting my head, only in my bra and underwear, I assert, "I can wear whatever I want."

Niel emits a deep groan knowing they are not mine, protesting, "We can get you women's. Give these to…"

This Second Life really thinks he's going to have say in what I wear? I spat out, "Don't you dare give my clothes to someone else. These were a gift to me."

Lavender quickly chimed in, "Everything you own will come back to you, and I will even bring some extra women's clothes."

Her words seem more like a peace offering between Niel and I to release the tension rising in the room. Niel click uncontrollably, slightly coughing to stop himself. Brushing his hair back, his eyes wide, a palpable pain washing over him. A familiar expression, one I wore when I discovered the truth about his past.

Realizing that the person before you isn't who you once remember. The difference between him and I, I never hid the truth.

With a swift pull of the door, Niel left the room. Lavender quickly running behind with the pile of clothes. The room fell into a moment of silence, the nurses doing their thing without talking.

Tobias broke the silence, "Don't tell me that's the people you know that got us in here?"

My body sank into the bed I was guided to, feeling the nurse's pressure on my stomach, I reply, "Yup, that guy use to be my best friend."

Tobias groaned as the nurse applied ice on his swollen ankle, "What happened to the two of you?"

My lips tightened as I met his gaze, "Too many secrets…I feel I don't even know who he is anymore."

Extending his hand, I met him with mine, our palms meeting as he gently squeezed, "You just need to talk to him. It looks like he wants to be close again."

Letting out a hmmm, I withdrew my hand. There is a wedge between us now, not only with me, but Niel is distant. I have no clue what Tobias just saw, but from my eyes he does not want to be close.

After the physical and some blood taken for testing, we were taken to our rooms for a two - week quarantine. Tobias on the other hand has to stay behind to go into surgery for his ankle. I can't believe Wanderers have the resources to do a surgery like that to save his leg. Though I am beyond happy for it.

Dropping the empty bag to the ground, the room is only a little wider than the door. Long and narrow bed in the corner, enough just to fit one person. On the same wall as the bed is a narrow but taller dresser. At the headboard, covering the rest of the narrow wall stand an end table. Collapsing on the bed, fatigue from the little over week - long hike for our lives.

*

Standing there is the person who woke me up from my sleep. Lavender held a bag filled with clothes and a tray of food. Drowsy, I look at her my hand loosening its grip from my knife I took from the end table.

With a warm smile, she ask, "Do you mind if I come in?"

Stepping aside to let her in, I shut the door. Her eyes linger on the knife in my hand.

Lavender reassured, "No one will hurt you here."

I respond with a tired laugh, "No one was supposed to hurt me inside the City either."

Sitting the food on the end table, Lavender took the liberty of putting my clothes in the dresser. I noted silently pieces Ieronim gave to me; making sure Niel didn't have his way taking them. If he did I can't promise I wouldn't try to fight him. Scratching the back of my head, I'm not even sure why I am so attached to these clothes. Maybe because it's my last remembrance of my life before now?

Picking at the small portion of food, it's the most I've gotten for a meal since leaving the city. Lavender pulls some feminine clothes out of the bag. They are almost new looking, the lace completely in tack, and a few slips to sleep in.

"Niel was adamant in getting you more clothes." She mention, " He helped pick them out."

I raised a brow, muttering to myself, "Of course, the Second Life did. It's just memories." That last part was for myself.

Shutting the drawer, Lavender turn, addressing me by his name "Um, Infinity,"

Glaring up, I stopped her, "My name is Snitch."

"Oh, Snitch. Yeah, I'm so used to Niel calling you Infinity." She admitted. Sitting at the end of the bed, Lavender continue, "Do you have an issue with our kind?"

Midway through raising a fork to my mouth, I pause. My eyes soften as I turn my body to face her, "This has nothing to do with what you guys became. I am sorry if that is what it looks like. I have nothing against you, Lavender. I am grateful honestly you didn't let um…whatever her name was attack me."

Her expression looks doubtful as she cocks her head to the side, "Then why do you keep calling him Second Life?"

My shoulder drop, head lowering as I say, "He isn't the Niel I once knew, so I call him that, since I know it hurts him. I know it's stupid ,but can you understand?"

Is it petty, childish, stupid, yes to all. I can't help it. I've been mourning his death for three years before I knew he was alive.

She nods, her expression solemn, "I was with my brother when I turned. Even though I was speaking, he couldn't accept me and stabbed me in the gut. By the way, we still feel pain. It hurt like hell, pardon my language."

Waving my hand, "Don't be polite with me, I cuss."

Lavender continue, "He left me there bleeding, calling me a monster. If he ever saw me again, he would stab my brain next time. Never once did I think my brother would do that to me, so yeah, I felt betrayed, like I didn't know him.

"Unlike zombies, luckily we heal. Fortunately, my teacher found me and taught me what we are. Then he found Niel on the pile of rotten bodies, moaning just waking up with a nasty gouge in his head." Her words wrap around my heart squeezing it. I am the reason he has the scar on his head. I almost killed Niel, not someone who would turn to a zombie, but I almost killed my best friend.

Lavender patted my leg seeing the remorse I feel, "Niel never was mad at you for what you did. All these years, he always talked about you. I am a little envious honestly.

"We were lucky to find him. After he became accustomed to this new life, he went right to work to finish what he did in his first life. He's remarkable, his mind, that body," Her lips moved as she lick the inside of them, I raised a brow at her reaction, "All of him drives so many insane, wanting him. Yet, he'll hardly ever give anyone the time of day.

"He brought us into the light, living with humans again as we did in our first lives. He's talked about you so much I feel like I know you personally. Niel done all this to see you someday." Her cool hand pulled away from my leg, "Do you have any questions for me? Niel said how you like talking."

I flash my teeth, "That was the person I once was…but…I am curious. Why are you guys so cool?"

Lavender looked down at her hand, "Our hearts beat slowly, and our body temperatures are lower than that of a humans. Neat, honestly. I don't get hot or cold easily anymore. We can withstand extreme temperatures."

Lavender leaned in closer, she smile like a highschooler about to gossip, "So, were those your boyfriend's clothes? You know, girl to girl?"

Tilting my head to the side, I scoff. I am smarter than that to fall for façade of casual girl talk. I reply, "Someone I know who's been by my side when I felt lost after all my friends died." What should have been a statement came out almost like I question, remembering the connection of Ieronim's lips on mine, "A friend."

Her lips pucker, holding back a smile before shooting up, "I never seen Niel get so jealous before. Honestly, I am envious, how you are always in his mind. Anyway, if you walk all the way to the end of the hall, there are shared bathrooms." She pulled out a bar of soap and shoes with straps on top, "Wear these in the showers. We try to keep it clean, but sometimes people just don't care, so it's better just to keep these on. I suggest to wash up before sleeping anymore."

Lavender personally delivered every meal for the past few days. During dinner, she always wants to sit down and have 'Girl talk.' I haven't found it in myself to ask her about her age when she changed to a Second Life. Perhaps she didn't get to talk to many girls being a Wanderer.

A heavy knock on the door jolts me awake. Glancing at the clock above the door, I've slept through breakfast. Getting out of bed Lavender must be worried since I didn't answer before.

"Sorry Lavender, guess my body needed more…" I started to say as I opened the door, only to be met my Niel instead, "Oh, it's you."

Niel's shirt hung haphazardly, as if he didn't have time or inclination to put it on, "You skip breakfast."

A part of his stomach shows, remembering how he once walked around my apartment without a shirt, I averted my gaze.

I let out a "hmm" as I took the tray, "I needed more sleep, Second Life."

He isn't my Niel, I need to remember that.

He push his way into my room stopping a few steps in scanning as if he's searching for something. Stepping into the bed I sat down, placing the tray on the end table beside my knife.

He stood there observing me as I eat, without asking, he picked up the knife, holding it firmly in his hand.

"Who gave to you?" He ask, his speech still slow.

I reply, not looking at him, "The same person who gave me the clothes."

Niel grumbled then pointed at the shaft and darts, "These too?"

I shook my head still avoiding eye contact, "I stole them."

Putting the knife down, he sat on the bed at the very end, maintaining a distance, much like Lavender does. I am curious if that is for respect or if they can't stay too close to humans due to hunger. I don't think I'll ever be able to ask just in case it's the latter.

Niel took the empty plate, his thumb rubbing the edge of it. Niel's dark blue eyes looking up from beneath his hair.

Pretending like I didn't see his gaze, I lean on the bed watching the clock.

"Don't skip meals, you need to gain strength." Niel slowly stated, "I've missed you, Infinity."

My eyes shot to him, glaring at his continuous use of that name. "I miss my friends too. I lost them almost four years ago.

Had to kill two of them, one looked exactly like you, Second Life."

I know these words hurt him, it hurts me too, but I never can keep them down. Niel did die that day, the one who never kept secrets from me, made me smile despite hating myself for snitching on my family. This new person isn't my Niel.

Niel put the plate on the bed, leaning forward. I press into the headboard, his hands squeezing too tight on my arms pinning them down. His jaw chatters, and fear washes over me, letting out a squeal as I turn my head. He's going to bite me like in the nightmare. To get his revenge of what I did to him.

Niel leaned closer, his skin radiating a coolness caught between life and death.

Releasing my arms, both hands cuffing my cheeks, he beg, "I *am* Niel. Fuck, Infinity, see me."

Keeping my eyes closed, desperately keeping my voice steady, "I stabbed him in the head. It's been almost four years since he died. Four years of drinking and numbing it all with Lily.

"You can't just come into my life, not after knowing that you *knew* everything. You continued my parents' work. You lived a life I knew nothing about, lavish, filled with money from who the fuck knows where. I thought I loved you, but I couldn't love someone who has so many secrets. My friend, Niel, would never kept secrets like that."

Opening my eyes to see his lips are in thin lines, two lines between his brows, not of anger but a pain I can't explain. He didn't let go of my face still, cupped between his hands.

Without a word he leans in, his lips on mine stealing a kiss. They are soft, just like how I always imagined late at night as I was alone in my room - yet not warm like others I've tasted. Moving with him, a heat rising as he pressed deeper. Taking more of me, his tongue slips inside wrapping around my own. Pulling away gasping for air he came for more. His teeth gently bit down on my bottom lip.

He pause braking the kiss, pushing my hair back roughly with both hands. Gulping holding himself back from doing more. "I didn't come back to protect you. Infinity…" He swallowed hard, "I love you, and I know you still love me."

Breathing slowly, masking all the feelings pushing to the surface.

He *isn't* my Niel.

Calmly, I state, "I loved the Niel I thought I knew, not the one standing in front of me."

His lips parted then closed as if he wants to say something. His head facing the floor, it finally came out. "In a few days, I'll see you. I will take you to him, and any questions we will answer. Bye Infinity."

As he shut the door behind him, I collapse. On my side, I touch my lips with just my fingertips.

Muttering to myself, "He isn't Niel. Not the one I knew."

Tears fell to the side of my face. He isn't Niel so why did his kiss feel that good?

*

The sun kisses my face aiding the early harvest of crops. Wearing slightly oversize shorts with rope tied around my waist to keep them from falling. I had a belt, but someone took it claiming they deserved more. Some of the kids are too trusting, letting it slip that I lived inside a city my whole life. They didn't know better so I can't get mad at them, but it is making my life here a little bit difficult.

As I go to pick up the basket filled with crops, the bottom broke. Everything tumbling on the ground. I let out a sigh rubbing the back of my neck. In front of me, a group laughs as they pick up their perfectly fine baskets, one of them is who took my belt.

Flashing my teeth, I say with a joyful tone, "Looks like I picked more crops than any of you, judging how easily my basket broke. Maybe next time you can pick up the slack where this doesn't happen."

Their snickers came to a halt, leaving me behind. I flip the basket to see if I can fix it. There's a perfect cut to cause it to split. Of course, one of them did this, I'm not surprise.

Rushing into the cafeteria after messily fixing the bag to receive an earful of how I need to be more careful. Once again, the cook brought up how this isn't Alpha City. I didn't bother arguing, knowing he never listens to a word I say, nor do I want to risk him skimming more food from me than he already does.

Sitting with Tobias and Sophie, Brent is still absent almost two weeks with the exploratory group. Brent had mentioned the mission might take anywhere from a week to four and a half weeks.

Sophie scoffed, looking at my plate. My food is less than ever before compared to everyone else.

I calmly say, "Don't make a fuss it's fine."

Tobias staring at my already half empty plate before I even taken a bite, "He gave you less than last week."

"He cut more of my rations because my basket broke." I ate my food wanting to drop the subject.

"Why don't you tell the Second Life's what they're doing to you."

I shook my head, "I haven't even seen that guy since we came out of quarantine."

He lied to me again. He say he would talk to me in a few days and never came. I saw him outside once walking with Lavender and others, but it was as if I never was there.

Tensing my jaw, taking another bite of food as the kiss rang through my head. Ieronim never lied to me like Niel has. He taught me how to evade unnecessary information, but for the most part he always told me the truth. At least I think he did, just how I thought Niel did. Lowering my head a little voice sounds in my mind, you can't trust anyone.

My body shook as a hand slams on the wooden table we sat at. I didn't look up from my food. It's become a routine - someone stealing our meal at least twice a week.

Taking another bite, ignoring them.

"You think you can eat like a king, limp?" A woman says, as she sticks her thumb into his food.

She has a nasty burn scar on her neck, disappearing beneath her clothes.

Tobias responded in a friendly demeanor, "I get the same rations as everyone else."

"Not exactly, limp. You got to sit in your bedroom for we don't know how long." She kick his leg under the table causing him to jerk, "Cause you came defective. Bringing a bunch of snot nose brats, and a lazy wall dweller with ya."

Her head sways looking at me, seeking a reaction so she has a reason to mess with me too. Tobias reaches over Sophie, keeping her from standing.

My eyes flutter shut, hoping that she will walk off if I give no reaction. Tobias grunt in pain as she kick at his bad leg again.

Her stomach lays slightly on the table moving as she laughs. "I think its best I get your portion for lunch now on." Sophie opens her mouth, "That isn't fair. He works hard like everyone else."

A man tall and buff and a scrawny woman came behind her, she scoffs, "They don't let anyone hurt in here. Whoever the fuck you know, suck their cock to get an extra meal."

"Ha," I couldn't help myself, grinning up at her. "I don't think I have a cock for him to suck, sorry."

In a fit of rage, she shove my scraps across the table.

My nose flared as I look at her. Her body looms over me once again, her stomach still resting on the table.

Her lips peeled about to speak, but I cut in, "You know, you wouldn't need to take food if you just let them know you are knocked up. What, three months along? Congratulations."

Her brows rose to her hair line. My hair pulled from the back and a searing pain radiates as the other girl snuck behind me knocking me to the ground.

My body hoist up as Sophie screamed, "That was a cheap shot!"

Getting to my feet, the woman yells, "People from within the walls don't belong with us. You only protect her cause she got your asses here."

They didn't even know who I was, and yet that night, they pulled me into their group. The least I could have done for them was get them somewhere safe.

Rearing my fist, I quickly struck her nose. Tobias limped over, pushing the two of us back. The guy and the two girls kick Tobias. He push us back collapsing on the ground. He's just received the okay to start helping around. What they don't know is he's been begging the doctor to be release early, and the doctor had been forcing him to stay in bed.

Tobias shouts in pain the sickening sound of cracking bone fills my mind.

Losing my breath my blood heated with rage. Tobias, a man who these kids we brought with us comes to him every night so he can read them a bedtime story. Even the older kids come for a story. Though they are too old for that - they just want to spend time with him. He is a dad they all imprinted on. A man who is most deserving to be a father. Now, curled up, grabbing his leg cursing in pain.

Lunging forward, only to be smacked to the ground by the muscular man. The woman I called pregnant kicked me in the head, causing my vision to blur. Shouts erupt from the crowd, people calling for doctors. As the girl went to kick at me, I got her stationary leg, pulling her to the ground. There's a loud thud as her head hit the concrete floor. People mimicked a painful sound.

She cry out on the floor, "Crazy bitch."

Laughing, I slowly press my foot onto her throat, my bottom and top teeth showing as I smiled at her, "You have no fucking clue who you've pissed off, nor what I am willing to do to protect the ones closest to me."

The man hands grab for my neck while I wasn't paying attention. Before he could wrap his thick fingers around I move back, releasing my foot from her throat. He moves quicker than me. His hand around my shirt hosting me upwards before I knew it. My stomach exposed to everyone around.

I dug my nails into his arm. "Tobias is a better man than you'll ever be." Inhaling sharply, the world spun. For a split second, everything was upside down, and then all the air left my chest as I lay flat on the table I just sat at. Still, no one dare to stop this.

A vain pop out of his forehead. His face upside down. "Our lives will be better without wall dwellers taking our supplies, thinking they are entitled to everything." His hand reached up to my neck, pressing down cutting off my air.

I bit out my last bit of breath, straining, "Get behind the line, others want this O'Salves dead too."

His arm cascading over my face, lifting my neck upwards, my lips brushed his arm hair. Opening my mouth wide, chomping on as much skin as I can get.

Chapter Eleven

As he hollers in pain, flesh tearing as I got a chunk of him. He let go of me, releasing my teeth from his skin. A familiar voice yelled from the other side of the cafeteria. My eyes flutter shut as my skull feels as if a fire has been set on my skin. A headache where everyone screams made me want to black out. My chest rises and falls, finally getting oxygen through my blood again.

"What is going on in here?" Niel comes in as if he owns the place. His voice like needles on my temples

The woman who started all of this groaned in pain, "That one from one of the cities, she started it."

I grumbled, half - smirking, "Not my fault she's pregnant and trying to take others' food."

She bit back, "I'm not pregnant."

Flashing my teeth, my voice rose, pretending to be surprised, "Oh, then you are just a glutton taking peoples' food."

Niel gently lays his hand on the back of my head, and my face wince as it sent pain from my skull down my spine. I moved away from his touch, and Niel stood in front of me blocking my view.

My words slur as my nostrils flared, "Tobias needs help. That man, he broke his leg."

Niel's voice eerily calm. He laid his hand on my cheek to look up, "It is all okay, Infinity."

"You don't know how we've been living." I say, as my brows furrow. "They've been treated badly for sticking by me. Get off, let me go to him."

His fingers tighten around my shoulders as his forehead rested on mine, "Just stay still. It's not your fault." He whispers.

"What are…" I pull back his eyes inches from mine. "Get away now." Niel shook his head, "Niel, fucking let go of me."

His throat bobbed, the sign of being worried. My bottom lip quiver. Standing, Niel blocked my view every turn, and no matter what way I moved, he blocked me. Dipping down, he pulled me back up.

All the voices are meshing into one chaotic hum. Niels' clicks stands out as he speaks to Lavender. He is hiding something from me. The crowd closes in, and the table I had been lying on is now obscured by people standing on top, wanting a better view. I have to see Tobias. Closing my eyes, I pushed Niel out of the way. He grab my wrist to spin me around.

Sophie being held back as Tobias is surrounded, a mask around his face, pumping air into his lungs. The bone in his leg protrudes out, blood displayed on the floor.

"No," I say more as a demand than a plea, "He can't die. You can't let him die."

Niel trying to turn me away, but my gaze is fixed on Tobias. As they move his body to the stretcher, his hand fell limp. Watching them manually making him breathe, my knees wobbled. I want to take a step forward, want to get close to him, but I can't.

I cry out, "Tobias, the kids need you, don't leave them." They can't lose another person. "I know you hear my fucking voice. You better make it. Those kids can't lose another dad. Tobias, don't leave your kids!"

Tears stream down my face as Niel's hand wrapped around my torso, my body leaning in, no longer wanting to stand.

The crowd morph back into place, covering him and Sophie as they left. Niel lifted me up, his hand on my forehead, keeping me against his body.

Niel repeatedly says, "It's not your fault, Infinity, it's not your fault."

It is the same reassurance he gave me when I cried in my room after my family died. He found me whimpering, trying to stay silent so no adults would come into my room. My apartment was filled with so many strangers that day. Niel laid beside me, keeping my back on him, petting my hair constantly telling me that it wasn't my fault.

He told me that, knowing I didn't truly understand what they were doing. He didn't even blame me, knowing I thought I was doing the right thing. He believed me when I told him I thought they were going to be safe. He was working with my family, never was mad at me for snitching them out.

"This place will be better without another mouth to feed," The man who broke Tobias leg says with pride, "Maybe them kids will commit suicide now."

The woman snickers as the nurses took care of them. On the sideline stood another nurse, waiting for Niel to allow her to help me. The tears cease, watching as they take delight in their cruel actions. Niel finally let go of me, thinking that I calmed down enough for medical attention.

Something Ieronim taught me - never let them see your next move. Never reveal how angry they've made you until you strike. I observe the nurse as she put her bag on the table, rummaging through it. Getting a flashlight she checked my scalp. Moving my hair around my face crunch as she poked at the spot that was hit.

Laing at the top of the nurses bag is a pair of silver scissors. Darting my gaze back to the man and the scissors. The nurse of the man got up, she looked through her own bag, her back turned to him. I stepped forward. My temples throb, my throat sore from where his hand tried to choke the life out of me moments before.

Taking the scissors, they shimmer as the lights hit the entirely silver surface made strong, medical grade steal. Spreading my fingers apart opening the mouth. Not raising my hand high for everyone to see. Each step I took made my head throb. He lays on the ground, his arm already wrapped blood seeping from my bite mark, legs wide open, unaware.

Pushing my weight forward, fabric tearing as the sharp scissors slide past the fabric with no restraint. His leg kicks upward, hand already on my shoulder about to push me off.

A feral grin crossed my face as I watch all the blood drain from him. Pure horrors knowing it is too late. The blades closing quickly on his shaft. Pulling upward, the once clean blades now stained with blood. One last stab in the leg, the scissors left in his inner thy as Niel hoisted me upward. I heard nothing. No one calling my name, and I didn't even realize Niel was behind me. As that man mouth open, all the sounds came back.

The man screamed, rolling on the ground, the blades digging in deeper.

"You want to wish that onto children then..." I spat at him from behind Niel's shoulder, "I took away your chance to have kids."

Niel fought with me as I started to climb his shoulder to look at the bastard as the nurses panic to stop the bleeding.

Seething with anger, I say through my teeth, "Don't fuck with an O'Salves. We do anything to protect our friends."

"O'Salves?"

"She can't be."

"She is lying."

"It makes sense why she's violent."

"No, she is using O'Salves name to look important."

Never before have I heard my last name said so much in one setting. The mutters filled with confusion, questioning how I could have that name. Not with dread, as people in the Alpha City did, but with wonder. The name rolls off their tongues smoothly, as if they had said it all their lives.

Niel tossed me over his shoulder, carrying me away. Pushing myself upwards just for my hands to slip. Every hard thump on the ground caused needles to shoot through my head.

Niel says, his voice drip with irritation, "Why would you do something," He paused as he stumbles over his words. "So...so rash for a person you knew only for a few months?"

Eyes closed, I reply, "They saved me as a stranger, and that bastard out there deserved what he got."

"I would had taken care of, of both of them. What you did, it's not part of our rules."

Grinding my teeth, I shot back, "Could have fooled me.

"No one has done shit for any of us these few months. They all turn a blind eye to our torture."

Niel puts me down, his brows scrunch at my words. "There's been no reports."

Rolling my eyes, I retort, "The kids have been treated like shit, Tobias and I been getting the butt end of everything. Practically I get two meals a day cause the chef doesn't like me. Over half the crap you given me has been taken. Maybe if you told me the truth, and came when you said you would been here for me... Maybe then you would had seen it for yourself."

"I had to..."

I flicked my wrist not wanting to hear anymore lies. "I don't care for the excuse." Pinching the bridge of my nose, turning to get away from him, my voice calmed. "Just get out of my life, Second Life. He deserved getting his dick cut off. He's a big enough one even without it."

"Infinity, why," he paused as if trying to find the words, "What happened to turning the other cheek?"

I froze in place, my fingers curling into a fist. Everything inside of me wants to charge at him. To scream at him with everything I have gone through practically alone. Everything boiling up, ready to spew out of my mouth. Then, it fizzles to nothingness as if a plug had been popped releasing it all.

I smile, where he couldn't see, as he still looked at the back of my head, "What happened was I was alone. I got abused once too many times.

"At your guys' one year anniversary is where I broke." Over my shoulder, I finished, my eyes hazed over, "It took five people to tear me off that cunt who pushed me to my limit, and it was the best feeling in the world."

Niel step forward slowly closing the distance. I waited for his hands to wrap around me in a comforting hug, like he had always done.

Instead, Niel grabbed underneath my armpit, dragging me off to an area I've never been. A hall with no other doors but one at the very end. Double doors painted a deep red, rounded at the top. Bursting in without knocking, a grand room unfolds before me, unlike anything I seen before.

Built before the first wave, the room is luxuriously large. Niel dragging me through it, his hand squeezing my arm the entire way. My body lifts off the ground as he threw me onto a couch dark blue in color, wooden outlines where fabric purposely did not cover.

The room is adorned with artwork. No inch of the stone wall is exposed, keeping the art of the past alive. The room is only lit by oil lamps and a fireplace, not burning wood, but a long display of oils burning in a line. Large flames coming from it lighting up majority of the room.

Niel pacing around clicks coming out of him in a rapid spitfire. His arms cross, as if this is now his first language, forgetting that he is speaking to one who isn't versed in it.

"I've only seen one person who could get Niel this worked up." A man stepped out from behind some curtains. Extending my head trying to peak how much further this place went, he continues, "Of course it's my little sister. You always knew how to push his buttons."

Swaying forward the man who stood in front of me, a familiar sight and yet so foreign, as fishtail lines cascade from his eyes and lines around the corners of his lips.

He wore a blouse, loose to his body, frays at the bottom and on the cuffs. His hair neatly cut on the side and shaggy on the top, wet as if he'd just got done with a shower. My breath halted as the memory flashes. Diverting my eyes from him, I bury my face in my hands. Too shocked to cry, feeling like I am hallucinating.

"Niel, calm down now." He says in a warm tone.

Niel huffed, "I didn't… I mean… She try to kill someone."

I whip my head, bearing my teeth, "Cutting his dick won't kill him."

Niel pointed his whole hand at me. "You stabbed his thy too."

I stood facing only Niel, "He may had killed a man who's a father to many."

My expression relax remembering who's in the room with us. To see my brothers painful stare. A familiar sight he would give me when I couldn't hold my tongue any longer around adults.

Dread fell over me, another secret that been kept. My *brother* is alive.

Pinching my lips together, trying to hold all my emotions back. My brother is *alive*. Avoiding their gaze, I watch the oil flames. They didn't step any closer as my nostrils flared. How many secrets have been held from me?

It's been fifteen years since I've been alone. Haunted by the name 'Snitch,' 'murderer,' and the pain of my actions all of these years.

My chin tilted to where the sky would be, slowly asking, "How long have you known he's been alive?" Mason side eyed Niel, giving him permission.

Niel closed the distance, speaking slowly to get the words out correctly. "I told you I'll be honest… Even if that honesty may hurt you. Do you want to hear it?" I stared at him, scared of what would happen if I open my mouth, "I will take silence as a yes…"

Niel stood beside me, the pause in speech making my heart leap out of my chest. Niel says, "I knew the hole time."

Sharply exhaling, feeling as if a knife has been plunged into me. Could it be true…I forced the next question out. "Mom and dad?"

Tears forming in the corners of my eyes. Niel and mason are alive, so that means there is a chance my parents are. I wouldn't had killed them, but it does mean they abandoned me. I force a mask on my face shoving all the sadness down, quickly replacing it with anger.

Mason answer that one, "They didn't make it."

"How?" My voice cracked. How is it they did but my parents couldn't?

Niel, reaches for me, "My parents helped him."

Moving away my fingers curled into fists. My nails digging into my palm. He had looked at me all the years as I cried, as I spiraled into depression, where I couldn't even eat.

Every time I mourned their death, thinking I was alone, he knew the truth.

Clipping Niel's jaw, he stumble to the side. My brother calling my name wanting me to stop. Before that sharp tone of his would work but not now. Clenching my fist harder, I spun around. Walking to the far side of the couch, my body heated, keeping my distance from hitting him again. Niel stood there watching, raising both of my hands, cutting off any words.

Tears fell down my face, beyond broken, only one thing I could say, "Fuck you. Fuck all of you. You aren't my fucking brother. He wouldn't have left me alone. He would had come for me.

"If I see you again, Second Life, I will cut your head off. I am getting out of this pit of deception."

Making it to the door, I stumbled back as my brother somehow cut me off. I didn't see him cross over.

Another second he stood at the door, as if it took him only a step. Stumbling backward, the ground connects with my ass. I have to be hallucinating.

Mason replies, somehow squatting in front of me, "Trinity, you are old enough to know. Just listen to our reasoning, please."

I say ignoring the voices, "I need to go to the doctor I am hallucinating."

Unable to breathe, before I even blink my brother is gently lowering me down on the couch.

Mason says as worry laced his words, "I can check you out, sister." Slapping his hand away, I swore, and he covers my mouth, glaring, "Stop cursing so much sister." His lips curled upward as he pet my long hair, "How I missed calling you that."

Lowering my head, ashamed of every memory I have. How much time we have lost. How he just got into college to become a doctor. He would had graduated and been practicing by now. Mason is treating me like I wasn't the one who snitched them out to the Luners.

Niel went to a large table covered in papers on the other side of the room to give us space.

Looking up I ask, "Why are you not mad at me?"

His smile wobble before saying, "For a few years I was. Then Niel handed me a photo of you." His eyes redden, "My little sister broken without her family. All my hate melted away in that moment."

I pushed, "Despite knowing I was broken. You didn't come for me."

Mason took out a small photo from his pocket. It's wrapped in plastic. Handing it to me I flip it over.

"You were young," Mason says, "We kept it a secret because mom and dad wanted to give you a normal life."

I can't remember when this photo was taken. My eyes swollen as I forced a smile, it's something I practice in the mirror for many hours after they died.

I didn't pretend not to be hurt, "Look how that worked out. Niel is my age, but he knew…"

Mason interrupt, irritation lacing his words. "He found out because Gabe told him. Mom and dad were against it, but it was too late. Trinity, look, I will explain it all."

He drag me over to some paintings high up on the wall, where many wouldn't have notice. He position me in front of him his arm extending past me, showing me where to look.

A pyramid, where the back half is crumbling in the painting, shadows on the ground larger than humans, clearly displayed.

"They are the firsts. The ones who seen humans before the rest. Part of nature and animal. They seemed to be rejected by humans. Only artworks exist of them, and a language we no longer know." He pointed guiding my vision slightly upwards. "They are the seconds. Wings flew them down braking open the skies, and the ground crumbled, releasing ones from below."

The things coming out from the ground were shaded much darker, smudged as if they wouldn't stay still. Where the wings of the ones above were smudge in the same fashion. On the ground, clearly drawn humans. Fear filled their faces as they saw the ground split open. While the ones looking up smile as if they been waiting to see the sight.

My brother then spun me around with a similar - looking painting of the rest on the other side of the room. This one is different from the rest. It's not an action portrait. In a room, they stood taller, with pointed ears. They posed for the painting to be done. A pointed - ear human man arm around a woman without pointy ears, both smiling down at each other, joy radiating out of the painting itself.

Mason says as he rub my shoulders gently, "And we were the third, sister. We came and created peace for the rest. We are descendants of Fae. We are *Fae*."

My eyes flutter as I peer at him, "What do you mean Fae? We are O'Salves." Did something happen to his mind since he been out here? How did he forget what his last name is.

His eyes sparkled, "Yes, yes, that is our last name, but what we are isn't human. We are Fae. So is Niel and his family. That is why they helped Mom and Dad, and there are many more still like us who held onto their past.

"As years past on Earth and our lineage mated with humans, we lost our immortality. Thankfully, our family retain our gifts." Mason looked over to Niel carrying sorrow "Not all families were as fortunate."

Mason guided me to the table Niel stood. Pushing some of the papers towards me, saying "This is our origin language. Few can still read it, and I have taught Niel, and others like us. Now, Trinity, you will learn."

Interlocking my fingers, my nose flare as I stare at the wavy symbols sprawled across the papers, in up and down movements.

Brushing his fingers through my hair, Mason kept talking, "We need to cut your hair soon Trinity. This is posing a risk."

I pulled away, taking a step back, declaring, "I don't want to cut my hair."

Mason shook his head, "Oh no, you have to Trinity. Our abilities are hindered by our hair. Our rule to cut it at eighteen is because that's our pinnacle. Beyond that, it can become too potent, potentially driving one to madness. I'm relieved you didn't because it's scary to deal with it alone. Now you are here, I can take care of you, like mom and dad took care of me.

"You've brought the work we needed to reclaim our immortality. Next winter, we should be able to travel with the finalize product to help our kind. It's what our ancestors were trying to do when they created the first wave, but they failed, creating zombies. Now, almost seven generations later, we're closer with every test."

My fingers raise slowly up to my mouth, "You are insane… Mother Earth, you have gone insane out here." I spun going for the door, where all of a sudden Mason stood in front of me. Dodging him, I say, "I got hit in the head. I need to see a doctor. I'm hallucinating. Maybe You'll vanish from my mind. Maybe I am asleep."

Niel calmly says as I left. "Give space and let her think."

Not bothering to close the door behind myself, I went straight to the doctor. My eyes wide not blinking once as I lay back getting a checkup. The world I once knew, the life I once believed, it's all crumbling beneath me.

My head on the flat pillow my mind feeling heavy. Sophie sat on a chair beside my bed. Her eyes puffy from crying not for me, but for Tobias. They gave me a mixture of Lily to keep me calm, as I was a panic when I rushed in an hour ago.

In a scratchy whisper, Sophie says, "Tobias is breathing… They aren't sure."

My words slurred as I say, "Don't…I can't."

"Inside the city." Sophie thought about the question before slowly saying, "Do they believe in a higher being? Is that how you stay safe?"

Tilting my head to look at her, the room spun. Her disheveled hair allowing me to peek past the strong outer shell, revealing a scared person beneath.

Not knowing how to answer, we sat in silence for a few minutes. Sophie's bloodshot eyes filled with desperation for an answer.

Finally, I say, "We stay safe with the wall and all the cameras." Her lips tightened, I add, "Some do, Niel, his family believes in something called God."

Her lips relaxed, as her hazy eyes stare deep into me, "What did the God do?"

"Um…I don't know." I admit. I never asked them about the God. Reaching out to touch her shoulder. She wrap her hand around my arm tightly, "When Niel died, they brought a man to pray for his soul. I didn't go, so I don't know what happens. They believe once you pass, you meet him, and you live a good life with him, I guess."

"I like the sound of that, where this isn't all for nothing." She mused "Not only to go back to Mother Earth, the end, but instead we go somewhere that's better."

"He isn't allowed to, but if he passes, and if this God is real… Tobias is the most deserving."

Her smile wobbled as she says, "He would be able to see his Wife and kid."

I laugh, "He would adopt any kid without parents until they were re united again."

Tears trace down my cheeks. This feels weird because despite knowing Tobias may die, we are both smiling softly with the idea his soul may live on.

*

My head no longer throbs with each step. Whatever they gave me last night worked.

Securing my leather around my waist, concealing both knives beneath a loose - fitting tee. After what happened yesterday, others may go after me. While carrying a weapon is looked down on, there are no rules against it. Rubbing my fingers on the unique leather work. Mistress was right when she told me she knew a good leather worker. When I approached him with the blades, he was more than happy to take the challenge. It took many tries to get it to lay flat and to unsheathe quickly, but he did it perfectly.

Walking through the halls to grab a basket, only one remained. My eyes scrunch at the newly made basket, not the one they cut yesterday. Stepping outside, the others are in the yard, as if they purposely agreed to work early.

"You are late. We agreed to work thirty minutes early yesterday." The cook says.

They didn't even let me get through the gate before starting stuff. I say, "No one told me that."

"Maybe if you weren't cutting up others, you would had known."

Glaring at them, I didn't bother to say another word. No matter what happens; they have it out for me. Guess that is a familiar theme outside and inside the walls.

The sun beaming down on me, sweat drips off my forehead. Clear blue skies where the eyes can see. Birds surround us in the trees and on the gates. Inside Alpha City, there were very view birds, but out here there's small and big ones all around. Even large animals are around, ones I still don't know the names of. At night when I come out I can catch glimpses of the glowing eyes peaking at me.

Laughter erupts ahead of me. Even though I was late, I am quickly catching up. A shadow crept up from behind.

Ignoring them as the person didn't seem to be slowing down. They probably are coming to get the cook.

"Are you still hallucinating?" Mason say as he squatted by me.

His clothes are eccentric. That is the nicest way to put it. He wears an almost translucent black tee, pleated at the front, loose fitted tan pants, hat atop his head protecting from the harsh summer weather.

Fluttering my eyes to hide my eye roll, I say, "With that outfit I say yes…I can see your nips."

He ruffled my hair, how he once always done. My heart softens at the act I haven't felt in forever. The last time he did this was the night the Luners took them.

I dreamt of it last night everything he told me. I tried to force it out of my mind but couldn't. Unable to deny the speed my brother poses, I dreamt of myself smiling into a stream. No since of danger. Mason too far away , and seconds later splashing water on me. Saying 'we did it.'

The others stood gawking at my brother and the clothes he wore.

Mason flashed them a smile, "Is there something needed by the group I can help with?"

The cook hastily replies, "It is very rare for you to show yourself…" He paused before adding, "Especially alone without your people."

"Looks like you just haven't been in the rights places to see it until now."

"It is a pleasure to have you. Would you like to see the gardens?" The cook gloats, "O'Salves, it's been the best it's ever been."

Mason glance at me, we shared a small smile, mine more subtle than his.

"No, I was here to check on this newcomer."

I could feel their glares on top of me as I kept working. They are going to be so embarrassed when they find out how their naughty thoughts are wrong. "Is it because how she cut someone's dick off?" The bluntness left my mouth ajar. Mason, now looking at me, "What?"

I don't have to look at him to know his head is cocked to the side.

Another chimed in, "You didn't know? She is violent."

"As the rest of the wall dwellers are."

Do they not know he once lived there too? Mason rub his neck of his unspoken past.

He cleared his throat, then a second time. Slowly, I stood, my lips stretched thin.

Mason responded, his head cocked to the side looking at me, "I wonder why I was not informed of it by my people."

"He may had killed my friend, then said how the kids should commit suicide. Less mouths to eat. I say I reacted accordingly by making sure he can't have kids." I mutter, "He's a big enough dick without one."

Mason let out a rough sigh, crossing his legs slightly. "Trinity, that isn't how you are supposed to act."

My eyes widen as he called me by my name. A new heat waved over me as they snicker.

"Trinity, that's such a weak ass name." Jenny, the one who cut my basket yesterday says, "I can't wait to..."

"It's Snitch," I reminded them, "You have no right to call me anything else."

Taking a step forward, Mason put his hand on top my head. Rejecting his affection they gasped.

"Here comes his dog to take care of you." Jenny smoothly says, "O'Salves is the man who runs this place. How dare you show him disrespect."

Behind my shoulder, gray skin and blond hair approaching. They call Niel my brother's dog. Wonder where that comes from?

The cook snitching on me. "She used your name as her own, O'Salves."

My brother wrapped his arm around my shoulders, "Well, she is my little sister, so she is an O'Salves. Now, do you have an issue with me because I am as well … a violent wall dweller?"

Mason removes his arm from around me, and in an instant, he stood in front of the cook.

"I did hear how she's been cut off from rations by you. Starting today yours will be cut in half for the next six months, and my people will make sure of it."

I snorted, relishing the fact of the big - bellied man sweating, realizing all the extra food he's gotten from me is being taken away plus some.

Niel scowled as we turned, the sight jarring me slightly. I understand the statement from before, but it should be 'scary dog.'

Moving down the hall, we laugh at their expressions when Mason told them I am his sister.

Walking backwards hand moving around, I laugh, "Jenny's jaw practically fell on the floor."

The sound of crying put spikes in my heart. Turning slowly, Sophie stumbling out of a room, her face red. Leaning against the wall, she slid down, letting out painful cries.

In an airy voice, I say, "No…No not Tobias."

Running away from the joy I felt, folding myself over Sophie, she clawed at me, crying and I held her desperately wanting to take her sorrows.

My face wrenched at the cry of a heart breaking; wishing that it wasn't Tobias. I'd been through this too many times myself. My fingers intertwining in her hair as I held her head closer to mine.

Niel leaned in, whispering "I will be in my room." Then, both my brother and he left us.

She laid in my lap, huffing, trying to catch a breath between cries.

The doctor finally emerges from the room, flanked by two nurses. "Now is the time to say your final byes before he goes to quarantine."

"Why would he be sent to quarantine?" I ask, helping Sophie up.

The doctor reply with a straight face. "To see what he turns into."

The nurse clarified, "You are a wall dweller, correct Snitch. Here, we wait after death to see if they become a zombie, or Second Life's."

Sophie grabs the nurse suddenly, crying out, "I forgot, he still has a chance."

The doctor slowly pulled her off, with the other nurse as he clarifies trying not to get her hopes up. "The chance is very slim, but yes."

Her bottom lip quiver as she mindlessly went back into the room, muttering to herself. She sat in the chair taking his hand crying.

I stood at the door, watching as his skin is already taking on a grayish hue. Slowly, I took a breath and came closer, my eyes burn as tears threaten to spill over. Placing a hand on Sophie's shoulder, still muttering to herself.

Softly, I say, "Don't tell the kids. Not until we know if he turns or not."

Sophie nod her head, keeping the room silent as if Tobias is only sleeping.

We stay by him as long as we could before we had to leave. Guiding Sophie to her room, tucking her in bed, she only mutter to herself.

As I walk down the halls, the doctor and nurses came into view.

I ask, "When you get time can you check on Sophie. She won't stop muttering."

The nurse gave a sorrowful look, "She just lost the father to her baby. I bet she's broken in more ways than one at this moment.

I'll talk with her for you, Snitch. She will be in good hands."

Keeping a still expression as they pass me no longer hearing their footsteps.

"Fuck, no wonder." I mutter.

My eyes soften, Mother Earth don't take him. Tobias is most deserving to become a Second Life.

Hall after hall I went down looking for Niels' room. He told me where to go before, but I haven't ventured to find it before now. Abruptly stopping, my brows scrunched. This is close to where I met my brother after all of these years. As I get close, the rooms become further apart. I paused at the door that's cracked open.

Niel had a habit leaving his door open so I can walk in whenever I needed. Smirking, perhaps there is a lot of Niel left in this Second Life's body. Opening the door my breath hitch at the sight displayed in front of me.

Niel laid back on the couch, one leg on the ground and the other cocked upwards. Lavenders' head bobbing up and down as his hand clenches a fist full of her hair, pushing her down a little longer. He groans, leaning his head back. It's as if my body has frozen. It isn't like I want to look, but something in my chest tightens at the sight of this act.

It isn't like we are dating. It had been three years since we last met. To hear him groan in pleasure again sends heat up my body. His eyes slowly opens, showing the whites as he sees me standing there. Clicks came from him as Lavender squirms away, covering herself with a shirt that isn't her own. Niel jumps up, tucking his dick upwards into the waistband.

My trance broke, gasping for air as if I forgot to breathe. Turning on my heel, my body stiff as I walk away.

Unable to control the tone of my voice, I scream at them. "I am sorry, I didn't mean to." Before slamming the door behind myself.

I ran through the hall as Niel calls my name. Each time his voice got closer.

Taking my arm, he turn me to look at him. Shoving him off, I stared at the ground. My lips thin as my heart aches.

Stuttering, I say, "I, I didn't, I mean, I, huff," I stopped, trying to get my words, "I didn't mean to walk in on you and your girlfriend."

"Lavender, we aren't dating." Niel clarifies, "We do this to let off steam. We are both Second Life's, it's easier this way." Somehow, his words didn't make me feel better.

I reply, unable to look up, "You don't have to explain yourself to me. I understand, I just, I got to go."

"Why are you acting like a virgin? You weren't scared showing your body off when you first got here."

My breath sharpen at his accusing tone. His eyes darkened as he took a step back.

Niel eyes soften realizing the truth. "It's for show."

Lifting my chin high masking all my emotions. "It's different when you are in control of a situation."

I lean in watching his face, my breasts against his body, taking back control. "See its different when you expect the action." His jaw ticked, "I can tease men all I want, and feel nothing."

Pushing off his body, I gave a wobbly smile, "I can't go pass this because then I am no longer in control."

Niel took a step closer, "You don't always need…to be in control." Both our feet touch and I didn't back away. "It's okay to just feel," He tucked my hair behind my ear, "To enjoy the moment." His lips grazing my ear as he finished, "It would be my pleasure to be your first. I will be gentle."

My heart lodged in my throat, stopping any words from escaping. My face heated as my gaze didn't lift from the ground.

He tilted my head up, his eyes darting over every inch of my face. He was just in bed with another, now flirting with me. Biting the inside of my cheek, my breath catches, unable to move once again. My heart tightens as his hand touched my waist.

"Infinity." Niel whispers, his voice cracking, "I never stopped loving you. When I awoke for the first time, all I saw was the redness in your eyes. The pain it caused you, and the curdling screech as my skull broke. I smelt nothing but you. Months, only you were here." He pointed at his head then touch my chest, "I wanted to find you, to hold you - everything drawn me to you, and I fought every day not to see you.

"Lavender and our teacher taught me not to react to hunger like zombies do." Niel licked the bottom of his lips, "I couldn't tell if I wanted you, or was wanting to feed on you. That's why I stayed away, Infinity. When I had you for the first time, smelling you again, that urge to take flesh, it was overwhelming." I swallow my mental question being answer if they are always in control of their hunger. "Until I realized exactly who was in front of me. Than it all went away, and the urge to want you near me like the past was there. To see you happy."

He rubbed the edge of my forehead, "I hurt you that day. You looked like an animal being hunted…You still look like scared prey. Eyes shifting, never steady, always ready to run or fight at any moment." His brows furrowed, "I want to protect you. To prove my love, and if you allow me you'll be the only one I'll ever hold. The only one I will save. I will be all of yours, and you can relax once again."

He kept me looking up at him despite me wanting to look away. The Niel I once knew is still here in front of me.

Lifting my heels off of the ground, staring up at his beautiful eyes. Noting for the first time his blue eyes are almost gray. My heart races to a gallop as we get closer. Niel leaning in then stopped. His gaze fixated on my lips, awaiting me to close the rest of the distance. Pausing, lowering myself down on the ground.

He was just in bed with another person. How do I know if she is not in love with him? That she is wanting more from him then stress relief. Shaking my head, Niel kiss the top of it.

His eyes shimmer as his grin grew, "Take your time, my Infinity."

Opening my mouth to correct him to call me 'Snitch.' Alarms blared through the halls.

The double doors push open as my brother walks out, carrying a duffle bag filled with guns. Already dressed in patted black clothes, tight around his body. He has muscles…Mason always said how lean is best, but I guess in this environment he changed his mind. A quarter down the hall a blur happen.

A small yip came from me as he reach out holding me in his arms. His body radiating heat, holding me a little tighter before pushing off tossing Niel the duffle.

Mason says, pain itching his voice, "Luners found us."

No, they can't be here. This was supposed to be the safe place.

Niel asks, "How did they get here with no warnings from the scouts?"

He swallowed before biting out, "They turned their backs on us."

Brother sound more hurt than angry about the situation.

We have to leave. I need to get my things and get to our meeting spot Tobias ingested on. Turning, Niel and my brother grabbing me by one arm, each lifting me off the ground. Kicking my legs, they wouldn't put me down.

"If they are here I need to get my things and leave." I shout at them, but they did not listen.

Mason replies, "You need to stay here while we make sure they don't get below ground. See the lights." I looked up at the lights shining from within the walls, "They are green, meaning they are inside the building you first came in. Yellow means they found the way in and then that's when you need to get out. Red means… no way out and fight for your life."

Niel reassures, "It won't get pass green. Just sit and relax you will be safe down here."

They took me inside of the room, already turning to leave.

Following behind them, I say, "You don't understand; I need my things."

Niel turns to look at me. "Leave it and stay here." My voice rose in protest. "It's all I have left."

Mason's eyes soften, and his shoulders sagged at my words. "I will get them for you. Just wait here and I'll bring them when I can."

Nodding, that's good enough for me. Waving bye, they both shot me small smiles before shutting the door.

My breath hitches every other moment being alone, hearing the alarms going off muffled on the other side. Spinning around, the moody lighting shows nothing that's going on. I won't be able to know when the lights change in here.

I read Elizabeth's books more than enough times. They had no mention of this place or where to find it. Mason mentioned something about scouts turning their backs. Is that how Luners found out? They couldn't have followed me all the way out here. They wouldn't had come all the way here for me.

Peeking out of the door, my breath quickens to see the lights yellow, and the alarms have a shorter beat. Closing the door, moving to the other side of the room. Yellow, I can't remember what yellow means. Red means get the hell out, but yellow... Raking my hands through my hair, my lips quiver with fear. Whimpers escape from deep within. Going to the desk, filled with papers much like the ones my parents had in the room. Shaking, I focus on them, words I can't understand, attempting to ignore the muffled alarms.

Papers tremble in my grip. Staring at curvy waves vertically written. Lines between my brows creased as something clicked. Not all of these are about the mixture they made – there's cities, kingdoms, villages, districts. The writing looks to be maybe talking about different times. Putting the papers down, a pinch of pain hits behind my eyes, struggling with the odd writing.

"What do I know. I'm just guessing." I say to myself, wanting my voice to tune out the alarm.

Niel said they wouldn't go past green. I need them to come back and tell me it is all okay. That they delt with the issue and we are safe.

Looking around for something I can get into. My brows raise slowly at the curtain on the back wall. My brother walked out of them, the first time I saw him in years. He shouldn't get mad at me looking around just a little.

Moving the curtains to the side, this room is darker, with dim blue lights shining from lamps scattered about. A neat chaos, almost like his newly found style. Mismatched objects, new and old somehow coexisting. A full - size bed with pillows all on the headboard, each with patterns sewed in, one black maybe gray, it is hard to tell with how dark this place is.

Feeling the wall, there's no light switches for me to flip. Shuffling my feet on the ground, making sure nothing is underneath me. Another curtain hung on the side wall, peeking in quickly before retreating. Closing my eyes, blue, yellow, purple lights filled the very small room. Resembling the room of my parents I wasn't allowed into. Memories flooding my mind. Turning my back knowing exactly what's going on in there.

The front door shuts with a heavy hand. A smile hit my lips for just a heartbeat, they are back. The next, anxiety floods as my nostrils flare. Sliding my feet across the floor, I strained my ears, but I didn't hear Niel or my brother. Going closer to the thick curtain covering the two rooms. Just a few steps away, the curtain pulls back with a menacing smile from the same man I cut the dick off of. My eyes widen with fear. What is he doing here?

He yells signaling others, "She's in here!" Before I could get my knife, his hand trace my neck, slamming me on the ground.

A sharp exhale and pain hummed through my body. Two others rushed into the room before I can get on my knees. Are they really using this time to go after me? I've seen them before, but we never interacted. They would glare at me from afar. I don't think I even know what their names are.

"You weren't joking that others wanted you dead too." Then it hit, a conversation I overheard. Hunt, that is his name. He is the one I cut the dick off of. "It's good that kids are chatty. The Luners been searching high and low for you."

Standing tall masking my fear despite my stomach being in my pelvis. I ask, "Are you the one who caused this?"

Yanking me by my hair, I scream in pain. Hunt grins as I gave him the reaction he was wanting. "Ah, yes scream for me…" I puff out the pain, muting myself. "They turned their backs on us when they left a wall dweller in charge, than them Second Life's." "Let's get out of here before O'Salves come back or that dog. We will be dead if they catch us."

Grinding my teeth, I say, "Whatever they promised you is a lie."

Hunt tossed me down. I slid hitting my brothers dresser wobbling it almost fell on top of me.

I didn't kill him last time because there was a hope that Tobias would make it. Wrapping his hand around my long hair, I stayed still, just for him to be close enough. Tobias is dead because of him. Now everyone in this place is at the hands of Luners because of him. Turning my body into him. The same arm I bit in reach.

My hand firmly wrapped around my blade; a quick smirk slides across my face as I unlatched the leather. Blood pours down as I fell to my feet. Backing away, my once clean blade is covered in blood.

Hunt cursed, "Fucking psycho."

I retort, "That's good, your self - aware."

I am trapped here. There are two others ready to grab me if I try to run for the exit. Not to mention all of the Luners who can be waiting for me, Mother Earth knows where.

I don't know if my brother and Niel are safe or fighting for their lives. Gripping the knife harder. Sophie is all alone with the kids perhaps waiting for me, or already vanished like the plan into the woods. I have to do something. Dragging my brothers dresser down, blocking the other room as I retreat.

Hunt shouts as I stare at the cauldron on the table mucked up with goop. My throat tightens at the sight of the ready – to – be tested material sitting there. Picking a few up, I held them tight, eyeing the curtain ready for them to come at me.

The table has papers listing all who they have tested. It's only a little over twenty tests since I arrived. Theres been no successful trials. Many turning within twenty minutes, some as quick as five. A few were able to make it a few hours before succumbing to the infection. Hunt's voice has silence to nothingness. Gulping, I have made my decision. These papers give me enough hope for what needs to be done.

The two jumped over the dresser. My hands behind my back keeping a needle in one hand, the rest in the other. Both of the guys' clothes are covered in blood now.

I say callously, "Is he dead?" The strangely colored lights made it hard to see their expressions, but their silence told me all, "Good, he is a murderer. The world is better without him."

Unable to see their mouths moving, the only thing clear was two different voices speaking.

He wasn't from around here. His words short and sharp, "This world will be better without *you* in it."

"You'll suffer plenty with the Luner's. They were more than accommodating with our demands to retrieve you." He on the other hand speaks like anyone else.

"A spit fire like you, I can imagine what hell you did for them to chase you all the way out here." The quick snips of words halted with a laugh.

My grin grew feral as they close the distance. They are unaware what a person will do when they have nothing to lose. They will not torture me like they did my parents. I did nothing wrong in the beginning to be treated like this. I followed the rules and stayed to myself. I never even had fun with my friends outside the walls. Always too scared what the Luners would think of me.

They created this animal I have become.

Elizabeth won't get her hands on me. She won't have the satisfaction of witnessing my suffering or forcing me to say whatever twisted thoughts are in her mind. They closed in on me slowly.

I hissed as the needle plunged into my backside, pressing down the plunger, until there was nothing left. I threw the vial on the ground, glass shattering. They didn't think twice other than lunging forward at me. Separating the other two needles, sticking the other guy in the ribs with one, plunging half the mixture in.

Before I could hit the buffer one, he squeezed my hand braking the vile in it.

The man with the snappy sharp tone says, "What the fuck did you stab me with?"

Glaring I say nothing. No longer fighting, they took me out of there each holding me up by an arm. Smirking as I lay eyes on Hunt's lifeless body. That's the ending he deserved.

Lowering my head, I am taken from the underground district that was supposed to be safe. I only got to see my brother for a moment - a fleeting glimpse before this utter end. This time, I would be the one who leaves his life. I will leave Niels life. They will suffer the pain I endured for many years. The difference is, I won't be alive, keeping it secret from them.

Kicking a shoe off as they dragged me further; deep into the woods, slipping another off. Hopefully, they can see my wandering body. I don't want to be an undead for too long before returning to Mother Earth. We kept going, and I manage to get a sock off. It has been almost twenty minutes since they have been dragging me away. Then the glimpse of her standing with an armored vehicle. I slipped my last sock off. The guy I stabbed has been sweating profusely. I think he's going to change soon.

I should be turning too at any moment. I wonder if it is painful or is it like drifting into sleep. My head is feeling fuzzy, but that guy looks like he is in pain. Maybe it varies per person? The stronger of the two, the one I couldn't stab, force me to the ground. My body sways trying to stay on my feet. I want to turn closest to Elizabeth. To be just aware when I bite her to end her reign.

"Do you have our new identity?" He says in airy breaths. It's going to happen soon.

Elizabeth calmly replies, "It is all in place for the three of you. Thank you for your efficient work, but where is the other man?"

The one I injected gasping for air, "She killed him."

Elizabeth raised one brow at me, "Interesting." With one head twitch, she continued, "Then you two enjoy your new lives." With that, two Hazard Prevention shot their shafts, and the men behind me fell.

Scoffing, I mutter, "I told them that you lied."

Her dead eyes stare at me. "I can't believe you got this far, Trinity. I can't wait to pick that brain of yours to know what you learned." Glaring, I didn't let anything show, "No worries, that tough girl act won't last long."

I got put into the back, my arms chained upwards on the side wall. I didn't take my eyes off her, and she maintained her calm composure towards me.

When I turn, I won't get the satisfaction of taking her life like this. Well, it won't matter. At least she won't get me.

Mother Earth, I am about to be returned to you. May my body rest soon after my mind. I don't know if you do this, but maybe you can send everyone in my life a sign. That I have passed, so they will stop looking for me.

The heaviness of my head falling forward, the vibration of the vehicle keeping me from completely going. My throat tightens with a stench filling my sinuses.

Clearing my throat, the smell wouldn't leave. The hum of the vehicle - now no longer audible - faded, and soon the vibration I couldn't feel. The weight of my head dissipate, leaving only the rancid smell to remind me that I am still in my body.

Chapter Twelve

She's still breathing." Randal says almost disappointed.

Elizabeth hisses, "Get her ass up."

Their voices sound distant, as if they are in separate rooms. Slowly inhaling, I'm met with an even worse stench filling my senses. Jerking my head back, coughing as Randal pulls away a container filled with a clear liquid, sealing it before putting it into a bag beside him on a metal table.

I don't let my disappointment show, keeping a neutral expression glaring at the woman who brought me here. Shifting, my arms are strapped down, and my legs immobilized. The room is barren, with the same gray stone walls I am getting used to seeing.

I should have turned by now. That shot better have not work with that crazy idea. I don't feel immortal or anything. I'm still very much myself. Maybe it's going to be a huge delay, and Elizabeth is going to be able to have her fun with me. Perhaps it worked, in the end I won't turn at all. Not like any of that matters I am about to be tortured to death. Screaming out in pain, I didn't see it happen.

Elizabeth approach the table, and the next moment her hand was on me. My pinky wrench upward, popping it out of its socket.

"That's just the start of this session," Elizabeth leans forward, casually popping my bone into place, evoking another scream.

Thinning my lips, a guttural growl emerges deep within, refusing to release its grip on my body. Randal, unable to face me, gripping the metal table.

She reaches for my pinky, which she just broke, and I scrunch my eyes shut. She let out a deep laugh, than pops it out of place for a second time. Leaning forward, she jumps back as I bear my teeth. Now, my pinky stuck out to the side, swelling rapidly as my hand trembles.

Taking a phone call, Elizabeth walks away from me as if I am nothing. Randal's back facing me as I struggle to suppress sounds of pain.

After hanging up, she spins to look at us. "Randal take over, and don't go easy." She pats his shoulder. "You know what will happen if I'm not satisfied."

Minutes passed before he half – turns. My eyes widened to see his eye blackened. Calming my expression, sealing my lips shut.

"There are no mics here... They blamed me for you getting out…You know with the code you used." Randal quickly pops my pinky into place. Surprisingly, it didn't hurt when he did it. "I told you to get far away."

"I did." Speaking through my teeth, "She chased me down to the furthest district."

He sighs as he pulls out random metal objects.

My mind spun, why of all times, the serum spanning seven generations didn't work. Mother Earth has truly dealt me the short stick.

Randal says as he starts to clamp down both sides of my arm. "Just tell her what she wants to hear."

The ridges from the clamp tighten more as I ask, "What is that?"

Randal won't look me in my eyes, keeping them lowered on what he's doing.

"That you are following in your family ways and want to take down the city with a second wave."

But that wasn't what they were trying. "She hunted me down like I am an animal. This is more than the 'following in my family footstep' she could had just said I was dead. I was never planning to come back."

He ignores my words. "That is what we all are - intelligent animals. Where she is a strong predator and…"

I finish, my lip twitches as the words played on my tongue, "I am just a pray."

He neither confirm nor denied that I am prey to her. He presses the contraption onto my arm tighter. That's all we are, prey or predator, where some are weaker or stronger than the last.

I ask, "Why can't you just let me go? Come with me this time."

He shook his head as a defeated man, "Since she went to hunt you down, she would go to the ends of the earth for the both of us."

"I think there are places that we can go to get out of the hands of Luners." I am going to die anyway, why not say it all, "My family wasn't trying to create a second wave as I thought. They were trying to make people live longer."

Randal tilts his head, looking at me with a soft expression, "I think you became as brainwashed as them."

I let out a whimper as he turns the clamp more. Quickly, I spat out, "I think it is insane, but the first wave, we don't know how it happened. It was sudden. They thought it's part of mad cow disease. Then we eradicated all cows hoping it would fix us." I bit out my words as my arm felt like it may break, "I learned it was my ancestors. They were the ones starting it, they created the first wave. But they messed up."

Loosening the clamps, he takes them off. Panting as some blood brakes through my skin into little balls. It is still red as it always been. Not like I am infected at all.

In any control substance, you need placebos to get better results to see who may fake it. Even though in this, you can't fake turning into a zombies, but they can fake that it worked. Mother Earth, don't tell me I took a placebo.

Randal took out a knife, and my back sweats at the sight, "How did you find that out, Trinity?"

My shoulders sag, "You already knew this. You have always known why my family had been targeted."

Sliding the dull edge of the knife up and down my skin. He finally answers, "That O'Salves believe they could make people immortal. They allowed only elitists to know, and when they kept failing, they got kicked out, sending them to the bums without the tools to finish their tests. That's at least what we thought until your parents found a way to restart the testing."

Randal still won't look at me. His voice went to a whisper, "They were wanting to kill you too, wanting to cut off everything that happened in the past. Because the elitists did not teach what they knew to their kids or grandkids, having the memory dying. Only a select few know within our ranks, and because of that, we can never truly leave Luners, always bidding to their commands.

"I convinced the rest that your family passion would die with you because they kept you in the dark. To not to eradicate another family name. There's been so many lost to history. I couldn't watch as another one got erased since most of society didn't know the truth."

I stare at him, "And is that all you know?"

He cut a thin layer down the top of my arm as he says, "You won't make it out of here alive, and I will try to make it as bearable as possible. I told you everything because." He shrugs his shoulders.

I won't make it out alive to tell anyone what I learn in here. Though he doesn't realize they don't have the full information. I don't know exactly what we are or where we came from, but my brother's speed sure wasn't human. I can't deny that.

Elizabeth pushes through the door with a grin on her face. She holds the knife that was strapped to my side and the leathers.

The other I dropped in the foyer where my brother left me.

"This is dated way before anything we have on record." Elizabeth struts to me, "Where did you get this? Somone outside these walls, and what else do they know about the past?"

I look her in the eyes, speaking through the pain, "Something my parents hid, one of the only things I managed to keep."

I can't let them know Ieronim given it to me when he help me escape. Keeping a relaxed expression, Elizabeth admires the knife eerily too close to my face. Sweat beads down my head bidding a smile from her.

She places the tip on my cheek. Biting my lip as she cuts deep into my skin screaming from within my throat. Wetness dripping down. She wants to get more information about the districts. Use what I know against them.

Elizabeth glaring to see only red irritated skin where Randal didn't draw blood. She dug my curved knife a little deeper, slowly peeling my skin open. I hiss as my arm feels like it's on fire. Jerking in the chair she paid me no attention, her gaze on Randal for his reaction. She stopped at my wrist, flicking upwards. His expression didn't warry as she hoped. "Why didn't you do more?" Her eyes squinting in annoyance. "I warned you if you went easy."

He blurts, "I got her to talk."

My nose flares with that rancid smell. Picking up almost a sweaty undertone. Blowing out I couldn't get the smell to go away.

Tilting her head to the side, Randal told her everything I said. He betrayed me quicker than I was expecting. Luckily, I didn't say anything about the districts.

She prunes her lips before saying, "You think the Wanderers can keep us out. That's disgraceful."

She takes my next finger, breaking it. Screaming, she goes to the middle finger, this time slowly, until there is a pop and crack. Burning as if fire is between the joints.

Seething in pain my head flew back. She went to the next finger slower this time making me feel every joint.

"Where are these wonderful safe havens?" Elizabeth asks.

"All I said was *think*. Just how I thought where I was staying was safe and look how that turned out."

Braking my thumb I pull forward, screaming as all my fingers on one hand points the wrong way. Tears of rage stream down.

"Thank the guy you killed for ratting them all out. He was more than happy to get rid of you, no matter what it costs others there, as long as he was free. Randal, peal back her skin."

I yell out unable to keep my panic at bay. My voice cracking, "That will kill me."
Elizabeth laughs at me as if I said something funny, "It won't kill you right away. It's sure as hell going to hurt."

"Why are you doing this? You already know the truth. Why not just kill me get it over with?"

Her fist connects to my cheek not once but twice before saying, "You got away and made us look like fools, your family went underneath our noses for years, and somehow your little friends are squeaky clean… I will peal you layer by layer, having you squeal all the truths. Hang you out for all to see. For no one to fuck with us anymore."

Her eyes have red veins popping out of the whites. Anger consuming every fiber in her body.

Randal says in a low tone, "That has been illegal for two and a half generations."

Elizabeth spits in his face, "Do you want to be hung with her? If not start slicing."

She squeezes my cheeks. Digging her thumb in the cut, "You'll regret ever being alive." My voice shook, "I already do."

Quick, shallow breaths, my body shakes in pain. Both arms pealed, the skin flops over, the underlayer of raw skin exposed as blood covers every inch. My leg twitches as my shirt was cut with my own knife. Two long chains connected to the ceiling unraveling in front of me.

"You won't stay quiet with this." Elizabeth is holding large hooks in her palms, "This is what broke your brother." My eyes flutter, tears of pain falling, "What happened to him?"

"I helped to peal his skin, down to his stomach, and he died as he cried out that they wanted a second wave of infection."

I couldn't stop the laughter, maybe it was the pain I felt these hours making me go crazy. Knowing he's alive, that she is full of shit, it is amusing me more than it should.

My eyes felt heavy, and the chuckle became softer. I mutter, "Lies."

She sticks the hook into me slowly pulling the chain upwards.

I scream, "Fucking bitch, he's alive! All you do is lie. You knew of Second Life's and didn't tell the people. You knew there is a chance and still kill the brain before seeing what happens. Scared of my family because we kept to our roots!"

The weird superstitions aren't that at all it was our roots. Don't cut the hair till eighteen or your body will be weak, believe in your gut feelings - they'll bring you to the truth, and never be too still, or they will know your fear. They were always letting me know we weren't human. Who else needs to be told not to keep too still. Always being told I look like a statue, reading their minds, eerie to be around. It is because we are not human.

Elizabeth has Randal yank the chain tearing the skin as I scream. That stench fills my senses as my nose flares. Elizabeth quickly undoes my wrists, about to put the other hook in. I pull her to me, my hands digging into her as I manipulate the hook, breaking the skin on her arm. I freeze as the pain shoots through my body, too painful to scream, as she holds my arm skin in her grasps. My mouth agape, and my breathing shallow, as if I am not breathing at all.

She pulls the hook out of her arm, not showing an ounce of pain. That calm demeanor slowly evaporating as her hair falls over her eyes. My skin hit the floor as she rushed to stop her bleeding.

Elizabeth whips her head at me, "Rip the rest of her skin off."

Randal did as she says with little hesitation. Quickly taking my skin off of my own body with a quick motion. One after another, not giving me enough time to gasp for air before the third and final skin tears from my body.

My throat closes as I wish to scream, Elizabeth yanking my head back. No longer able to lift my arms, shaking uncontrollably. She twists the chain in her hand, pulling the hook down and around. Deep inside my throat groaning at the mind - bending pain.

Elizabeth whispers, "Where is he?"

I couldn't answer due to the agony, even without it I wouldn't answer.

She screams in my ear, "Where is Mason!"

She place my knife Ieronim loaned to me at the base of my neck. Letting out a long, slow breath, my throat unclenches itself as sweat beaded out of every pore.

I say, "He may not been able to keep me safe, but he will be. You'll never know."

Elizabeth bloodshot eyes darts over my face. "I will get him."

My lips slowly curl, "So this is all because my brother got away from you all these years ago."

Her brows raise, "Shut up."

"You failed to get my brother, in hope getting me would lure him out."

"Shut up!" Her voice cracks, "I will kill you."

"Secrets will die with the dead. Killing me will never get you closer to my brother."

"You O'Salves are the plague of the Earth."

I grin as she looks down at me, pressing the knife up to my throat, "You lost him, and you have been in fear every day because of it. I remind you of your failure. That is why you hated me and been pinning everything you can on me."

"I did not fail. I will get him and kill every last of your kind." She pulls the knife away from my neck, pushing my head forward.

"Your powers come from your hair, and I will destroy it. That's how my family did before, trying to get rid of every filthy thing that didn't belong on earth. Muddying our bloodlines."

My brows nits, then slowly relaxes, "You know of my bloodline?"

"The earth became cursed with you things. Then came the first wave, and that's when we were able to eradicate the majority, destroying that history. After you are dead, your adoptive family is next."

She had already known we weren't human, long before I even knew. This is why she has been coming after me left and right. After I am gone she's going to kill Niels parents because she thinks that's what's left of his bloodline.

Slowly, I say, "Randal, did you know that O'Salves are rumored to be Fae? Sounds like Elizabeth knew this long before I even found out."

Eyeing him as my head is still force back, the curved blade at the nape. His face pale with a small gap between his lips.

I mutter, "I wouldn't do that if I were you."

If my brother is correct that this is the source of our powers, I am overdue for a haircut.

"Your powers are with your hair." The blade slices upwards, my hair cutting in layers. "And you will lose it all."

My body slumps forward, chest touching my knees as my freshly chopped hair cascades down as leaves fell from a tree.

"Trinity?" Randal's voice cuts through my mind.

My body is limp, unable to move as my blood heats to temperatures I'd never felt before. Even out in the hot summer sun in my uniform outside the walls where I thought I overheated isn't anything close to now. It hurts. My veins are as if fire itself is being pushed through.

No longer did my heart beat, and more of my muscles relax. Elizabeth pulling upwards on the chain; only part of my body moves with it as if I had died.

Randal voice cracks, booming in my head. "Trinity?"

Elizabeth says, as if she speaks in one ear, "Do not approach her. Their kind stills to make one think they are dead."

Randal in my other ear, "What the hell are you talking about, Elizabeth? You have lost your mind. The stress of this job got to you."

Their voices were as if they spoke directly into one ear, while the other is in a different. Not in the same room at all, yet at the same time like they are in my head.

Randal has no clue what she is talking about. She pulls the chain again, and half my body slumps over. I can feel the skin tugging, the breaking of the muscle, but I feel no pain.

Elizabeth say, too eagerly, "We keep it from the public. This is why my family created the Luners, to make sure these vile beings don't gain traction. We had wiped the knowledge out, ensuring there were little to no traces." She spits at me. "They are like cockroaches, never able to truly eradicate."

Her hand touches my neck as she let out a chuckled - not one of joy - the sound of relief.

Unable to blink, staring at the ground, my arms slump to my side, as my chest still touches my knees. The red pouring out of my body staining the ground at an eerie sight. "Don't get any closer, or I will make sure she dies." Elizabeth threatens.

Randal voice cracks again as he begs, "I don't understand the vendetta you have with her, but you are out of this. You are taken off the task."

"You won't make it out of here to get me off this case, you sympathizer, and I deem you a threat of the Alpha City." She screams, my body involuntarily jerks at her shrieking voice, busting my ear, "Oh, oh see I told you these things pretend to be dead."

She hauls me upwards, her arm against my chest, as I still have no ability to move. My breathing shallow. I can't even pick it out when I am exhaling - all out of my control.

My body feels like it's on fire, every cut burning as if my skin is melting away. My eyes forever open, unable to move even my pupils. Why is my body reacting this way just by her cutting my hair?

"Come on now, snap out of it, show him the monster your kind is." Elizabeth urges.

She slaps my face once, twice, thrice, and she let go. My body slumping over to the side. I feel absolutely nothing. I can't move any part of my body despite me willing them to. Yelling at my hands to move, but they remain at my side.

It is as if my mind is not my own, and I am telling someone else to move. In front of me, she holds a chain, the one connected to my shoulder, and yanks with all her might. Randal's voice in one ear, "You are going to tear it out of her."

Elizabeth's voice in my other ear, "Maybe then she will react."

She pulls, and the sounds of my muscle and skin tearing. My body lifts out of the chair, my ankles still tied down, keeping me from standing, as she jerks the chains.

The ripping sound fills the room, and I fell down, somehow managing to sit upwards slightly at an angle. Blood pours out of my body, burning as it covered my naked torso, with only my bra remaining. I couldn't look down, but out of the corner of my eye, the eerie sight that my blood is almost becoming translucent.

Randal pushes Elizabeth out of the way, his head lowering to look me in my eyes. His hands gently cupping my face, trying to get me to focus on him.

"Trinity." His voice blares in both ears, "Trinity please don't…"

Elizabeth pushes him back, the knife in her hand ready to strike, going right for his throat. Screaming in my mind, telling him to watch out, none of it surfaces. Randal disarms her in an instant.

Randal has her turned around, Elizabeth hands behind her back, overpowering her every movement. His black eye isn't because he is weaker than her, but he knew when and when not to fight. A leader in his fullness, now, choosing to fight.

Randal has chosen to fight for *me*. Willing any part of my body to move in its frozen state, I can't let him do this alone. Elizabeth getting her leg up, kicking Randal. As he pushes her off, she lunges for the hook dangling there. My eyes slowly rise as she goes for his head, I can't warn him. Randal side steps, the hook barely missing him.

I can't be a prey, waiting for my demise at the hands of her. My eyes close as Randal screams. The hook digging in his forearm as he try to dodge. Forcing my body forward, a muffled scream came from deep within as my mouth wouldn't open. My lips finally peel apart, a holler emerges as my mouth finally listens to my brain.

My nostrils flares, and my lungs expend for the first time ever. Exhaling, I taste it on my tongue - the stillness as no airflow came through. Breathing for a second time in my life, a true breath, stench filled my lungs.

I can pinpoint it. Finally, that stench I keep getting whiffs of weren't from me turning into a Zombie.

My voice, scratchy, emerging, "You are scared. Truly scared of me... Of us."

The odor becomes stronger as her back stiffens, turning slowly, as if she heard a ghost. The stench is mixed with salt, garlic, and sulfur. The scent of fear is choking me out.

My head slowly tilts to the side, pushing my back up against the chair.

Randal yanks the chain out of his arm, backing far away from her. My nose flares as I detect the same three smells from him but something I can't identify. Narrowing my vision, as she steps in front of me.

My head jerks as her breathing is too loud. My eyes squint; the lights became brighter, irritating them. My blood, mixing with white, pouring out of my body.

This isn't normal. My parents and my brother bled normally. I saw blood come out of them when my mom got a cut from a knife, my brother playing too hard with his friends hurting himself, and my dad when he fixed a few things around the house. They all bleed red like anyone else. Not this white blood, if blood is even what you can call this.

About to speak, I stop as my own voice sounds like a shriek. Everything is too much for me - every step shakes my body, every sound hits my eardrum, and the lights are the worst of it.

In a soft whisper, I say, "Cutting the hair doesn't make my family weaker. It releases our powers, and you, Elizabeth, are the one who cut my hair for the first time." Her mouth moves, but no words came sealing her lips. She points my knife at me like it's a normal knife, the dull outside sliding up.

Heat radiates from my core. Wiggling the leathers around my ankles, they became too tight, I broke them with the slightest of pressure. My body sways as I stood, every step reverberated through me tickling me to the bone. Despite the slight trimmer in her hands, her hair messier than normal, Elizabeth keeps her calm expression. I smile, truly smiled, breathing in that lovely fear.

I say in a whisper, "You don't have to pretend anymore. I smell your fear. There isn't anything you can hide." I held my hand out. "That belongs to me."

Forcing myself forward, swaying from the white blood that won't stop flowing. I still don't feel any of the wounds on my body. Only the burning heat coming from my core.

Elizabeth lunges at me, grinding her teeth in pure rage. Too slow to move, she gets my arm, again, she keeps going, slicing me, even getting my chest and stomach. I can't move like my brother. Why can't I move like him? Isn't that freaky Fae thing. I am too weak to even move normally.

The whites of Elizabeth's eyes bulging, her voice shrieks, "I won't give you the chance to become a Second Life."

My head jolts downward, cuffing my ears, and even then her voice pierced through.

"You will die, and the rest of your friends will die for sticking up for your kind. They will die because of you, like Niel, and the rest of them."

As she lunges, I reach out, my mouth open wide, tearing her flesh with my teeth. Dropping the knife, I pull her into me.

She bore her teeth at me holding back the pain she's feeling.

My lip twitch, not using my vocal cords to talk, "You are keeping a hate that doesn't belong, something from the past that doesn't involve you."

"You muddied our bloodline."

I say wispily, "If anything, you muddied ours, for we no longer have immortality."

"Trinity!" Randal yells out.

I couldn't cup my ears to protect them from his loud worried tone. Elizabeth somehow is looking down at me now. A knife in my abdomen, white blood pouring out, the blade smoothly pulling out as white blood mixes with the red from before.

"It's a shame to kill you." Elizabeth mutters as she ran her fingers across the blade, "There have been no mentions of white blood in my families journals."

My vision blurs as I stumbled back. My knees buckle as I try to keep myself from hitting the ground. I am loosing too much blood at this rate. My hands cupped over the wound, it feels weird, there's no pain.

Elizabeth mutters as if she was alone, "Maybe I could keep you. Train you to find others." I growl, "I am not a pet."

Squeezing my face, forcing my head in a straight - up angle, "No, not a pet. A prisoner. If you live, you'll do what I want."

"Never." I bite out.

"Oh, but you will," She pushes me to the ground, "Unless you want me to kill everyone you know, starting with Randal. Than your friends, and then…"

A primal snarl comes out, stopping her words. My jaw slacks; unaware I could make that sound. Coming from deep within awakening an animal that's been asleep.

The muscles pulls at my face as her odor increases. Garlic, salt, sulfur the wonderful smell of fear.

My voice silk as oil slipping off of my tongue, "How can you imprison something that you are terrified of? You reek of fear every time a syllable slips off my tongue."

Her eyes widen just for a second before masking it. Taking my hands off the wound, my blood still seeping. If I die today, at least I am able to take her down with me. The knife sits alone on the floor. The familiar feel, I stand, my body swaying as I twirl the blade in my hand. Elizabeth holding out her pocket blade.

"You'll feel pain when I feel none." My oil - dipped tongue rolling off with ease, "You can keep attacking and I won't die until the blood ceases. Where your pain, agonizing and all, will stop you way before death."

She lunges. My feet slide on my blood, smearing it, and dodging her dagger. My nostrils flare with her beautifully reeking smell.

Making a three – sixty turn, sliding my knife underneath her neck. Her blade lodges into the peeled part of my arm, sinking deeper. Pulling my arm away, taking her knife with me leaving Elizabeth weaponless.

My voice is still as low as its been this whole time, any louder than this I'll hurt my own ears.

Silky smooth, I say, "I could have let you go just for threatening me. But, no. You threatened the ones I love. Threatened a predator to be a slave to a lesser."

I press a little harder, feeling her heart race as if it's my own. All of these years, her calm demeanor was just a mask she carefully disguised her fear with.

My hand slides the blade not too deep where she will die right away. I learned that mistake from the last man. Pushing her away, she stumbles trying to keep her balance.

"I. Will. Kill." She bit out every word as her knees hit the ground, "You."

Her body fell on the ground, the blood seeping out from every side. Stumbling backwards, gasping for air, unknowingly I'd been holding it this whole time.

Theres rustling behind me. I look over my shoulder to see Randal trying to get to his feet. His face pales in all color. Garlic, salt, and a sweet scent. Tilting my head to the side in a bird - like manner, my chest expanding.

I ask, "Fear…and sweet? Randal, are you scared of me?"

He clears his throat with tightening vocal cords, "You, what are you, Trinity?"

Straightening my head, noting all the white blood on the floor, "I'm not exactly sure." Am I a Fae, or something else? "Elizabeth knew what I was, who we are, this whole time."

My feet sliding in my own blood, I should be dead, and somehow I am still standing.

I say, "Glad, happy, cheerful, sweet… Why do you smell sweet?"

I can't wrap my mind around why his odor has a sweet scent to it. My focus remains only on the smell. The sight of my blood isn't bothering me. My fingers on one hand have been pointing directions they shouldn't.

Randal's hand extends, palms up. "I am scared what they will do to you, to me, but I am grateful you are able to protect yourself. Give me that hand so I can put your bones back in place."

"Grateful?" That's what that oddly sweet smell is.

I took another deep breath in as the salt and garlic lightens. The bones pop back into place with resistance, stinging as I close my hand into a fist. I shake as they relaxed.

It's the first pain I felt since my blood turned white.

"Now get out of here, run far away."

Stumbling I say, "They will kill you if they know you let me go." I grab the hook, "I am sorry, but if not this, they will suspect you."

He bows his head, I position the hook, pushing it through. The hilt became lodged into him. My hands trembles from how easily it went through.

Randal whistles, covering both my ears as the sharp spikes shoots into my head, he says, "My leg - brake it. Pull the chain where I can't touch the ground. If we don't report back in thirty minutes, they will come." I hesitate with his request. "Don't look at me like that, Trinity, just do it."

My voice shakes in a wispy tone, "I don't want to hurt you anymore."

"This will save us and everyone you know."

He grunts in pain as I shut the door behind me. I broke his ankle, and his feet barely touched the ground below as he instructed me.

Stumbling out of the emergency doors, the darkness of night blanketing me. The hissing of pipes, doors slamming, the high - pitch chuckles coming from a few drunk girls down the street. My hands cup my ears, but it's still braking through, hurting every fiber of me.

Chapter Thirteen

Navigating the familiar paths my body remembers so well, nothing has changed since I've been gone. Except it's all louder.

I used to love walking down the streets late at night to calm my mind. When did it become so loud? My ears are on the verge of bleeding and my hands can't keep any of the noise out.

Getting to the very top of the building I once lived in, peering into Ieronim's bedroom. Even in the darkness that blankets his room, I can make out the surroundings. Taking the hilt of the knife and rearing back, I pause before braking the window. It's the same one I was rushed out of a little over a year ago.

I should see if it's unlocked first. Sliding the window upwards with ease, my brow raises. Luckily, I didn't break the window for nothing. Inside his room, blinking slowly seeing the outlines of everything around. My eyes are no longer irritated from the harsh lights.

Smacking my lips at the sight of water on his end table. I can see him lying there with a blanket over his body and a foot sticking out. Somehow I am able to see him without the lights on.

Creeping over, I drink the glass of water my body begs me for before waking him. Laying the knife on his end table. My arms are on fire, my shoulder won't let me move it without agonizing breath - stopping pain, and every movement tore at my stomach. I am in agony. Guess that wasn't a Fae thing from before, just pure adrenaline.

"Who paid you?" Ieronim's voice brakes my mind.

Dropping the glass, it shatters on the floor. Falling back, a silver blade shimmers and Ieronim leaps out of the bed. My eyes water as my eardrums ring. Screaming in a panic, my own voice makes my spine tingle like nails on a chalk board.

Books tumble over me as I cover my ears. I didn't care about protecting my already beaten body. His voice raises to an ear - splitting decimal, no longer able to understand his words. It's all too loud.

Leaning into myself, I keep repeating, "Too loud, too loud, too loud, too loud."

Everything is hurting me. My own voice raises higher, my vocal cords can be felt, but the words lost me. Trying to get him to stop, my body trembles. Breathing heavily, my body growing weaker as if I may pass out.

Burying my eyes in my knees as Ieronim flicked the lights on.

Ieronim asks, "Trinity?" He reeks of garlic and a pleasant scent of lavender I didn't mind at all.

I beg in an airy voice, "Too bright, too loud." His footsteps booms as he walks on the floor. Swooping me up, I didn't react although my body is screaming at me, only keeping my ears covered. Everything hurts.

Keeping my eyes shut and ears covered, my body rests inside of the bath. Ieronim reaches over to undue my pants, quickly pulling back as he feels me tremble. His eyes trace over my body of the torture I have endured. Panic traces every tense muscle in his body.

It hurts.

As the water rushes , I jerk upwards, but Ieronim keeps me down. As the warm water reaches the top, all the humming is too much. Squinting, I can't see Ieronim's expression. Everything is smeared in front of me as if its overexposed film.

Dread fills Ieronim's words, "What happened?" Less than a whisper, I reply, "Too loud."

The water is the only comforting thing for me. It's all too much. I can't muffle it out. Dunking my head underneath the water, bubbles tickles my lips as they went to the surface. The sounds are muffle just enough where I can release my grip on my head.

What am I supposed to do if everything hurts me? I need my brother by my side. My lungs straining, I kept myself under a little longer. I don't want to go back up to hear all the hums. The voices in other rooms I can't block out.

Opening my eyes as my body begs for air, the lights are no longer on. Peeking my head out of the water, a few candles flickers inside the bathroom and bedroom.

Ieronim whispers, "Is this better?" I nod slowly, "Can I ask you some questions?"

Looking away, barely audible for another, I reply, "Not enough time."

His voice cracks, "Have you been okay?"

"No, yes, both…" I can't lie, or maybe I am just so sick of being lied to myself. I want Ieronim to know everything but there is not enough time to explain. "My brother is alive, Niel is too, my parents are dead. Wanderers call us wall dwellers. Most don't like us, some don't mind."

Ieronim says almost to himself, "You aren't okay."

Slowly I shook my head, tears fell down my face, "I killed Elizabeth. She tortured me, threatened to kill you guys, Gabe, Sandra… I couldn't" My voice hitches, "… I am scared."

Ieronim falls over me gently hugging my body. His hands grips around my bare skin as if I may disappear. Nudging his head into me, my shoulders relax as I hug him back. Squeezing him, Ieronim lets out a grunt.

He chuckles, "You are stronger than before."

Pushing him away, I say, "I didn't mean to."

Shooting out of the bath as there's a knock on the door, Ieronim put his hands out keeping me at bay. Sinking back into the tub with water rushing over my ears, I hear familiar hushed whispers coming up the stairs. One, two, three, four people are here.

Vixen bolts into the bathroom, shrieking. Submerging my head entirely, her voice ripples, "You are alive…what are you doing? What's wrong with her. Ieronim what's wrong with her?"

Ieronim's his voice is panicky but keeping it hushed as he says, "Keep to a whisper. Everything is… sensitive with her."

Henery whispers, "Why is the tub white?"

Slowly poking my head out of the water, I reply, "It's my blood."

Henery corrects, "Blood isn't white."

"When you took an unknown shot, and not being completely human, apparently it is."

Ieronim shoulders slack, "Not completely…" He pause in mid thought before starting up again, "Trinity, are you a Fae?"

A primal growl bubbles out of me. Both my hands curls the lip of the tub, lifting myself out. My raw skin has healed since I've been here. My stab in my stomach is half the size as before, and blood isn't coming out.

Turning my head slowly, I bare my teeth, "If you say it, I will kill you."

The smell of fear fills the air, my nostrils flaring.

Ieronim took a step back, "I didn't know, Trinity."

Seething I ask, "How long have they kept this a secret from the people?"

Ax asks, "What the hell is going on?"

Ieronim puts both his pointer fingers up, "No, it isn't like that. If I knew you were one, I would had told you."

I bite out, "Our dear, Ieronim, a friend and foe. Keeping life and death between his lips. How dare you not tell me?"

I continue not wanting to hear excuses, "He knew of Second Life's and the beings before. He himself is a Fae. You reek of lavender - a stronger odor than any human."

Water rushes over my body as I step onto the tile floor, the flickering of candles able to see the fear on everyone's faces.

Ieronim says, "I am nothing like what you are - no abilities, slightly heightened senses, but *you* are like the ones before."

Shaking my head, "I don't have time to argue. I need to leave. If you find out Elizabeth is alive, get out of here and run far away."

Henery steps forward blocking Ieronim from me. "I'll get Ieronim to explain more later, but you can't go anywhere in this condition."

"I won't die. It just hurts."

Alarms blare out of their phones. Jerking my head downwards, up, and around, it's so sudden my arms couldn't lift to my ears to muffle the sound. Somehow then everything sounds normal. Touching them, headphones protect me from the outside world.

Ieronim is slowly backing away. He got them to protect me.

Ax jaw flexes before saying, "They are on the hunt for you again."

Still in a whisper, I say, "Randal held it off as long as possible. When or if I can come back I will explain more. Until then none of you seen me."

Vixen gives me a hug, "I am glad you are alive, but next time don't come battered like this." I smirk, "I will try."

Ax hugs me next, "Whatever's going on, Ieronim better tell us everything after today." He looks over to Ieronim like they will know everything by the end of the night. "I hope it means you are more of a bad ass."

"After I figure it out myself, I'll let you know."

Henery pulls me in, "Shit Trinity…I wish we could go with you. Just somehow give us updates."

I gulp, unsure if that would ever be an option, but nodded.

Reaching for the headphones, Ieronim touches my fingertips. My eyes flare as his lips press against mine. Stealing yet another kiss from me as his tongue slips between my lips.

Ieronim says, "Take it with you. It's going to help as you get use to this new normal. If I knew O'Salves were Fae, I would had told you. I'm telling you, they took you out of our history."

Tension creeps around each corner as I navigate the alleys. No sign of Luners searching for me. A few from Hazard Prevention roam the streets casually. The alarms sent out didn't mention me, just to be wary of shady activities. I have to thank Randal for that. My heart finally relaxes. Knowing he is now in charge, my friends, the people I keep dear, are going to be safe.

The strip where black and white mixes to gray. Looking up at Vixen's club, I have to leave the safety of alleys. People stood outside waiting to go in. It is as if the alert never went out. Passing the group, a ball cap on top my head, a shirt and pants Ieronim gave me, with a small bag that he made me take, and my knife tucked within the waistline.

"Hey, have you… Oh, forget them, they have headphones on they can't hear us. This duty sucks ass."

"I know, let's just jot down if anyone saw anything suspicious. Quicker we get fifty people to talk to us, quicker we can head home."

I smirk as I keep going, keeping my head lower as if I am listening to music. They don't even have a clue what's going on. I am going to owe Randal big time for doing this.

Out of sight, the smallest crack in the wall is my salvation. No wonder the Luners haven't bothered with it.

The darkness of the woods welcomes me. Keeping my eyes open with no irritation from unnatural fluorescents. Despite only the glow of the half - moon above, I am able to see the bats flying, attacking the bugs they deem for meals.

Slipping the headphones off, no longer are the hums of man - made objects banging at my temples. Truly able to smell the earthy tones of Mother Earth, not only dirt but the unique aromas of plants as I pass each one. No longer do I feel pain.

My nostrils flares as rotting flesh punches me in the face. My body stiffens as a small horde of zombies pass me. Slipping the blade out of my waistband, hoping I will not have to use it. They click, communicating with one another as one looks my direction. Pulling my elbow back, jabbing something behind me. A squeal tries to escape, biting my lips making sure it wouldn't. Clicks beside my ear as the zombie takes a breath. Turning its head not like the monsters I grew up learning about. Its jaw doesn't unhinge to attack me. It turns to the herd, leaving me in its wake.

My heart lodges in my throat as I watch this thing I've been terrified of all of my life pass me as if I was one of them. It moves on, aware that I am no longer human, like I am undead myself.

Reaching a stream, my body ripples beside its energy. Dipping my bare feet in, leaning back, relaxing for the first time ever. Daniel told me stories from outside the walls, encouraging me to go next time. It had always been next time. He showed his true self, true joy right after coming from the outside. I wanted to but fear always stopped me, choking me before I could even stutter a yes. Alone at night, I would imagine being here, where zombies weren't a threat to us. Niel, Daniel , June, Alix, and I sitting at a stream much like this.

To be free, like Daniel always talked about. Where we took care of each other in nature. I understand what he meant now about how lovely nature truly is. Why he was here every chance he got.

This is where life is. Where what's within the walls are lies.

About The Author

K. N. Chambers has been told she could never be an author due to her Dyslexia, but she refuses to let something like that stop her passion. Using her constant nightmares for inspiration in her stories she writes. Getting married in 2021 her loving husband has supported her being an author from the very start. Her parents as well saw her passion and believe what she could do. For as long as she can remember she's been writing, and her mom saved many of her unfinished works knowing they were worth telling. Unfortunately, her dad had pass in 2023, so he couldn't see her achieve this dream in person. She knows he's watching her cheering her on alongside her grandparents in heaven. One thing she lives by is "Anything and everything is possible, and at the same time it's not."

www.ingramcontent.com/pod-product-compliance
Lightning Source LLC
Chambersburg PA
CBHW022007310726
48972CB00006B/1556